# SHIRLEY ROUSSEAU MURPHY's

sensational Joe Grey Mysteries are the cat's meow!

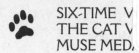

"**MAGICAL WHIMSY AND DEFT WRITING.**"
*Cats* Magazine

"**M**urphy's raised the stakes of the
feline sleuth genre."
*Kirkus Reviews*

"**T**ry the Joe Grey series . . . It is entertaining to see
cat behavior from the inside out."
*Houston Chronicle*

"**DELIGHTFUL.**"
*Library Journal*

"**V**ery successful . . . Murphy's sentient cats have
attracted a lot of attention and a large
following of appreciative readers."
*Monterey County Herald*

"**M**urphy has hit on an excellent recipe for keeping
her series fresh and popular . . .
The combination of interesting human characters
and cats with human characteristics
ensures that these Joe Grey mysteries
will stay popular for many years to come."
*Tampa Tribune*

Books by
Shirley Rousseau Murphy

# CAT
# FEAR NO
# EVIL

## A JOE GREY MYSTERY

# SHIRLEY
# ROUSSEAU
# MURPHY

## AVON BOOKS
*An Imprint of HarperCollinsPublishers*

This is a work of fiction. Names, characters, places, and incidents, are products of the author's imagination or are used fictitiously and are not to be construed as real. Any resemblance to actual events, locales, organizations, or persons, living or dead, is entirely coincidental.

AVON BOOKS
*An Imprint of* HarperCollins*Publishers*
195 Broadway
New York, NY 10007

First Avon Books paperback printing: January 2005
First HarperCollins hardcover printing: March 2004

Avon Trademark Reg. U.S. Pat. Off. and in Other Countries, Marca Registrada, Hecho en U.S.A.
HarperCollins® is a registered trademark of HarperCollins Publishers Inc.

Printed in the U.S.A.

12

For Pat.

And for a pair of black feline brothers who were
kinder and more simpatico than Azrael:
Fluffy, who ate crackers and cheese in bed with me.
And Scrappy, who warned me of a prowler outside my
open window when I slept alone on a summer night.

The wonderful thing about the cat is the way in which, when one of its many mysteries is laid bare, it is only to reveal another. The essential enigma always remains intact, a sphinx within a sphinx within a sphinx. . . . My own belief is that cat was created to encourage us to dream. . . . Like poets, cats lead us along the margins of the everyday, visible world. By following in their footsteps we can slip behind the looking glass, to find, as often as not, that the reflection in the mirror is our own image. He who knows the cat surely understands himself a little better.

—ROBERT DE LAROCHE, *The Secret Life of Cats*

# CAT
# FEAR NO
# EVIL

 1

During the first week of October, when an icy wind blew off the Pacific, rattling the windows of Molena Point's shops, and the shops, half buried beneath blowing oaks, were bright with expensive gifts and fall colors, residents were startled by three unusual burglaries. Townsfolk stopping in the bakery, enticed by saffron-scented delicacies, sipped their coffee while talking of the thefts. Wrapped in coats and scarves, striding briskly on their errands, they had left their houses carefully locked behind them.

Burglaries are not surprising during the pre-Christmas season when a few no-goods want to shop free of entailing expense. But these crimes did not involve luxury items from local boutiques. No hand-wrought cloisonné chokers or luxurious leather jackets, no sleek silver place settings or designer handbags. The value of the three items stolen was far greater.

A five-hundred-thousand-dollar painting by Richard Diebenkorn disappeared from Marlin Dorriss's ocean-front home without a trace of illegal entry. A diamond choker worth over a million vanished from Betty and Kip Slater's small, handsome cottage in the center of the village. And the largest and hardest to conceal, a vintage Packard roadster in prime condition was removed from Clyde Damen's automotive repair shop, again without any sign of forced entry.

Police, searching for the 1927 Packard that was valued at some ninety thousand dollars, combed the village garages and storage units, assisted by Damen himself. They found no sign of the vehicle. Police departments across the five western states were alerted to the three burglaries. Now, three weeks after the events, there were still no encouraging reports, and police had found little of substance to give detectives a lead. And Molena Point wasn't the only town hit. Similar thefts had occurred up and down the California coast.

With most of Molena Point's tourists gone home for the winter, and local residents settling in beside their hearths in anticipation of festive holidays, the disappearance of the valuables made people nervous— though certainly the victims themselves were above reproach. All three were law-abiding citizens well known and respected in the community. Clyde Damen ran the upscale automotive repair shop attached to Beckwhite's foreign car dealership. He took care of all the villagers' BMWs and Jaguars and antique cars as if they were his own children.

The owner of the Diebenkorn painting, Marlin Dorriss, was an urbane and wealthy semi-retired attorney, active on the boards of several charities and local fundraisers. Betty Slater and her husband, Kip, who reported the diamond choker missing, ran the local luggage-and-leather shop and were long-time residents who traveled to Europe once a year and gave heavily to local charities.

Both residences and the Damen garage had alarm systems. All three systems had been activated at the time of the thefts, but no alarm had been set off. Considering this, the citizens of Molena Point thought to change the locks on their doors and to count the stocks and savings certificates in their safe deposit boxes in the local banks.

When there was a lull in the thefts for a few days, people grew more nervous still, waiting for the next one, waiting for the other shoe to drop.

But maybe the sophisticated thief had moved on, tending to the similar thefts along the California coast. All California police departments were on the alert. The newspapers had a field day. However, Molena Point police captain Max Harper and chief of detectives Dallas Garza offered little information to the press. They pursued the investigation in silence. The MO of the thief was indeed strange.

In each instance, he left all valuables untouched except the single one he selected. In the case of the diamond choker, he had ignored pearl-and-ruby earrings, a sapphire bracelet, and five other pieces of jewelry that together totaled several million dollars. In the theft of the painting, only the Richard Diebenkorn landscape had disappeared—it was Dorriss's favorite from among the seven Diebenkorns he owned. And Clyde Damen's Packard was only one of twelve antique cars in the locked garage, several of them worth more than the Packard.

Clyde had purchased the Packard in rusted and deteriorating condition from a farmer in the hills north of

Sacramento, who was later indicted for killing his grandfather. It was now a beautiful car, in finer shape than when it had come from the factory. Just before it disappeared, Clyde had placed several ads in collectors' magazines preparing to sell this particular treasure. At the time of the theft, the gates to his automotive complex had been locked. The lock and hinges did not appear tampered with, nor had the lock on the door that led to the main shop—Clyde's private shop—in any way been disturbed. The deep-green Packard with its rosewood dashboard and soft, tan leather upholstery and brass fittings was simply gone. When Clyde opened the shop very early, planning to spend the morning on his own work, the space where the Packard had stood beside a half-finished Bentley was empty. Shockingly and irrefutably empty. A plain, bare patch of concrete.

Before calling the cops Clyde did the sensible thing. He locked the shop again and went out into the village to find his housemate, a large gray tomcat. Finding Joe Grey trotting along the street headed in the direction of the local deli, Clyde had swung out of the car and rudely snatched him up. "Come on, I have a job for you!"

"What's with you!" Joe hissed. "What the hell!" He had been headed to Jolly's Deli for a little late snack after an all-night mouse hunt. He was full of mice, but a small canapé or two, a bit of Brie, would hit the spot—then home for a nap in his private, clawed-and-fur-covered armchair.

"I need you bad," Clyde had said. "Need you now."

At this amazing announcement, too surprised to argue further, Joe had allowed himself to be hoisted into

Clyde's yellow Chevy coupe and chauffeured around to the handsome Mediterranean complex that housed Beckwhite's Foreign Car Agency and Clyde's upscale automotive shop. Joe was a big cat, muscled and lithe. In the morning sun, in the open convertible, his short gray coat gleamed like polished silver. The white triangle down his nose gave him a perpetual frown, however. But his white paws were snowy, marked with only one stain of mouse blood, which he had missed in his hasty wash. Standing on the yellow leather seat of the Chevy, front paws on the dashboard, he watched the village cottages and shops glide by, their plate glass windows warping in the wind. His whiskers and gray ears were pinned back by the blow. His short, docked tail afforded him a singular profile, like that of a miniature hunting dog. He had lost the tail when he was six months old, a necessary amputation after a drunk stepped on it and broke it—Clyde had been his savior, rescuing him from the gutter, taking him to the vet. They'd never been apart since.

Clyde pulled up behind the shop, unlocked the back shop door, and slid it open. "Don't call the station yet," Joe said, trotting inside. "Give me time to look around."

But, prowling the scene, he found not the smallest detail of evidence. Not even the faintest footprint. No scent, no smell the cops could not detect—except one.

Just at the edge of the bare concrete where the Packard had been parked, he caught the smell of tomcat.

Staring up at Clyde and growling, he crouched to sniff under the remaining cars. The scent was far too familiar—though it was hard to be certain, mixed as it was with the smell of oil, gas, and fresh paint. All of which, Joe pointed out to Clyde, were death to cats.

"You won't be breathing them that long. You've only been in here three seconds."

"Three minutes. It doesn't take long to damage the liver of a delicate and sensitive feline. You're buying me breakfast for this favor."

"You had breakfast. Your belly's dragging with mice."

"An appetizer, a mere snack. Are you asking me to work for nothing?"

"Kippers and cream last night, with cold poached salmon and a half pound of Brie."

"Half an *ounce* of Brie. And it was all leftovers. From your dinner with Ryan. Actually from Ryan's dinner. She's the only one who—"

Clyde had turned on him, scowling. "She's the only one who *what*? Who pays your deli bill when you have your goodies delivered? May I point out to you, Joe, that no one else in Molena Point has deli delivered to their cat door."

"The deli guy doesn't know it's the cat door. I tell them—"

"What you *tell* them is my *credit card number*. If I weren't such a sucker and so damned kindhearted—"

"I just tell them to leave it on the porch. Why would they suspect the cat door? What I do with the delivery after they leave can't concern them."

"*No one* else in the world, Joe, pays his cat's deli bill."

"No one else in the world—except Wilma Getz—lives with a cat of such impeccable culinary—"

"Can it, Joe! Tell me what else you smell. Not

merely some wandering neighbor's cat that probably came in yesterday when the garage doors were open. Can't you pick up the scent of the thief? If *you* can't track him, no one can," Clyde said with unexpected flattery.

But in fact Joe could smell nothing more. He wondered if perhaps the thief had worn gas-and-oil-covered shoes to hide his own scent. And if he had, why had he?

Maybe he thought the cops would use a tracking dog? But Molena Point PD didn't have any dogs, tracking or otherwise. Everyone in the village knew that.

Or did the thief hide his scent because he knew about Joe himself? That thought was unsettling. Nervously he watched Clyde call the station.

By the time three squad cars pulled up, Joe was out of sight in the rafters. He stayed there observing from the deepest shadows, watching Detective Garza photographing and fingerprinting, listening to him question Clyde, Garza's square, tanned face serious, his dark eyes seeing every detail. Officers lifted prints from every available surface. They went over the shop inspecting every car. They examined both the front and back entrances. The thief sure hadn't taken the car out through a window. Nor did it appear that he had entered that way. Best bet was, he knew the combination to the back door's state-of-the-art numerical lock, or was very good at lock picking. The prints that did not belong to Clyde or to one of his mechanics would be duly checked. Garza would do his best to obtain prints on the prospective buyers who had answered Clyde's ad for the Packard. Only after the officers had left, a matter of several hours, did Joe pick up the scent of aftershave around the big double doors, a splash of Mennen's Original that likely was left by one of the cops, a brand so common that half the men in the village might be wearing it. But then he found the scent down the alley as well, along with a faint breath of diesel fumes.

"I think Garza's right," Joe said. "I think they loaded the Packard on a truck bed." Detective Garza had found a partial tire mark farther down the alley, the track of a large truck in a bit of dust out near the street. He had photographed that and had made a plaster cast. Garza did not wear Mennen's Original.

The upshot was that, except for the scent of tomcat that continued to worry Joe, he found nothing else that the cops missed, and that fact deeply annoyed him.

"You're starting to think you run the show," Clyde said. "That the law can't function without you."

He only looked at Clyde, he need not point out that he and Dulcie and Kit were the best snitches the department had. That they had helped Molena Point PD solve more than a few burglaries and murders. That the evidence they had supplied had allowed the city attorney to prepare for solid convictions, that many of those no-goods were presently enjoying cafeteria meals, free laundry service, and big-screen TV supplied by the state of California. He need not point out to Clyde that Max Harper and his officers did not make light of the anonymous information that was passed to them by phone. They no longer questioned the identity of the callers, they took what was offered and ran with it—to the dismay of those criminals subsequently prosecuted.

But now, as Joe prowled the rooftops long after mid-

night, it was not only the theft of Clyde's Packard roadster and the other high-class burglaries that bothered
him. The identity of the elusive tomcat whose scent he
had detected in Clyde's garage continued to prod at
him. As did the problem of Dillon Thurwell.

Fourteen-year-old Dillon was deep into some kind
of rebellion that, because she was Joe's good friend
and a friend of Joe's human friends, worried everyone.
Cat and human alike were amazed at her sudden
change of character, at her angry defiance toward those
she had seemed to love—yet no one could blame Dillon's anger on her age or on crazy hormones; her sudden rage at life was more than that. The unexpected
disruption of her seemingly close and solid family had
been a shock to the village. Who would have imagined
that Dillon's quiet, businesslike mother, who seemed
to manage her home life and her real estate work with
such happy efficiency, would suddenly be slipping
deep into an affair with one of the village's most
prominent bachelors? Because of this, Dillon had
changed overnight from an eager and promising young
woman to a surly, smart-mouthed teen running the
streets at all hours as she had never done—or been allowed to do. Dillon's sudden apparent hatred for herself, and for everyone she had cared about, deeply
frightened Joe.

Beneath the bright half-moon Joe stalked the roofs
fussing and worrying as only a sentient cat can, as only
a cat—or a cop—with a compulsion for asking hard
questions can chew on a puzzle. As above him the
moon and stars glinted sharply in the cold black roof
of the sky, the three problems racketed around in his
head like fast and elusive ping-pong balls tossed out by

some demonic tease: Dillon; the scent of a tomcat that did not belong in the village; and the mysterious burglaries.

Around him the moonlight struck pale the crowded, angled rooftops, and gleamed white below him across the sidewalks and across the faces of cottages and shops, slanting moonlight that threw stark tree shadows along the bleached walls. And the shop windows shone softly, their lights glowing across their bright wares like miniature movie sets. The village at three in the morning was so silent and still that it might lie frozen in some strange and uneasy enchantment. Prowling the roofs, Joe Grey himself was the only sign of life, his gray ears laid back, his yellow eyes narrowed to slits as he paced and worried.

But then, as he stalked from peak to peak among a forest of chimneys, he was suddenly no longer alone. He paused, sniffing.

Beneath his paws the shingles smelled of tomcat, of the worrisome intruder.

Flehming at the stink that was already far too familiar, Joe scanned the night, studying the dark shingled slopes and shadows, hoping he was wrong and knowing he wasn't. He moved on quickly, prowling block by block, searching, crossing high above the narrow streets along branches of ancient oaks as he scanned the streets below. Pausing beneath second-floor windows, he peered in where the tomcat might have stealthily entered. *This* tomcat could jimmy almost any lock, and his intentions were never charitable. Around Joe Grey nothing stirred, no faint sound, no hush of another cat brushing against a window frame. And though the shadows were as dense as velvet, they didn't move—shadows that could hide the black tom the way the darkest pool hides a swimming snake.

2

The cold wind off the sea blew up Joe's tail and flattened his ears and whiskers where he stood watching the shadows and convincing himself he'd been mistaken, that he hadn't scented the black tomcat. And suddenly a quick black shape slid into the gloom beside a penthouse. A big, muscled shadow vanishing into an ebony cleft of night. A beast taller and broader than any village tomcat. Joe remained crouched, his gaze glued to the inky tangle of rooftop vents and air ducts and converging overhangs. It was over a year since the evil black tomcat and his thieving human partner had first appeared in the village, and Joe had hoped he'd seen the last of them.

He waited a long time. Was about to turn away when the animal reappeared, slipping through a wash of starlight, his belly caressing the shingles. He was quite aware of Joe, his ears flat to his broad head, his long thick tail lashing with menace. On the ocean breeze the tomcat's stink was as predatory as any hunting leopard.

A subtle shifting of his weight, and Joe could see his yellow slitted eyes.

A year ago last month, the black tom had appeared in the village with his human partner, old whiskey-sodden Greeley Urzey, the pair having flown up from Panama to Molena Point so Greeley could visit his sister. The old man had taken Azrael's carrier right on board the PanAm 727, right into the cabin—an action tantamount, in Joe Grey's opinion, to carrying a loaded assault rifle across international borders.

But then, Greeley himself was no innocent. Ragged old Greeley Urzey, despite his resemblance to a penniless tramp, was highly skilled at his chosen craft. He could gently manipulate the dial of a safe, listen to the tumblers fall, smile that stubbled lopsided smile, and open the iron door right up. And his sleek black tomcat partner was equally skilled at his particular brand of break-and-enter. Wrenching open a second-floor window or skylight, slipping through and dropping down into a jewelry or liquor store, the black cat would fight open the front door's dead bolt. And *voilà*, Greeley was inside with his clever drills and lock picks.

Joe Grey smiled. After only a few of those midnight raids, he and Dulcie had nailed those two like hamstringing a pair of wharf rats, and the thefts had stopped.

But Joe and Dulcie hadn't alerted the department. That one time, they hadn't called the cops. They didn't need news of an amazing talking black tomcat to hit the news media—to hit the fan big time. They had, instead, watched the thieving pair sneak quietly out of the village to return to their home in Central America, had celebrated Azrael and Greeley's departure praying they would never return.

Now, crouched low, intent on the shadows, Joe watched those burning yellow eyes scan the rooftops and he was filled with questions. Had these two stolen Clyde's Packard? Were they behind these clever thefts? Such virtuosity, and the sophisticated contacts needed to fence the jewelry, to say nothing of the resources to dispose of such a large item as a Diebenkorn painting or the Packard, did not seem in character for those two. Greeley liked to steal cash and disappear, liked to drink up the profits, then steal again, that was Greeley Urzey's style.

As he watched, the black tom disappeared as quickly as he had slid into view. Studying the darkness, Joe could taste the beast's testosterone-heavy stink. He remained still, listening for the nearly inaudible pad of a paw, for the scuff of a careless claw or the shift of a piece of loose gravel.

Tensely waiting, he heard nothing. Only the hush of the breeze among the oak leaves. Moving across the roofs he followed Azrael's scent, tracking him in a circuitous route up steeply slanted peaks and around platoons of chimneys, drawn on over the rooftops for three blocks, four, in and out of narrow clefts and across twisted limbs high above the empty streets— tracked him until the trail suddenly and insolently turned back to Joe's own roof. To the bright new cedar shingles of the Cape Cod cottage that Joe shared with his human housemate.

There on the roof Azrael stood boldly facing him, stood barring the entrance to Joe's private tower that rose above the new shingles, his cat-sized penthouse, his own private rooftop retreat. The tomcat blocked his entry with gleaming teeth and bared claws.

The tower, rising above the new master bedroom, was an architecturally pleasing hexagon four feet across and four feet high. Its six glass sides supported a peaked hexagonal roof. Within, Joe's aerie opened by a cat door to the master suite below. Joe's private tower was off limits to all village cats. It was marked by his own scent and defended when necessary, no prisoners taken. Only Joe's tabby lady, Dulcie, and their pal the tattercoat kit, were welcome here. Watching the black tom blocking his private property, Joe tensed to spring.

The second-floor master suite, which had doubled the size of Clyde's single-story cottage, included a large bedroom with wood-burning fireplace, a second fireplace in the spacious study, a bath, and dressing room. The contractor had included ample high shelves and beams where a cat could climb. The largest beam gave to a ceiling niche above Clyde's desk, from which opened Joe's door to the tower. Contractor Ryan Flannery had tackled the challenge of a cat-friendly structure with amused delight. Over a late dinner, she and Clyde had designed the glass-sided aerie, allowing ample space for deep cushions, a water bowl—and the door out onto the roof where the black cat had now insinuated himself, his acid-yellow eyes challenging Joe, his hissing smile as evil as the name he liked to call himself, the death angel.

Azrael's voice was as hoarse as scuffed gravel. "So, little kitty. Your Clyde . . . *Damen*, is it? . . . has added onto his house. Isn't he clever. And this little pimple sticking up here, what is this? A dovecote? Have you been reduced to raising tame pigeons for your hunting, birds too fat to fly away?" Azrael's sulfur-yellow eyes were as belligerent as those of an underworld gang leader.

Considering the defiant beast, Joe felt much the same as a cop would observing some street scum whose dirty hands were smearing his patrol car.

The fact that Azrael had been born far more skilled and intelligent than ordinary cats had fostered in this animal not joy and goodness but a keen hunger for evil.

An ordinary cat was not expected to be moral, your everyday household kitty was not supposed to behave with the welfare of others in mind. Certainly many cats were blessed with sensibilities that led them to warn their families of burglars or fire or a leaking gas line. But for a speaking cat of Joe Grey and Azrael's talents, far more, it seemed to Joe, was expected—if you were dealt a winning hand, you were expected to sweeten the pot. That was Joe's opinion. If you were given the extra talents, you were committed by the power that made all life to give back in kind. Expected to make the lives around you brighter. To help take down the no-goods, not to join them.

Stepping boldly in through Joe's cat door and leaving a tuft of black fur on the metal rim, Azrael lifted his tail. Joe leaped, enraged, as the tom sprayed Joe's favorite cushions with a stink powerful enough to corrode a steel building. Joe hit him, knocking him away as the beast sprayed Joe's water bowl. They were clawing and raking, the force of Joe's attack soaking them both. Sinking his teeth into Azrael's neck, Joe forced him against a window, clawing and ripping at him. Hanks of black and gray fur flew. Locked together, yowling and screaming, the tomcats thundered against the small windows threatening to break glass, a spinning ball of raking claws and torn and shredded cushions. Below, in the master bedroom, Clyde shouted.

Brought up from a deep sleep, Clyde yelled again and leaped out of bed. "What the hell? Joe, where are you?" He stared toward the ceiling of the study that seemed under siege by a small and violent earthquake. "*What* the hell's going on!" Racing into the study in his shorts, he climbed atop the desk and peered up through the cat door, where a ruckus like fighting bulls shook the ceiling.

Above him, in the little glass house, whirled a dervish of screams and spinning fur. "Joe! What the hell—" Reaching up inside the tower, he tried to separate the fighters. Grabbing the black tom, he tried to pull him off Joe.

"Get away from him!" Joe yelled. "He'll take your arm off."

The cat's claws raked Clyde. Hot with anger, Clyde jerked the black tom down through the cat door. He wasn't sure whether he had hold of head or tail until teeth sank into his thumb. Swearing, he snatched the cat's neck between tightening fingers. He had him now, one hand gripping the cat's tail, the other hand clutching the beast's thick black neck. Holding the twisting, screaming tom away from his own tender hide, Clyde stood on the desk nearly naked, his arms oozing blood, his black hair tousled from sleep, his bare feet scattering papers and bills like autumn leaves. In his hands, the flailing black monster clawed the air and swore like a stevedore. Clyde hadn't heard such creative invective since his rodeoing days; the beast swore in Spanish as well as English, the Spanish expletives sounding far nastier. Gripping the flailing cat was like holding a whirling radiator fan with knives embedded in the blades—a machine Clyde didn't know how to turn off. He was tempted to keep squeezing until the cat stopped yelling and hopefully stopped breathing. He knew what this cat was, and he didn't like him any better than Joe did. It would be so easy to collapse that vulnerable feline throat.

He couldn't do it. He couldn't kill even this lowlife who, if he were set free, would likely go for Clyde's own throat.

Maybe if Clyde had been convinced that the tomcat was totally evil, he would have done the deed. In Clyde's view, Azrael was an irritation, but he didn't see the cat yet as the pure, deep evil that demanded without question to be eradicated from the known world. That, Joe Grey would later inform him, was a serious flaw in Clyde's judgment.

Easing his grip on Azrael's throat but continuing to clutch tightly the nape of the cat's neck and his tail, holding the screaming, flailing animal away from him to avoid ending up in the emergency ward, Clyde stepped down off the desk.

Standing in the middle of the study, he wondered what to do with the beast. If he tossed the cat across the room, it would spin around and leap at him; he could clearly imagine Azrael tearing at his face and at other tender parts. Above Clyde, Joe Grey crouched peering down through his cat door, his white nose and white paws red with blood, his cheek torn in a long, bleeding gash, his yellow eyes blazing with rage.

But now, as well, alight with deep amusement.

Ignoring Joe's silent laughter, Clyde found himself wanting to reach up for the gray tomcat, hold him close, and wash the blood from his face—a gesture impossible at the moment, and one that at any time would meet with indignant resistance.

Joe looked down at Clyde. Clyde looked up at Joe Grey. In Clyde's hands Azrael fought and flipped and twisted so violently that Clyde felt every jolt.

"Help me out, here, Joe. What do I do with the beast?"

Joe stifled a laugh. "The cat carrier? Or the bathtub filled with water? My suggestion would be to squeeze real hard and put an end to him."

"I can't do it."

Joe's yellow eyes burned with a look that was all wild beast, that said *kill*, that contained no hint of civility.

"It would be like lynching a killer without due process."

"You think the California legal system would give *this* lowlife due process?"

Clyde shrugged, engendering a moment of miscalculation in which the black tom raked his hind claws down Clyde's shoulder, bringing new blood spurting, one claw dug deep. Joe stopped smiling and leaped from the tower like a swooping eagle, knocking the tomcat from Clyde's grip. The two cats hit the floor locked in screaming battle, then Joe flipped the tom twice, forcing him into the cold fireplace.

Crouched over Azrael among the ashes, Joe blocked his retreat with a degree of viciousness Clyde had never before seen in his feline pal. Azrael, driven by Joe's frenzied attack, backed against the firewall pressing hard into the bricks—as if wishing the wall would give way and let him through into the dark chimney.

Watching the two tomcats, Clyde stood clutching his arm and applying pressure to the wound. The cats communicated now only in silence, their body language primal. Clyde could read Joe's superiority of the moment as Joe goaded and stalked his quarry. The black tom showed only uncertainty in the twitch of his ears and the drop of his whiskers.

Joe moved from the fireplace just enough so Azrael could step out. His meaningful glance toward the glass doors at the south end of the study was more than clear. As Joe herded the flinching black tom toward the roof deck, Clyde stepped to open the door.

Silently Azrael padded past them onto the deck, as docile as any pet kitty. Silently Joe Grey stood in the doorway beside Clyde watching as Azrael crossed the wide deck over the roof of the carport, leaped into the oak tree, and fled down it to the sidewalk. As Azrael disappeared up the street, Joe Grey turned back inside, never looking to see which route the cat would take. Azrael had left the premises cowed and obedient, and that was all he cared about—for the moment. If, before the black tom was driven from the village, he presented more serious problems, Joe would deal with trouble as trouble arose.

**3**

It took the rest of the waning night for Clyde to clean and doctor Joe's wounds and tend to his own lacerations. He just hoped the black tomcat didn't have rabies or some exotic tropical disease. When he was finished with the disinfectants and salves, he sported seven oversize adhesive bandages on his hands and arms and shoulder. Joe Grey's injuries hardly showed, hidden beneath his short, dense fur. One could see only a few greasy smears where his silver coat parted, plus the bloody bare patch on his nose that was already beginning to scab over.

Joe's vet would have shaved the torn areas and maybe stitched them. Joe didn't want to see Dr. Firetti, preferring to appear in public as undamaged as possible. He was not through with Azrael, and he had no desire to be observed around the village looking like the walking wounded. He hoped his nose would heal fast.

Watching Clyde set up a ladder and climb from the upstairs deck to the roof, Joe wondered what had

brought Azrael back to the village. He knew for a fact
that Greeley was still in Central America, as Wilma
had had a letter just last week from his wife, who
owned the Latin American shop in the village.

The tomcat had returned to the village just once since
he and Greeley sneaked away after robbing the village
shops; traveling with them was Greeley's new wife-to-
be. Sue flew often to Latin America on buying trips, so it
was no problem for her to leave her shop in the hands of
a manager. The couple were married in Panama and settled down in a Panama City apartment; but their conju-
gal bliss had, apparently, not appealed to Azrael.

Dumping Greeley and Sue, he had taken up with a
little blonde he found in a tourist bar, and soon Azrael
and Gail Gantry headed back to the States. Ending up
in Molena Point, they had pulled some slick burglaries
until Gail was arrested for the murder of a human ac-
complice. Immediately Azrael had slipped away and
disappeared, had not been seen in the village again until last night.

Now, licking a scratch on his shoulder, Joe peered
up into the tower. Above him, on the roof, Clyde had
set down his bucket of hot water and cleaning rags and
opened the tower windows. Joe watched him remove
the shredded, ruined pillows and drop them in a plastic
garbage bag. Joe had liked those pillows. Clyde removed Joe's water bowl and scrubbed it, then washed
the inside of the tower, the walls, the floor, the ceiling
and windows. The place would smell like Clorox for a
week. Better that than tomcat spray. Clyde left the windows open so the tower could dry and air. Neither Joe
nor Clyde had any idea what would prevent Azrael
from a second foray, other than the smell of Clorox.

Joe wondered if one black ear hanging from the peak of the tower's hexagonal roof would serve to keep the beast away.

He wished that he had obtained such a trophy.

Clyde finished cleaning the tower as the first blush of morning embraced the rooftops. Coming down the ladder and returning to the master suite, Clyde showered and dressed. Joe, waiting for him, prowled the two big rooms. The suite, with its pale plastered walls and cedar ceiling, with its dark hardwood floors and rich Turkish rugs, was really more than a bachelor needed. Joe wondered, not for the first time, if Clyde would ever, finally, settle down with a wife.

There had been plenty of women, for a night, a week, not pickups but good friends, lovers who, having ceased to be lovers, were still the best of friends. That said something positive about Clyde, something Joe liked. But he did wonder if Clyde would ever take a wife. If, in building this comfortable upper floor, Clyde was preparing for just such a move.

If he was, Clyde hadn't confided in *him*, in his steadfast feline housemate.

Joe had thought for a while that Clyde and Charlie Getz would marry, but then Charlie had fallen head over heels for Clyde's best friend, police chief Max Harper. An old story, Joe guessed, the guy's friend gets the girl. The stuff of fiction. But it had worked out all right, all were still best friends, and Charlie and Max's love was powerful and real.

Maybe he'd marry Ryan Flannery, Joe thought. Maybe Ryan, unknowing—or maybe hoping?—had built this upstairs addition as if destined to live here with Clyde herself?

So far, Joe could only wonder. Clyde had been as close-mouthed as a fox with a squirrel in its teeth. But the two got along very well, had fun together, and had the same sense of humor; they were comfortable together, and that meant a lot. And of course Joe never pried—not to the point where Clyde swore at him and threw things.

They went downstairs together, Joe padding quietly beside Clyde's jogging shoes, feeling Azrael's bites and scratches across every inch of his sleek gray body.

In the big remodeled kitchen Clyde started a pot of coffee and gave old Rube and the three household cats their breakfast. All four animals were nervous, the cats skittery and quick to startle, the old black Lab growling and staring up at the ceiling as if afraid whatever riot had occurred might yet come plunging down into the kitchen.

Sucking on his first cup of caffeine, Clyde fetched the morning paper from the front porch, spreading it out on the table so they could both read it—an act so magnanimous that Joe did a double take. "Why so generous? As you've said in the past, it's *your* paper, *you* pay for it."

Clyde glared at him. "You don't need to be sarcastic. This morning scared me. He's a big bruiser, Joe. I hope you can stay away from that cat. Next time, he might not back off so easy."

Joe shrugged, pacing the plaid oilcloth. What a downer, to find that beast prowling the village just before Christmas.

"What do you want for breakfast?" Clyde said diffidently.

"Any salmon left?"

"You ate it all last night. Settle for a cheese omelet?" Joe yawned.

"With sour cream and kippers?"

Joe thought about that.

Clyde rose and began to make breakfast. "You look terrible. You're all frowns and droopy whiskers."

"You don't look so great yourself with adhesive tape stuck all over."

"Maybe the cat is just passing through," Clyde said. "Anyway, you don't need to be worrying about some mangy alley cat. You should be feeling like the proverbial fat feline, with the church bomber *and* Rupert Flannery's killer both set to go to trial."

Clyde was being so kind and complimentary that Joe found himself waiting for the other shoe to drop.

Though he had to admit, their work on the church bomber and on the murder in Ryan Flannery's garage *had* been satisfying. No human cop could have done what they did, could have slipped in through Ryan's narrow bathroom window to spy on a prowler. Or could have trotted into the scene of the crime on the heels of a prime suspect, listened to his phone conversations, and passed on the information to the detective division. With those cases wrapped up, Joe knew he should be feeling as smug as if his whiskers were smeared with caviar.

But he didn't feel smug; he felt edgy.

Turning from the stove, Clyde looked deeply at him. "It's not just that tomcat that's eating you. It's those high-powered burglaries."

Clyde gave him a lopsided grin, shaking his head. "You think Azrael was involved in those thefts? No way, Joe. That wasn't Azrael. No cat, not even a beast of *his* caliber, with *his* thieving talents, could have pulled off those robberies."

Joe said nothing. He wasn't so sure. Joe was thinking about Azrael and what the unscrupulous black tomcat might be up to, wondering what had brought him back to Molena Point, and his stomach was full of nervous flip-flops.

Well, but maybe he was just hungry. Maybe he'd feel better when he'd stoked up some fuel, when his killer genes were appeased with a nice helping of fat and cholesterol.

Turning back to the skillet, Clyde said, "If you're going to count worries, what about my missing Packard? That car's worth a bundle; I spent almost a year restoring it. For that matter, if you want to worry, what about Kate? This search for her family is upsetting her big time."

Kate was another of Clyde's good friends whom, at one time, Joe had hoped Clyde would marry. Joe himself had a lot in common with Kate; for one thing, she knew his secret, she knew that he could speak, that he was more than an ordinary cat. And Joe, in turn, knew the equally bizarre secret of Kate's own nature.

Kate had, nearly three years ago, moved from the village up to San Francisco, and there had begun searching for some clue to her parents, whom she had never known. The adoption agency and foster homes had supplied just enough facts to frighten her. Personally, Joe thought she was more than foolish to be prying into a history that was best left alone.

But curiosity was just as much a part of Kate's nature as it was of Joe's own feline spirit.

Skillfully Clyde folded the omelet. "Since she

started this search for her history she won't talk to you, she won't talk to me. She's so damn stubborn. When she called last night sounding scared, wouldn't *say* why she was scared . . ." He turned to stare at Joe. "She calls, then will hardly talk."

Clyde dished up the omelet. "You were listening, you know how she sounded. You were all over me, stuffing your ear in the phone."

"Maybe you should go up there. Two hours to San Francisco . . ."

"She'll be down for Charlie's gallery opening on Sunday. Maybe I can find out then what's going on." He set their plates on the table. He had added kippers only to Joe's part of the omelet.

Crouching on the table, Joe waited for his breakfast to cool; he didn't like burning his nose. "I still don't see why Sicily has her openings on Sunday. You'd think that earlier in the weekend . . ." Cautiously he licked at the edge of his omelet.

Clyde shrugged. "Those parties spill out the door. Since she's changed to Sunday, the crowd has nearly doubled."

Joe didn't reply. He was too busy tucking into breakfast—a good fight made him hungry as a starving cougar. But after several bites he looked up at Clyde. "Kate's situation is the same as Dillon's."

Clyde looked at him. "I don't see the two situations as even remotely the same. Dillon's mother has broken up their family. Kate has no family, she . . . Oh well," Clyde said, shrugging, "both are family problems."

Joe twitched an ear. "Both shattered families. Only in different ways."

Because he'd been an abandoned kitten, Joe had done a lot of thinking about family. Had wondered how life would have been with that kind of security, a mother to take care of him, other kittens to play with . . .

Maybe his mother had been run over in the San Francisco streets. He always told himself that was what happened, that she hadn't simply abandoned him. He didn't remember if he'd had brothers or sisters. Whatever, with no mother to fetch him up past the first couple months of life he'd had nothing to depend on but his wits. Catch a meal or a one-night stand wherever he could con some apartment dweller, then off again searching for something better. Not until he was lying fevered in the gutter nearly dead from a broken and infected tail, and Clyde discovered him, did he see the world as more than the pit of hell.

And not until he was grown and learned suddenly, after a rude shock, that he could speak and could understand human language—not until he began to think like a human and to understand human civility, did he realize what a family was all about.

He was getting so philosophical and sentimental he made himself retch—but the fact remained, he could now understand why Kate wanted to know her heritage, why she wanted her past to be a part of her no matter how bizarre—just as he understood why Dillon was so shattered by the destruction of her family, by her mother all but abandoning her.

That was the trouble with thinking like a human. You started empathizing. Suffering the pain of others. Compromising your autonomy as a cat. You were no longer satisfied to slaughter rats, get your three

squares, and party with the ladies. Even his previous
promiscuity he now found juvenile and boring. Now
his partnership with Dulcie was deep and abiding.


When Kate called last night, Clyde had been sprawled
in bed reading the latest thriller. Joe, lounging on the
pillow next to him reading over his shoulder, had reluctantly left the aura of the story and pressed his ear to
the phone.

"You sound way stressed," Clyde said. "What's the
matter?"

"Just need to talk, I guess." Kate's voice sounded
tight and small. "Maybe need a change, maybe I'll
move out of the city for a while, come back to the village." She had sounded so deeply upset and off center,
that Joe went rigid listening.

"Is it your job? Has work gone sour?"

Joe had rolled his eyes. Clyde could be so impercep-
tive.

"No, the studio's wonderful."

*"It's the search for her grandfather,"* Joe had whispered, nudging Clyde.

"Is it the search for your family?"

"Maybe. I guess. I don't want to talk about it. I just
want to get away, to be with—with friends."

"Kate . . ."

"Well I'm coming down," she'd said, putting more
spunk into her voice. "Even if just for a few days. I
want to see Charlie's show—her first one-man exhibit.
At the Aronson. I'm coming to the opening; I can't
wait. While . . . while I'm there, maybe I'll look at
apartments."

"You can stay here while you look. In the new guest room. Strictly platonic."

Well, Joe thought, it had always been platonic, their friendship had never gone any further. One thing about Clyde, when Kate was married and living in the village, and she and Jimmie saw a lot of Clyde, it was just friends and nothing more. Clyde would never have gotten involved—but there had always been that spark between them, Joe had seen it even then.

"Thanks for the invitation." Her voice started to sound weepy again. "I've already called Wilma, already arranged to stay with her. But can we have dinner?"

"I'd like that. You . . ."

"I know you're dating Hanni's sister. Could we make it a threesome? Or why not everyone? Ryan, Hanni, their uncle Dallas, Charlie and Max and Wilma . . ."

Clyde stared at Joe. Joe stared back at him. Now she was gushing. She didn't sound at all like herself.

"Royally scared," Joe had said when Clyde hung up. "Maybe she'll talk to me, maybe I can get a line on what's bugging her."

"Maybe you can meddle."

"Maybe I can *help*."

"In your case, helping *is* meddling. Leave it alone, Joe. She doesn't want to talk, she just wants company. Kate's a big girl. If she wants to keep this private, she can handle her own problems."

"Well, aren't you out of joint. And she doesn't seem to be handling them, she's scared out of her pretty blond head."

"Just give her some space. Don't overreact." Clyde's nose, in other words, had been royally put out of joint.

Joe had tramped across the bed to his own pillow, kneaded it with a vengeance that threatened to send feathers flying, and curled up for sleep with his back to Clyde.

Kate was *his* friend, too. Thinking about her problems left him as irritable as a trapped possum.

But now, finishing breakfast in a withdrawn silence, neither Joe Grey nor Clyde imagined that soon the lives that touched them would fall into a deeper tangle. That at Charlie's gallery opening they would be treated to a glimpse of future events as dark as the leer of the black tomcat.

# 4

The party was in full swing, the champagne flowing, the talk and laughter in the Aronson Gallery rising louder than the three cats found comfortable; despite the din they peered down from the loft far too interested to abandon festivities: three furry people-watchers taking in the glitter, the excitement, the popping of corks, and the women's elegant gowns.

Of course the guest of honor was most elegant of all. The cats seldom saw Charlie in anything but jeans and workshirts. Her transformation was impressive, her gold lamé sheath setting off her tall, slim figure and picking up the highlights of her red hair.

"Oh, to be an artist," Dulcie said, "to have your own exhibit, with all the lovely people and champagne and delicious food, and to wear gold lamé like a movie star."

Joe cut her a tolerant look. Dulcie's dreams ran heavily to silk and cashmere and gold lamé.

"And the gallery's never been more elegant. I'm sure," she said with a little grin, "that Sicily Aronson built the loft just for us."

"Right," Joe said, laughing.

"Well we *are* the star models, with our portraits in the window," she told him. As well as the drawings of the three cats in the window and in the gallery below, many of the works on the loft walls were of them: small, quick sketches of the cats playing and running.

But the real ego trip was the large portraits in the gallery below, hanging shoulder to shoulder with some very handsome horses and dogs. Peering down through the rail watching the crowd, the cats tried to look everywhere at once. The opening was mobbed with Charlie and Max's friends, art patrons, and animal lovers—and of course there were lots of cops present. The cats could see how pleased Charlie was that the department had turned out for her—well, for Max, she'd be thinking. For their chief. But then, the whole department had been at their wedding, just three months ago, where the head of detectives had given the bride away, and Clyde had been best man.

Clyde and Max Harper had been friends since high school, when during summers and on weekends they followed the rodeos up and down California, riding broncs and bulls. Harper, lean and sun-leathered, still looked very much like an old bronc buster. Clyde had mellowed out smoother, but he was still in good shape. Strange, Joe thought, how things happened. When Charlie arrived in the village two years ago, to stay with her aunt Wilma, Clyde had at once started dating her. It wasn't until much later, and, Joe thought, quite by accident, that Charlie and Max fell in love.

Tonight, none of Harper's officers was in uniform and the chief himself was dressed in a pale suede sport coat, beige slacks, and a dark silk shirt—a perfect complement to Charlie's gold lamé. He stood across the room talking with two of his men, his tall, slim figure military straight; his tanned, lined face that could look so stern tonight was only proud and caring as he looked across at Charlie and moved in her direction.

Charlie tried not to let everyone see quite how thrilled she was by her first one-man show; she was so excited her stomach was queasy. As she watched Max work his way through the crowd toward her, she watched Sicily Aronson, too. From the moment the doors had opened this evening, the flamboyant brunette had been everywhere, flitting from group to group, her diaphanous skirts and shawls floating around her, her tall figure set off by the usual collection of dangling jewelry, tonight an impressive mix of silver and topaz and onyx. Sicily had taken care of the party details personally, the invitations, the press releases, the hanging of the work, down to the selection of appetizers and wines.

"You're gawking," Max said, coming up behind Charlie. "You're supposed to look sophisticated and cool."

"I don't feel sophisticated *or* cool." She grinned at him and took his hand, moving with him to a far corner where they could have a little space. "How can I not be excited, when everyone we know is here, and so many people I don't know, have never seen before."

"Maybe collectors, come to buy out the show."

Laughing, she studied the long, lean lines of his face, her throat catching at the intimacy of his brown eyes on her.

"I'm glad I married you," he said softly, "before you got so famous you wouldn't look at me."

She made a face at him.

"You will be famous. Of course, with me you're already famous. Particularly in bed."

She felt her face color, and she turned her back on him, studying the crush of viewers that was already overflowing onto the sidewalk. Max ran his hand down her arm in a way that made her catch her breath. Turning, she breathed a sigh of pure contentment.

"It's a fine show," he said seriously. "You know you have three prospective clients waiting to talk with you. That woman over by the desk, for one. The Doberman woman."

She nodded. "Anne Roche. I'll go sit with her in a minute."

"And would you believe Marlin Dorriss is here? That he's seriously eyeing three pieces of your work? That *would* be a conquest, to be included in the Dorriss collection. He's been looking at the gulls in flight."

She nodded, grinning at him. Early in the evening Dorriss had spent some time looking at the drawings of seagulls winging over the Molena Point rooftops. They were not romantic renderings, but stark, the dark markings of the gulls repeated in the harshly angled shadows of the rooftops.

"That would be very nice," she said softly, "to hang beside work by Elmer Bischoff and Diebenkorn." She looked up at Max. "I still find it hard not to warm to Dorriss, to his quiet, sincere manner. Find it hard not to like him, despite his unwelcome affair with Dillon's mother."

Dillon was Charlie and Max's special friend; Max

had taught her to ride, helping to build confidence and independence in the young teenager who, they had sometimes thought, might be a bit too sheltered.

She was not sheltered now. The sudden breakdown of her family had turned Dillon shockingly bad mannered and rude. Charlie hurt for her, but she grew angry at Dillon, too. An ugly turn in life didn't give you license to chuck all civility and let rage rule—even when it was your mother who had betrayed you.

But Charlie hadn't had a very good relationship with her own mother, so maybe she was missing something here. Certainly she hadn't had anything like Dillon's fourteen years of warmth and security. Maybe that made the present situation far worse. Until her mother went suddenly astray, Dillon never had to cope with a problem parent.

Surely Helen's transgression with handsome Marlin Dorriss was understandable—plenty of women were after him. A well-built six-foot-four, he was a man whom women on the street turned to look at, a well-tanned, athletic-looking bachelor with compelling brown eyes, always quietly but expensively dressed, his voice and manner subdued, totally attentive to whomever he was speaking with. Busboy or beautiful model, Dorriss seemed to find each person of deep interest. He had an air of kindness about him as if he truly valued every human soul.

"Hard not to like the man," Max said, giving Charlie a wry grin and putting his arm around her. Warm in each other's company, they stood quietly watching the crowd. "Kate Osborne just came in," he said. "There by the door talking with Dallas. She'll be pleased that you're wearing her hairclip."

Charlie touched the heavy gold barrette that tied back her red hair. Set with emeralds and carved with the heads of two cats, it was a handsome and unusual piece, part of a collection of jewelry that Kate's unknown parents, or perhaps her mysterious grandfather, had left to her. She had stopped by the ranch that afternoon for a few moments to drop off the barrette; they had stood by the pasture fence petting the two Harper dogs and talking. Charlie hadn't wanted to accept the gift. "I can't take this, Kate, it has to be worth a fortune. It's very beautiful."

"It's not worth a fortune, it's only faux emeralds. I had the whole lot appraised the week after that attorney gave them to me. So strange . . . but I'll tell you about it when we have more time." Turning, her short blond bob catching the sunlight, she removed the plastic clip from Charlie's hair and fastened on the gold-and-emerald confection.

"Oh yes," Kate said, stepping back. "It's beautiful on you, it will be smashing with that gold lamé."

"But . . ."

"Charlie, I'll never wear this, I'll never have long hair, long hair makes me crazy. Jewelry is meant to be used, to be worn." Taking her compact from her purse, she held up the mirror so Charlie could see.

Charlie had been thrilled with the gift. "I still think it looks terribly valuable. Even if the jewels are paste, the gold work is truly fine."

"If you like primitive," Kate said. "As we both do. The appraiser—he's top-notch, was recommended by several of my clients in the city—I don't think he goes for this kind of work. He did say the pieces were unusual in style. When I pressed him for some date, some idea what the history of the pieces might be, he seemed uncertain. Said they didn't really belong in any time or category, that he really couldn't place them as to locale."

"Strange, if he's so knowledgeable."

"Yes." Kate had looked uneasy, as if she found the lack of any background for the jewelry somehow unsettling. "He assured me the jewels were paste. He said that wasn't uncommon, and I knew from my art history that was true, that during the 1800s real gold and silver settings were made with great care, but often set with paste jewels."

Kate gave the two dogs a parting pat. "I gave the other barrette to Wilma, the silver and onyx one for her silver hair."

"But if there's some clue to your parents here, if they were connected somehow to the jewelry . . ."

Again, that uneasy downward glance. "I have ten more pieces to solve the puzzle. *If* that's why the jewelry was saved for me, if it does hold some clue."

"But why else would they keep it all those years, if it isn't of great monetary value? Do the other pieces have images of cats?"

"I . . . five do," she said, frowning. "There's . . . an emerald choker with cats." Kate shook her head, seeming distressed. "If the stones were real, I'm sure it would be worth a fortune."

So strange, Charlie thought now, that mysterious collection of jewelry waiting for Kate for over thirty years, tucked away in the back of a walk-in safe, in a hundred-year-old law firm. A firm that seemed, Kate had said, on its last legs, fast deteriorating. The jewelry had been put away in a small cardboard box to wait for an orphaned child to grow up, to come of age.

Standing on tiptoe to look over the crowd, Charlie waved to Kate. And a waiter by the door moved in Kate's direction with a tray of champagne, rudely shouldering aside another server—the same waiter who, half an hour earlier, had watched Charlie herself so intently. What was he looking at? Kate's choker? Charlie's own barrette? Surely Sicily hadn't hired a thief among the caterers.

*My imagination*, Charlie thought. *Everyone's looking at the jewelry, because it's so different with its primitive designs.* Even from across the room, Kate's silver and topaz choker was striking against her pearly dress and her silky blond hair. Kate was so beautiful, with the gamin quality of a Meg Ryan or Goldie Hawn, a perky, carefree perfection that Charlie greatly envied.

"What?" Max said. "What are you staring at? Kate? But you are the most beautiful woman in the room."

"You, Captain Harper, are the biggest con artist in the room." She smiled and touched his cheek. "I'm so glad Kate came. She drove clear down from the city for tonight—well, other errands, too. But she planned her time specially for tonight."

"Maybe she plans to buy a drawing or two before her favorites are gone, or maybe to take back for some client—maybe she plans to do a whole interior around a group of your drawings."

"You're such a dreamer. I know she loves San Francisco, but I do hope she moves back to the village—that she rents the other side of our duplex." Charlie had bought the run-down duplex last spring, before they were married, as an investment. Ryan Flannery, her tenant in one apartment, had done considerable repairs in lieu of rent.

"It's *your* duplex," Max said. "You're grinning. What?"

"I still don't feel like a landlord."

"What does a landlord feel like? Does this take special training? You think you're not mean enough, tough enough?"

She gave him a sly look.

"Tough as boots," Max said. "You don't mind having friends as tenants? With Ryan in the other unit . . ."

"I love having Ryan there. We haven't disagreed yet. The few improvements . . . We settle the cost over a cup of coffee. Ryan does the work, I buy the materials. What could be simpler?"

"I married a sensible woman, to say nothing of her beauty."

The biggest improvement so far to the duplex, after the initial painting and cleaning up, had been the backyard fence for Ryan's lovely weimaraner, an addition well worth the money. It was a real plus to have a guard dog on the premises. Ryan's side of the building had already been the scene of a kidnapping, and, just a month ago, the scene of a shocking murder. Such events were not all that common in their small quiet village, but Charlie and Max both hoped the big, well-trained dog would put a stop to any unsettling trend.

The other tenants, in the one-bedroom side, would be leaving in February, four months hence. Charlie wondered if Kate would want to wait that long. She watched Kate and Ryan, and Ryan's sister Hanni, with their heads together laughing. Golden hair and dark, and Hanni's premature and startling white hair. The three young women had started in her direction when they were sidetracked by Marlin Dorriss, who seemed to want to escort them all to the buffet table—Charlie guessed Dillon's mother hadn't accompanied him; the two did not overtly flaunt their relationship.

It was amazing to Charlie that since moving to the village, she had acquired three close woman friends her own age, trusted friends even besides her aunt Wilma. She had never had girlfriends in school, had always been a loner. She hadn't known how comfortable and supportive female friends could be—if they were women who didn't fuss and gossip, who liked to do outdoor things, who liked animals and liked to ride. Women, she thought amused, who preferred an afternoon at the shooting range to shopping. Though Charlie had even begun to enjoy shopping, when she had the spare time.

She could never get over the fact, either, of her sudden success as an animal artist. After giving up a commercial art career at which she had been only mediocre, and moving down to the village to open a cleaning-and-repair service, she had suddenly and without much effort on her part been approached by a gallery that loved her work. Her animal drawings and prints had been warmly accepted in the village and far beyond it, in a way almost too heady to live with. Even Detective Garza, that very discerning gun-dog man, had commissioned her to do his two pointers, and she considered that a true compliment. She watched Garza start through the crowd now, as if to speak to Max; she supposed the detective would take Max away from her. The square-faced Latino looked very handsome in a pale silk sport coat, dark slacks, white shirt, and dark tie, particularly as she was used to seeing him in an old, worn tweed blazer and jeans. She could see a tiny line of pale skin between his short-trimmed dark hair and his tan.

Easing through the crowd to them, Garza gave her a brief hug and turned his attention to Max. As Max squeezed her hand and moved away with him, Charlie turned toward the curator's desk where Anne Roche, the Doberman woman, had made herself comfortable in one of the two leather chairs.

Anne was a frail, fine-featured woman, cool to the point of austerity. Everything about her spelled money: her glossy auburn hair sleeked into a perfect shoulder-length bob, her creamy complexion and impeccable grooming. Her easy perfection made Charlie uncomfortably aware of her own freckles and kinky, carrot-red mane. Anne was interested in a portrait of her two champion Dobermans. Anne's looks might be intimidating, but her love of animals and her shy smile put Charlie immediately at ease. She spent some time telling Charlie how much she loved her work, particularly the quick action pieces.

"And the cats," Anne said, her brown eyes widening. "Some of your cats look so perceptive they make me shiver. And your foxes and deer and raccoons—so wild and free. Those aren't zoo animals."

Charlie laughed. "I watch them from our porch and from the kitchen windows. We live up in the hills above the village, so there's open land around us. The fox comes almost every night, though we don't feed him."

"Well, he's very fine. I have to say, your work is the best I've seen, and I'm quite familiar with the drawings of Pourtleviet, and of Alice Kitchen. Have you thought of producing a book? A coffee-table book?"

Charlie smiled. "I do have a small project in the works, not a coffee-table book, but with cat drawings."

"I'm glad to hear that. I wish you well with it. When can we get together for some sketches of the dogs? I'd like you to do them on the move, at least for the first work, some of those wonderful quick sketches."

They were discussing a time convenient to them both and were going over Charlie's fees when the waiter who had approached Kate so rudely, and who had eyed Charlie's barrette, started toward the desk with a tray. He was young, maybe thirty, dressed in white jacket, black slacks, and black bow tie. His stark blond hair topped a perfect tan, as if he surfed or played tennis. Maybe a sports bum working as a waiter to support his habit? His handsome, tanned face was closed of any expression, withdrawn and bland. But as he held out his tray of champagne, his look changed to one of surprise.

He crumpled and fell suddenly, dropping the tray, scattering glasses in a spray of champagne, landing hard across Charlie, hurting her leg as she fought to steady him and herself. It happened so fast she couldn't hold him. His weight twisted them both as he slid from her grip to the floor, pulling her with him; she went down in a tangle of sprayed wine and breaking glass.

He lay white and still beneath her. He had made no sound as he fell, no cry of distress or pain. As Charlie untangled herself and felt for a pulse, Max was beside her pulling her away, his lean, lined cop's face frightened, his demeanor stern and quick. "Get back, Charlie. Get away from him. Now."

Charlie struggled up, her gold sheath soaked with wine, and she slid fast behind the desk as Max's officers herded everyone back. Max knelt beside the tall, liveried man feeling for a pulse, feeling the carotid artery, turning back the man's eyelids. Around them the din of voices had stopped as suddenly as if a tape had been turned off, the crowded room so still that the running footsteps of the two officers who had moved to secure the front of the building echoed like thunder. Detective Garza's voice was a shout as he called on the police radio for paramedics. Charlie watched the scene numbly. The client she had been talking with had disappeared into the crowd. As sirens came screaming from a few blocks away, Max performed CPR, and his officers secured the front and back doors. The gallery windows blazed with whirling red lights. Sirens still screamed as two medics pushed through the crowd to crouch over the waiter. As Max rose, the look on his face told her the man was dead.

Anne Roche had been right there. Had she been involved, in some inexplicable manner? She stood now with the rest of the crowd waiting to be questioned.

After a long interval of feverish work with CPR, oxygen, and electric shock, the medics rose. Max nodded. The younger medic spoke into his radio, calling for the coroner. Max reached for Charlie, taking her hand. As she moved away with him, she felt cold, disoriented. Looking up at Max, she had to question the forces that were at work here.

This was the second disaster to occur during a ceremony of special meaning to her and Max. The first had been their wedding, when she and Max, along with most of the Molena Point PD and half the village, had narrowly escaped being killed at the hands of a bomber.

Before that, Max had been set up as the prime suspect in a double murder, had been cleverly and almost successfully framed. And now . . . another calamity at a celebration involving Captain and Mrs. Max Harper.

Was there some pattern at work beyond her understanding? Some mysterious force that invited such ugly occurrences? But that was rubbish, she didn't believe in cosmic forces ruling one's life; and certainly such an idea would anger Max. Free souls ruled their own lives. Both she and Max believed that. Despite what Max called her "artistic temperament," she prided herself on being totally centered in fact and reality—except of course for the one fact in her life that was beyond reality, the one aspect of her life that was so strange that Max would never believe it. The one amazement that she could never share with him, the secret she could never reveal to the person she loved most in all the world.

Glancing above her to the balcony, she looked into the eyes of the three cats, their noses pressed out through the rail, chins resting on their paws. Joe's sleek gray coat gleamed like polished pewter, marked with white paws, nose, and chest. Dulcie's dark tabby stripes shone rich as chocolate. The kit's fluffy black-and-brown fur was, as usual, every which way, her yellow eyes blazing with curiosity, her long fluffy tail lashing and twitching. The three cats watched Charlie knowingly, three serious feline gazes. And while Joe Grey stared boldly at her, and Dulcie narrowed her green eyes, the kit opened her pink mouth in a way that made Charlie's heart stop, made her slap her hands over her own mouth in pantomime so the kit wouldn't forget herself and speak.

But of course the kit didn't speak. Slyly she looked down at Charlie, amused by her panic. And the cats turned to watch the newly arrived coroner at work, three pairs of eyes burning with conjecture, three wily feline minds where a hundred questions burned, where theories would be forming as to the cause of the waiter's death.

Before the waiter fell, the three cats had seen no one very near to him except Charlie and her client. The moment he fell, the cats had searched the crowd for any action that might be missed from the floor below, a furtive movement, some sophisticated and silent weapon being hidden in purse or coat pocket. But it was already too late: by the time the man fell they would surely have missed some vital piece of evidence.

It deeply angered Joe that he had been looking directly at the victim and had seen nothing. As soon as the man dropped, Joe had studied him, seeking anything awry that might, the next instant, vanish. Had there been an ice pick in the ribs? A silenced shot? Or did the waiter die from some poison that did not cause last-minute pain or spasms? Apparently neither cops nor coroner had found any such indication. The guy had gone down like a rock, *as if* he'd been shot. But neither police or coroner had found a wound.

The man worked for George Jolly's deli, which had catered the party; the cats had seen him in there serving behind the counter. They were well acquainted with the deli, and with the charming brick alley that ran behind its back door, where George Jolly set out his daily snacks for the local cats. Jolly's alley was the most popular feline haunt in the village, although villagers and tourists as well enjoyed its potted trees and flowers, its cozy benches and little out-of-the way shops. Mr. Jolly wasn't present to help serve tonight. The two other waiters had knelt over their coworker after he fell, until detectives ordered them away.

Joe glanced at the kit, who crouched beside him. The young tortoiseshell was leaning so far out between the rails that Dulcie grabbed a mouthful of black-and-brown fur and hauled her back to safety.

"You want to drop down in the middle of those cops and medics?"

The kit smiled at Dulcie and edged over again, watching everything at once. For a cat who had not so long ago been terrified of humanity, who had sought only to escape mankind, the kit had turned into a brazen little people-watching sleuth. If Kit had a fault, it was her excesses. Too much curiosity, too much passion in wanting to know everything all at once. As the three cats peered over, Max Harper looked up suddenly to the balcony. He looked surprised to see them, then frowned.

Joe turned away to hide a smile. Harper could look so suspicious. What were *they* doing? Just hanging out to watch the party. The whole gallery knew they were up there, they'd been camped on the balcony all evening. Wilma had brought them up a plate loaded with party food, and they had received dozens of admiring looks, to say nothing of typical remarks from the guests: *Oh, the cute kitties . . . they look just like their portraits, aren't they darling . . . That tomcat, he looks just as much a brute as in Charlie's drawings, I wouldn't want to cross that one . . .*

Joe looked down at Max Harper as dully as he could manage, scratched an imaginary flea, and yawned. With effort he remained a dull blob until at last Harper turned away.

Only when all the guests had been questioned and names and addresses recorded and folks were allowed to leave, only then did the cats abandon the balcony and trot down the spiral stairs. While the police remained to finish their work, Charlie's little group headed for the door, anticipating late-dinner reservations. Max would be along when he could. He and Detective Garza stood in the center of the gallery with a dozen officers, both quietly giving orders. It would be hours before anyone knew whether this had been a natural death or murder. Until that question was resolved, the department would treat the Aronson Gallery as the scene of a murder.

"If it *was* murder," Dulcie said softly, "who knows how long the gallery will be locked down? And Charlie's show has just opened."

Joe Grey licked his paw. "The coroner should know by morning. Charlie's already sold seven drawings and four prints. By morning, Garza should have photographed, fingerprinted, done the whole routine. Let's go, before we miss supper." They moved quickly to the front door, where the party was shrugging on coats and winding scarves against the late October chill. But as the three cats slipped diffidently around their friends' ankles, preening and purring like pet kitties, Joe's thoughts remained with the dead waiter. Allowing Clyde to pick him up, Joe purred and tried to act simple for the benefit of those who did not know his true nature; but as he snuggled against Clyde's shoulder, his sleek gray head was filled with questions as sharply irritating as the buzz of swarming bees.

5

Joe lay across Clyde's shoulder absorbing the warmth from his housemate's tweed sport coat, which smelled of aftershave and of dog. Around them along the village streets, the wind hushed coldly, and above their heads the sheltering oaks rattled like live things; a few tourists lingered looking into the bright shop windows, but the shadows between the shops were dense and still, for no moon shone beneath the heavy clouds. Clyde's tweed shoulder was rough against Joe's nose. Dressed in his usual party attire, a sport coat over a white cashmere turtleneck and Levi's, Clyde had had a haircut for the occasion. His dark hair was short and neat, with the obligatory little white line of non-tan— the general effect a clean, military look that Ryan liked. Ryan walked close beside them, Clyde and Ryan holding hands. Joe observed them with interest.

"What," he had asked Clyde just last week, like some overprotective parent, "are your intentions? You're dating Ryan, neither one of you seeing anyone else. I know it's not all platonic, but where's the wild abandon of passion? A couple of years ago, it was a different woman every week, in bed, cooking your supper, and in bed again. What happened to all the debauchery?"

Clyde had scowled at him, said nothing, and left the room. But Joe thought he knew. Clyde had had a sea change, a complete turnaround in the way he viewed his woman friends.

It had started with Kate, when she left her husband after he tried to kill her. She had been so very frightened, so distraught, had left the house in fear and come to Clyde for shelter and for comfort. Clyde had made up the guest bed and cooked a midnight supper for her, had tried to soothe and calm her, but when Kate exhibited her alarming feline nature, trying to make him understand the extent of her fears, when she took the form of a cat, she had put Clyde off royally.

After her move to San Francisco, there had been months when she'd been out of touch, when she wouldn't answer his calls or return them. Then Clyde began dating Charlie. That had lasted until Charlie and Max, unplanned and unintentionally, had fallen madly in love. And Joe smiled. They had been so distressed that they had hurt Clyde, so relieved when Ryan came on the scene, moving down from the city, and the two hit it off.

But where this romance was headed, Joe wasn't sure. Clyde had become far more circumspect in his relationships. No more one-week stands, no more wild partying—and Ryan, recovering from a miserable marriage, seemed just as reluctant to commit.

As they headed across the village to a late supper, strolling past the brightly lit shops, Wilma carried Dulcie wrapped in her red cloak, and Hanni carried the kit. Hanni had covered her jade-green sequined dress with a long cape made from a Guatemalan blanket—tacky on anyone else, smashing on Hanni Coon with her lean model's figure and tousled white hair. Hanni, definitely a dog person, carried the tattercoat with considerable deference. Consorting with cats was new to her. The kit was so thoroughly enjoying herself looking over Hanni's shoulder into the shop windows that Joe wanted to tell her not to stare. When passersby greeted them, Joe looked totally blank and mindless, but the kit was incredibly eager, accepting the petting of the locals and smiling at them in a far too intelligent manner. The few tourists they met stopped to stare at the bizarre little group carrying three cats, but then they smiled. Molena Point was famous for odd characters.

Ahead of Hanni and Wilma, Charlie walked with Kate, Charlie wrapped in a long, creamy stole over her wine-damp gold lamé. Kate wore a black velvet ankle-length wrap. In the wake of the waiter's death, the party of six was silent and subdued. Strange, Joe thought. When the waiter fell across Charlie's lap, Kate had registered not only alarm but fear, a quick shock visible for only a moment before she took herself in hand.

Beside Joe, Ryan moved so close to Clyde that her dark, blowing hair tickled Joe's nose. She was growing more used to him, more comfortable with Clyde taking his tomcat around the village, carrying a cat in the car just for the ride or allowing Joe into a restaurant. No matter that Ryan took her dog into restaurant patios, that was different. After nearly a year of dating Clyde she hadn't quite decided what to make of Joe—Joe knew he shouldn't tease her and set her up, but his jokes gave him such a high. Nothing so bizarre as to reveal the truth, nothing to imply that he understood Ryan's every word and might have something to say in return.

But dog people were such suckers for the inexplicable behavior of cats, for the unfathomable mysteries of the feline persona. There was, in the minds of most dog addicts, not the faintest understanding of the logic of feline thought. And that made them ridiculously easy marks. The simplest ruse could bring incredulous stares: *I never saw a cat go round a garden smelling the roses, standing up on its hind paws like that. I never saw a cat sit up like a dog to beg, or fetch a ball like a dog.*

Well of course ordinary cats did all those things, when they chose to; he had demonstrated for Ryan nothing extraordinary. But in that ailuro-challenged young woman, his little dramas had stirred amazed responses. Dulcie kept telling him to watch himself. "You're going to blow it, Joe. Blow it big time. Ryan isn't stupid. How do you think Charlie found out that we can talk, that we're not ordinary? By watching us when we got careless, that's how. Just as you're getting careless with Ryan."

"Don't worry so much. I'm never careless, my jokes are totally harmless. And Ryan isn't Charlie, Charlie's the one with the imagination. Not everyone would come to the conclusion Charlie did. Ryan's a cop's kid, she likes a logical explanation for everything. Facts are facts. She would no more believe a cat could carry on a conversation than Max Harper would believe it. And you have to admit, we're in Harper's face all the time."

"But . . ."

"There's no way," Joe had said, "that either Ryan or Harper would ever buy the truth about us—unless, of course, we sat down and had a little heart-to-heart with them."

He looked up as they approached the restaurant's brick patio, and he licked his muzzle, tasting the good smells of steak and lobster. The patio was crowded with diners at small tables beneath its sprawling oaks. The host was all smiles as he escorted them through the patio, through the main dining room, and up the stairs. The eyes of everyone were on them, not only because Charlie was an up-and-coming artist in the community and the wife of the chief of police, not only because of Hanni's theatrical good looks and her status as a top interior designer, but because how many dinner parties, reserving the upstairs private dining room, included on the guest list three cats?

The smaller upstairs room with its paneling, high-peaked ceiling, and rafters, featured a long skylight along one slanting side, above which heavy clouds drifted, edged with light from the hidden moon. A fire was burning on the brick hearth. Bay windows formed three sides of the intimate dining room, looking down on the village's bright shops and dark oaks. A long table filled the room, draped with a white cloth and set with heavy silver, flowered china, and a centerpiece of red pyracantha berries. On a window seat in one of the bays, among a tangle of flowered cushions, three linen napkins had been laid open beneath three small flowered plates. There, no silverware was required. As the cats settled into their own places and the human diners took their seats, Max Harper hurried up the stairs, giving Charlie a grin, the two as delighted to be together as if they'd been parted for days.

"Dallas is still at it," Max said. "We just got the coroner's prelim."

"That was fast. What did he say?"

Harper's thin, lined face was expressionless, a cop's face that you had to know very well to decipher. He looked irritable, as if some vital question was still begging. Joe watched him so intently that Dulcie nudged him, pretending to nibble a flea. Immediately he stuck his nose in his supper, concentrating on his salmon mousse—the rich, creamy confection was far more delicious than any sweet dessert mousse that so delighted humans. Salmon mousse, in Joe's opinion, was one of the great inventions of mankind.

"Could have been accidental death," Harper said. "Could be manslaughter. No way to tell, yet. He died of blunt trauma, a blunt blow to the head."

"But there wasn't . . ." Charlie began. "No one . . ." She grew quiet, letting Max continue.

"As near as Dr. Bern can tell, so far, the blow occurred three or four days ago. There was slow bleeding within the skull where multiple small capillaries had ruptured. The pressure can build up slowly, over time." He took a bite of salad. "Pressure pushing down around the spinal cord. Bern thinks that happened over several days. At the last, while he was serving drinks at the party, the increase of blood became rapid.

"When Bern called, he was still looking for the sudden rupture of an artery or vein, which would have been the final event in a long drawn-out trauma." He spooned more dressing on his salad and took a sip of beer, a frustrated frown touching his face. Harper had quit smoking over a year before, but sometimes Joe saw him itching to reach for a cigarette, his fingers moving nervously, the creases along his cheeks deepening.

"The guy's ID was faked," Max said. "He's been using the social security number of a man who died three years ago. Strangest thing, his prints are not on record in any of the western states. It'll take us a week or two, maybe more, to get fingerprint information for the rest of the country. Department of Justice is always backed up."

Charlie said, "He could have been hit in the head anywhere, then? Several days ago?"

Harper nodded. "There's a rectangular bruise on the side of the head, the shape of a brick. It was already fading, but there were brick particles in the skin. Could have been an accident, maybe he stood up under a low flight of stairs, for instance, and cracked himself on the head. Or it could have happened in a fight, some guy bashed him with a brick. He was using the name Sammy Clarkman. He's worked for George Jolly for three months, has done several catering jobs during that time."

Ryan leaned forward, looking at Max. "Lucinda Greenlaw knows him."

Max gave her his full attention.

"I knew I'd seen him in Jolly's Deli," Ryan said. "I'd forgotten, until just now, that last month when the Greenlaws were here, Lucinda and I were in there, and she knew the guy."

Max listened quietly. The whole table was silent.
Beside Joe, the kit was so alert and still that he kept an
eye on her—he never knew when the kit would show
too clearly her eager enthusiasm.

Lucinda and Pedric, a pair of tall, bone-thin eighty-
year-olds, had married just a year before, after Lucinda's husband Shamas died in an unfortunate
manner for which one of his nephews went to prison.
On the day of their wedding the Greenlaws had
adopted the kit. They knew her special talents, they
knew that she, like Joe Grey and Dulcie, was not in any
way ordinary. The kit's command of the English language, her off-the-wall ideas, and her opinion on almost every subject were, in the eyes of the Greenlaws,
deserving of admiration and respect.

Setting out to travel at their leisure up and down the
California coast, they had planned to have the kit with
them, but she was so prone to car sickness that she had
turned wan and miserable. For the kit, the pleasure of
travel wasn't worth the distress. The Greenlaws had
arranged that she stay for a while with Dulcie and
Wilma. Just at the end of September they had returned
to the village for a short layover before the holidays,
had stored their RV in Wilma Getz's driveway, and,
scooping up the kit in a delirium of pleasure, they had
checked into a suite at the Otter Pine Inn, the nicest of
several village hotels that catered to pets. The kit had
spent a delirious week enjoying herself with her human family. And, to the kit's great joy, the elderly newlyweds had decided it would soon be time to fold away
their maps of the California coast and build their
Molena Point house as they had promised the kit they
would do. The tortoiseshell had been ecstatic, a whirl-

wind of anticipation. When she spoke of the house, her round yellow eyes shone like twin moons, her bushy tail lashed and switched. She was a wild thing filled with exploding dreams: Their own home, a real home, her beloved Lucinda and Pedric forevermore near to her.

But now, what was this? What was the connection between the footloose Greenlaws and the dead waiter? Glancing at Dulcie, Joe intently watched those at the table.

"We had ordered a picnic," Ryan was saying. "We picked it up and spent the day on Hellhag Hill laying out their new house. Seeing how the sunlight falls, how to cut the prevailing winds. That hilltop house could be truly desolate and cold if it isn't set right on the land.

"When Lucinda and I stopped at Jolly's to get the picnic basket, that guy—Sammy—was behind the counter. You could tell he was new, didn't know where things were, like the small plastic containers. I thought maybe he'd just been working in the kitchen, not at the counter, he had to dig around in the cupboard forever to find what he needed.

"Lucinda called him by name," Ryan said. "He didn't seem to recognize her until she reminded him that they'd met in Russian River, and then he seemed pleased to see her. She told me later he'd worked at the inn where she and Pedric stayed this past summer.

"I thought," Ryan said, "that the guy wouldn't have acknowledged Lucinda at all, if she hadn't nudged him. That maybe he didn't want to be recognized."

Harper looked around the table, waiting to see if anyone else knew the man. No one did, and no one else had seen him at Jolly's. Kate had been in the village at the same time that Lucinda and Pedric were, but she hadn't been in Jolly's. Clyde said, "I ordered takeout last weekend, but Jolly's son made the delivery." He glanced inadvertently across the room to Joe Grey, as if wondering if Joe knew Sammy. The tomcat stared, wondering at Clyde's carelessness. The expression on Clyde's face, when he realized what he'd done, was embarrassed and shocked. To cover Clyde's social blunder Joe yawned hugely, pawed at his ear as if it itched, and belched.

That got a laugh. He'd have to talk to Clyde; his housemate was getting careless.

Harper studied Ryan. "Did Lucinda tell you anything about him?"

"She said he'd been interested in a locket she'd bought somewhere north of Russian River. That he'd wanted to know where she got it. She said she'd picked up several pieces of really nice costume jewelry in a little shop up around Coloma. She showed me the gold locket. It was set with topazes, and had a cat's face in the center. Beautifully made, rich, heavy gold all carved in leaves and flowers." She looked up at Kate. "It was, in fact, very like your choker. Same style, that heavy baroque look but . . . well, but different than baroque."

Kate was very still.

Ryan said, "Could the pieces have come from the same place originally? Old jewelry, some of which found its way to San Francisco? Maybe from the same group, the same jeweler?"

"The appraiser thought my pieces were made in the last century," Kate said. "He reminded me there were a lot of Italian immigrants along the coast then, and that some were fine jewelers."

Max turned to Ryan. "Did Lucinda tell you anything else about Sammy?"

"Not that I remember," Ryan said, pushing back her short, dark hair. Her resemblance to her uncle, Detective Garza, was most striking when she frowned, when she looked thoughtful and serious.

Rising, Harper moved out to the foyer, flipping open his cell phone. The cats could see him standing just at the head of the stairs, punching in a number. Joe counted ten digits. Maybe he was calling Lucinda and Pedric's cell phone. He tried the number twice, waiting for quite a few rings each time, then spoke briefly, apparently leaving a message, and returned to the table.

"It's midnight," Charlie said. "Would they turn off the phone at night?"

Max said, "Maybe they leave the phone in the kitchen at night, and don't hear it?"

"Maybe they checked into a nice inn somewhere," Wilma said, "and left the phone in the RV. They stay at an inn or motel every few nights."

On the window seat, the kit, always jumping to the worst conclusions, moved between Joe and Dulcie, nervously kneading her claws. It took stern stares from both cats to make her settle down again. Above them the sky brightened as the clouds blew past, revealing the thin moon.

"When I mailed the preliminary drawings to them last week," Ryan said, "they were in Eugene." She looked at Kate. "Aren't they coming through San Francisco?"

"They are," Kate said, "so I can show them the Cat Museum. It was nice they were here in the village the same time I was; Lucinda and I hit it right off. I'd never known her well when I lived in the village. Just to speak to. I had no idea she was so . . . that we'd have so much in common. We're some forty years apart, but that doesn't matter, I feel like I've known her forever."

As you should, Joe Grey thought, exchanging a look with Dulcie. And Wilma glanced across at the cats, knowing exactly what they were thinking: that Kate and Lucinda, because they shared special knowledge, would naturally be friends.

Those who knew the cats' secret had grown to a number that was sometimes alarming to Joe Grey. Secrecy was the only true protection he and Dulcie and Kit had against the wrong people knowing their true nature. They had learned that the hard way. Certainly, if ever the news media found out about talking cats, the fur would hit the fan big time.

Though as for their true friends, it was deeply satisfying to be surrounded by six staunch supporters, to have human allies who understood them. With Clyde and Wilma, Charlie and Kate, Lucinda and Pedric Greenlaw playing backup, as it were, they were not alone in the world.

As for the three criminal types who knew their secret, the cats tried not to think about that. If fate were truly to smile, not only convicted killer Lee Wark, but Jimmie Osborne, Kate's ex-husband, would remain behind bars in San Quentin for the rest of their natural lives. And old Greeley Urzey, if indeed he had not accompanied Azrael back to the States, would stay in Central America for the rest of *his* evil days.

Well, Joe thought, he wasn't going to ruin his supper thinking about those no-goods. The salmon mousse was far too delicious. Licking the creamy confection from his whiskers, he would, like Scarlett, think about his enemies tomorrow. He listened to Ryan, Charlie, and Wilma make plans for an early breakfast and had almost finished his large helping of mousse when a black shadow appeared on the window seat, cast down from the moonlit skylight, a pricked ear and feline profile striking across his plate. Staring up, Joe met the blazing yellow eyes of the black tomcat; the beast's presence made Joe swallow his supper with a shocked snarl.

Beside him Dulcie hissed, crouching and looking up. And beside her the kit cringed low, staring up through the glass where the black tom poised predatory and still, intently watching them, his eyes blazing with the reflected glow of the restaurant's soft lights. In the backlight of the moon Joe could not see the beast's wicked face, only his broadly extended cheeks and flattened ears; surely a cold smile played across that evil countenance. As the three cats stared, rumbling low in their throats, the humans at the table looked up, too; and Charlie caught her breath; Wilma and Clyde half rose as if to chase the beast away, then glanced at each other and sat down again.

Max Harper put his hand on Charlie's arm. "It's only a cat, some cat wandering the rooftops." He looked at her strangely. "What did you think?"

"I . . . I don't know. It's so big, it appeared so suddenly up there."

The cats knew well that she was thinking the same as they; they could see her flash of shocked dismay that the black tom had returned, before she hid her true feelings and smiled at Max.

"Nerves, I guess," she said softly. "More stressed over the show than I'd thought."

Harper nodded. He did not look convinced. Glancing puzzled at Clyde, he hugged Charlie. She relaxed against him, smiling as if she had been flighty and silly.

Above them Azrael hadn't moved. Joe imagined him highly amused by the stir he was causing—to Joe, and to those who understood Azrael, the presence of the black tom cut through the companionable evening like claws ripping velvet. Beside Joe, Dulcie's green eyes glinted and her low growl was deep with rage, her angry rumble hiding a keen anxiety. But now that the kit's first startled fear had passed, she looked from Joe to Dulcie wide eyed, and extended a soft paw to Dulcie, a silent question. Joe watched her uneasily.

The kit had been told about Azrael; but Kit did not like to take others' word, she wanted to experience every new thing for herself. Joe glanced at Dulcie. The kit would need some talking to.

The delight of the evening, Charlie's joy in her first one-man show, and the friends' happy celebration, had, with the waiter's death, turned chill and worrisome. Now with the dark presence of the half-wild beast who called himself the death angel, Joe Grey felt his skin crawl with an ugly portent of disaster.

**6**

Charlie's late supper party was long over, the guests departed and by now sleeping deeply, the predawn village deserted. The time was five A.M. The courthouse clock had just struck, as the black tom left the roof where he had slept.

Pacing the streets through the muted glow from the shop windows, he looked up with interest at interminable arrangements of holiday confection, leather coats displayed among autumn leaves, hand-knit sweaters and bright jewelry framed by golden pumpkins—every window so full of fall excess they made a cat retch. Swaggering as he approached the windows of the Aronson Gallery, he considered with disdain the seven pieces of Charlie's work that hung facing the street, the large drawing of Joe Grey dangling a mouse from his teeth, the color print of Dulcie reclining on a paisley cushion like some 1940s girlie calendar.

These little cats were too high above themselves, they had grown far too vain with all this attention. It was time they were taken down.

At five o'clock on this dark winter morning the streets were still deserted, no lone gardener working along the sidewalk tending the shop-front flowers, not even a seagull careening and diving across the inky sky. The only living creatures in view besides Azrael himself were a couple of homeless men huddled in a doorway trying to keep warm, trying to maintain a low profile in this village where police did not encourage nonpaying overnight guests.

Azrael had slept quite comfortably on the roof of the Patio Café tucked between the steeply slanting shingles of a small penthouse and the restaurant's chimney, which had held its warmth until long past midnight. The brick-and-shingle cave, conveniently out of the wind, had been scented pleasantly with aromas from the restaurant, with the heady smell of steak and lobster and fried onions.

He hadn't slept hungry. Before he retired to the roofs he had taken a leisurely supper from the restaurant's garbage bins, probably scrounging the leavings, he thought sourly, of Charlie Harper's dinner party.

From the roof last night he had watched the party break up and emerge from the restaurant in twos and threes, Charlie and Captain Harper pausing to bid good night to Wilma and her houseguest. Very nice. Wilma had invited Charlie to an early breakfast, so that Charlie could then show Kate Osborne the duplex that Kate wanted to rent.

No one but these weird women would invite company for breakfast at six on a winter morning—all this human camaraderie made Azrael retch.

Now, swarming up an old, thick bougainvillea vine, he prowled the rooftops again. They were barely beginning to brighten. To the east, the first light of dawn smeared bloody fingers across the dark hills. Heading across the roofs for Wilma Getz's cottage, he shivered in the cold wind that whipped in off the sea—felt like it came straight out of the Arctic. He never would get used to the damp chill in these northern regions, he could never shake the longing to sidle up to a sunny wall or to a rooftop heat vent. This part of the continent was fine for a short visit, for a brief session of snatch-and-grab with one human partner or another, but he would never want to live here.

He had tolerated the chill when he knew that he and Greeley would soon be taking off again for warmer climes, but this trip without Greeley was another matter. Having severed relations with the old drunk, he now had no sure promise of a return to that comfortable latitude; he didn't in fact know just where he was headed.

But something would turn up, something always did. The longing for a place of one's own, that senseless yearning that beset most cats and most people, had never troubled him. Meanwhile, his present situation was more than tolerable. Excellent food, excellent sleeping arrangements when he chose to take advantage, and some most interesting ventures.

Staring over the gutter where the two homeless men had left their lair to check out the trash cans, Azrael understood perfectly their wanderlust: those two might be scruffy and smelly but they had the right idea. Adventure was far more important than walls and a roof. The lure of what was out there around the next bend, the challenge of whatever lay beyond the shadows, of thrills yet untasted, that was the true quality of life.

He had parted from Greeley in Panama City to look

for just such fresh vistas after a bellyful of Greeley's newly wedded bliss, a sickening surfeit of Greeley's prissy bride and her attempts to domesticate Greeley's sweet little cat. Expecting him to drape himself around the house and purr on cue—he'd had enough of that in a hurry. Walking out for the last time, he'd taken up with that blond floozie in Panama City, had found her in a local bar, spent the evening winding around her ankles and had gone right on home with her to her poky little hotel room. By the time she headed stateside again, he'd not only revealed to her his conversational talents, he'd convinced her that he was the partner of a lifetime, that she couldn't take full advantage of her light-fingered skills without him. Oh, Gail had had a lust to steal. He'd greatly admired her talents. He'd picked her out of the crowd at the bar, as sure of her nature as if he'd caught her in the act.

Traveling with Gail to the States, he'd endured the kitty carrier and the nine-hour plane ride only because of the challenges that lay ahead. In San Francisco, where Gail had a boyfriend, they'd burgled a few shops and pulled off some amusing shoplifting gigs. And he had discovered a colony of cats that deeply interested him—he'd learned a lot in the city before they hit the road again traveling south, to enjoy a few easy heists along the coast. The weather had been warm for that part of California. Settling for a while here in the village while Gail entered a contest for would-be starlets, they had hit the jewelry stores and the upscale shops smooth as butter—until the dumb broad killed a guy and got herself sent to prison.

Then he'd split again, making himself scarce. But he hadn't gone far; this wealthy part of the coast was full of prospects. He'd remained on his own until he took up with his present associate, a partner far smoother than Gail or Greeley. Though both the blonde and the old man had been good for laughs.

His present colleague was much more talented than either of those two, a thief as cold as an Amazon boa. This partnership could, in fact, be the most interesting venture yet in his varied career. And now, concentrating his attention on Kate Osborne, he might really be onto something.

Leaping from a café balcony to the slanted roof of a bay window, he dropped down to a patio table, one of a dozen that the restaurant kept filled even in winter months. Tourists would freeze their figurative tails off to be seen eating al fresco in a sidewalk café as if they were in Europe. Thumping heavily to the brick paving, he headed up past the crowded shops, where cozy, close-set cottages took over.

Approaching Wilma Getz's small stone house, he slipped in among the masses of flowers that forested the woman's front yard beneath the oak trees. The old girl got up early; already the kitchen window was brightly lit, its glow reflecting blood-red from the bougainvillea flowers that framed the glass. The gaudy blooms stirred within the tomcat a painful longing for the hot streets of Panama.

Charlie Harper's van was not yet in sight; but Kate's car of course stood in the drive, the cream-colored Riviera silvered with dew. He found it interesting that she drove a seven-year-old vehicle. Maybe Clyde Damen kept it in running order for her. Azrael had learned a good deal last night about Kate Osborne.

Before the gallery opening, wandering in that direction to have a look, he'd been sidetracked by an appealing white Angora. She had insisted on leading him on a circuitous route of hide-and-seek, sickeningly coy. Why couldn't females simply accept what was offered and forget the foreplay? When he followed her under the deck of the Bakery Café, he had recognized Kate and Wilma's voices above him and caught a snatch of their conversation.

Promptly abandoning the Angora, driving her away when she returned to him coyly rolling over, he had listened with rising interest to the conversation above him. Kate was saying something about a cat museum, then mentioned some unusual pieces of jewelry carved with cats. That had brought his ears up.

The two women were apparently enjoying a light, early dinner on their way to the gallery opening. Lashing his tail with interest, he had settled under the deck just beneath their table.

The dining deck was crowded, all the tables were full, the tangle of conversations assaulting his ears like the dissonant caws of a flock of unruly crows. As he sought to isolate Kate and Wilma's discussion, he was nearly overcome by the aroma of broiled salmon—one didn't get fresh salmon in Panama, the waters were too warm, although the local fish and fresh prawns were quite superior. Pushing up between the supporting timbers of the deck, peering up through the cracks between the slats, he had studied Kate. The slim, blond young woman had an air about her that deeply interested him, that set her apart from other humans, that made him want to observe her closely. She was leaning across the table speaking softly, "Of course it's foolish. Why do I relate the jewelry to such an idea? Why do I keep imagining the jewelry linked to some impossible lost world? Except," she said uncertainly, "McCabe's journals—the man I think was my grandfather—speak of such a world as if he believed in it. Strange remarks, Wilma. Why do I keep returning to those entries? Surely I misread them. What is it in my nature, that wants to believe such things?"

*What, indeed?* Azrael had thought, observing Kate and smiling.

Having been raised in Latin America where unusual tales were believed, where wild stories had substance, where myth was a powerful part of life, the tomcat was a strong believer in matters supernatural. And why not, given his own surreal nature.

"The gold work," Kate was saying, "is so unlike anything else I've ever seen, like nothing I've found in any book on jewelry." But she laughed. "I take one class in the history of jewelry, ten years ago, and I know it all."

"But you did research it," Wilma said. "You spent hours in the city libraries."

Kate had leaned back, sipping her tea. "I'm being so silly. Those twelve pieces, even if they're a couple of centuries old, were very likely made right here in California. And even if the jewels are paste, the appraiser *was* interested in them—as curiosities, he said."

"Who was he? You had them appraised in San Francisco?"

"Yes. Emerson Bristol. He came highly recommended."

The tomcat stiffened and remained still, watching Kate through the cracks. *Emerson Bristol. Well doesn't that win the gold cat dish.* And as he considered this

unlikely happenstance, some interesting pieces began
to fall into place.

"I know who he is," Wilma said. "Yes, he has an excellent reputation."

"Bristol showed me some pictures from different
periods. That, with what I remember from art school
and then what I found on my own, made me see clearly
what he meant. The style of my pieces is almost Art
Deco, yet very different from that, much more primitive. Yet not medieval. Or baroque or Spanish, but a little of all of them. Not anything like nineteenth-century
European work."

She looked intently at Wilma. "Whoever made that
jewelry had his own ideas. Maybe some lone jeweler
emigrating from Europe, wanting to work alone, to do
his art *his* way. I can understand that, that he did not
want to follow tradition."

She broke a French roll, dropping a few crumbs
down onto Azrael's nose. "Maybe he produced a small
body of work that found its way into private collections
but never into any big collections or museums. And
then it got scattered again when people died off, and
was all but lost."

"Did Bristol think that might be the case?"

"We didn't discuss that. He simply said he found the
work different and interesting." Kate had leaned forward again, as if looking intently at Wilma, her face
hidden above the table. "Could that lone jeweler have
been my ancestor? And those twelve pieces stayed
within his family? Then through their attorney, they
found their way to me."

"I'm no authority," Wilma said, "but if others found
it interesting, as your appraiser did, why was it ignored

and forgotten? When the jewelry is so unique, why *didn't* some collector search it out? You said Bristol wanted to buy it?"

"He said he has a small collection of oddities. He didn't offer me much. After all, the jewels are paste." Kate paused. "Well the gold, of course, is worth something. It's lovely, but . . ."

"You have the other pieces safe, not lying around your apartment?"

"They're in my bank box, because of the gold and the workmanship. Until I know what they're all about."

"You said five other pieces, besides the barrette you gave Charlie, are designed with the images of cats?"

"Yes. But lots of designers use cats, have done, all through history." Kate sat very still at the table. The setting sun piercing down through the slats had warmed Azrael. Kate said, "Perhaps the pieces *are* older, from some European village that was very fond of its cats. Or maybe the jewelry was made in some isolated community here, by talented immigrants who settled back in the mountains, a little enclave where cats were valued."

She was, Azrael thought, denying the very world he sought, denying the very world from which she surely had descended. "Folk who stayed together," she said, "a little pocket of civilization that preferred to remain off by itself."

"But why," Wilma said, "when the pieces are so beautifully made, weren't they set with real stones?"

"A common practice in the seventeenth and eighteenth centuries, and even today, I guess. It didn't seem to make much difference whether the jeweler was working with real stones or imitation, the craftsmanship was equally fine." Kate set down her teacup. "The most amazing part, to me, was to finally track down the legal firm that gave them to me. The firm that served my grandfather—if McCabe was my grandfather. It's changed its name twice, and it looks to me like it won't be around much longer. The one remaining attorney is ancient. I can't imagine hiring him. I understand he does mostly grunt work now.

"But for him to simply give me the jewels, to haul out those old photographs of me as a child, and the names of the foster homes, and to feel that he had adequately identified me—" Kate shook her head. "Poor old thing. He must have been well over eighty, and had palsy, and . . .well I have to admit, when he gave me the box of jewels and said they were mine, I signed a release for them and got out of there as gracefully fast as I could manage. Before he changed his mind.

"And when I saw Bristol," Kate said, "I didn't give him my real name or phone number. I know that's bizarre. I— This whole thing, that doddering attorney, the jewels hidden away like that, all of it has me edgy, but strangely excited."

"It would have me edgy, too. And very interested. I think you were wise, keeping your identity to yourself until you know more."

The Getz woman *would* say that. She didn't trust anyone, Azrael had thought, scowling. Now he knew why Bristol hadn't been able to find his mysterious client after she left his office. The tomcat had licked his whiskers—his partner would be pleased to hear the answer to that little puzzle.

*If*, he had thought, *if I choose to share what I know.*

"Why," Wilma was saying, "hadn't the lawyer ever

been in touch? Why had he never contacted you, when apparently the firm, in its better days, kept track of you as a child?"

"The instructions he read to me said I was not to be given the jewelry until I was eighteen. By that time there was only the one partner; he didn't explain but I'm guessing he was already letting things slide, forgetting things. That walk-in safe—anything could be stashed in there, from the year one.

"When he opened its door and we went in, there were boxes of files in the back that looked like they'd been there since the place was built, in the eighteen hundreds."

"Were there no papers for you, nothing besides the jewelry?"

"There were two yellowed newspaper clippings. Something about Marin County, about a large number of cats disappearing and a tide of cats racing away in the night through a garden. The other clipping was the same kind of thing, in the city. Both from the same year, half a century ago." She was silent a moment, looking at Wilma. "Cats disappearing where? It gives me the shivers. And the strange thing is, ever since I saw the appraiser, I have this idea I've been followed."

Beneath the table, Azrael was riven with interest. *Cats racing away to where?* To what mysterious place? To the netherworld that he felt certain lay deep beneath northern California? And could *Bristol* know of such a world? Was this why he wanted the jewels? Or did he want the jewelry for its value? *Had* Bristol hired someone to follow Kate? But how could he, when he didn't know who she was? And that wasn't Bristol's style. The man *was* an upscale appraiser, he *was* well accepted in the city, very proper and circumspect. His under-the-table ventures were always accomplished at arm's length, by a man who knew far more intimately how to circumvent the law.

"The first time," Kate said, "I was coming out of Macy's, juggling some packages and trying to find my car keys. When I looked up, a man in the park was watching me. A thin, shabbily dressed man, very ordinary looking. Dull-colored hair, brown I guess. And a prominent nose, I remember that. I looked away and hurried the three blocks to my car. When I glanced back he had left the park and was half a block behind me. I was more curious than afraid. I stopped for a coffee so I could watch him; I wanted to see what he would do.

"He stood in a doorway looking away in the other direction, but when I left the coffee shop he followed me again. He was half a block away when I unlocked my car. By that time I was scared, I wanted to get away. Of course he would have seen the make and color of my car, the license. I was foolish to lead him to it, but I really didn't think . . ."

"When you pulled away, did any car follow you?"

"No, no one followed. I did watch for that."

"And the next time it happened?"

"Three days later. I was going into a fabric house, returning an armload of samples. When I turned into the door and glanced back, there he was half a block behind me.

"I dumped the samples inside, went back to approach him. But he slipped into a store and was gone. Just gone. I went all through the store. Apparently he went out the back through the stockroom. The three clerks were busy, and I was late so I went on.

"Maybe I'd have been foolish to confront him. Now, since I've glimpsed him twice more, the idea frightens me."

Azrael didn't know who this was. He didn't know if the stalker was, indeed, connected to Bristol. When the two women left the Bakery, heading for the gallery, he had followed above them, trotting across the rooftops.

From the roofs he had observed the gathering at the gallery, the fancy clothes, the expensive cars pulling up. Then much later he had looked down through the skylight on the Harper party's cozy little supper, and heard Kate and Charlie make their date for breakfast.

Turning away to pace the midnight rooftops, his black tail lashing, his nerves rippling under his skin like electrical shocks, the black tom had devised a plan so audacious, so perfect in its concept, that even when at last he settled down beside the brick chimney, mightily purring, he was so wired he found it hard to sleep. Stretched out against the warm bricks he lay for a long time perfecting the details, the tip of his tail flicking with challenge.

7

Dawn had not begun to bloody the sky when Azrael brushed through Wilma Getz's daisies, trampling the white blooms, and paused beneath her lighted kitchen window. The front yard had no lawn, just stone and brick walks, which he avoided, and flower beds as tangled as a Panamanian jungle and so heavy with dew that immediately his fur was soaked. Scowling, he moved swiftly up the back steps.

Both the front and back doors of Wilma Getz's stone cottage opened to the front garden. The house didn't have any useful backyard, in human terms. The hill that rose nearly straight up behind it was wild with tall grass and heavily populated with small creatures: a serviceable hunting spot. He had seen Dulcie and the tortoiseshell up there just yesterday dragging out a fat rabbit.

Pausing on the back porch, he sniffed the plastic flap of Dulcie's cat door, drinking in the sharp female scents—though he didn't need that message to know that Dulcie and the tortoiseshell had already left the house.

Coming down from the roofs he had seen them racing away, likely going to hunt. The tortoiseshell had been talking a mile a minute, making Dulcie drop her ears in annoyance, then turn to hush the younger cat before they were overheard. The young tortoiseshell was so eager, so filled with curiosity. The black tom smiled evilly.

Slipping under the flap, he stopped its swinging with his nose and moved through the shadows of the small laundry room, pausing behind a cardboard box filled with newspapers. How civic-minded of the old woman to dutifully recycle her copies of the Molena Point *Gazette*.

Though maybe *old woman* wasn't the term for Wilma Getz, even if she did have white hair hanging down her back. Maybe *gun-toting granny*, the way Greeley called her. The woman had taken no guff from Greeley, that time he came here to see his sister.

Greeley had been drunk as a boiled owl, stinking of booze and needing a bath. No wonder the woman had treated him like dirt. Though she hadn't messed with him, with Azrael. It took more than some white-haired ex–parole officer to run *him* out of a house.

From the shadows of the laundry, he looked through the open door to the kitchen. Wilma Getz stood at the sink, her back to him, mixing something in a bowl. He could smell raw eggs, and milk, and the sharp aroma of bacon sizzling in the skillet, sending tremors of greed through the tomcat. He licked away some drool. Wilma Getz's long white hair was tied on top her head with a yellow scarf, her sweatshirt printed with yellow flowers; the woman was as wild for color as some Panamanian maid, wearing red and purple and dragging her ragged bouquets.

Padding silently across the blue-and-white linoleum behind her, he could hear a shower running from deeper in the cottage. Moving on past Wilma to the dining room, he slipped under the cherry buffet, where he stretched out on the thick Kerman rug, tucking his paws under trying to keep warm. Why the hell didn't people turn up the heat?

He knew the layout of the house from his visit here with Greeley. That had been a year ago this last summer, when Greeley's sister Mavity got herself hit on the head and had come here from the hospital to recover. Neither Greeley nor Azrael had had anything to do with that little caper. Greeley was drunk the whole time, the old man laying up in that storeroom among those stacked cases of liquor, drowning himself in Scotch and rum—though Greeley *had* come to visit his sister that once, before they took off again for Panama.

But then Greeley had dragged that shopkeeper woman along on the plane and had married her down there. What a laugh. Couple of old farts playing at being newlyweds, trying to act like spring chickens.

Peering out from beneath the buffet past table and chair legs, he scanned the living room on his left, with its stone fireplace and blue velvet furniture and the painting of Molena Point rooftops over the mantel. Its dark green trees and bright red roofs reminded him of Panama. A wave of homesickness filled him, deeply angering him. He had no use for such sentiment.

Across the dining room from him, the door to the hall stood open, leading to Wilma's bedroom on the left and the guest bedroom on his right. Wilma's big room, where he and Greeley had gone to visit Mavity, was furnished in white wicker, flowered chintz, and a red metal woodstove. A room that, despite his disdain for human trappings, touched within him some regrettably cloying hunger, some weak aspect of his nature that made him want to curl up in there, purring.

He heard the shower stop.

In a minute the bathroom door opened; a cloud of scent reached him, as soft barefoot steps went down the hall. From the guest room came little rustling sounds as if Kate were getting dressed. He imagined her stepping out of her towel naked, beautiful Kate with her creamy skin and silky golden hair, and her golden eyes—unusual for a human. He imagined her as cat, golden and creamy, and again he smiled.

After dressing in pale jeans and a cream polo shirt, Kate pulled on her sandals and flipped a brush through her short hair. She needed to make a decision this morning on one of the three apartments—Charlie's, or one of the other two she had already looked at. If she was really serious about moving, she needed to put down a deposit. In Molena Point, as in the city, nice rentals didn't last.

The thought of moving again, of starting life over once more, though in a smaller way, wasn't pleasant. Moving out of her pretty Molena Point house after Jimmie tried to kill her, hiding from him, then later selling the house and furniture, at the same time being involved in his trial and conviction, had been more than traumatic. She had thought that when she moved to the city that would be the last move.

But now again everything was changed. Now, when

she returned to the city, she'd be followed once more, the strange man appearing in the shadows, in dark doorways, always with her like some incurable illness.

She had never really thought, until these last weeks, that when someone threatened you, they stole your freedom; that by following you they confined you, hindering your movements, limiting your options.

Heading down the hall for Wilma's bright kitchen, badly wanting coffee, she paused in the dining room, startled.

Was someone here? Someone in the house besides Wilma and herself? What did she sense? What a strange feeling. A sense of something unwelcome, someone who did not belong here.

Stepping into the living room, she found it empty. She moved back down the hall to Wilma's room. That room, too, was empty; the light, bright room with its red stove, its white wicker furniture and flowered chintz, seemed undisturbed. The bath and the open closet were empty. Yet the feeling of a foreign presence, of being watched, persisted.

This was not at all like when Dulcie or the kit watched her, not a friendly and amused little awareness, no sense of camaraderie.

Surely she was imagining this—yet the sensation was so real, she felt goose bumps. Strange that last night talking with Wilma over dinner she'd had the same uncomfortable idea that someone was watching them and listening—though the patrons at the surrounding tables had all been deep in their own conversations, paying no attention to them.

Taking herself in hand, she moved into the warm

kitchen where Wilma stood at the stove making pancakes. The first pale light of dawn had begun to brighten the diamond-paned windows. Wilma's homemade orange syrup was warming on the back burner, sending out a heavenly scent to mix with the aroma of pancakes and frying bacon. Wilma, in her yellow daisy-printed sweatshirt and her white hair pinned on top, looked as ragtag as a girl. Wilma moved like a girl, long and lithe despite her sixty-some years.

As Kate poured herself a cup of coffee, Charlie pulled up out front, driving her company van, the old blue Chevy that Clyde had rebuilt and made to look like new. He had fitted the inside of the van with specially designed storage for Charlie's cleaning and repair equipment, all beautifully planned between the two of them, every shelf and cupboard secured so nothing would jar loose and fall as Charlie plied the steep Molena Point hills. Kate wondered, now that Charlie and Max were married, and Charlie's career as an animal artist had taken off, whether Charlie would still run Charlie's Fix-it, Clean-it. Maybe she'd keep the business but turn the management over to one of her employees. As Charlie swung out and headed for the back door, Kate reached for another cup.

Pouring coffee for Charlie as she came in through the laundry, Kate added milk and sugar. Charlie was wearing a pale blue sweatshirt over a thick white turtleneck and fleece pants. Setting a covered bowl that smelled of fresh oranges on the table, she hugged Wilma and Kate. "Cold out. I'm sure it's going to snow." She smelled of horses from having done the morning feeding and cleaning the stalls, chores that she and Max shared equally since they had returned from their honeymoon. One of them got breakfast, she'd told Kate, while the other did the stable work. "There were in fact a few flurries," she said, "as I was getting in the van."

Wilma laughed. "It might snow in the hills but it better not snow on my garden." Snow in Molena Point might happen once every ten years, and then melted at once. Wilma dished the bacon onto a paper towel and handed plates of pancakes to Kate and Charlie, pouring another batch onto the griddle for herself. The two younger women settled at the table feeling cozy and pampered; yet even as they sat comfortably talking and enjoying Wilma's good breakfast, Kate had the feeling of a foreign presence. She looked up at Wilma. "Where's Dulcie? And how come the kit's not out here with her face in the pancakes?"

"They're off hunting. Bolted out of here almost before daybreak—as if the mice and rats couldn't wait to be slaughtered." Wilma shrugged. "When I ask Dulcie her hunting secrets she just smiles, and sometimes pats my cheek with a soft paw."

From beneath the buffet, Azrael's view of the kitchen was primarily legs—chair and table legs and human legs: Kate's slim, tanned ankles below her jeans, Charlie's leather paddock boots that smelled of horse even at that distance, Wilma's jogging shoes, scuffed and worn. He grew still and intent when Charlie asked about Kate's search for her family.

He had no idea why being adopted was so traumatic for humans. What difference if your mother took off, and whoever sired you was long gone? Except he did wonder, sometimes, about those cats that had produced him. But Kate was saying, "Every time I go through McCabe's papers, I grow uneasy." The smell of pancakes and bacon was making him drool.

"He was a construction contractor in San Francisco?" Charlie asked.

"Yes, and something of a philosopher. He wrote a regular column for the *Chronicle*, on all manner of subjects. McCabe and his wife—my grandmother, I guess—died in the 1939 earthquake. Apparently their baby survived, though I have found no birth certificate for her, nothing about her in the city records."

"It must be hard, with your foster home records so incomplete," Charlie offered. "But what led you to McCabe's journals?"

"The adoption agency was finally willing to release what information they had. It wasn't much, just the name McCabe who, they said, might have been my grandfather. I guess, with the earthquake, records were destroyed.

"The *Chronicle* archives produced some of his columns on microfilm. I found no address for him, no social security number, though that wasn't signed into law until 1935, no bank records, not even his contractor's license, and that is so strange. There were city records destroyed in the earthquake, but . . . I don't know. It's discouraging.

"I found a few relatives of people who had run the foster homes, but no one could tell me much. The *Chronicle* offices had nothing else, none of the vital information you'd think would be in their files. But I did find his connection to the San Francisco Cat Museum. Strange, I had visited the museum when I was in art school, studying the paintings and sculpture. Of course I hadn't a clue that the man who designed and built the museum might be my grandfather."

Kate broke a slice of bacon, eating it with her fingers. "It was in the museum that I found his journals, in their archives. And in the journals I found the name of his lawyer.

"The firm was still in the phone book—well you know the rest," she told Charlie. "That old man, the shoddy old office, the box of jewelry at the back of that walk-in safe."

Wilma rose to fill their coffee cups. Beneath the buffet, Azrael crouched, fitting the fragmented pieces together; not much yet, but he knew her parents were not of this world, and that deeply excited him. Then as the conversation turned from Kate's search to the three apartments that she was considering, he began to yawn, his pink mouth gaping wide in his sleek black face. Even the death angel needed an occasional nap.

"There's a big living room," Charlie said, "with a high, beamed ceiling. A small kitchen, and one bedroom at the back. A double garage underneath each unit, a deck along the front with a view of the village and the ocean. And of course Ryan is next door in the studio unit, with her lovely big weimaraner—if you don't mind occasional barking. Rock is a good stand-in for an alarm system, if that's ever needed, and he's a real love."

Azrael yawned again, so hard he nearly dislocated his jaw. He was dozing when he heard the slap of Dulcie's cat door. The sound jerked him to full attention. And before he could slip away, Joe Grey shot through the room, under the dining table, and past Azrael straight for the living room. Azrael heard him hit the top of the desk. Either the gray tom had fled by so fast that he didn't smell Azrael—not likely—or he was too preoccupied to care. Azrael heard Joe knock the phone from the cradle, and heard from the kitchen Dulcie's hastily whispered question and Wilma's casual reply.

"Anyone else here?" Dulcie hissed.

"Just us three," Wilma said. "What's the matter?"

*So,* the black cat thought. Both Charlie and Kate Osborne knew that these little cats could speak. Interesting. Apparently Joe Grey and Dulcie hadn't been very careful.

"What *is* it?" Wilma repeated.

*"Gas leak,"* Dulcie mewled. "A house up the street. Really strong, not like when you catch a sniff of it on the street."

Azrael could hear Joe Grey talking into the phone, giving the location, most likely talking to a police dispatcher. Telling her how strong the gas stink was and from which side of the dwelling. The next moment, some blocks away, a siren began to scream, and a fire engine went rumbling through the narrow village. He could feel the tremors in his paws as it passed, sharp as the precursor to an earthquake.

Listening to the blasting horn and the siren's final shrill scream just a few blocks away, Azrael flattened his ears. He could hear men shouting, then two more sirens, probably emergency vehicles in case there was an explosion. All these conscientious do-gooders flocking to help, so dedicated they made him gag. He imagined firemen searching for a gas cutoff, plying a wrench to stop the gas at the street. Imagined them gingerly pulling open front and back doors, ducking away and covering their faces in case the gas exploded. All that drama to save a few human lives, when the world was already overpopulated. In Azrael's view, the human herd could stand some thinning.

He froze, closing his eyes when Joe Grey streaked past. The gray tom didn't pause. Had Joe Grey caught his scent, even over the smell of fried bacon? Azrael heard Joe hit the kitchen and keep running. The plastic door flapped once, twice, and both cats were gone— and Wilma and Kate and Charlie were running out, humans and cats gripped by the urge to *rescue someone,* to *help people.* Enough smarmy goodwill to sicken a crocodile.

Now, with the house to himself, he left the shadows with leisurely insolence, and strolled into Wilma's kitchen. Leaping to the table, he polished off three pancakes and two slices of bacon. He licked the plates clean, then licked the cube of butter and drank the cream from the pitcher, nearly getting his head caught. Why would anyone make a pitcher so ridiculously small? He sniffed at the cooling coffee but it smelled inferior, not the rich Colombian brand he preferred.

Dropping to the blue-and-white linoleum again, he sauntered back through the dining room and down the hall to the guest room. Likely both humans and cats would be up the street all morning preoccupied with helping their neighbors. The black tom smiled. Fate couldn't have planned it better.

Alone in the guest room he set about a methodical search, pawing among Kate's silk lingerie bags and rooting in the gathered elastic pockets that lined the sides of her suitcase, his agile black paws feeling carefully for a small metal object. For what could be his passport to a greatly elevated position in the eyes of his current partner. For what, possibly, might also be a source of information that could prove most interesting.

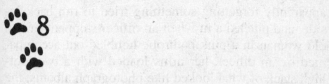

**8**

The yellow-and-white Victorian cottage stunk so powerfully of gas that the two cats thought it would go up any minute in an explosion of bricks and splintered wood and shingles. They'd seen such a disaster before. They didn't want that experience again. But with typical feline curiosity, they were too interested to leave. Cops were on the scene now, and that generated more questions.

Once the fire crew had cut off the gas, having circled the house peering in, they had broken the lock and gone inside. Shortly thereafter a rescue vehicle pulled up in front, then two police cars came screaming.

The house belonged to James Quinn, a Realtor with Helen Thurwell's firm. Quinn was, in fact, Helen's partner, handling sales with her as a team. The air around the handsome Victorian cottage was, even from a block away, so heavy with gas it made the cats retch.

Scorching up a pine tree, they clung in the frail branches side by side, where a breeze helped clear the air. Watching the police evacuate the houses along the block, they were both alarmed and amused by people running out of their homes loaded with valuables and carrying their pets. A frazzled-looking young woman apparently forgetting something tried to run back inside, and pitched a fit when an officer stopped her. An old woman in a pink bathrobe hobbled out accompanied by an officer, her arms loaded with a two-foot-high stack of what looked like photograph albums, the little tie cords at the spines flopping in her face. As if she was saving all the family pictures. A portly lady in a red-and-black sweat suit clutched three cats, the frightened animals clawing her as she hurried down the street. When Wilma and Charlie saw her, they took two of the cats and ran with her, carrying the cats three blocks to a neighbor and handing them inside. Neither Joe nor Dulcie had seen the kit. Scanning the street looking for her, Joe moved from paw to paw, growing so nervous and restless he seemed about to explode, himself.

"The kit's all right," Dulcie said. "She won't . . ."

"You don't know what she'll do. And it isn't only the kit . . ." Joe's yellow eyes narrowed. "Coming through the dining room—I think I caught the scent of that black beast."

"Azrael? In the house? Oh, but why would he . . . ? Where, Joe? We have to go back."

"As I passed the buffet. Just a faint whiff of scent— the whole house smelled of bacon."

Her eyes wide, she crouched to leap down. But he reached a paw to stop her. "I'll go back, Dulcie. Stay here, watch for the kit. Who knows where she's gotten to. You know how she is, she'll be in the middle somewhere . . ." He sounded truly worried, his frown deep and uneasy.

"I'll watch, I'll find her. But you . . . Be careful, Joe. Why did he go into Wilma's house? What's he up to?"

Joe's eyes were filled with conflicting concerns. "Watch for the kit but don't go near that house. Promise me!" He gave her a whisker rub and was gone, backing fast down the rough bark of the pine tree and streaking for Wilma's house. Dulcie stared after him, her ears flat with frustration, then she turned to search the gathering crowd again and the surrounding rooftops for the dark small presence of the tortoise-shell kit; the kit could vanish like a shadow among shadows. And, by her very nature, she was powerfully drawn to any kind of village disaster.

Dulcie looked and looked for a long time, but didn't see the kit. She saw no cat at all among the bushes or slipping between the feet of the thickening crowd or concealed in the branches of the surrounding trees. No cat hidden among the angles of the rooftops. Growing more and more worried, she left the safety of pine tree at last, and galloped across the roofs toward the gas-filled house.

Crouching on a shop roof just across the narrow street from the yellow Victorian house, she watched several officers in the front yard gathered around a paramedic's van. Below her hung a striped awning that bore, along its front edge, the name of the antique store it sheltered. Dropping down into the sagging canvas, crouching belly to stripes like a sunbather in a giant-size hammock, she studied the windows of James Quinn's yellow house.

All the windows were open to let out the gas, as was the front door, and still the air stunk of gas. She could see Captain Harper and Detective Garza inside. She could not see the medics, they were not around their van. Were they in there working on someone? Was Mr. Quinn in there? Dulcie's skin rippled with dismay. If he was still there, if he had not run out . . .

*Had he been asleep when the gas leak started, had he perhaps not awakened? Was he dead in there?* Dulcie thought, sickened. James Quinn was an elderly man, though he still worked as a Realtor. He was a very nice single man living alone, with no one to wake him if he slept too soundly during such a disaster.

Or, she thought, had he already gone to work when the leak started? Maybe he didn't even know about the leak, maybe he had left the house really early, to show a distant piece of property, maybe he had no idea what was happening here. James Quinn did not seem to Dulcie the kind of person to have carelessly left a gas jet on, to have not turned it off properly. According to Wilma, Quinn was if anything overly careful and precise.

Helen Thurwell's real estate partner was a short, gentle, wiry man, thin and bald, with leathery skin from hours on the golf course. His tee time was dedicated as much to business as to pleasure. Though pushing seventy, Quinn was still a top salesman with the firm, low key, easy, never pushy. That was what Wilma said. A man to whom clients came, as they came to Helen, when they wanted to avoid the hard sell. Playing golf with his clients, Quinn made many a casual, million-dollar deal.

Where was the kit? She was always in the front row

when anything happened in the village. Searching the block for Kit, from her high vantage where she could hardly miss another cat, Dulcie began to entertain a sick feeling. Was the kit in that house?

But why? Why would she be in there?

A crew from PG&E was working at the curb where, earlier, the fire crew had removed a concrete cover and turned off the gas. Most of the utility trucks and squad cars were parked down the block, safe in case of an explosion. The crime tape the police had strung was not enough to keep back onlookers without the officers who were politely but firmly directing them. She saw Wilma and Charlie and Kate standing with the crowd waiting for any opportunity to help. But where was the kit? Surely she had heard the sirens, there was nowhere in the village where she couldn't have heard them.

The medics were bringing someone out on a stretcher. James Quinn lay unmoving, his face and hands strangely red. They set the stretcher down on the lawn and the medics knelt over him. But soon they rose again; they did not work on Quinn. He lay waiting for the coroner's attention.

Dulcie knew that under other circumstances the body would not have been moved until a detective had photographed the scene and made sketches and notes. She supposed with the house full of gas, that hadn't been an option. But to leave him lying here on the lawn seemed strange, even with a police guard around him. Maybe Detective Garza wanted to photograph the body and let the coroner have a look before they moved Quinn again. How could Quinn have died in there? How could he not have smelled the gas? Even in sleep, one would think the stink of gas would wake him. He wasn't a drinker. Never touched liquor; so he had not slept in an alcoholic stupor too numbed to wake. And from what she had heard of Quinn's careful nature, it would not have been like him to leave the gas on accidentally. She saw Dr. John Bern's car being driven over the lowered police tape, coming slowly up the street; she glimpsed Bern's bald head, the glint of his glasses.

Dulcie was watching Dr. Bern kneeling over the body when a thumping on the shingles above her jerked her up. The kit came galloping straight at her and, hardly pausing, dropped down onto the awning, rocking the canvas and digging her claws in. Dulcie was so glad to see her, she nuzzled against Kit, licking her ears and whiskers. The kit stunk of gas.

"You've been in there," Dulcie hissed.

The kit looked at Dulcie, shivering. "He's dead." She stared across the street at the stretcher and the body. "I was in there when you came the first time, I looked out and saw you and Joe, I saw you sniff at the gas, then turn and race away. I knew you'd call the station so I . . . but listen, Dulcie . . ."

The tattercoat's round yellow eyes were wide with the news she had to tell. "The gas stunk so strong I went in through the back door—to see if he was in there, to wake him if he was still asleep, to . . ." The kit stared at her with distress.

"You could have died in there."

"I pushed the back door open to get in, a little breeze came in. I wasn't there long and I stayed low against the floor, but it choked me and I felt dizzy. He was lying on the kitchen floor. I stuck my nose at his nose and there was no breath and he was cold, so cold, and the gas was making me woozy so I got out of there fast and you and Joe were there, then running away up the street so I knew you'd call for help. Why was there gas in there?"

Dulcie sighed. "You didn't paw at a knob, Kit? And make the gas come on?"

"No! I never! The gas was all in there. Why would I do that!" she said indignantly. "I smelled it from the street. That's why I went in." Her eyes darkened with pain. "But he was dead. Cold dead."

Dulcie looked and looked at the kit. The kit settled down beside her, pushing very close. She was quiet for a long while. Then in a small voice Kit said, "Where's Joe Grey?"

"He's following someone." Dulcie didn't mean to tell the kit more. For once, the kit could keep her nose out. Below them, the coroner still knelt over James Quinn, Dr. Bern's bald head and glasses reflecting the morning light.

Down the block within the growing crowd, the cats saw Marlin Dorriss pushing through. The tall, slim attorney was dressed in a pale blue polo shirt and khaki walking shorts that, despite the chilly weather, set off his winter tan. His muscled legs were lean and brown, his white hair trimmed short and neat. He was a man, Dulcie thought, that any human woman might fall for—except that Helen Thurwell had no business falling for anyone. In doing so she had royally screwed up her daughter's life, had sent Dillon off on a tangent that deeply frightened Dulcie.

It was hard enough for a fourteen-year-old girl to grow up strong and happy. In Dulcie's view, human teen years must be like walking on the thinnest span

across a vast and falling chasm where, with a false
step, you could lose your footing and go tumbling
over—as the kit would say, falling down and down.

The cats didn't want that to happen to Dillon.

Watching Marlin Dorriss approach the stretcher,
seeing the concern and kindness in his face as he observed from some distance the body of James Quinn, it
was hard for Dulcie to imagine him willfully destroying a close little family. The matter deeply puzzled her.

Dorriss had lived in Molena Point for maybe ten
years, in an elegant oceanfront villa. A semiretired
lawyer, Dorriss served only a few chosen clients, rep-
resenting their financial interests. He was gone from
the village much of the time, keeping a condo in San
Francisco, a cabin at Tahoe, and condos in New York
and Baton Rouge. He was a sometime collector of a
few select painters, mostly those of the California action school, such as Bischoff, Diebenkorn, and David
Park. He collected a few modern sculptors, and bought
occasional pieces of antique furniture to blend into the
contemporary setting of his home. Dorriss was charming, urbane, easy in his manners, but a man deeply
frustrating to the local women. If he dated, the relationship never went far.

Certainly he had woman friends across the country
if you could believe the photographs in the Molena
Point *Gazette*, the San Francisco *Chronicle*, and one or
two slick arts magazines. Dulcie imagined Dorriss
consorting, in other cities, with wealthy society
women as sleek and expensively turned out as a bevy
of New York fashion models.

So what was it about Helen Thurwell that so attracted him? The tall, slim brunette was nice enough

looking, but she was not the polished, trophy-quality knockout that Marlin Dorriss seemed to prefer. And why was Helen ruining her own life and Dillon's for a high-class roll in the hay when Dorriss had dozens of women?

As she crouched in the sagging awning studying the attorney, she saw Helen Thurwell approaching from the alley behind Jolly's Deli. At the edge of the crowd Helen paused, standing on tiptoe trying to see. When she realized which house was surrounded, she began to force her way through the crowd.

She stopped when she saw Quinn's body, then started forward again, her hand pressed to her mouth. At the same moment she saw Marlin Dorriss.

Even now, at this stressful moment, there was a spark between the two. They stood very still, as if joined by an invisible thread, both looking at Quinn but sharply aware of each other.

Then Dorriss turned away and headed up the street.

Helen remained looking, her face very white, her fist against her lips. Behind her, Detective Garza emerged from the house carrying a clipboard and a camera, his square, serious face and dark eyes filled with a stormy preoccupation, with an intensity that Dulcie knew well.

Pressing forward on the sagging canvas, Dulcie didn't take her eyes from the detective. As she watched Garza, he in turn watched Helen Thurwell.

Not until Helen turned away from Quinn did Garza approach her. The two spoke only briefly, then they moved up the steps and inside the house.

Across the street, half a block away, Helen's daughter stood watching them, pressed into the crowd with three of her school friends. Dillon's look followed Helen with an anger that made Dulcie shiver. The same expression, the same hate-filled resentment with which, moments earlier, Dillon had observed Marlin Dorriss as he turned and left the scene.

Glancing at Kit, Dulcie dropped from the awning to a bench, then to the sidewalk. With the kit close behind her, they skirted through the bushes past the uniformed officers and the coroner and the body. Crossing the porch in shadow, within moments they were inside the house, silent and unseen. Following Detective Garza and Helen Thurwell through the house, Dulcie and Kit glanced at each other, their curiosity equally sharp, equally predatory and keen.


Joe Grey trotted fast up the four blocks to Wilma's stone cottage and, avoiding the front garden, galloped around behind where the wild hill rose steeply at the back. Leaping up through the jungle of tall grass, its dry swords laced through with new green shoots, he spun around, standing tall on his hind paws and peered over the rustling jungle, in through the guest-room window.

He could see Kate's tan wheeled suitcase lying open on a luggage stand. The only clothing not folded into it was her blue velvet robe, which was thrown across a chair. The black tom crouched just beside the bed. Even as Joe watched, Azrael slid up and into the open suitcase among her sweaters and silk lingerie bags, and began to paw through them, his black tail lashing as he prodded and poked with demanding paws. Joe watched him, frowning. Kate was all packed to head home, the hangers in the closet empty, the bedding turned back, the sheets and pillowslips removed and piled in a heap in the corner. That, Dulcie had told him, was the way Wilma liked her guests to leave a room. Neither Dulcie nor Wilma could understand why a house guest, on departing, would make up the bed with dirty sheets when his host would only have to strip them off again, to put on clean ones for the next round of company.

When the tom had finished patting and pawing at the sweaters and lingerie, he turned his attention to the side pockets of the suitcase, sliding his quick black paw into one pocket after another, searching as thoroughly as would any human thief.

But searching for what? Why would this feline thief waste his time with maybe a few hundred dollars in cash, say, when he was accustomed, working with a human partner, to robbing far more productive safes and cash registers? And why Kate?

Kate had told Wilma that the choker she wore last night was paste, fake jewels. So why would this black beast want it? And where was his human partner? Who was Azrael running with now, if old Greeley was out of the picture? Joe watched, fascinated and filled with questions as the tomcat rooted and dug.

When the cat had investigated nearly every inch of the suitcase and had slyly smoothed each item back as it had been, when he was rooting in the last small pocket, he paused.

With his paw deep in the smallest pocket, he remained very still. His mouth was open, panting, his ears shifting in every direction, seeking for the faintest sound.

The tip of his tail twitching with excitement, Azrael

withdrew his paw, claws extended. Dangling from those curved rapiers was a round flashing key fob attached to a long silver key.

Dropping his prize on the carpet, he stood looking down at it. A very plain key and curiously flat, no little ridges as most keys had to fit into the mysterious depths of their given lock. This key did have little protrusions to code the tumblers, but each was precisely cut, at right angles. And Joe Grey smiled.

Clyde carried a key like that, struck from a flat sheet of metal, each straight cutout with only right angles and precise corners, a key that looked as if it would be easy to reproduce but, for reasons Joe didn't understand, was apparently hard to duplicate—or maybe locksmiths did not keep that kind of blanks, in some universally agreed-upon deference to security.

Leaving the safe deposit key lying beside the suitcase, Azrael leaped to the dresser. Pawing through a sheaf of papers that were weighted down with a hairbrush, he was once more thorough and intent. He sorted carefully through the stack but, not finding what he was seeking, he abandoned the papers at last and tackled a leather briefcase that stood leaning against the mirror.

Poking his black nose in, then all but climbing inside, the tom wiggled and shook the bag as if fighting some inner fastener. Pawing and nosing, he backed out after some minutes, gripping in his teeth a small blue folder. A checkbook? Joe was so fascinated that he stepped on a thistle hidden among the grass, the barbs stung like needles. Flinching at the pain, he watched Azrael open the folder and stare down at the pad of checks.

Was he reading the bank's name and location? Joe watched him remove a check carbon with a careful paw and pat at it until he had folded it into quarters. Pressing the creases with his paw, he retrieved the key, laid it on the folded carbon and took them both clumsily in his teeth.

Holding his head high so as not to drag the key and maybe not drool on the carbon, Azrael left the room flaunting his prize as he might flaunt a pigeon he had captured on the wing.

Outside on the hill, Joe Grey moved fast, leaping down through the grass, heading for Dulcie's cat door. He was around the house by the corner of the garage when he heard the cat door flap, and the black beast burst out and down the steps, flashing away through Wilma's garden.

Silently Joe followed.

Metal and paper are not mouth-friendly, the one brutally hard, the other inclined to become soggy. But, heading across the village and keeping to the shadows, Azrael was on an incredible high. What he carried was practically an engraved invitation, a passport to jewels that, according to Emerson Bristol's *true* account of the matter, were worth a hefty fortune.

The scenario was quite different from what Kate Osborne believed. And that should lead to ridiculously easy pickings; as simple as snatching baby birds from a sparrow's nest.

9

The body had been taken away. On the trampled front lawn of the yellow Victorian cottage, the coroner stood talking with Captain Harper. Inside the house could be seen, through a front window, Detective Dallas Garza and Helen Thurwell standing in a book-lined room, talking. In the same room, unobserved, Dulcie and the kit lay sprawled beneath a leather easy chair, peering out, watching and listening.

The cats weren't sure whether Helen was some sort of witness, or a suspect. Though of course Garza would want to question her, she was Quinn's sales partner. Dulcie looked around the study, mentally yawning. Quinn's house was dullsville.

One would think a real-estate agent would have a lovely home, maybe small and modest but certainly designed with character and imagination. James Quinn's residence looked as if Quinn, who was a widower, cared little about his surroundings. As if the living room were no more than a wide passageway to the bedroom or kitchen but otherwise of no use. The furni-

ture was old and cheap, the colors faded almost to ex-
tinction; there were no pictures on the walls, no books
or flowers or framed photographs on the end tables.
She imagined Quinn bringing home a bag of takeout
for his supper, eating it alone in the kitchen or on the
couch as he watched TV on the relic set, imagined him
coming into his study to do a little paperwork, then off
to bed.

Maybe his social life and nice meals, whatever ele-
gance he might enjoy, centered around the golf course.
Certainly Quinn had nice clothes, certainly he dressed
very well; she had seen him around the village.
Whether dressed for work showing houses or for the
one sport in which he indulged, he always looked well
turned out.

Quinn's study was just as dull as the rest of the
house, furnished with scarred and mismatched furniture and cheap plywood bookshelves. Helen stood
looking down at Quinn's battered oak desk, which was
strewn with folders and papers lying every which way
atop a black leather briefcase.

"He never kept his papers like this, in such a mess.
James might not be . . . have been much for a pretty
house," she said almost as if she'd read Dulcie's
thoughts, "but he was a neatnik when it came to work."

Helen Thurwell was a few inches shorter than
Garza. Her cropped, dark brown hair was straight and
shining, her black suit neatly tailored. She wore flat
black shoes, simple gold earrings, and she still wore
her thick gold wedding band. Dulcie watched her cover
that now, with the cotton gloves that Dallas Garza
handed her.

"We've fingerprinted and photographed," Garza

said. "Even with the gloves, please handle the papers by the edges. I'd like you to go through them, tell me if anything looks strange, or if you think anything is missing."

Watching the detective, Helen was quiet for a long moment. "As if someone . . . As if this wasn't an accident?"

"Until we learn otherwise," Garza said shortly.

"I'll have to sort them into some kind of order."

Garza nodded.

Standing at the desk, Helen began sorting through Quinn's papers, arranging them into stacks, each atop one of the empty file folders that were mixed in with loose sheets. "He was always so neat, he never made this kind of mess. Each sale has its file with several pockets for offers and counteroffers, for miscellaneous notes, for the inspection and related work. He . . . he used to tease me about my haphazard ways." She compared several sheets, stood thinking a moment, then put the papers in their proper files. When she had finished, she moved away from the desk, turning toward the window. The cats could see her face now, her dark eyes filled with distress. She looked up at Garza.

"I see nothing missing, all the clients we were working with are here. Their files seem complete. His field book is here and doesn't look tampered with. The only thing that's strange, outside of the mess, is a notebook seems to be missing. Not part of our work but a small personal notebook. Maybe it's somewhere else in the house. I don't know what it was for, I'm sure it didn't have to do with business. It wasn't anything that the rest of us kept."

Helen shook her head. "I didn't see it often, and he never shared it with me. Occasionally I would see him making an entry, but it seemed a private thing. A small brown notebook maybe three by five inches. Sometimes he carried it in his coat pocket. Reddish brown covers . . . what do they call it? *Deal?* A slick mottled brown, sort of like dark brown parchment, but heavier. Black cloth tape binding. The kind of notebook you'd get in any drugstore or office supply."

"Did you ever see the entries?"

"No. When I came in he was usually just putting it away. Not hiding it, but as if he'd finished whatever he wrote there. Possibly something to do with his clients' personal likes and dislikes, that was my guess. Not about what they wanted in a house, that we kept in a mutual binder. But maybe for little gifts, you know? What kind of flowers or candy. We send a little gift when a sale is completed.

"And yet that does seem strange," Helen said, "to take that much care with those routine presents. He usually let me handle that."

She looked with desolation at Garza. "James was a very matter-of-fact guy, not a lot of imagination. Honest—a good person to work with." But as she said this, her face colored and she turned away.

Watching from the shadows, the kit put out a paw as if to comfort her, then quickly drew it back out of sight. Dulcie considered Helen with interest. Had mentioning James Quinn's honesty embarrassed her because of her own cheating? Why else would she blush like that?

When Detective Garza and Helen had left the house, the cats trotted to the far end of the living room and leaped to the sill of an open window, ready to follow them out. But, hitting the sill, they saw who was out there and dropped again to the floor. Dillon Thurwell stood in the shadows not six feet from them.

Unwilling to miss anything, the two cats hopped up onto an end table that stood behind the dusty draperies. Crowding together, they could just see out where Dillon and three of her girlfriends were giggling and whispering rude remarks—as if they had been there for some time watching the coroner and ogling the dead man, as if they had seen Quinn taken away to the morgue and found the tragedy highly amusing. In the morning light, Dillon's red hair shone like copper against the dark hair of two companions, and against the long, pale locks of the one blonde. The girls were dressed in low-cut sleeveless T-shirts that showed their bellies. Their remarks about the pitiful dead man were filled with rude humor.

Dillon seemed so cold and hard, Dulcie thought sadly, compared to the young girl she knew. Last year, Dillon had been among the first to suspect the murders of those poor old people at Casa Capri Retirement Home. Acting with more compassion and more responsibility than most of the adults involved, and far more creatively, she had helped to uncover the crimes. Then this last winter during the Marner murders, when Dillon was kidnapped by the killer, she had again kept her head better than many adults would have, defying her captor, and quick to move when Charlie and the cats helped her escape.

Now Dillon seemed not at all in charge of herself, as if suddenly she was letting others totally rule her. She was no longer someone Dulcie wanted to be near, no longer a person whom a cat would love, whom a cat would go to. Dillon Thurwell seemed now ready to explode into an emotional hurricane.

And one of Dillon's friends greatly puzzled Dulcie. Consuela Benton was not a classmate, but was several years older, a beautiful Latina, her long, black, curly hair rippling in a cloud around her slim face. She must be at least eighteen, to Dillon's fourteen. In every way she seemed a world apart from the other three.

Consuela's lipstick was nearly black. She wore such heavy eyeliner that she looked more like a vampire than a human girl. Why would an older girl like this bother with younger children? What did she gain from their company? Dillon and her friends, even with their attempts at sophisticated dress and cool makeup, compared to Consuela, were like scruffy kittens next to a battle-hardened alley cat.

These last months, Consuela had surely become a leader for the oldest junior high girls. Dulcie had seen her hanging around Dillon's school or with a crowd of young girls in the shops, where they were loud and rude. Both Dulcie and Joe, following the girls casually, had seen them shoplifting.

The first time, Dulcie didn't want to believe that Dillon was stealing. By the third time she followed them, she was trying to figure out where they were stashing the stolen items. At one of the girls' homes? Neither she nor Joe wanted to call Captain Harper. As proud as they were of their impeccable record of solving local crimes, they didn't want to tell Harper this. Dillon was Max Harper's special friend. Harper had taught her to ride, on his own mare, Redwing. He had helped her to become a capable horsewoman, had tried to help Dillon move easily and surely through her teen years without falling.

But then the kit had followed the girls and, apparently, had seen something so upsetting the kit would not talk about it. Dulcie had found her at home curled up in a little ball beneath the blue wool afghan looking wan and forlorn.

Pawing at the knitted throw, Dulcie had nosed at her. "Are you sick, Kit? Are you hurt?"

"Fine. Not hurt."

"Sick?"

"No."

"Then what's the matter?"

"I don't want to tell."

"You must tell me. I can help."

"Must I? Can you?" That was all the kit would say.

"Did someone hurt you? Did someone do something to you?"

The kit had shaken her head. Dulcie, having seen Kit following the four girls earlier that morning, could only suspect that she was upset about something Dillon had done. But Kit refused to get Dillon in trouble or to dismay the captain.

Well, Dulcie had thought, no one could force her. Kit would have to decide in her own time. Now, as she glanced at the kit, the tall, broad-shouldered girl with the black braids laughed loudly. "I bet he killed himself. Turned on the gas and sucked it up and croaked." She clutched her throat as if strangling, gagging and sticking out her tongue. *Leah*, Dulcie thought. The girl's name was Leah. Dulcie wanted to claw her.

"If *I* was that old and wrinkled," Consuela said, "*I'd* kill *my*self."

The three younger girls doubled up with merriment, their giggles self-conscious and loud.

"The dead guy's your mother's partner," said the blonde.

"I guess," Dillon snapped. "It stinks here, let's go."

"And that was her lover." Leah giggled. "That tall guy who left a while ago, that was your mother's squeeze."

"You have a big mouth," Dillon told her. "A big cesspool mouth."

"So *isn't* he her lover? *You* said . . ."

Dillon slapped the girl. Hit her so hard that Leah reeled. Catching herself Leah swung at Dillon.

Consuela stood leaning smugly against the side of the building, watching them, grinning slyly when Leah grabbed Dillon's hair. As Dillon swung to hit her again, she was grabbed from behind.

Max Harper was quick and silent, holding Dillon's arm. The captain's thin sun-creased face was drawn into an unforgiving scowl. He stood, thin and muscled and tall, staring down at Dillon. "Go home, Dillon. Go home now. And go alone."

"You can't make me," Dillon said tremulously, her face flushing.

Harper looked hard at her, and at the other three. "Leah and Candy, you get on to your own homes. *Do it now.*"

Leah and Candy backed away from him, and left.

Redheaded Dillon stood still, defying him. Consuela stood watching, still smirking.

Ignoring Dillon, Harper fixed on Consuela. "Miss Benton, I don't want to see you around Dillon anymore. You have no business with these girls."

"What I do is not your business!"

"It is my business if you are arrested for a crime."

Consuela flipped Harper the bird, turned away, and sauntered insolently up the street. Max Harper stood looking after her, then looked down at Dillon. All the closeness between them, all the easy companionship, was gone. "Go now, Dillon."

At last Dillon headed away in the direction of her own house, sullenly scuffing her feet like a young child. Harper, watching her, looked so sad that Dulcie wanted to reach out a paw and comfort him. He looked as if his own child had fallen in front of him and refused to get up.

The kit watched the captain, too, very still and frightened. Was there nothing she could do to make him feel better? She knew how to tease the captain, but she didn't know what to do about his hurt. She watched the girls fade away through the village wondering why Dillon ran with those others. Did you call a group of human girls a clowder, like cats? Why were those girls so angry? Why had Dillon turned so mean? The kit was so full of questions she began to shiver—but part of her shivers were hunger, too. The deep-down belly-empty hunger she always felt when her head was too full of fear and questions.

Behind them, an officer had come into the house and

started closing windows; soon the house would be secured and additional crime tape strung around it. Dulcie and Kit looked at each other, slipped through the drapery, leaped out the window and up the nearest tree—and they raced away across the rooftops and along sprawling oak branches until they reached Jolly's alley.

On the roof of Jolly's Deli they paused with their paws in the gutter, their pads sinking down into the mat of wet leaves, looking down into the pretty brick paved lane with its flowers and benches, anticipating the usual nice plate of treats that Mr. Jolly put out for the village cats; after the stressful morning, a cat needed comfort food.

Mr. Jolly himself was just coming out the back door, dressed in his white pants and white shirt, white shoes and white apron. Bending over with a grunt because his stomach got in the way, he set down a paper plate loaded with smoked salmon and shrimp salad and roast beef, all smelling so good the kit drooled. The cats were ready to scorch down the jasmine vine and enjoy the feast, when Dulcie nipped the kit's shoulder and pulled her back quickly onto the shingles where they would not be seen.

Below them, Consuela was entering the alley pushing irritably past the flowering trees in their big clay pots. The black tomcat swaggered in beside her. Consuela, swiveling her hips, sat down on the little wooden bench. Azrael, glancing the length of the alley, crouched before the plate of deli scraps, and in seconds the food was gone. He scarfed it all the smoked salmon and roast beef and the nice shrimp salad. The kit wanted to fly down there and cuff him away but he was pretty big. His purrs of gluttony filled the alley as loud and ragged as another cat's growls. Behind the rudely slurping beast, Consuela sat impatiently waiting, tapping her booted toe and tossing a key in her hand. Each time she flipped the key, it clinked against its dangling metal fob. With her frowzy black hair and black lipstick and black-lined eyes, the two were as alike as human and cat could be. Watching them, the kit looked up when Dulcie nudged her; and she looked where Dulcie was looking.

Across the chasm of the alley on the opposite roof, among the leafy shadows of an acacia tree, Joe Grey stood so still that he seemed at first glance no more than a smear of gray shadows among the dark leaves.

Had he been there all the time? His yellow eyes gleamed intently, telling the kit to be still. Then his gaze dropped to the alley where the black tomcat was cleaning the paper plate with a rasping tongue, holding it down with his paw.

As the black tom turned and sauntered across the bricks and leaped onto the bench beside Consuela, Joe Grey came to the edge of the roof, listening.

"Well?" the black tom said, watching her.

Coldly Consuela studied him. "What do I get? What's in it for me?"

"You'll greatly impress our friend, I can guarantee that. I expect he'll split with you."

Jingling the key, she looked unconvinced.

"A blond wig, a little practice with the signature, you're in *and* out and no one the wiser. Banks don't

bother to see if you have your checkbook or if you remember your account number. They just want you in
there with your money. In this case they want you in
and out fast. Opening the vault makes them edgy."

"You're an authority, you've cased a lot of banks."
She whipped out a little mirror and applied another
layer of dark lipstick, then spit on her little finger and
smoothed a perfect black eyebrow. "What if she misses
the key?"

"What if she does? She'll think she misplaced it.
Who would come into her room there at the Getz house
and know to look for a safe deposit key?"

"You did," she said fluffing her hair.

The cat shrugged. "She'd never think of that."

The two continued in this vein for nearly half an
hour before Consuela agreed to pack a bag, gas up her
car, and head for the city while Kate was still in the village. The three cats listened in amazement to Azrael's
persistent and artful barrage; but only Joe Grey had the
full story. Dulcie and Kit glanced across at him, impatient for him to fill in the blanks. As Azrael painted for
Consuela visions of her wearing mink and driving a
Jaguar escorted around San Francisco by any man of
her choosing, both Dulcie and Kit had to clench their
teeth to keep from collapsing in fits of giggles. Whatever scam Azrael was pushing, they thought he ought
to stick to robbing antique stores and stealing the savings of little old ladies. Banks were big time, out of his
and Consuela's league.

Or were they? By the time the two left the alley,
Azrael was strutting beside Consuela lashing his tail
with triumph.

# 10

Late September rains had turned the hills above Molena Point from summer gold to the clear bright green of winter. To visitors from the East Coast, where the summer hills are green and the winter hills brown, the reverse in color seems strange. Gold rules the California summers, green paints the colder months. High above the village rooftops the Harper pastures glowed as green as emerald.

Charlie stood at her kitchen window looking down the verdant slopes past their neat white pasture fences to the village and the far sea, waiting beside the bubbling coffeepot for Ryan Flannery's red pickup to turn into the long drive, waiting to go over the blueprints so that Ryan could start the new addition.

Having moved to the ranch as a bride just a month earlier, to the home where Max had lived with his first wife until she died, Charlie had been reluctant at first to suggest any changes in the house. But when she did broach the subject, Max had been all for it. This home was their retreat, their safe place, their serene and private world. The new addition would make that haven even more perfect, a lovely new space in which they were together, and in which she could do her own work while Max was off locking up the bad guys.

Max's wife, Millie, had been a cop. She hadn't needed space to work at home, other than the small study that she and Max had shared. That marriage had been nearly perfect. Max's friends, Clyde in particular, had thought Max would never marry again.

Charlie had no notion that she could take Millie's place, nor would she want to. She had married not only Max, she had married the good and lasting presence of Millie, the woman who so deeply loved him and had so strongly shaped his life. That was not a matter over which to be jealous, she wanted only to treasure Max as Millie had done and to love him.

The house had been Max and Millie's retreat. Now it was Max and hers; she thought the change would be positive and healthy.

There was Ryan's red truck, right on time. Charlie watched the big Chevy king cab, with its built-in tool-boxes and ladder rack, approach the house between the pasture fences, watched Ryan park and swing out of it carrying a roll of blueprints. The big silver weimaraner that rode beside her did not leave the cab until Ryan spoke to him; then he leaped out, all wags and smiles, dancing around her. Laughing, Charlie watched Ryan cross the yard to the pasture gate, and carefully open it. Pushing the two resident dogs back inside, she re-leased the weimaraner; the three took off racing the pasture wild with joy, secure behind the dog-proofed pasture fence.

This small ranch was Charlie's first real home since

she'd left her childhood home. She'd lived in rented rooms while she was in art school, then in several small San Francisco apartments nattily furnished with a folding cot, a scarred old dinette set, and the cardboard grocery boxes that served in place of shelves and dressers.

At the pasture fence, Ryan stood a moment watching the three dogs race in circles, then turned toward the house. Coming in, she gave Charlie a hug and spread the blueprints out on the table, weighting the corners with the sugar bowl and cream pitcher, and with her purse. Ryan's dark hair was freshly cut, a flyaway bob curling around her face. Her green eyes were startling beneath her black lashes, her vivid coloring complemented perfectly by a green sweatshirt that she wore over faded jeans. Ryan's mix of Irish and Latino blood, from her Flannery father and her Garza mother, had produced great beauty, great strength, and vivaciousness.

"Anything more on the dead waiter?" Ryan asked, sitting down. "I haven't talked to Dallas."

"Nothing," Charlie said. "Strange that Max hasn't been able to reach Lucinda and Pedric, that they haven't answered their cell phone messages."

"That is strange. And what about James Quinn?"

Charlie had no hesitation in relaying information to Ryan. Max would do the same, as would Ryan's uncle, Dallas. "There were no prints at all on the handle of the gas valve," Charlie said. "The gas starter in the fireplace had been full open, apparently for some hours. When Sacks and Hendricks first arrived on the scene, the doors and windows were all locked. When Wilma and Kate and I got there, Sacks was very carefully working on the lock, and we were all afraid the place would blow. Just one spark . . . Well, when they got inside and opened up, when they were able to go through, there was no sign of forced entry."

Ryan shook her head. "What a pity, if it was suicide—and more the pity if it wasn't. This will keep Dallas and Max busy for a while." She turned the blueprints to a page of elevations, and laid it out facing Charlie.

The new addition soared to a raftered peak with long expanses of glass looking down the hills to the sea and, at the back of the room flanking the stone fireplace, plain white walls for Charlie's framed drawings and prints. Before they came down on a final design, Charlie and Max and Ryan had spent nearly an hour standing on ladders in the front yard seeing just how high the room should be raised, how it should be oriented for the best view.

From the new raised floor level they would see the village rooftops to the west with the wild rocky coast beyond. The old living room would become the new master bedroom, retaining the original stone fireplace and bay windows. Ryan would cut a new door to the existing master bath and closet, and those would need no change. The old master bedroom would become Max's larger and more comfortable study. Ryan was, Charlie had learned, very skilled at saving what could be saved, but running free with what should be added.

Charlie greatly admired Ryan Flannery. Ryan had done something practical and exciting with her art degree, while Charlie's own art education had certainly gone awry, or had seemed to until recently. Her attempt at a commercial art career had been a royal bust, had at last sent her scurrying to her only living relative, to her aunt Wilma—for moral support and for a roof over her head. She had been living with Wilma when she started Charlie's Fix-it, Clean-it service. Not until much later did she have this surprising success with her animal drawings. Animals had always been her one great pleasure in the arts.

They sat studying the elevations, looking for any undiscovered problems. As Charlie watched Ryan red-pencil in a change they had agreed on, she could see, through the bay window, the three dogs playing in the pasture. The two young Great Dane mixes still acted like puppies. The presence of Ryan's beautiful weimaraner with his devilish cleverness made the two mutts act far more juvenile. Rock was smarter than they were, a year older and far quicker, a handsome canine celebrity who had come to Ryan quite by accident—or maybe by providence, Charlie thought, if you believed in such matters. The dogs were chasing one another and chasing the sorrel mare, when she agreed to run from them.

Charlie studied the plans again but could find nothing to be improved upon. In her view the design was perfect, and she could hardly wait to get started. She had risen to fetch the coffeepot, glancing out at the lane, when someone on a bike turned in, heading for the house.

"Dillon," Charlie said with curiosity. "She hasn't been here in a while."

"Surprised she's here now, after Max scolded her this morning at the Quinn place. You heard about that?"

Charlie nodded. "Max wasn't happy with her." Charlie had stopped by the station after she showed Kate the apartment. Max had been glum and silent, hadn't much wanted to talk about Dillon. Charlie watched the pretty redhead bike slowly up the lane, hardly peddling. Even at a distance, Dillon looked sour and unhappy.

"Sullen," Ryan said. "I'm sorry to see that. Consuela Benton is not a good influence."

Dillon walked her bike to the porch and leaned it against the porch rail. Slowly she slumped up the steps. Dillon was tall for fourteen. Her red hair was piled atop her head, tied with a purple scarf. Her tan windbreaker was tied by its sleeves around her waist, hiding her bare belly under the very tight T-shirt. She mounted the steps with a belligerent swagger. Charlie rose to let her in. No one used the front door. With the new addition, that, too, would change. Back and front entries would become one, with a large mud room for coats and dirty boots. Entering the kitchen, Dillon crossed in silence and plunked down at the table, staring at the blueprints that drooped over the edges. "What's all this?"

"Plans for the new addition," Charlie said. "You want coffee? Or make yourself some cocoa."

Dillon rose, slouched to the counter, and poured herself a cup of coffee, dumping in milk and three spoons of sugar. Charlie was deeply thankful to have gotten past that age long ago—too old to be a child, too young to be a woman, caught in a world where you were expected to be both but were offered the challenges of neither. In ages past, at thirteen you were *learning* to be a woman, learning the needed survival skills, the small simple skills involved in everyday living and in raising a family and, in the best of times, the urgent intellectual skills so necessary to human civility. Charlie found it hard to conceal her anger at the change in Dillon. Observing the girl's attitude, she found it difficult to remember that only a few months ago she had considered Dillon Thurwell nearly perfect, had thought Dillon was working very hard at growing up. Training the horses under Max's direction, Dillon had been mastering the skills of concentration and self-management, building confidence in her own strength—absorbing the building blocks that she would so badly need as a strong adult.

To see Dillon now, to see the change in her, to see the twisting of her strong early passions into self-destruction, angered Charlie to the point of rage.

All because of her mother—and yet that was so lame. Dillon was still her own master, she still had the luxury of choice in what she would make of herself, no matter how her mother behaved.

Sipping her coffee, Dillon stood by the table staring at the plans and elevations, then glanced down the hall toward the living room and three bedrooms. "What's the point? This house is big enough already." She stared at Charlie. "You starting a family? You pregnant?"

"I am not starting a family. Not that it would be any of your business. I need workspace. A studio." Charlie couldn't help feeling confrontational. She watched Ryan, who was studying Dillon, probably fighting the same impulse to paddle the child.

"So what was this murder last night?" Dillon said. "Some guy fell dead in your lap?"

Charlie managed a laugh. "That's putting it crudely but accurately. You missed the excitement. I was hoping to see you at the opening."

"I don't go to art exhibits. I suppose my mother was there with what's-his-name."

"I saw Marlin Dorriss. I didn't see your mother."

"So who died? Some waiter? What, poison in the canapés?"

"He worked at Jolly's. Sammy something. Blond, good-looking guy." Charlie's voice caught at Dillon's expression. "You know him?"

"Why would I know some waiter?"

"Why not? Something wrong with waiters? You never go in Jolly's? Who knows, he might be—have been, some college student working his way through. Not that it matters. Did you know him?"

Dillon stared at her.

"What?"

Dillon shrugged. "Maybe he hung out around the school. Some tall, blond guy hung around the high school."

"Not around your school? Not around the junior high?"

Another shrug.

Charlie wanted to shake her. "He was a bit old to be hanging out with school kids. What was the attraction?"

"Maybe he has a younger brother."

Charlie just looked at her. Ryan turned the blueprints around, laying the elevations of the new living room before Dillon. Dillon, in spite of herself, followed the sweep of the high ceiling and tall windows.

"This is what we're doing," Ryan said. "This will be

the new living room. There," she said pointing to where the new arch would be constructed, "off the kitchen and dining room."

"That's gonna cost a bundle." Dillon had grown up knowing, from her mother's business conversations, the price of real estate, and knowing what it cost to build. "I didn't think a cop made that kind of money."

Charlie and Ryan stared at her.

"I guess it's none of my business what you do with the captain's money."

"I'm spending my money," Charlie said quietly. "And *that* is none of your business. However, for your information, we're using money from the book I worked on after the author died. And from my gallery and commission sales." She wanted to say, What's with you? You think dumping on me is going to solve *your* problems? You think belittling me is going to make you feel better about your mother or yourself? With heroic effort, she said nothing.

Ryan said, "The two smaller bedrooms will be joined to make Charlie's studio. Tear out this wall, here, we have a fifteen-by-thirty-foot room. Add a couple of skylights and voilà, Charlie's new workspace. You have a problem with that?"

Dillon looked at Ryan with interest. Charlie watched the two of them face-off, Dillon a defiant, angry young lady; Ryan both angry and amused. Charlie thought that Ryan was a far better match for Dillon Thurwell's rage than she herself. She didn't much like confrontation—but Ryan had grown up with cops, and she knew how to give back what she got.

Charlie would have liked to share with Dillon her

excitement over the new studio as she shared it with her other friends, to relay her delight over simple details like the big adjustable shelves to hold drawings and prints and paper supplies, the new printing table, her anticipation over a new (used) desk, over a decent place for her computer.

She studied the girl, looking for a spark of the old Dillon. "I'll be working on the building project as carpenter's helper, under Ryan's direction. I want to improve my carpentry skills. I'm already pretty good at Sheetrock, from helping with Clyde's apartment building." She wished she could hone her people skills as easily. She wished she could master the moves to make the world right again for Dillon.

Dillon looked at her and rose. "Can I ride Redwing?"

Charlie nodded. "Don't let the dogs out of the pasture. You want company? We're about through here."

"Could I call my friend? Could my friend ride Bucky?"

Charlie stared at her. Bucky was Max's big, spirited buckskin. The sun rose and set with that gelding, no one else rode Bucky. "What friend is that?" she said carefully.

"From school. My friend from school."

"A girlfriend?"

Dillon said nothing. The child's stare made Charlie very glad she didn't have a teenager to raise. "You know that no one rides Bucky. Even I don't ride Bucky, without a very special invitation."

"I guess I'll go home then." Dillon turned on her heel, heading for the door.

Ryan rose, moving quickly around the table. She put her arm around Dillon. "Christmas vacation isn't far off."

"So?" Dillon turned a sour look on her. But she didn't move away.

"You have a job for the two weeks of vacation?"

Dillon shrugged. "Who needs a job? Who wants to work during vacation?"

"You want to work for me?"

"Why would I want to work for you? Doing what?"

"Carpenter's gofer. Fetching stuff. Sweeping up, cleaning up the trash. Maybe some nailing. Learn to lay out forms and mix cement. I can get a work-learning permit through the school. I'll pay you minimum, which is likely more than you're worth."

Dillon stared at her. "Why would I want to do that kind of work?"

"Something wrong with it? It's the way I started, when I was younger than you. At about the same time I began to learn to shoot a gun and to train the hunting dogs—carpentry skills might come in handy, whatever you do with your life." Ryan looked hard at Dillon. "What you do right now—while you're hurting—will shape the rest of your life. You want to spend it sneaking around shoplifting?"

Dillon pulled away. Ryan took her hand. "You are not your mom, Dillon. And she's not you." Ryan's green eyes flashed. "You plan to mess up your life just to punish her? What do you get out of that? If you're a survivor, as I hear you are, you'll stop this shit. You'll not let the dregs of the world plan your life for you, you'll write your *own* ticket."

She drew Dillon close and hugged her. "Charlie and

Max love you. Clyde and Wilma love you. I don't love you but I'd like to be your friend." She tilted Dillon's chin up, looking hard at her. "You come to work for me, you'll have more fun with my carpenters than with your smarmy girlfriends—I bet *they* wouldn't have the guts to tackle construction work."

Dillon said nothing. She stared back at Ryan, her jaw set, deeply scowling.

But something was changed. Charlie could see it; deep down, something was different.

Ryan said no more. Dillon moved away and out the door, swung on her bike, and took off up the lane. Charlie watched her pedal away alone. But maybe her shoulders were less hunched, her back not quite so stiff. Ryan glanced at her watch and rolled up the plans. "I'll leave one set. If you can go over them with Max tonight, if you're happy with everything, call me and I'll be at the building department first thing Monday morning." She gave Charlie a twisted smile. "To start the permit process rolling." They both knew that the county building department was hell to work with, that weeks of officiousness might be involved, enough unnecessary bureaucratic red tape to break the spirit of a marine sergeant.

Ryan shrugged. "I can only hope we get a good inspector, hope he doesn't find some trumped-up excuse to trash the whole plan." She grinned at Charlie. "It'll be okay, I'll sweet-talk him, as disgusted as that makes me. I can hardly wait to get started, I'm as excited as a kid—as enthusiastic as a kid *should* be," she said, glancing toward the lane. She slipped an elastic around the blueprints. Charlie unplugged the coffeepot, and they walked out to the pasture gate, discussing the

work schedule and where the building materials should
be stacked. At the gate, the three dogs came bounding.
The big silver weimaraner weighed eighty pounds and
stood over two feet at the shoulder, but he was dwarfed
by the Harpers' half-breed Great Danes. The three
dogs charged the gate like wild mustangs, but Ryan
and Charlie, with fast footwork and sharp commands,
got them sorted out, got Rock through the gate without
the pups following. Ryan loaded Rock into the passenger seat of her pickup. "You still planning on a ground-
breaking party?"

"The minute we have the permit. Max needs some
diversion."

Ryan grinned, gave Charlie a thumbs-up, and took
off up the lane. Charlie stood by the pasture gate petting the pups and scratching behind Redwing's ears,
thinking about Dillon, about the building project, about
the several commissions she'd promised, including the
Doberman studies; and about the two recent deaths in
the village. All the fragments that touched her life,
both bright and ugly, seemed muddled together like the
contents of a grab bag: You pay your money and you
take your chance. Or, as Joe Grey would put it, whatever crawls out of the mouse hole, that's your catch of
the day.

**11**

The only luggage the black tomcat required was a canvas tote containing a dozen assorted cans of albacore and white chicken, and a box of fish-flavored kibble. A little something to snack on, between room service. His traveling companion, by contrast, had packed three suitcases, effectively filling the entire trunk of her pale blue Corvette.

Consuela hadn't been thrilled about him coming along on this little jaunt. He had prevailed, however, having more plans than he had mentioned to her—far more than cleaning out Kate Osborne's safe deposit box.

Traveling north from Molena Point, Consuela preferred Highway 101 to the coast route, despite the heavy traffic and the preponderance of large tractor-trailers. She was a fast driver with flash-quick reactions and a competitive take on life. Azrael studied her with interest.

She no longer looked like the bawdy young woman who had hung out with those younger girls; her transformation was, as always, remarkable. She looked her true age now, of twenty-some. Without the frizzed-out hair and theatrical makeup, her sleek, fine-boned beauty was startling; and the transformation hadn't taken long. She had scrubbed her face and now wore very little makeup, just a touch of pink lipstick. He had watched her dampen her dark hair, twist it tightly around her head, and cover it with the sassy blond wig that she had styled like Kate Osborne's hair. She was wearing a tailored beige suit, much as Kate might wear. She looked serious and businesslike, and in fact far more interesting than the painted child who had run with Dillon and her friends. She had wanted to make reservations at the St. Francis, on Union Square, but Azrael had quashed that notion. The Garden House on Stockton was just a block from Kate Osborne's apartment.

He slept during much of the two-hour drive, waking in San Jose, where Consuela stopped at a Burger King. She ordered orange juice and coffee for herself, and a double cheeseburger for him, hold the pickles. That would tide him over until they hit the city and had visited Kate's bank—though as it turned out, their errand didn't take long.

The branch that Kate frequented was old, with round marble pillars in front, its floors and walls done all in marble. Azrael, not trusting Consuela, rode into the bank in her carryall. No one questioned her when she presented the safe deposit box key, read off the number, and waited to sign in.

But when the clerk gave her the signature card, a hot rage hit Azrael, and Consuela went pale.

The card had been signed just an hour earlier by Kate herself.

"Forgot something," Consuela told the clerk, smiling and shaking her head at her own pretended inefficiency. The bank clerk looked hard at her but accepted the signature card.

Playing dumb, Consuela followed the clerk into the vault. This was apparently not the same teller who had helped Kate an hour earlier; that clerk would have remembered her, or at least remembered what Kate was wearing. Azrael watched the other clerks warily, looking for some trap; his paws began to sweat. These tellers might, for all he knew, know Kate personally. It was a small branch, and Kate did work right in the building. He'd considered that before but had thought, what were the odds? You couldn't cover every contingency.

Moving into the vault, waiting for the teller to open up the little drawer, both Azrael and Consuela were strung with nerves. Before they were alone in the locked room he'd nearly smothered in the damn bag.

Opening the metal box, Consuela stared into the empty container. Not a scrap of paper, not a paperclip or a speck of dust.

"Nothing," she said, having expected as much. "Nothing. What did you do! How did you tip her! This is your fault," she hissed, her face close to his. "You stupid beast. You drag me all the way up here for *this*, for *nothing*. Either you tipped her or . . . What did you hear last night, that made you think . . . You'd better start explaining."

"Keep your voice down! You're supposed to be alone in here! Kate *said* the jewels were here. Plain as day."

She just looked at him.

He raised his paw, wanting to slash her. She might look like a refined lady now, but she was still little more than a streetwalker. "Are you calling me a liar?"

"If they *were* here, she's cleared them out. An hour ago, you stupid beast. Did she burn rubber getting here before us? And why? Who tipped her? Is there another name on the box? Did she call someone here in the city?"

"*You* were looking at the card. I was inside the damn bag."

"They don't keep that information on the sign-in card. I looked." She stared hard at him. "How the hell did she *know*! What did you do when you took that key, leave black cat hair all over her room? Paw prints on the dresser?"

He extended his claws until she backed away. She closed the box, and held the carryall open, looking at him until he hopped in. *Well, screw her,* he thought hunkering down in the dark bag. And they did not speak again until they hit the Garden House and Consuela turned into the parking lot.

The place was so typically San Francisco it made him retch, all this Victorian garbage to impress the tourists. And he was hungry again. A bad gig always made him hungry. He waited in the car while she signed the register, then rode in her carryall up the elevator. They did not learn until later that the hotel allowed pets, that he would have been welcome, that catering to domestic animals was their specialty. Though one might have known from the smell of the room. It stunk like poodle poop.

When the bellman departed, Azrael hassled Consuela until she phoned for takeout of cold boiled crab legs and sushi. Before he got down to the work at hand he wanted sustenance. Even now, despite Consuela blowing it with the safe deposit box, this little trip held promise.

Their room was on the south side of the building, a location for which Consuela had paid an extra ten bucks a night, as the manager had at first said those rooms were all taken. From this vantage, Azrael would have a perfect view down the block to Kate Osborne's apartment. When the bellman left, Consuela dumped the carryall on the nearest chair, dropped his bag of food in the closet, picked up the phone, and ordered his takeout. Then, changing into jeans and a T-shirt, she turned on the TV and sprawled on the bed. She was still scowling. He got the feeling too often that the woman didn't like him.

Well, she was going along with his plan all right, the mercenary little bitch. Maybe she just didn't like cats. The times they'd worked together, he'd never bothered to ask. Now, after the bank fiasco, her mood was as dark as the murky worlds that filled his late-night longings.

Kate must have missed her key shortly after she returned to Wilma Getz's house this morning, after she'd looked at that apartment.

Why didn't she simply assume she'd misplaced it? What made her hustle on back to the city?

*Right,* he thought. *That meddling gray tomcat.*

Somehow those little cats had spied on him when he was in the Getz house or when he and Consuela were in the alley. When he finished with those three, they'd be dog meat.

Listening to the inanity of some late-afternoon sitcom, he clawed open the window and slipped out onto the fake balcony, crowding against the metal rails in the four-inch-wide space, looking across the flat roofs to Kate's apartment building. Consuela had at least had the decency to slow the car as they passed, to make sure of the number. From Kate's description to her friend Wilma, the apartment at the north front was hers. At least, that seemed to be the only one with a view of both Coit Tower and Russian Hill. The windows in that apartment were open, the white curtains blowing in and out, stirred by a rain-scented breeze. Above him, thick gray clouds were gathering.

He waited a long time jammed against the rail before he glimpsed Kate moving around inside, hurrying as if preparing to go out. He waited until she turned away, then dropped to a lower portion of the roof, and leaped to the flat roof of the next building. Fleeing across the hard black tar among air conditioner units and heat vents, he reached the wall of Kate's building.

The window above him must open to the kitchen, he could smell bananas, and lemon-scented dish soap. Crouching out of sight, hidden by the blowing curtains, he was about to rear up and peer in when he dropped again fast and flattened himself against the roof.

Kate stood above him, looking out just where he would have appeared. He lay very still, his eyes slitted, a black shadow against the black tar.

## 12

Kate stood at the kitchen window waiting for her kettle to boil, looking out at the darkly striated cloud layer that was moving above the city rooftops, taking a moment to calm herself. She was still all nerves and anger. The hurried drive to reach the city before Consuela did, and rushing to her safe deposit box . . . The sense of invasion knowing that Consuela had her key had left her shaky with nerves and anger. And she felt watched again, too, as she had at Wilma's house.

But Consuela wouldn't have the nerve to follow her home. Surely the woman would think she'd be ready to call the police, or already had called them.

Through the trails of gray cloud the late-afternoon sun threw vivid glances of light onto the flat roofs, reflections so sharp they blurred Coit Tower and obscured her view of the Oakland hills. Selecting an English Breakfast tea bag, she poured the boiling water into her cup and, letting it steep, took the cup to the bedroom to sip while she unpacked her small bag.

An hour earlier, returning to San Francisco, she had

headed straight for the design studio. Parking in her marked slot, she didn't go upstairs to her office but hurried around the corner to the branch where she did her banking, praying she wasn't too late. Having borrowed Wilma's duplicate safe deposit box key, she had given it to the teller and signed in. She had shared her box with Wilma ever since she opened it, when she'd left Molena Point three years ago. Having no living relatives that she knew of, she had wanted someone to be able to take care of business if she were in an accident, if something unforeseen happened.

Following the overweight, pale-haired teller through the formidable iron gate of the vault, impatiently waiting for her to wield the pair of keys, she had pulled out the metal box, nearly collapsing with relief when she saw the thick brown envelope in which she kept her important papers and the small square cardboard carton that held the jewelry. Stripping the safe deposit drawer of its contents, dropping the box and papers in a leather carryall, she had debated about reporting that an imposter might try to open her box.

But there was nothing in it now for Consuela to steal. With the time and fuss such a report would take, she had decided not to do it. Surely the bank manager would be summoned, forms would have to be filled out, the police brought into the matter. The rest of the day would be shot when she had other things to do. Leaving the box empty, she had settled for the smug satisfaction that she had arrived before Consuela.

As she left the bank she had scanned the parking garage for Consuela's blue Corvette, or for anyone who might be watching her as she hurried up the three interior flights to the design studio and her own office.

The lights were on in several offices but she saw no one. Shutting her office door behind her, she slit the tape that sealed the little cardboard box to make sure the jewelry was still inside. Fingering the lovely, ornate pieces, she had longed to keep them out in the light where they could be admired, longed to wear and enjoy them. But at last she put them back and sealed them up again.

Opening the bottom drawer of her fireproof file, she tucked the little box at the back and locked the drawer. Not the safest place, but better than any SD box, if that woman was able to copy her signature. She really didn't understand what this was all about, when the jewelry was paste. The whole matter made her feel so invaded and helpless. Was nothing secure anymore? Leaving the office and hurrying home, she had wanted only to tuck up safe in her apartment and shut out the world.

Kate's apartment building was a stark, ancient structure with two units upstairs and three down, and a parking garage underneath, a tan stucco box so old that one wanted to sign a long-term lease hoping the landlord would be forced to honor it, would not give in to the sudden urge to level the building and go for a high-rise. Kate's apartment was reached by a concrete stairwell that held smells she did not like to think about. The apartments themselves, though, were in prime shape, freshly painted and with new carpet. The large windows opened without sticking, the kitchen appliances were new, with granite countertops gracing the pale pickled cabinets.

Opening up her hot, close apartment, she had sorted through four days' worth of mail and made a quick trip to the corner Chinese market for milk, eggs, some vegetables, and frozen dinners. She planned to spend the rest of the week wrapping up two interior design jobs and doing the preliminary house call for a couple who were moving out from the East Coast. That job, which she had committed to some weeks ago, was the last new work she meant to take. The Ealders had bought a lovely town house facing Golden Gate Park, and she was looking forward to that small but interesting installation.

She had been approached by two other prospective clients but had turned both over to other designers. She could take on nothing new. She wanted, when she left the San Francisco firm in March, to have all her work completed. She expected she would move back to the village. She had been offered an enticing position as head designer, if she would move to the firm's new Seattle office; but that was so far from her friends.

In Molena Point, she had given Charlie a deposit on the duplex apartment and had made arrangements to start work for Hanni the first of March. That gave her four months to finish with all her clients. She didn't want to hand over any last-minute items to her successor.

During the next busy months she would have little time for personal concerns, little time to follow the confusing leads to her family; and maybe that was just as well. Anyway, the most pressing matter at the moment was to clear her desk and calendar before Lucinda and Pedric arrived—and hope that whoever had followed her was gone, and that Consuela had returned to Molena Point, out of her sight. She wondered if Lucinda and Pedric could shed some light on the jewelry, on its age and background. The fact that Lucinda had bought similar pieces in that small shop up the coast invited all manner of speculation.

Russian River was just a tiny vacation village, but it had a colorful past filled with strange stories from the Gold Rush. So many immigrants had ended up there, panning for placer gold or working the mines, people from dozens of countries and divergent cultures. She wanted to go up there later in the year if she had time, dig around and see what she could learn.

She chose her clothes for work the next morning, then straightened the apartment, picking up papers she'd left scattered and doing a little dusting. The cool serenity of the cream and beige rooms welcomed and calmed her, the simple white linen couch and chair and loveseat, her books and framed prints. She had brought nothing with her from the Molena Point house when she left Jimmie, had wanted nothing from that old life that had gone so sour, not a stick of the furniture she had taken such care to select. She'd had an estate dealer sell it all, the Baughman pieces, the handmade rugs, everything that had at one time meant so much to her.

She *had* wondered if Jimmie would like her to ship the furnishings up to San Quentin, for his new residence. If a convict had free access to large-screen cable TV and the latest computers, if he could make and receive all the phone calls he pleased, and could, in the prison library, study for a law degree with which later to sue the prison authorities, if he could place bets on the horses and professional sports and buy lottery tickets, maybe he'd like to customize his cell, redesign his personal environment in keeping with his new mode of living.

Clyde would say she was bitter.

Clyde would be right.

Filling her briefcase with the needed papers and work schedules, and setting aside a stack of sample books, she moved about the apartment with an increasingly uneasy sense of being watched again, even in her own rooms. Oh, she didn't want that to start, that awful fear that had stopped her from taking the cable car or walking to work, that had made her cling to the comparative safety of her own locked vehicle whenever she left a building.

Finishing her housekeeping chores she fetched a favorite Loren Eiseley, a copy in which she had carefully marked the passages she loved most, and she curled up on the couch under a quilt.

But she couldn't concentrate for long; she kept looking up from the pages toward the kitchen where the north window was open to the breeze.

Of course there could be no one there, she was on the second floor.

Except, the roofs were flat out there and, she supposed, easy enough to access if one knew where the fire escape or maintenance stairs were located.

Rising, she closed and locked the window, then got back under her quilt holding the book unopened, listening.

And later when she checked the window before she went to bed, the lock was not engaged. The closed window slid right open, though she was sure she'd locked it. She locked it now, testing it to make sure—it was not a very substantial device, just one of those little slide clips that sometimes didn't catch, that she would have to press hard with her fingers while she slammed the window, to make it take hold properly.

That night she did not sleep well. And every night for a week, arriving home after dark, she checked the kitchen window first thing. It was always locked. But then on Friday evening, she discovered that her extra set of house and car keys, which she kept in her jewelry box, was missing.

She looked in the locked file drawer in her home office where she sometimes hid the extra keys and extra cash. The cash was there, but not the keys. She looked in the pockets of her suitcase—where that black tomcat had been poking around, hooking out her safe deposit key.

The pockets were all empty.

Well, she'd misplaced her extra keys before, and later they'd turned up. Only this time the loss frightened her. She felt chilled again, and uncertain.

But what was Consuela going to do, let herself into the apartment and bludgeon her? How silly. Bone tired from the week's intense work and late hours, but more than satisfied with the Ranscioni house, she gave up the search. The keys were somewhere. No one had been inside the apartment. If they didn't turn up, she'd change the lock. Making herself a drink, she slipped out of her suit and heels and into a robe, thinking about the Ranscioni job.

The buffet installation and fireplace mantel and new interior doors were perfect. She was more than happy with the work the painters were doing. The furniture had been delivered on time, and today the draperies had been hung, right on schedule. Tomorrow she'd place the accessories herself. She did so enjoy doing the last details on a house by herself, wandering the rooms alone for a leisurely look at the finished product, uninterrupted even by her clients; a little moment to herself, to enjoy and assess what she had created.

A young woman, Nancy Westervelt, had come in just this morning wanting her to take an interesting small job. Kate had regretfully turned her down. The woman—handsome, dark-haired, and quiet—had wanted Kate to incorporate her South American furniture and art into a contemporary setting. Nancy was mannerly and soft-spoken and, given that their tastes were so similar, would have been fun to work with.

She had thought a lot that week about the safe deposit box incident. She had paid close attention to her office file drawer, often checking to see that the cardboard box was there in the bottom drawer at the back, and that the tape hadn't been disturbed. She had gone back to her safe deposit box twice to see if Consuela had returned. After that once, just after she'd cleared the box herself, the girl had not been back. But the presence of that frowzy, thieving girl there in the city, presuming she was still there, bothered her more than she wanted to admit.

She had once glimpsed the man who had followed her before she left the city. He was watching as she left work. And that was a plus, although she had not found her spare house and car keys. And then on Saturday morning, leaving the Ranscioni house, coming up the stairs with her grocery bags she opened the door—and paused, feeling cold. That prickly sensation as if her hair wanted to stand up. Had she heard a small, scraping sound? Had she felt some unnatural movement of air against her face?

She stood for a long moment trying to identify what was disturbing her, what held her so rigid and still. She sniffed for some strange scent, a hint of cologne perhaps. She listened for the faintest brushing, the tiniest shifting of weight on the wooden floors.

Silence.

But someone was there, she could feel the difference on her crawling skin. The way she had felt in Wilma's house that morning when she had paused in the dining room, certain that someone was present.

Setting down her groceries on the hall table, she snatched the vial of pepper spray from her purse and walked slowly through the apartment opening each door, pushing back the two shower curtains, checking the window locks and looking in the closets. She even opened the wall bed in her office.

There was no one; the rooms were empty, the windows locked as she had left them. Quickly she put away her groceries, all the while listening.

Returning to her study where she'd left the wall bed down, she opened a package of new white sheets and made it up, although Lucinda and Pedric wouldn't arrive until Sunday evening. Covering the taut sheets with a thick, flowered quilt, she cleared off her oversize wicker desk, stashing papers and samples in her bedroom. She always brought work home, room layouts, catalogs and price lists, and the heavy books of fabric and carpet samples.

In the living room she cleared away the week's newspapers that she'd hardly had time to look at, then tossed the pillows from the window seat into the dryer for a good freshening. A few short, dark hairs clung to one of the pillows.

A friend had brought her poodle over a few weeks ago, a small black toy that had snuggled on the window seat. She hadn't thought that poodles could shed, but maybe she was wrong. She removed the hairs with a damp sponge and tossed the pillow in with the others.

On her way to the trash with the papers, an article caught her attention. Pulling that section out to read later, she laid it on the kitchen counter—something about a jewel robbery. Shoving the rest of the papers in the trash and straightening up the kitchen, she thought how good it would be to see Lucinda and Pedric.

How excited the old couple had been, planning their tour through the Cat Museum's gardens and galleries. Picking up the phone, she made lunch reservations for Monday at an elegant Chinese restaurant near the museum, a small place that she thought would please them. She was so looking forward to their visit, this elderly couple with their twinkling eyes and dry wit, this pair of eighty-year-old newlyweds with their Old-World knowledge about cats that made her want to know them better. And she had to smile. How thrilled the kit was that the Greenlaws would soon return to the village to stay. Lucinda and Pedric were the kit's true family, and now at last she would have a home with them, in a brand-new house atop Hellhag Hill.

The cave within the hill that frightened Joe Grey seemed not to have dampened the resolve of the Greenlaws to live there. They connected that dark fissure in some way to the ancient Celtic tales they collected, to the myths that had been handed down from their ancestors. The day after they were married they had bought the entire hill, some twenty acres.

Kate had, when she first saw the cave, been as intrigued as the kit, wanting to go down into it. But then she had grown frightened, and had ended up leaving quickly. On later visits to the village she had stayed away from that part of the hills.

When she had the apartment in order for the Greenlaws, she made a cup of tea, then pulled on a warm sweater over her jeans and walked up Russian Hill to the Cat Museum, wanting one more look at her grandfather's diaries. Maybe to winnow out some overlooked clue to her heritage. The afternoon was cool and sunny, with a brilliance one could find, she thought, only in San Francisco, the sky a clear deep blue behind a scattering of fast-running white clouds. When she looked down the hill behind her, the shadows of the crowded buildings angled crisply across the pale sidewalks; the dark bay was scattered with whitecaps, the bridges glinting with afternoon sun. The breeze off the bay tugged at her like a live thing. She kept thinking about the dark hairs on the cushion of her window seat; she had found, when she cleaned out the lint catcher of the dryer, a wad of straight, black hairs, not really like poodle hairs.

Had Consuela brought that cat to the city? Joe Grey had said only that Azrael had been the instigator of the bizarre effort—the dismally failed effort, she thought with satisfaction. Why would Consuela have brought the cat here?

Entering the wrought-iron gates of the Cat Museum, she stepped into a world that seemed totally removed from the city. Between the various gallery buildings, its gardens were as lush and mysterious as the secret garden of her favorite childhood book. The cats who lived there watched her from where they sunned themselves lying on the low walls or atop various pieces of cat sculpture. Today, she did not linger in the gardens, but went directly to the desk to sign out McCabe's diaries.

She spent several hours in the reading room but found nothing she'd missed before. From his early years as a stevedore, then as a building contractor and newspaper columnist, through his marriage, to the weeks just before the earthquake in which he died, he had written what he observed of the city but offered no fact about himself. Kate could not even find his wife's name. Several entries mentioned their baby girl, but nowhere did McCabe write her name. Had he had some superstition, some objection to setting down the names of those close to him? Or had there been deletions in the journals, pages removed? With such short entries, that might be easy to do, and sometimes the flow did seem disjointed. The passages to which she kept returning were vague: McCabe's occasional offhand mentions of *the other place*, or *those grim kingdoms,* and *one day will I make that journey?* These, and mentions of not liking to be shut in, not liking a low, heavy sky—and of dreams that disturbed him in the small hours so that he rose to prowl the streets.

But those *were* dreams, perhaps nightmares. Not facts about his life. *I dreamed last night of a granite sky lit by a green haze . . . I have dreamed of caverns falling, and of the echoing cries of beasts in a world I have never seen . . .*

Kate left the museum frightened. She must give up the search. Whatever lay in the tangle of her heritage was not for her, she had learned nothing about her parents and she was only upsetting herself.

Arriving home, she meant to put on her robe, fix herself a drink, have a light supper, and tuck up on the couch with a book. When she turned into the kitchen, the newspaper she had left on the counter had slid to the floor. She picked it up, puzzled.

A stain of grease darkened the article that had interested her, grease smeared across the account of a downtown jewel robbery. Frowning, she wiped the counter more thoroughly where she had earlier prepared some chicken, and wiped the paper as best she could.

The robbery had occurred ten days ago as the owner was locking up to go home. When he stepped outside and turned to lock the door, two men pinned him against the building demanding to be let in. He grabbed one of them, and there was a fight. Apparently someone, perhaps a neighbor, called the police. The store owner, James Ruse, said it was just seconds until he heard sirens. He told reporters that as the cops belted out of their car, grabbing one man, the other seemed to go insane, jumping on Ruse and beating him. Ruse grabbed the brick he used to prop open the door on hot days and hit the man hard in the head. That didn't stop the burglar; he beat Ruse again, injured one of the cops, and escaped. Police captain Norville said it was likely the man was on drugs, that he had been almost impossible to subdue.

The article unnerved her, the city was getting so violent. She didn't understand why the police didn't shoot the man, when he had almost killed an innocent shopkeeper, had been trying to kill him. She didn't turn on the kitchen TV for the news as she usually did when she fixed her dinner, but put on a CD while she made her salad.

When she went to the refrigerator for the bowl of chicken, she saw that it was empty.

Someone *had* been here. Had eaten the chicken, apparently while reading the newspaper.

Quietly she reached for the phone, meaning to dial 911, then to leave, to wait for the police on the street or in her locked car. She had started to phone when she saw the paw prints.

Greasy paw prints on the stove, catching the light when she stood at an angle. And when she examined the back of the newspaper, there were greasy prints there, as well.

Checking all the window locks, she angrily searched her apartment, looking in every tiniest niche, under every piece of furniture. In the living room she found the cat's black hair matted on her white couch: a stark and insolent greeting. She imagined the huge black creature riding in the car beside Consuela, peering coldly out the front window—laying what kind of plans?

Because they had missed stealing the jewelry, he had come here into her apartment, had very likely searched the entire apartment looking for it. What next? Her office? And where had he been when Consuela entered the bank? Riding on her shoulder snarling at the tellers? Following her on a leash like some pet jungle cat, commanding irate or amused stares from tellers and customers? Although most likely he had kept out of sight.

If he had jimmied her window, he had probably let
Consuela in through the front door, and Consuela had
taken her extra keys. They had most likely locked the
window and locked the door behind them when they
left; and now they could enter at their pleasure.

Searching again, she could find nothing else disturbed. Whatever they had done in here, that black
beast frightened her far more than that little snip Consuela could ever do.

Well, she couldn't tell the cops that a cat had broken
in, and she had no evidence that any human had been
in here. Unplugging and removing her kitchen phone,
and then her office extension, so that neither phone
could be taken off the hook, she carried them into the
bedroom, setting them down beside the nightstand
where she left the third phone plugged in. Locking the
bedroom door behind her, she checked every small
hiding place once again, behind the boxes on the closet
shelf, behind her clothes. She was thankful she'd had
the bedroom lock installed; it gave her a sense of security after she'd been followed. She didn't like sur-
prises; she would not want to wake with someone in
her room.

Certain that the cat was not in the room with her, she
washed her face and brushed her teeth. She was tucked
up in bed, reading, by 8:15, the dark winter evening
shut away beyond the draperies—wanting to lose herself in a favorite book as she had done when she was a
child in one foster home or another.

But, again, the book didn't hold her. Putting out the
light, turning over clutching her pillow, she wanted to
sleep and didn't think she could. Then when she did

sleep, her dreams were filled with Azrael, and with phantom worlds that beckoned to her from the darkness. She woke at three and lay sleepless until dawn, her mind racing with unwanted questions.

13

Long after Kate slept, that Saturday night, down the coast in Molena Point, rain swept in torrents along the rocky shore, turning sodden the cottages and rooftops and, south of the village, bending double the wild grass on Hellhag Hill, drenching the two friends who climbed through the black, wet tangles, desperately searching.

Joe Grey heard it first, a lonely and mournful weeping as he reared up in the tangled wet grass. He and Clyde were halfway up the hill, Joe's paws and fur were soaking. In the driving rain, he could see nothing. Leaping to Clyde's shoulder, he stared up through the windy night toward the crest. The weeping came and went in the storm as unfocused as the cries of spirits; the gusts pummeled him so hard he had to dig his claws into Clyde's shoulder. Clyde grunted but said nothing. Above them, the grieving lament increased: somewhere in the cold blackness the kit sobbed and bawled her distress. The time was three A.M.

Scuds of rain hit their backs fitfully, then were gone

again. Of course no stars were visible, no moon touched the inky hill. Pressing a paw against Clyde's head for balance, Joe prayed the kit hadn't gone into the cave. Crouching to leap down, to race up to the crest, he peered down into Clyde's face. "Can you see her? Can you see anything?"

"Can't see a damned thing. *You're* the cat. What happened to night vision?"

"It takes a *little* light. I'm not an infrared camera!"

The yowl came again, louder, making Clyde pause. "You sure that's the kit? Sounds like the ghost itself." The ghost of Hellhag Hill was a treasured village myth, one Joe didn't care for. Rising tall against Clyde's head, Joe peered harder into the black night. Had he seen an inky smudge move briefly? Clyde stunk of sleep, a sour human smell.

"There," Joe said. "Just to the left of the cave."

Clyde moved to stare upward, clutching Joe tighter. The trouble had started an hour ago with the ringing phone in their dark bedroom. Burrowing beneath the covers, Joe heard Clyde answer, his voice understandably grouchy. "What?" Clyde had shouted into the phone. "It's two in the morning. This better not be a wrong number."

There was a long silence. Clyde said, "When?" Another silence, then, "Are you sure?" Then, "We're on our way." Joe had peered out as Clyde thudded out of bed and stood looking around the dark room, then staring toward the study and Joe's aerial cat door. "Joe! Where the hell are you? *Joe!* Come down here! *Now!* Wilma just called. It's the kit, she's run away!"

Joe had crawled out from under the blanket yawning. "What do you mean, she's run away? She's probably out hunting. She doesn't mind the rain. Where's Dulcie? Isn't she with Dulcie?" But the feeling in his gut was uneasy. The kit had disappeared last winter for several days—and had fallen, paws first, into trouble.

"What happened?" he said, stalking across the blankets. "Why suddenly so distressed? What else did Wilma say?"

Clyde was pulling on his pants and a sweatshirt. Joe leaped to the top of the dresser, waiting for an explanation.

"They're dead," Clyde said, staring back at him. "Lucinda and Pedric. There was an accident—somewhere north of Russian River. The minute the kit heard, she ran out of the house bawling and yowling. Dulcie raced after her, but apparently she lost her, couldn't track her in the rain and wind. They don't know where she went or what she'll do. She was so upset, Dulcie thinks she'll head for Hellhag Hill." Clyde pulled on his jogging shoes. Hastily tying them, he grabbed his keys.

In the downstairs hall Clyde dug his parka from the closet, snatched Joe up in his arms, and headed for the car. Racing down the hall, they heard Rube huffing behind the kitchen door. Clyde double-timed it through the dark living room and out the front door, not bothering to lock it. Sliding into the old Buick sedan that he'd driven home that night—to avoid putting up the top in his yellow antique roadster—he dropped Joe on the passenger seat like a bag of flour, hit the starter, and fished a flashlight from the glove compartment.

Shining the light along the sidewalk, Clyde headed for the hills, man and cat watching every shadow, every smear of darkness. Joe, crouched on the dash where he could see the street, glanced over at Clyde.

"How could there have been a wreck? When did this happen? How could they have a wreck at night? Lucinda and Pedric don't drive at night. Never. At eighty, that's smart. So how—"

"Wilma didn't give me details, she was frantic for the kit, I've never heard her so out-of-control. The Sonoma County coroner called her. A wreck, a tanker truck—gasoline. A nighttime wreck, a fire. My God, those two innocent people. The kit was wild, hysterical."

"Watch your driving. I'll do the looking. Why did Wilma *tell* her all that? Didn't she know the kit would—"

"Kit had her ear stuck to the phone, you know how she is. She heard before Wilma could snatch her away. And even if she had—"

"There! Slow down."

Clyde skidded to a stop.

"Is that her in the bushes?" Joe had been ready to leap out when he saw it was not Kit but a raccoon—and his concern for the kit escalated into a sharp fear. The car lights picked out raccoons' masked eyes, an unwelcome gang of midnight predators.

Joe had shouted and shouted for the kit as they moved on between the close-crowding shops and houses. "I think she headed for Hellhag Hill," he had said tightly, hoping she hadn't bolted down into the caves that, as far as he knew, might go clear to the center of the earth. Because the kit could, in her volatile grief, mindlessly run and run and keep running. Even at the best of times, the kit was all emotion—and Lucinda and Pedric were her family.

Trying to see out of the slow-moving car, Joe had been weak with nerves by the time they reached Hellhag Hill. Clyde parked along the dropping cliff where the waves slapped and churned below them, set the hand brake, and snatched Joe up again. The minute he opened the door, both man and cat were drenched. The hill humped above them like a bloated black beast. Impatient with human slowness, Joe had leaped from Clyde's arms and raced blindly upward through the forest of wet, blowing grass.

But now, perched on Clyde's shoulder again where he could see better, he tried to identify that faint smear of blackness. *Was* that the kit, rearing up for a better look down at them? But as he watched, the black speck disappeared, was gone. Now, not a sound from above. Only when Clyde paused again and stood still did they hear one tiny sob.

Rearing up taller against Clyde's head, Joe shouted, "*Come down, Kit. Come down now! Right now!* I have something to tell you. Something about Lucinda and Pedric." And he leaped down into the tall wet grass and raced ahead of Clyde up the black hill.

Only when they were very near the tumble of boulders on the crest did the kit peer out, crouching and shivering. This was not their fluff-coated, flag-tailed tortoiseshell, their sassy, brightly animated friend. This rain-soaked, forlorn little animal was dull and spent, a miserable ragged beast who, with her wet fur matted to her body, seemed far smaller, far more frail.

"Come here," Joe said, shouldering through the wet grass. "Come *now*."

The kit came to Joe, with her head down, slow and grieving. She looked like the first time Joe had ever seen her, a terrified feral animal afraid of humans, afraid of other cats, afraid of the world, totally alone and without hope. She stood hunched in the grass before him.

Behind Joe, Clyde stood very still. Then in a moment, he took two careful steps toward her. She didn't spin away. Two more steps, and another, and he knelt beside the kit, where she cowered with grief before Joe Grey.

Gently Clyde picked her up, gently he held her. The wind beating at them made her shiver. Unzipping his jacket, Clyde tucked her inside, then zipped it up again. Only her dark, lean little face could be seen. Pitifully the kit looked up at Clyde. "They never drive at night. They would never be driving at night. Why were they out at night on the highway?"

She stared into the wind and up at the stormy sky. "How could your strange human God cause Lucinda and Pedric to be dead? Why would he do that?" She looked at Clyde, and down at Joe Grey. Around them, the black hill rolled away, uncaring. Above them the black sky stormed uncaring and remote. To the vast and incomprehensible elements this small cat's mourning went unheard, her pain unheeded. What possible power, so beyond mortal ken, would bother with this insignificant beast? What power in all the universe would care that she was hurting?

They had started down the hill, Clyde snuggling the kit close, Joe Grey shouldering through the wet grass beside him, when lights appeared on the highway below coming slowly around the curve.

When Clyde and Wilma, Kit and Joe and Dulcie, were all together, sitting in Wilma's car, the kit crawled out from Clyde's jacket. Obediently allowing Wilma to towel her, she was quiet, very still. As Wilma worked, her yellow slicker made crinkling sounds over her soaking pajamas, and her wet boots squelched with water. As the kit began to dry and grow warmer, when her small body wasn't quite as rigid, Wilma said, "I don't know much more than you heard. I can't imagine why they were on the highway at that hour. It's been storming all night up there."

She looked at Clyde. "Sheriff's office called me just before I called you. The accident happened on 101 somewhere north of Ukiah. They had been heading north. A gas truck . . . apparently hit them on a curve." She looked desolately at Clyde. "Both vehicles rolled and burned. Just *burned* . . ." Wilma covered her face. "Exploded and burned."

She was quiet for a long time, holding the kit, her face pushed against the little cat. Still the kit was silent. Wilma looked up at last. "There was nothing left. Nothing. The vehicle's license was ripped off in the explosion, went flying with torn pieces of the RV. That's how the sheriff knew who to call."

Since Lucinda had sold her house just after she and Pedric were married, the newlyweds had used Wilma's address for all their business, for everything but interest income, which was handled by direct deposit. Wilma faxed their bank statements to them, and sent any urgent papers. Wilma's address had been on the couple's drivers' licenses and on their vehicle registration.

As the five sat in the front seat, close together, Dulcie nosed under the towel, into Wilma's arms, snuggling close to the kit. Around the car, the wind eased off, and the rain turned from fitful gusts to a hard, steady downpour. It seemed to Dulcie that fate had, since early in the year, turned a hard and uncaring countenance on their little extended family. First Captain Harper had been set up as a suspected murderer. Then that terrible bomb that came close to killing everyone at Captain Harper and Charlie's wedding. Then during Charlie's gallery party, that man dying. And now this terrible, senseless accident to Kit's human family. She felt lost and grim, she wanted only to be home with Kit, tucked up in Wilma's bed with hot milk and kitty treats, where nothing more could happen.

When Clyde and Joe slid into their own car and headed home, Joe settled unashamedly against Clyde's leg. He felt more like a pet cat tonight, needful of human caring. Not since his days as a stray kitten, sleeping in San Francisco's alleys, had he felt quite so in need of security and a little petting—it was all very well to have a solid record of murder and burglary convictions to his credit, but sometimes a little mothering of the bachelor variety was a nice change. The thought of Lucinda and Pedric gone, forever and irrefutably gone, had left him feeling uncharacteristically vulnerable.

Glancing down at Joe, Clyde laid his hand on Joe's shoulder and scratched his ear.

They'd been home for half an hour, Clyde had toweled Joe dry and used the hair dryer on him, and Joe was half asleep under the covers when Clyde came upstairs bringing with him an aroma that brought Joe straight up, staring.

Clyde set a tray on the bed, right in front of him. Imported sardines? He had to be dreaming. A whole bevy of those little pastrami-on-rye appetizers that Clyde kept stashed in the freezer, now warm from the microwave? He looked at Clyde and looked back at the brimming tray.

Clyde, who had showered and pulled on a robe, set his hot rum drink on the night table and slid into bed, propping the pillows behind him. "So tuck in. What? You're not hungry?"

Joe laid a paw on Clyde's hand. He gave Clyde a whisker rub, then tucked into the feast with a gusto and lack of manners that, tonight, Clyde didn't mention. If Joe slopped on the covers, Clyde didn't seem to care. With the wonder of Clyde's offering, and with the bodily nourishment as well, a wave of well-being surged all through Joe Grey. He began to feel warm all over, feel safe again; began once more to feel strong and invulnerable.

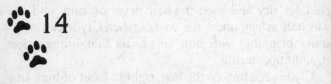

## 14

In the Getz house, the kit slept safe and warm, tucked in the blankets between Wilma and Dulcie, worn out from her grief, escaping into exhausted oblivion. The bedroom smelled of hot milk and hot cocoa and shortbread cookies, and of the wood fire that had burned down now to a few glowing coals. Outside, the rain had abated, but at four A.M. the cold wind still found its fitful way along the wet streets; wind shook drumbeats of water from the oak trees onto rooftops and car hoods—and on the cold and windy streets, others were about, who cared nothing for the windy cold, who cared only for adventure.

A giggle cut the night, then soft but urgent whispers as three girls moved quickly down the narrow alley that opened to the backs of a dozen shops.

Most of Molena Point's alleys were appealing lanes as charming as Jolly's alley, brick-paved byways lined with potted flowers and with the leaded- or stained-glass doorways of tiny backstreet stores. This concrete alley, however, was only a passage hiding garbage cans

and bales of collapsed cardboard cartons that awaited
the arrival of a sanitation truck. It was closed to
passersby with a solid-wood six-foot fence.

The gate wasn't locked. Candy pushed it open and
entered the long, trash-lined walkway, followed by
Leah and Dillon. They were on their own tonight; Consuela did not shepherd them. Flipping back her blond
hair, Candy fitted a key into the lock of Alice's Mirror.
The three slipped inside, Candy reaching quickly to cut
off the alarm system, just as the shop's owner would do
upon entering.

The girls were gone only a few minutes. They
emerged loaded down with velvet pants, cashmere
sweaters, wool and leather jackets, with plastic bags of
scarves and designer billfolds and necklaces. They had
known the location and distribution of the stock as well
as any store employee might know it. Dillon, swaggering
out with the biggest armload of stolen clothes, glanced
back as Candy locked the door. She was grinning.

Piling their loot into the trunk and filling the backseat of the car they had left parked at the curb, the three
slid into the front seat, the blonde at the wheel, and
moved quietly away. Watching the streets for cops, or
for a stray and observant pedestrian, they saw no one.

"Cops are all home in bed," Leah announced. "Or
drinking coffee at the station."

Dillon giggled. But as the car slid past Wilma Getz's
stone cottage and she smelled the smoke of a wood
fire, she sobered, studying the house. The sight of that
solid and inviting cottage where she had so often been
made welcome filled her with a sharp jolt of shame,
with a moment of clarity, an ugly look at what she was
doing.

* * *

In the stone cottage, Wilma was not asleep. She lay in bed in the dark, beside the two cats, thinking about Lucinda and Pedric. What *had* they been doing out on the highway at night? Kit had spoken the truth, the old couple never drove at night. And there could be no emergency that would account for a late-night run. Lucinda had no family and none of Pedric's relatives lived on the West Coast to take him racing to them.

Before the kit slept, she had looked up at Wilma suddenly, her round yellow eyes opening like twin moons, and had said decisively, "They can't be dead! Pedric is so clever. Lucinda and Pedric call themselves survivors. Survivors like me, that's what Lucinda says."

Dulcie and Wilma had exchanged a look.

Yet what Kit had said held some truth—everything Wilma knew about the Greenlaws showed how resourceful they were. She lay thinking about their well-appointed RV, where they always carried extra food, warm clothing, medical supplies, and of course their cell phone. Pedric had fitted out the RV with all manner of innovations to make life easier for them, from a bucket with a tight lid in which they put their laundry and soap and water, letting it bounce and agitate as they traveled, to locked storage compartments that could be opened from either the inside or outside of the vehicle. Pedric had grown up traveling all over the country in similar vehicles, and he was almost obsessed with self-sufficiency.

That did not explain why they were out in the storm at night. It was not as if they had been traveling to a new campsite. They had *been* at the one site for over a week and according to the registration had not checked out. The sheriff said they had left behind a folding camp table, two canvas chairs, and a large cooler. As she lay thinking, warm beside the two cats, she heard a car slide past the house and wondered idly who was out at four in the morning. Maybe a police car.

And as Wilma drifted off again into a depressed and anxious sleep, across the village the hardtop sedan pulled into the garage of a small rental cottage that stood behind a brown-shingled house. The cottage had once been servants' quarters.

The minute the ten-year-old Cadillac sedan entered through the automatic door, the door rolled down behind it. Inside, by the light from the door opener, the three girls unloaded the clothes. Most were still on their hangers, which Leah hung in the oversize metal storage lockers that lined the garage wall. She filled five lockers and snapped on padlocks. Four other units stood unlocked.

Leaving the car and letting themselves out the side door, which Candy locked behind them, the three girls headed away in separate directions, each to her own home. As Candy and Leah melted quickly into the night, Dillon, hurrying toward her own home, kept well away from the shadows. She didn't like being out in the small hours alone, though she would never let the others know that. Her girlfriends were about the only family she had now that she could count on. Her mother was zilch, a zero. And her dad had caved. He didn't fight back, he didn't do anything. He was just very quiet, turning away even from her—so patient and tolerant with Helen that he made Dillon retch. If she'd been her dad, she'd have packed up and hauled out of there, the two of them. Leave Helen to ruin her life any way she wanted.

Or she'd have booted Helen out and changed the locks, let her move in with what's-his-name.

But he wasn't doing either; he wasn't doing anything. Moving quickly along the dark streets, she was just a few blocks from home when she started thinking about that contractor, Ryan Flannery; when she saw suddenly a flash of green eyes and heard again the woman's rude comments, there in the Harper kitchen. *Bitch*.

Except, hearing Ryan's voice, for a moment Dillon was drawn beyond her anger. Ryan's retort had been almost exactly the same as Captain Harper's angry words.

And a small still voice down inside Dillon asked, what was she going to do about Ryan Flannery's challenge?

15

Kate Osborne didn't learn about Lucinda and Pedric's deaths until Sunday evening as she waited for the elderly couple to arrive for their visit. Lucinda had called two nights before, to say they'd be there by late afternoon, that they would be driving down from somewhere near Russian River, some little out-of-the way campground. And Kate had to smile. She was sure Lucinda hadn't had this much fun in all her adult life before she married Pedric. Her earlier marriage to Shamus, while busy with social functions and exciting for the first few years, had deteriorated as Lucinda aged, Lucinda staying home ignoring the truth while Shamus played fast and loose.

"I thought we'd eat in," Kate had told her. "That you might be tired, so I'd planned a little something at home. I make a mean creole, if you'd like that."

"That sounds like heaven," Lucinda had said. "A hot shower and a good hot creole supper. Couldn't be better. We'll plan to take you out the next night." Kate thought that maybe, with Lucinda and Pedric there, she

163

could get her head on straight, maybe could look at her own problems more objectively. This last week had been so strange and unsettling.

All week she had felt reluctant to go out after dark, and that was so stupid. Of course she'd had to work late, if she were to finish with her present clients in a timely manner. The work week would have been satisfying if she hadn't kept watching nervously for the man who had followed her to reappear.

At least she had found her extra keys in the drawer where she sometimes kept them; they had fallen down between the folds of her sweaters. That had eased her mind; and nothing in the apartment had, again, been disturbed. The windows had remained locked, and she saw no one lingering down in the street.

But still she was nervous. And then this morning, having gone into the office to do some paperwork, she saw him when she started out of the building, standing across the street in a shadowed doorway; and she stepped back inside the entry.

She couldn't tell if he was watching her, couldn't really be sure it was the same man. She had remained inside the glass door until he left the mosaic of shadows, ambling on down the street in plain view, a perfectly ordinary man wearing nondescript jeans and a brown windbreaker—but his face had been turned away.

She wanted to see his face. In spite of common sense, her fear had so sharply escalated that she arrived home cold and shivering. And then getting out of her car in the little parking garage, did she imagine a shadow slipping away behind the building? Steeling herself, she had gone on up the closed stairway, her pepper spray in her sweating hand. She was coming into the apartment when she'd heard a series of thuds, either inside or on the roof.

Gripping the pepper spray, and sick with fear, she had made the rounds of her familiar rooms. She found two desk drawers protruding, not pushed in all the way. And the couch and chair cushions were awry, and a kitchen cabinet door ajar. Then she found a wad of short black hair on the kitchen counter. She stood staring, filled with anger and fear, before she flushed it down the toilet and Cloroxed the countertop. She had no idea how the cat was getting in. No lock had been disturbed, and she had found her lost keys, though she supposed they could have been copied, then returned to her. But what was the purpose? Consuela knew by now that the jewels were not here; she must have learned that the first time she searched the apartment.

Kate was not afraid of Consuela. And she *should* not be afraid of the black tomcat. Badly shaken, but with Lucinda and Pedric due to arrive, she got herself in hand at last; she showered, and dressed comfortably in a velour jogging suit and scuffs. She wanted dinner preparations finished early, as they would be there before dark. She boiled the shrimp and made the creole sauce and measured the rice to be cooked. She set the table in the little dining room with her new paisley place mats, and put together a salad with all but the two ripe avocados she'd selected from her hoard on the windowsill. She set an amaretto cheesecake out to thaw. The scent of the freshly boiled shrimp and of the creole sauce filled the apartment, stirring her hunger. She filled the coffeepot, using a specially ground decaf, and curled up on the couch near the phone with a book, waiting for Lucinda's call that they were about to cross the Golden Gate. From the bridge, it was only ten minutes.

She read for some time Loren Eiseley's keen observations of the world. Strange that they were so late; it was growing dusky. Traffic must be heavy; not a good time to come into the city, with people returning from the weekend. When it was nearly dark, she rose to pull the draperies. Before closing those on the east, she stood a moment looking out toward East Bay, watching the lights of Berkeley and Oakland smear and fade in the gathering fog. She hoped Lucinda and Pedric arrived before the fog grew thick. Making a weak drink, she returned to her book. Only belatedly did she pick up the phone to see if they had left a message on the service before she ever got home.

She no longer used an answering machine; three power outages with the resultant failure of the machine had prompted her to subscribe to the phone company's uninterrupted reception even when the phones were out.

There was no beeping message signal. There was no sound at all from the receiver, no dial tone.

How long had the system been out? This happened every now and then, particularly in bad weather. As her apartment had not been disturbed, she didn't think anyone had tampered with the line.

Lucinda didn't have the number of her cell phone. Anyway, she realized suddenly, she'd left that phone in the car, plugged into the dash, the battery removed to keep it from turning to jelly. She had meant to bring it up with her; now she did not want to go out in the night to get it. She was disgusted that she had forgotten it when all this last week she had carried the phone even when she walked.

It was nearly seven thirty when she poured herself another mild drink and decided to fix a plate of cheese and crackers to calm her rumbling stomach. Lucinda had said they'd been up around Fort Bragg, poking along the coast. They did love their rambling life. For a pair of eighty-year-olds, those two folks were remarkable. Slicing the cheese, she reached to turn on the little kitchen TV that had been a birthday present to herself. She didn't watch much TV, but she liked to have the news on while she was getting dinner. Shaking out the crackers, she caught something about an accident in Sonoma County. An RV and a tanker truck. She glimpsed a brief shot of the wreck, the vehicles so badly burned you couldn't tell what they had looked like. Fire trucks, police cars, and ambulances filled the screen. She stood at the kitchen counter unmoving.

When had this happened? This couldn't be . . .

She relaxed when the newscaster said the collision had happened late last night. This had happened while Lucinda and Pedric were safely asleep in their RV, or in some cozy inn up the coast—not at a time when the Greenlaws would have been on the highway.

She didn't like to look at the TV pictures. It was a terrible wreck, those poor people hadn't had a chance. She had reached for the remote, to turn to another channel, when a cut of the newscaster came on, interviewing the Sonoma County sheriff. She paused, curious in spite of herself.

"Now that the nearest relatives have been notified,

we are able to release the names of the deceased. The tanker driver, Ken Doyle of Concord, is survived by a wife and two young children." There was a still shot of a dark-haired young woman holding a little boy and a fat baby. "The occupants of the RV were residents of Molena Point. Lucinda and Pedric Greenlaw had been . . ."

She couldn't move. Suddenly she couldn't breathe.

". . . vacationing up the Northern California coast. The eighty-year-old newlyweds, who were married just last year in a Molena Point ceremony, were returning home to the central-coast village . . ."

She needed to sit down. She stood leaning against the counter, holding on to the counter, staring at the TV.

She had seen Lucinda and Pedric only a few weeks ago. She had spent the evening with them. She left the kitchen, making her way to the living room and the couch, which seemed miles. Sat with her head down between her knees as she had been taught as a child, until the nausea passed.

Why would Lucinda and Pedric be on the road late at night?

A long time later she rose to put the shrimp and creole sauce and salad in the refrigerator. Standing in the kitchen with her back to the TV and the sound turned off, she made herself a double whiskey and took it into the living room.

But there, she couldn't help it, she turned on the larger TV mindlessly changing channels looking for more news, though she did not want to see any more. The wreck had happened Saturday night while she lay sleeping. Today she had gone about her pointless affairs while Lucinda and Pedric lay dead. She had stopped at the grocery, buying shrimp, flowers for the table, imagining the thin, wrinkled couple tooling along in their nice RV, stopping at antique shops, stopping to eat cracked crab . . . Staring at the TV, she didn't know what to do or what to think. She simply sat.

Did Wilma know? She ought to call Wilma. Should she call Clyde, ask Clyde to tell Wilma? Clyde was closer to Wilma than she was, they were like family. If they knew, why hadn't they called her?

And she couldn't call out; the line was dead.

She'd have to go down and get her cell phone. How stupid, to have left it in the car. Fetching her keys, she pulled on her coat, snatched up the pepper spray, locked the door behind her, and went down the stairs, hating this sense of fear. Reaching the garage she moved quickly, watching between other cars. Unlocking her Riviera she snatched up the phone, hit the lock, and slammed the door. She was up the stairs and in the apartment again before fear had immobilized her. This was crazy; she couldn't live like this. On a hunch, she tried the apartment phone again—and got the insistent beeping of the message service.

Sitting down on the couch with the now functioning phone, she started to play back her messages, then decided first to call Clyde. She needed, very much, to hear his gruff and reassuring voice.

The downstairs rooms of the Damen cottage were dark, but upstairs behind the closed shutters the bedroom and study were bright, the desk lamp lit, a warming fire burning in the study where Clyde sat at his desk filling out parts orders. Or trying to, working around the prone body of the sleeping gray tomcat where he lay sprawled across the catalogs. Far be it from Joe to move. Far be it from Clyde, who found the tomcat as amusing as he was exasperating, to ask him.

Ryan had left half an hour ago, after an early supper in the big new kitchen: takeout from their favorite Mexican café. Impatiently waiting for the building permit for the Harper place, she had gone home to her blueprints, anxious to finish putting together a design proposal for a remodel at the north end of the village. "I want to get that wrapped up, so I can concentrate on the Harper job."

"You are not," Clyde had said, "going to get so busy that you keep pulling men off one job to work on another, like most contractors? Delaying all the jobs?"

"No fear." She had grinned at him, flipping back her short dark hair. "I can manage my work better than that." She had given him a warm, green-eyed smile and laid her hand over his; her closeness led him, more and more lately, to imagine her always there with him. He sat at his desk now thinking about Ryan sharing the house, comfortable and warm and exciting.

Clyde's view of women had changed dramatically since the time, a few years back, when every conquest was exciting, when every new looker was a challenge even if he couldn't stand her as a person. Joe Grey had chided him more than once about bringing home some airhead. Well, that life was not for him anymore; the idea of bringing home some bimbo now disgusted him.

The change had started when Kate left her husband

and came to him for help. He had been so smitten with
her, and for so long, but after that night when he had
hidden her from Jimmie, he had been so confused by
her bizarre nature.

He had mooned over Kate for a long time after that,
but she had distanced herself. She had known better
than he that with the difference between them a relationship would never work; she had seen too clearly
his fear of her impossible talents.

The night she left Jimmie and came running here to
him, he would not believe what she told Clyde about
her alternate self, although her feline nature was part
of the reason Jimmie wanted to kill her. In order to
prove to Clyde what she could do, she had done it.
Standing before him, whispering some unlikely spell,
she had taken the form of a cat. A cream-colored cat,
sleek and beautiful, with golden eyes like Kate's and
marmalade markings.

His fear had been considerable. He had charged into
the bedroom and slammed the door and wouldn't open
it. He did not want to see her again in either form. The
next day he'd been better, although the concept still
shook him. He became civil once more; but he would
never get over it.

And yet even after that shattering incident, he had
longed for her, had tried every way to get her to come
home again after she moved to San Francisco.

Neither Joe nor Dulcie could take human form. Nor
did Joe Grey want to; the tomcat said he liked his life
as it was, that the talents he *had* were plenty. Well, the
upshot for Clyde was that he had begun to look at a
woman as a *person*. To want to know who she was and
what she thought about life.

While pining over Kate, he had dated Charlie, a woman as honest and real as anyone he'd ever known. It was then he had let himself realize, as he had known deeply all along, what the real values were. It was then he put away his shallow philosophy and turned, as Max had done years before, to look at what a woman believed deep down, what she cared about in life.

Joe Grey would say, big sea change. The tomcat had ragged him plenty about his earlier lifestyle. Clyde stared down at Joe now. The tomcat seemed to make himself twice as big when he sprawled across a desk where a person was working. "You wouldn't consider rolling over, so I can finish this order?"

Joe stared up at him, his yellow eyes wide and innocent. "You think you should try Kate again? The phone has to be out, it wouldn't be busy all this time, even Kate can't talk that long—but she has to be home, she's expecting Lucinda and Pedric, she'll be worried."

They had been trying all evening to get her, calling both the house and her cell phone. Clyde wished he had started calling that morning. Both he and Wilma had been waiting for more information, for the sheriff to find the bodies, for some assurance the old couple had indeed been killed. Then when he tried to get Kate this evening, busy signal. "I left messages on both phones. Why the hell doesn't she check her messages!"

Joe said, "Maybe by now she's had the TV on. If it's been on the news, she . . ."

Again Clyde hit the redial. If she *had* seen the news, if she knew, maybe she was talking with Wilma.

He got another busy. Five minutes passed as he tried to work, patiently lifting Joe's gray paw to check a price, peering under a gray ear to retrieve a parts number.

"Try again," Joe said. "I'm worried about her."

Clyde tried three more times before Kate's phone rang. Just one ring, and she picked up. Clyde left the speaker on so Joe wouldn't crowd him pressing against the phone. "Kate? You okay?"

"No, I'm not okay. Did you . . ."

"You heard the news."

"This can't have happened. It's impossible to believe. What were they doing out on the highway in the middle of the night? If they'd had some emergency, say one of them got sick, they'd have called the medics. Or the sheriff. Or a cab. They'd been staying in a campground, they could have called the manager. Have you talked with anyone up there? The highway patrol? The Sonoma County sheriff? What have they found? Couldn't it be some kind of mistake? The wrong RV. Or maybe they—"

Clyde said, "Wilma talked with the sheriff. They've had a crew there all day going through the wreckage."

"And?"

"They— So far, no bodies. Nothing much at all left." He glanced at Joe. "It was a terrible fire, Kate. Ashes, rubble. The truck driver . . . they did find his body, in his crashed truck. The truck wasn't burned as badly as the RV."

Kate was silent for a long time. When she spoke again, her voice was very small. "They were so happy together. Their late marriage was like a fairy tale, like one of their Old-World folktales. It isn't fair. They were having such a good time traveling. And planning to build their dream house . . ."

Clyde stared at the phone.

"It's all wrong," Kate said. "Their campsite hadn't been vacated, they left canvas chairs, a folding table set up under the pines. The late news said some towels were left hanging on a portable line, an expensive bear-proof garbage can."

The fur along Joe Grey's spine felt rigid. His paws were cold as he sorted through the facts—Lucinda and Pedric heading for San Francisco to stay with Kate, Lucinda with the same kind of jewelry that Consuela had gone to steal from Kate and that the appraiser had tried to buy.

Moving closer to the phone, Joe placed a paw on Clyde's hand, staring at the speaker.

Clyde scowled and shoved the phone at him.

"In spite of this mess," Joe said into the speaker, "one seemingly unrelated question. Did you get there in time?"

"I did," she said sadly. "I moved it all, thanks to you. I wanted to call but I . . . Joe, that cat has been here. Inside my apartment."

"The cat can't hurt you, Kate." He paused. He wasn't sure of that. "But Consuela could," he said staring at the phone. This whole gig made him edgy; this stuff was happening too far away, and there were too many loose pieces, events that didn't add up. "Come home, Kate. Come back to the village now." He glanced at Clyde. "You can stay with us."

Clyde looked surprised, then nodded.

"And I've been followed," Kate said.

"Followed where? When was this? Consuela? Who?"

"A man. I . . ."

Clyde nudged Joe away from the speaker. "Did you report it to the police? Do you know him?"

"I . . . No. And I didn't report it, not yet."

*"Why not?"* Clyde snapped. "Never mind. Kate, get a second appraisal on the jewelry. This is all too weird."

"Emerson Bristol has an excellent reputation, Clyde. He's a big name in the city."

"You researched the subject," Clyde said. "You know that such unusual work, made by a master craftsman, ought to be cataloged somewhere. Even if it is paste. You said you've been through all the catalogs, the books in San Francisco Public and in the museums. Don't you think it's strange that there's absolutely no mention of it?"

"Yes," she said in a small voice.

"I don't like this. Joe's right. Come home, Kate. Bring that stuff down here to someone in the village—someone Harper recommends."

"I have so much work, installations . . ."

"Come home, Kate. Come now."

"I . . . After tonight, I feel all in pieces. Will you call me when you know more about Lucinda and Pedric? More about what happened?"

Clyde sighed. "I'll call you."

"And . . . there's something else," she said. "I almost forgot. Likely it's nothing, but . . . I threw out some newspapers when I was cleaning up, but I saved one. It was dated three days before Charlie's gallery opening. There was a jewel robbery here, on Market Street. A cheap, touristy kind of place. It happened around six in the evening, just before the shop closed. The police got there before the three men could get away. They arrested two, but the third man got a cop down and escaped. The paper said he took a hard blow to the forehead, the store owner hit him with a brick. It's probably coincidence," Kate said, "but I . . ."

"Harper is checking the police records for fights," Clyde said with interest. "For batterings, anything like that. He's sure to catch it, but I'll tell him. Save the paper, the date. And come home, Kate. Where it's safe. We all miss you."

"I'll think about it, Clyde. Good-night, you guys." Her voice was weepy. "Good-night," she whispered. "I guess I feel better."

When Clyde hung up, Joe dropped off the desk and leaped to Clyde's new leather easy chair that sat before the fire. Clyde had brought the Molena Point *Gazette* upstairs with him. The Greenlaw accident filled the upper half of the front page. Scanning the article, he saw with disappointment that it gave no more information than the TV news had supplied.

The lower half of the page was devoted to Saturday night's clothing store burglary. Alice's Mirror had been relieved of its highest-priced stock. There was no sign of forced entry. The theft hadn't been discovered until this morning when the owner opened the store for the usual Sunday tourists.

Joe sat staring into the fire, wondering how much he should tell Clyde. It was just this morning, the morning after the Greenlaw accident, that Kit had told Joe himself, and Dulcie, about the missing key.

After their night on Hellhag Hill, Joe had awakened very late, alone in the rumpled bed. The bedside clock said 8:15, half the day gone, from any cat's point of view. Clyde would long ago have gone to work. Joe was crawling out from among the tangled sheets when the phone rang. He didn't knock the bedside phone from its cradle, but trotted through to the study. Leaping to the desk, he listened as the machine answered.

Only one word was spoken. "*Joe?*" Dulcie hissed.

He hit the speaker. "*Damen residence.*"

"*Jolly's,*" she said softly and immediately hung up.

He hit the erase button and was out of there, leaping to the rafter above the desk and up through his rooftop cat door.

Pausing in his private tower for a drink of water, he raced out across the shingles, then along an oak branch, across slanting and angled roofs until he was forced to descend to the sidewalk, at the divided lanes and grassy median of Ocean Avenue. Crossing Ocean among the feet of a group of tourists, he shied away from their reaching hands. *What a smart cat, crossing the street with us . . . Cute kitty . . . Do you think he's lost? We could . . .* Dodging away, he headed for Jolly's alley. Dulcie's voice had sounded desperate. All manner of disasters, most of them involving the kit, had raced through his tomcat mind as he swerved along the sidewalks and at last into Jolly's alley.

**16**

Belting into the alley, Joe found Dulcie and the kit crouched beneath the jasmine vine beside the deli's back door, their ears down, their eyes filled with distress. Though it was midmorning, the alley was empty. No other cats, no tourists. George Jolly's ever-present offering of delicacies stood untouched before the closed deli door. The kit had not even sampled the smoked salmon and egg custard. She sat staring listlessly down at her paws. Joe nudged at her, deeply distressed by her grieving for Lucinda and Pedric. Pushing in beneath the vine, he nosed at her. When she glanced up at him, the kit looked not only heartbroken, but ashamed.

"What?" Joe said. Dulcie, too, looked devastated. *"What?"* he repeated. "What's with you two?"

"She took the key," the kit said.

"Who did? What key?"

"Dillon. I should have told before but I thought . . . I didn't want her to be in trouble."

*"What* key, Kit? Key to what?"

178

But he knew.

"The key to the back door of Alice's Mirror," Dulcie said. "The store that was burglarized last night. It was on the local news this morning."

"I followed them," the kit said. "The four girls. One afternoon weeks ago. Followed them into Alice's Mirror. They were acting so . . . I just knew they were going to do something. I slipped inside behind a rack of satin and velvet and I watched them. Dillon looked so . . . sort of wandering pretending not to look all around. Like a bird when it's busy pecking the ground but really watching you. She was wandering just beside the door to the shop's office, admiring a rack of blouses, sliding them along—then she vanished.

"I could see her in the office where customers aren't supposed to go, so I went in there behind her. She didn't see me; I slid behind some boxes and watched." The kit sighed. "She took a key from a hook beside the desk and slipped out again and left the shop. Her two friends picked out some clothes, asked a clerk some questions about them and took them to a fitting room. I went outside and saw Dillon down the street, handing something to Consuela. Consuela turned and hurried away. I went up an oak tree until she came back and gave it back to Dillon; it was a key. Dillon went back inside the shop. I followed and watched her put it back in the office, hang it on a little hook. Then in a minute, all three girls left and they met Consuela outside.

"And I ran home.

"But I didn't tell anyone. I didn't want to tell Wilma or you or anyone. I knew I should call Captain Harper, but I didn't want to get Dillon in trouble and make the captain feel worse about her, so I didn't do anything. I curled up under the afghan and tried to sleep and pretend it didn't happen."

Joe Grey listened quietly. All along, Kit had carried this burden, wanting to protect Dillon. Kit looked up at him. "They copied it, didn't they? In one of those key places. It was all over the news. The burglary."

Joe nuzzled her and licked her ear, and the three cats looked at one another. What was happening to Dillon? And, more to the point, what were they to do about it?

Joe said, "It's time to tell the captain."

The kit's eyes widened; but she didn't argue. She just looked very sad.

"The closest key maker to Alice's Mirror," Joe said, "is Jarman's, just down the street behind the fire station. Otherwise she'd have to go out on the highway." Thoughtfully he licked his paw. "Mr. Jarman would remember her."

Harry Jarman was an elderly, round-faced, gray-haired, gentle old man who had been making keys for the village ever since he was a young fellow. He knew everyone in Molena Point. Even though Consuela hadn't been in the village long, the old man would know who she was, he didn't miss a thing. If he had made a key for Consuela Benton, he would remember that.

Dulcie licked the kit's ear. "Don't grieve, Kit. You did just right to tell us. This is best for Dillon, she can't go on like this, she'd have no life." Dulcie looked at Joe. "You want to call the captain, or shall I?"

"I'll call him. I can tell him Consuela took the key to be copied. I don't have to mention Dillon."

Dulcie's eyes widened. The kit's ears pricked up, and her tail lifted more cheerfully. But as the three cats headed for Dulcie's house and the phone, Joe himself felt frustrated and sad. Even if he didn't mention Dillon, Garza and Harper would know; they would quickly uncover the younger girl's role in the matter. And, glancing at Dulcie, he knew she was thinking the same.

Before Max Harper had the interior of the building that housed Molena Point PD remodeled, his desk had occupied a six-by-six space at the back of the open squad room. He'd had no walls for privacy, no bookshelves, preferring, then, a work area where he could see and hear everything that went on among his officers: a sacrifice of privacy for control that Harper no longer needed. Now, since the remodeling, the captain enjoyed the luxury of real walls and a solid door, which he had quickly come to appreciate. Charlie said he'd lived a spartan life long enough. She had bought the leather couch as an anniversary present: one month married, time to celebrate. She had added two red leather easy chairs and a bright India rug from their own home. Three of Charlie's drawings hung on the walls where Max could enjoy them, portraits of Max's gelding, Bucky. Harper's work calendar and charts stood in a rack to the right of his desk, at easy glance for the chief but not openly displayed to visitors— though that did not deter Joe Grey.

Joe entered Harper's office this morning on the heels of Mabel Farthy, the blond and portly dispatcher, as she delivered Harper's early lunch, her approach down the hall wafting the scent of garlic and pastrami like a long and diaphanous bridal veil behind her. As Mabel set the takeout bag on the desk, and Harper turned to slip some reports into the file drawer, a swift gray shadow slid behind the couch.

Charlie had carefully arranged the furniture with the cats in mind. The couch stood as near the door as she could manage, and she had chosen a style with legs high enough so Joe and Dulcie didn't have to squeeze down like pancakes. Feline surveillance didn't have to be an exercise in flattened spines and shallow breathing.

Joe, drinking in the heavy aroma of pastrami, watched two sets of shoes enter: Detective Garza's tan leather loafers and Detective Juana Davis's regulation black oxfords over black stockings. Garza settled into one of the red leather chairs, stretching out his long legs. His tan chinos were neatly pressed, his Dockers fashionably scuffed.

Beneath the couch, Joe made sure his paws were out of sight—he didn't want to appear to be spying.

Dallas Garza had a deep fondness for fine hunting dogs, but until recently he had never understood, or given much thought to, cats—until Joe Grey came on the scene. Working judiciously on Garza's attitude, Joe had seen the detective develop, over many months, an almost passable fondness for certain felines, at least for those cats who crossed his professional path.

Having spent a week freeloading in the Garza cottage closely observing the detective, Joe had decided that he could trust this new addition to the department. Of course Garza had no notion of the intimate telephone conversations and interdepartmental reports that he had shared that week with the gray tomcat.

As Joe pulled in his paws, Detective Davis sat down at the end of the couch just above him. As she slipped off her shoes and tucked her feet up under her, her shifting weight forced little squinching noises from the new leather. Protocol was not an issue with these three; you could take your shoes off if you liked. Only honesty and ethics mattered. Juana, Max, and Dallas played poker together, usually in Clyde and Joe's kitchen.

As the three tucked into their deli lunch, Joe couldn't help an occasional drool dampening Harper's new carpet. Listening to paper rattling and the sounds of their satisfied munching amid small talk, he had a long and hungry wait before Harper laid down his sandwich and picked up a file of reports. Covetously Joe eyed the sandwich, but told himself to forget it. He could see from his position beneath the couch a long reflection in the glass-fronted bookcase that gave him a view of Harper's desk. This thoughtful touch, too, had been Charlie's. She and Joe had tested it early one morning when Harper was downstairs on the indoor pistol range.

Harper looked up at Garza. "You have no indication that Quinn's house had been broken into."

"None," Garza said. "And no other prints besides Quinn's. Only Quinn's prints on the handle of the gas jet, where of course his prints would be."

Harper shuffled the stack of papers. "There seems nothing out of place here, among his real estate transactions. Both Helen and their broker have been over everything, found nothing out of the way, except for the missing notebook. You searched the real estate office?"

"Yes," Davis said. "The broker, James Holland,

helped Helen look for the notebook while I waited. They ransacked the entire office. We searched Quinn's car again, took out the seats, everything short of dismantling the vehicle."

"The notebook may be of no value," Harper said, "but the case is open until it's found."

The three were silent, finishing their lunches. Harper asked Davis about two identity thefts that had been reported, both involving scams on local residents. These piqued Joe's interest because this was the first he'd heard about them. Crimes like identity theft made him glad he was a cat without the encumbrance of a charge card, social security number, and other invitations to embezzlement.

"The victims are getting their papers together," Davis said. "Paid bills, canceled checks. Both have retained attorneys. The one woman, Sheila James, is looking at a five-thousand-dollar-a-month mortgage on a house that is, in fact, completely paid for. The other folks, Ron and Sandy Bueller, moved here just a year ago. Six new credit card accounts in their name, some sixty thousand in debts outstanding, so far, plus payments on a two-million-dollar piece of land in the north part of the county that they didn't buy and have never seen."

Davis shifted her position on the couch; the leather creaked again. "All of that within the space of a week. And we have nothing so far. Zilch."

That, Joe knew, was par for the course in these cases. The officers discussed every possible venue at their disposal to get a line on the guy; Davis and Garza were working on them all, and would keep digging; the loopholes, the lack of ways to nail these thieves was, Joe thought, like chasing mice through a metal grating:

the chasee escapes, the chaser bangs his nose on the barrier.

"What about the Greenlaw accident?" Davis said. "Still no bodies?"

"Not so much as a scorched bone," Harper told her. "Sheriff thinks, now, that neither of the Greenlaws was in the RV when it crashed. He's searching the area, thinking they might have been murdered and dumped before the wreck.

"If they were alive," Harper said, "someone would have heard from them. Wilma, certainly. She's not only Lucinda's friend, but her executor. She's ready to drive up there, car gassed up, suitcase packed. She'd like to help the sheriff's teams search but right now there's nothing she can do that they're not on top of. Sheriff has dogs out, the works."

"They're eighty years old," Garza said. "There are some desolate stretches in those forests."

"Eighty years old and tough as boots," Harper replied. "Certainly Pedric is. And Lucinda, since they married, has become just about as strong mentally and emotionally. When Shamus was alive, Lucinda was little more than a wilting violet, acted like she was scared of her own shadow."

Harper studied his two detectives. "I had a call this morning, about the burglary at Alice's Mirror.

"Our favorite snitch," Harper said, "suggested we ask Harry Jarman about a key he might have duplicated for Consuela Benton." The captain smiled. "I picked up a key from Alice's Mirror this morning, stopped by Jarman's with it. He remembered Consuela coming in a couple of weeks ago. I laid seven keys on the counter, six from my own pocket.

"He picked it out right away. Remembered he'd used the last blank like that, and had to order more."

Davis gave a little pleased *"All right!"* Dallas laughed softly.

"I have a *Be-on-the-lookout* for Consuela," Harper said. "Soon as we can print her, if we get a match, maybe we can make a case and get a warrant for the cottage she's renting up on Carpenter. I understand the garage is part of the rental deal."

Beneath the couch, Joe Grey grinned. *Right on, Kit,* he thought, both saddened and relieved. *You nailed her. And if the department can make Consuela for masterminding the burglary, maybe it will go easier for Dillon.* And, Joe thought, the cops might need a warrant to toss Consuela's rental. But a cat didn't.

The three officers moved on to the rash of coastal burglaries, and for over an hour they discussed the various reports from up and down the California coast, comparing MOs. The information from some two dozen fences was all negative. None of the stolen items had been traced to any of the known fences. The burglaries covered the geographic area from Malibu in the south to Point Reyes in the north, and inland as far as Oakland and Berkeley and Thousand Oaks. Garza had prepared a chart on the computer, listing the dates of the burglaries, the time of day they were discovered, the length of time since the items had last been seen. In the case of jewelry kept in a home safe, the lapse of time might amount to several months, the piece in question might have disappeared at any time during that period. There had been no report at all on Clyde's antique Packard.

Peering out from beneath the couch, Joe could

barely see the chart without being seen himself, without his gray-and-white nose and whiskers protruding. As the three officers talked, Davis swung one stockinged foot over, twiddling her toes just inches from Joe's nose. Her feet smelled of talcum powder. Dallas's chart showed all social gatherings at each address within the last three years, with size and description of events, from dinner parties to charity functions. An addendum provided guest lists, and lists of household help and maintenance people for each event.

None of the houses had been for sale, none had been shown to buyers. Joe was awed at Garza's thoroughness, and at the details possible when law enforcement from different cities shared information. Seven names surfaced as guests in more than two of the burgled residences. Joe grew so interested, pushing out farther and farther, that his whiskers brushed Juana's ankle. She jerked her foot away and leaned over, peering under the couch to see what was there.

Joe Grey was gone, curled into a ball among the shadows of the far corner, hiding the white markings on his face and chest and paws, and squinching his eyes closed.

When Juana decided there was nothing under there and settled back, Joe crept out again where he could see. It was interesting that, of the list of guests, three had themselves been victims of that rash of bizarre thefts. The statistics were broken down further into a morass of facts, which, without the written information before him, left the tomcat's head spinning.

He watched enviously as Garza printed it all out and stepped down the hall to the dispatcher's desk to make copies. He would dearly love to have that printout. But even without a copy, two names on the list held Joe's attention.

A woman up the coast in Marin County had attended four of the listed affairs, all charity events. And Molena Point's own Marlin Dorriss had been a guest at five of those houses, at private dinner parties.

In no case had the two been guests at the same function.

"Dorriss knows everyone," Detective Davis said. "He's all over the state, on the board of a dozen museums and as many charities." She laughed. "Until this business with Helen Thurwell, Dorriss appeared to be without flaw in his personal life. And that," she said coolly, "is all the more reason to check him out."

Dallas said, "Max, you talked with Susan Dorriss— Susan Brittain? Her husband was Marlin Dorriss's brother? Why did she suddenly change back to her maiden name, all these years after her husband died?"

"She's never been close to her brother-in-law," Harper said. "Something to do with Dorriss's two sons, her husband's nephews. Bad apples, Susan says. She didn't see much of Dorriss when they all lived in San Francisco. Said that not until after she moved down to the village to be with her daughter, did she know that Marlin had a place here.

"Then she had that accident and was in the nursing home, and she didn't think much about him. But after she recovered and was back in her own place she ran into Marlin. That distressed her, that he was living here. That's when she decided to drop the name, exhibit no more connection with him than necessary."

"All because of his sons?" Juana asked.

"She said they were impossible as young boys and she'd heard they were no better now. She was very critical of the way Marlin raised them. I got the impression that if she'd known he had a home in the village part-time, she might not have moved to Molena Point at all."

"Interesting," Garza said. "Didn't her daughter tell her?"

"No, she didn't," Max said. "Susan thinks that's because her daughter wanted her to move down, to get out of the city. I'd give a month's pay to see his phone and Visa bills, his gas station receipts. See if we could put him in those locations during the burglaries."

"That's stretching a bit," Dallas said. "No way the judge would issue a search warrant on that kind of conjecture. And if we went directly to the phone company and to his credit card people, if we got into that gray area . . ."

"I don't like to beat a dead horse," Davis said, "but life was simpler twenty years ago."

Garza grunted in agreement, then the three were silent. And beneath the couch, Joe Grey smiled. Marlin Dorriss might be as innocent and clean as driven snow, but the guy was worth checking out.

**17**

On a rocky point just at the south edge of the village, Marlin Dorriss's villa rose among giant boulders that had been tumbled there eons before by the earth's angry upheaval. Its montage of angles and converging planes reflected moving light from the sea's crashing waves. The pale structure seemed, to some, harsh and ungiving. Others, including Dorriss himself, admired the play of light across its pristine surfaces, the shifting shadows always changing beneath swiftly blowing skies.

Few windows faced the street. Those slim openings, like gun slits, glinted now in the morning sun as Joe Grey slunk among the boulders. Studying the house, he prayed that he hadn't left Dulcie in danger as she went to investigate Consuela's rented house. He had made her promise that if she heard any noise from within, any small hint of a human presence, she'd get the hell out of there fast.

"What can happen? So I'm hunting mice. If a mouse ran in through an open window, why wouldn't I follow?"

"Not everyone loves a prowling cat. Just be careful."

"You're feeling guilty because you suggested this gig and you're not coming with me. I think it's a blast. Who knows what I'll find?"

"I had hoped the kit—"

Dulcie had flashed him a look of green-eyed impatience. "*I* don't know where she is. And *you* know she'd only make trouble. She'd be into everything, and I'm always afraid she'll start talking a mile a minute."

But Joe had parted from Dulcie with an unaccustomed fear tickling along his spine, a taut wariness that almost made him turn back. Only the urgency of Marlin Dorriss's personal papers led him on, calling to him like the sound of mice scurrying in the walls.

It would set him up big time to lay his claws on the precise evidence that Max Harper would so like to obtain, papers that Harper's officers couldn't legally search for, and without which they might never have the lead they needed—if indeed Dorriss *was* involved in these high-class thefts.

And if Dorriss wasn't the thief, nothing lost. A few hours' adventure.

"You're courting trouble," Dulcie had told him. "Getting too bold. That place is huge, and built like a fort. Let me come . . ."

"We really need to know where the stolen clothes are hidden," he'd said, and had bullied until he sent her away; and now he couldn't stop worrying about her. She had left him, scowling, her ears back, her tail lashing, her parting words, "You're going to trip on your own claws if you're not careful," ringing in his ears as he crossed the village.

But what was life for, if not to balance on the edge?

He just didn't want to put Dulcie in that danger. Consuela's small house lent itself to quicker escape. Anyway, he had not the faintest notion that he would fail. With sufficient tenacity and clever paw work, why should he fail? Every human had bills to pay; every human kept his paid bills stashed in some drawer or cubbyhole.

"And how," Dulcie had said, "are you going to keep from implicating Detectives Garza and Davis? You daren't make it look like one of them broke into Dorriss's. They both were there in Harper's office when he talked about the bills."

Joe had been worrying about that. He'd told Dulcie, "No problem. I'll think about that after the deed." If he could find evidence that Dorriss had been in those towns at the time of the burglaries, Harper would have something to work on. It had to be frustrating to have a multimillion-dollar case like this and not a useful bit of evidence. Harper and Dallas Garza's strong cop-sense that Dorriss could be involved was good enough, anytime, for Joe Grey.

A granite-paved parking area curved before the front of the house, between the huge pale boulders and the natural, informal gardens. Granite flagstones led to the heavily carved front door that was recessed beneath a white slab. Above the door at either side, surveillance cameras looked down on Joe. To a master of break-and-enter, the place looked like Fort Knox. He hoped to hell those cameras weren't running at the moment, closely monitoring him. Even if he was only an innocent feline, electronic surveillance made him nervous—though Dorriss ought to be happy to have a stray cat wandering the property ridding the area of unwanted moles and gophers.

Passing the entry he trotted along the side of the house to the back, into a fine mist of sea spray. Crossing the stone patio he stood looking back at the house. Only here facing the sea were there wide expanses of glass looking out at the boulders and the crashing surf. The huge windows would, from within, afford an unbroken view of the Pacific.

The patio was protected from the wind by a six-foot glass wall, its panels skillfully fitted around the mountains of granite. From this sunny shelter a stone walk led down the cliff to the sea, doubling back and forth in comfortable angles until it reached the sand far below. For a few moments Joe crouched at the edge of the cliff rocked by the sea wind, caught in the timeless dance of the violent sea; then he turned away, approaching the house through the glassed patio.

He paused, startled.

Either luck was with him, or a trap had been laid.

Of the four pairs of sliding glass doors that opened to the seaward patio, the one at the far end stood open perhaps four inches, just wide enough for a cat to slip through.

Looking along the bottom of the glass he saw where it was locked in place so no one larger could enter. Higher up where the glass door joined the wall, he saw the tiny red lights of an activated security system, a strip of lights that rose from six inches above the floor to about six feet, a barrier impossible for a human to circumvent unless he was circus-thin and agile enough to slide in on his belly, or was a skilled high jumper.

Sniffing all around the open glass he could catch no animal scent, cat or otherwise, could smell only salty residue from the sea spray. He could see no one inside the room beyond the glass, but the place was huge, with angles and niches that might conceal an army.

Slipping beneath the electronic barrier ready to spin and run, he eased beyond the beam. Once inside, he expected his every move to trigger an interior beam, but no alarm sounded. Uneasily he rose to his full height, his gray ears pricked, his short stub tail erect, his yellow eyes searching every angle of the furniture, dissecting every shadow. Still no alarm—and talk about architectural bravado!

The walls of the soaring, two-story great room were hung with large and vivid action paintings from the mid-1950s. Thanks to Dulcie's coaching, he recognized several Diebenkorns, two Bischoffs, half a dozen Braden Wests. Opening from this soaring gallery were a dozen low, cavelike seating niches, cozy conversation alcoves that were tucked beneath the floor above. Each little retreat was furnished in a different style designed around some esoteric collection. One conversation area featured miniature landscapes. One was designed to set off a group of steel sculptures. In another, couch and chairs were tucked among huge six-foot-tall chess pieces. An array of carved wooden chests and small cupboards was arranged among soft velvet seating. Joe could imagine Dulcie and Kit prowling here for hours, riven with delight at every new discovery, rolling on every velvet settee and hand-woven cushion.

Keeping to the shadows, scanning every niche to make sure he was alone, he expected any second to see someone sitting among the exhibits, silent and still, watching him. Or to come face to face with whatever animal, most likely a cat, enjoyed access through the open glass door. At the back of the room, behind a vast, two-sided fireplace, was a dining room with dark blue-gray walls. The huge carved table and chairs were rubbed with white, the chair seats upholstered in white. He would not have noticed these niceties if he had not spent so many hours with Dulcie. At every break-and-enter, she had to admire, examine, and comment upon the decor.

In the left-hand wall of the dining room, a door stood open to the kitchen. Far to the left of the kitchen an entry hall led to the carved front door, and here rose a broad and angled stairway. Was Dorriss's office up there on the second floor, his desk and files? Or did Dorriss have a secretary hidden away in some village office to take care of business matters? Likely he relied on a broker in some large firm to tend to his investments, but he had to have letters, personal bills. Wouldn't a house of this size and quality have a safe? Did Dorriss keep his stocks and bonds at home, along with the valuable pieces of antique silver and jewelry that he was known to collect?

Skilled as he was with his paws, Joe's expertise did not, as yet, include safecracking. Anyway he was here for bills, not silver. Who kept their Visa bills in a locked safe? Contemplating the possible extent of Dorriss's security arrangements, and his skin rippling with nerves, he made for the wide stairway.

Leaping up the carpeted stair, he gained the top step and stood listening, sniffing the soft flow of air from open windows somewhere on this floor, seeking any waft of human or cat scent. The house was meticulously clean; peering into a bedroom, he could see that the spaces under the chairs had all been freshly vacuumed. He could smell the faint afterbreath of the vacuum cleaner, that dusty aroma ejected through the dust bag even in the most expensive of models—though this dust-scented air was perfumed, as well, with cinnamon. Likely the housekeeper added powdered cinnamon to the fresh dust bags. Joe knew that trick—both Clyde and Wilma did it, to delicately perfume the house. Surely Clyde had learned the habit from Wilma, he'd never have thought of it on his own. The spice was far superior to air fresheners, which made Joe and Dulcie sneeze.

The wide upstairs hall was lit from above by a row of angled skylights. Paintings were spaced along both walls, again work by Diebenkorn, Bischoff, West, and James Weeks. Each piece had to be worth enough to keep Joe in caviar for ninety-nine cat lives. Five bedrooms opened from the hall. Each was handsomely designed, but none looked or smelled lived in. Only the last room, on his left, smelled of recent occupancy and looked as if it were regularly occupied; the shelves were cluttered with books and papers and several small pieces of sculpture, the smell of aftershave mixed with the scent of leather, and of charred wood from the fireplace. The fireplace was laid with fresh logs over a gas starter. The paneled wall on either side looked hand-carved, the oak slabs thick and heavy.

The master bedroom joined Dorriss's study through an inner hall, which also opened to the master bath and dressing room. This suite occupied the entire south end of the second floor. Around Joe the house was silent, the only sound the dulled crashing of the sea and the whispering insistence of the sea wind. Intently listening he trotted into Dorriss's office and leaped to the desk.

The desk faced a wall of glass; one of the three panels was cracked open a few inches. Crouching on the blotter with his nose to the window, Joe had the sensation of floating untethered above the cliff and the sea.

A fax machine stood beside a phone. Dorriss's computer occupied an adjacent worktable of boldly carved African design. The monitor was the newest model, flat, slim of line, dark gray in color. There were no file cabinets, but the desk had one file drawer. How would all of Dorriss's various business and charity pursuits be conducted with no more file space than that one drawer? At home, Clyde's automotive interests overflowed four file cabinets and all the bookshelves, plus six more file cabinets at the automotive shop. Did Dorriss keep all his business records in the computer? For the first time Joe wished he'd brought Dulcie; she could get into that computer like a snatching paw into a mouse hole.

With her official position as Molena Point library cat, Dulcie's access to the library computers, and her interest in such matters, had allowed her to become more than conversant with the daunting world of megabytes and hard drives. That, plus her female-feline stubbornness, assured that no computer program would outsmart this sweet tabby.

Joe stared at the computer wishing that he'd paid attention. Instead, he tackled the desk drawers, surprised to find them unlocked. Clawing the top drawer open, he wondered if, any second, he'd trigger a screaming alarm. Or a silent alarm that would alert some private security company? Because why would Dorriss leave his desk unlocked unless he had it cleverly wired?

Or unless he kept nothing of value here.

The smaller drawers contained only office supplies: pencils, pens, paperclips, various-size labels, and thick cream-colored stationery embossed with Dorriss's elegant letterhead. Joe tackled the file drawer. As he clawed the drawer out, a noise above him brought him up rigid, ready to scorch out of there.

But it was only a bird careening against the window and gone, leaving a long smear of feathery dust. He scowled, annoyed at himself. He was a bundle of rigid fur, rotating ears, nervously twitching whiskers.

Why did he do this to himself? Why wasn't he out napping in the sunshine like a sensible, normal cat?

The drawer was neatly arranged with a row of hanging files—and talk about luck. Dorriss's paid bills were right there in front, in one of six color-coded files that were tucked into a hanging box folder. The packets of paid bills were each held together by a large clip: utility and phone, automotive and gas, Visa and American Express. Other receipts and documentation were filed behind these, the entire box folder marked "current year taxes." When income tax time came, Dorriss had only to haul this stuff out and add up the numbers.

How strange that he would keep his credit card bills in plain sight. Or were these fake bills? Decoys meant for prowlers, and not the real thing?

But that was so dumb, that was really reaching. How would Dorriss even make that kind of fake bill?

Glancing over his shoulder toward the empty hall,

he lifted out the packets with his teeth and spread them across the blotter. As he pawed carefully through, his ears went up and his whiskers stiffened—he was looking at hotel and restaurant charges in cities where the thefts had occurred.

He was pretty sure of the dates, though who could keep every burglary and every date in his head? The more he looked, the more he thought that the numbers did indeed match. The excitement made his skin ripple and his tomcat heart pound.

So what was he going to do now? Haul all the bills away with him, down the stairs, out the glass door, and around the house in the snatching wind, then drag them across the village in broad daylight?

Well, of course he was.

And of course Marlin Dorriss wouldn't miss the contents of these files. Particularly when, the minute he opened the drawer, there would be the empty file folder sagging like an abandoned mouse skin.

He studied the fax machine that stood beside the phone. Could he fax the bills to Harper, then put them back in the file?

But that operation, if he faxed all of them, could take hours. And were faxed bills adequate evidence for the judge to issue a search warrant?

Digging deeper back in the drawer he found files for previous years' taxes, each year carefully marked, each containing similar bills, credit card on top, phone bills at the back. Dorriss was so beautifully organized that Joe wanted to give him a medal.

Lifting a packet of paid bills from an earlier year, he dropped it into the front file in place of those he had removed. Voilà. Who would know? Unless of course

Dorriss had reason to refer to his recently paid bills. Digging a large brown envelope from the drawer of paper supplies, he pawed the bills into it, and worked the two-pronged fastener through its punched hole. Clawing the fastener closed, he tried not to think about possible tooth marks on envelope or bills. He was pushing the file drawer closed with his shoulder, bracing his claws in the carpet, when he heard a door open in the house below, and the breeze through the slightly open window accelerated as if in a wind tunnel.

Directly below, footsteps rang across the entry tiles, a man's heavy and hurried tread. Joe heard no voice. Dorriss didn't call out as if there was anyone else in the house—if it was Dorriss. The hard footsteps moved toward the stairs and started up, muffled suddenly by the thick runner to a faint brushing sound.

Gripping the heavy envelope in his teeth, lifting it free of the floor so as to make no sound, thus nearly dislocating his neck, he hiked the package across the hall to the nearest guest room. There on the thick antique rug he hastily dragged his burden under the bed; no dead rat or rabbit had ever been more cumbersome. Beneath the bed he paused, startled.

*Now he smelled cat.*

*Tomcat?* The scent of cinnamon was too strong to be certain. And the aroma was combined with the nose-twitching stink of a woman's perfume.

Helen Thurwell's perfume? But what kind of affair was this, if she occupied a guest room? Sniffing again at the expensive scent, he thought it was too heavy to be Helen's. Whose, then? Another of Dorriss's lovers, taking her turn when Helen wasn't available? He could hear Dorriss coming softly up the carpeted stairs. He hoped to hell the window above the bed was open. He could feel no movement of air, no breeze slipping in fingering under the bed.

This room would look down to the front entry, over the angles and juttings that faced the street, over descending roofs and ledges that should give him a quick passage to freedom—if he could get out. Listening to the approaching footsteps, he caught, over the numbing perfume, a whiff of Marlin Dorriss's distinctive aftershave, an aroma he had never smelled on any other human, that he had never encountered on the village streets; only those few times when he had happened on Dorriss in a patio or shop. Maybe Dorriss had it blended just for himself. The lawyer's soft footsteps on the thick carpet turned into the master bedroom.

Joe was about to slip out and check the window above him, when the sounds from the bedroom gave him pause. Stone sliding across stone? Wood scraping stone and wood? Dorriss coughed once, then Joe heard the heavy *clunk* of thick metal.

A safe? Was that why the desk wasn't locked? Whatever Dorriss wanted to keep private was locked away behind a wall of metal? Joe listened to papers being shuffled, then the scrape, again, of stone on wood. Then Dorriss moved into the dressing room; Joe heard the unmistakable snap of a briefcase or suitcase, then the slide of a zipper.

Leaving the brown envelope under the bed, he slipped out and padded down the hall into the master bedroom, watching the partially open door to the dressing room where papers still rattled. He could see, on a luggage stand, a black leather suitcase lying open. Dorriss stood over it, putting in folded clothes. On the stand beside the suitcase lay a sheaf of papers, and atop the papers a black automatic. A clip and a box of bullets lay beside it, the sight of which sent ripples of alarm through the tomcat.

He'd had enough of guns. His hearing hadn't been the same since he and Dulcie played moving target in the attic above Clyde's shop, chased and shot at by counterfeiting car thieves, and Clyde tried to rescue them. That was three years ago, part of that little caper during which he and Dulcie discovered their powers of speech, and their lives had so dramatically changed. The shock of seeing one human murder another had brought out latent talents in them that they had never suspected. One of those thieves had been Kate Osborne's husband, Jimmie, who subsequently took up residence at San Quentin.

Now, looking at the gun, he considered leaving the Dorriss house at once, even without the evidence.

Oh, right. Marlin Dorriss was going to shoot an innocent cat that happened to wander in? Dorriss must like animals, if he'd left the glass door open for some household kitty.

The more specific implication of that open door Joe did not want to think about.

Worrying only briefly about his own gray hide, wondering only briefly which of his nine lives he was living at the moment, Joe waited until Dorriss turned away, then slipped past the dressing room door deeper into the bedroom.

Creamy, hand-rubbed walls greeted him; a pastel Persian rug over blackish stained hardwood floors; a seating alcove arranged with a charcoal leather love seat and chair before a dark marble coffee table.

At the other end of the room stood a king-size bed with a pale brocade spread and a dull, carved headboard and matching nightstands. On the wall opposite the fireplace, next to the double dresser, stood a huge armoire inlaid with ivory, an antique cupboard that would be large enough to hold both a small bar and a thirty-inch TV. But it was the fireplace that held Joe's attention.

A portion of its ornate paneling stood open and a steel safe loomed within, its steel door also wide open.

Rearing up, Joe could see nothing inside. Before he could leap up for a better look he heard Dorriss coming. Diving under the bed he watched Dorriss's black oxfords cross the room, heard him slam the safe closed, heard the little clicks as he turned the dial to lock it.

Joe watched Dorriss return to the dressing room, then came out from under the bed again and began to check out the room.

The tops of the carved night tables were empty. These roughly made chests with their dull unpolished wood looked handmade and expensive, perhaps pieces that Dorriss had imported from South America.

Rearing up, he could see two dark, flat items on the dresser. Leaping up and miscalculating, he hit the small plastic folder, sliding so hard he nearly went over the edge. He froze, listening, sure that Dorriss had heard him.

When the sounds of packing continued, he guessed not. Examining the folder, he found it was a little loose-leaf booklet designed to hold a dozen or so photos of one's dog or cat or baby, depending on the holder's preference, each photo protected within a clear little pocket.

These pockets held credit cards.

Laying a silent paw on the slick plastic, Joe felt far more elated than if he'd discovered a warren of fat rabbits. Studying the cards, he found examples from half a dozen credit card companies, each card issued in a different name. Behind each card in the same little pocket was a white file card containing an address and phone number, social security number, birth dates, and a woman's name. A mother's maiden name, that universal code for certain identification? And, best of all, a driver's license issued to the cardholder, each one bearing Marlin Dorriss's photograph. Joe was so pumped he wanted to shout and yowl.

But even this prodigious find was not the most interesting. Next to the credit card folder lay what might be the real kicker, the veritable gold mine. For a moment he just stared. Then he started to grin; he could feel his whiskers tickling his ears. Right here beneath his paw was the ringer. The first-prize trophy. He heard again Dulcie's description: a small notebook with a mottled reddish-brown cover and a black cloth binding.

The notebook still smelled faintly of gas, of whatever substance PG&E put into their natural gas supplies so users would know if there was a leak in the line. Joe was reaching a paw to flip through the pages when he heard Dorriss coming back again, the scuff of his shoes on the dark hardwood. Joe had only time to leap from the dresser to the top of the armoire, where he crouched as flat as a pancake hoping he was out of sight. But then when Doris approached the dresser, he couldn't resist, he slipped to the edge to watch.

Picking up the notebook, Dorriss flipped through it as if reading random passages; the expression on his

face was one of deep rage. Glowering at the open notebook, he ripped it in half. Ripped it again, then tore
each half straight through the offending pages.

Scooping up the stack of torn pages, he moved to
the fireplace. From the top of the armoire Joe stared
down at Dorriss, his heart doing flips. *As sure as
queens have kittens, he's going to burn those pages.*

Dropping to the bed behind Dorriss and slipping
silently to the rug, Joe began to stalk the man. He
wanted that notebook, he wanted those little mysterious pages that could be, that his cop-sense told him
were, hard and valuable evidence to the death of James
Quinn.

**18**

The five freshly cut oak logs in the fireplace were art-
fully crisscrossed over the gas jet. Marlin Dorriss,
dropping the torn pieces of the notebook on the raised
hearth, turned to find a match or, more likely, Joe
thought, some sort of mechanical starter. As he
reached into a small carved chest that stood at the other
end of the hearth, Joe slipped silently behind him.

Closing his teeth on the wadded remains of the
notebook he was gone, a gray streak disappearing under the leather love seat. It wasn't the best place to hide
but it was the closest. If Dorriss came poking, Joe
hoped to slip out at the far end. Once concealed, he
carefully spit out the pages so as not to drool on the evidence, and crept to the edge of the love seat where he
could see his adversary. He hoped he had all the bits of
paper. The notebook cover still lay on the hearth, the
slick brown cardboard bent and twisted, victim of Dorriss's rage.

Dorriss turned, reaching for the notebook. He stared
at the hearth and searched the carpet and into the fire-

place, frowning and puzzled. He stared around the room, then moved swiftly to the dressing room and bath, looking for an intruder. Joe could hear him banging the glass shower door and the closet doors. The next minute he flew into the study, then out again and down the hall. Joe heard him swerve into the first bedroom. *Not under the bed! Oh please God don't let him look under the bed and find the bills! Cat God, human God, I don't care. This is a bona fide feline supplication. Please, please, please don't let him look under that bed.*

But why would he look there? The guest beds sat low to the floor. The frames that held the box springs were no more than six inches high, not enough space for a burglar to hide—at least, not for the kind of burglar Dorriss would have in mind. Joe heard the closet in that room slide open, then Dorriss was in the hall again searching the other bedrooms, banging open closet doors. Immediately Joe fled for the guest room and under the bed.

Fighting open the metal clasp, he shoved the notebook pages in. Laboriously, with an impatient paw, he managed to fasten the flap again. Next time around, he'd like to have opposing thumbs. Down the hall, Dorriss was making more and more noise, searching, then pounding down the stairs apparently to search the rest of the house—but he'd be back. Slipping out from under the bed, leaving his burden for the moment, Joe scrambled up to the sill.

There was no breath of air behind the closed shutters; no window was open. Balanced on the sill, he challenged a shutter's latch with frantic claws. But when he'd fought it open, the window behind it was not only closed, but locked. From the stairs, he heard Dorriss coming.

The lock was a paw-bruiser, invented by designers who had no respect for feline needs. He heard Dorriss turn into the study, heard him opening the desk drawers—maybe wondering what else the thief might have taken. Joe's paws began to sweat, slipping on the metal lock—and he began to wonder.

If, as unlikely as it seemed, the downstairs glass door had been left open for one black tomcat, if against all odds the opportunistic Azrael had somehow partnered up with Marlin Dorriss, Dorriss might well be knowledgeable enough to be looking for more than a human thief. Frantic, Joe could hear him shuffling papers.

By the time he got the lock open and slid the glass back, he was a bundle of nerves, and his paw felt fractured. Dragging the heavy brown envelope up to the sill, he balanced it against the glass. As he pulled the shutter closed behind him, he heard Dorriss coming out of the study, heard Dorriss pause at the door as if looking in. Joe wondered if his gray fur made a dark smear behind the closed white louvers? Or if the shutter humped out of line where he crouched? He wondered if cats were subject to sudden coronary occlusion? He was ready to leap out into space clutching the envelope, calculating how best to negotiate the twisting angles to the lower roof, when the phone rang.

*Thank you, great cat god or whoever.*

Dorriss let it ring twice, but then he crossed the hall to answer. Joe knew he should jump at once, but for an instant he remained still, listening.

"I can't talk now," Dorriss was saying, "there's someone in the house." Joe heard a sharp metallic snap, as when a bullet is jacked into the chamber of an automatic.

"I can't *talk* now. You're where?"

Pause. Against all good sense, Joe remained listening, gripping the envelope in his teeth.

"What the hell are you doing there? What the hell made you take off? Call me back, I can't *talk*."

Silence, then an intake of breath. Then, "You're telling me the truth?"

Pause. Then, "All right, get on with it. That's very nice indeed. Then you need to get back here. I told you not to play these games with your little friends. *They've* made a mess, and you'll have to clean it up. I don't want any more of your childish pranks, I can't afford to deal with that stupidity, and I won't have it rubbing off on me. Get back here fast, my dear, and take care of this."

A soft click as Dorriss hung up. Joe crouched on the sill, his teeth dug into the envelope, adjusting his weight-and-trajectory ratio, eyeing a lower roof. With the extra baggage, if he missed his mark he'd drop like a rock, two stories to the stone terrace.

But he didn't want to toss the envelope, let it fall and maybe split open, spill the evidence all over Dorriss's front yard, to be snatched and sucked away in the sea wind.

He took a deep breath and was airborne—airborne but falling heavily, his usual buoyancy gone. His ability to twist in the air had deserted him. He felt like a rock, a flung boulder. Falling, he was falling . . .

He landed on the little roof scrabbling with frantic claws, five feet to the left of the window and five feet below, coming down with a thud that shook him clear to his ears.

But he was all in one piece and, more to the point, so was the envelope. He was poised to jump again when a sound to his right stopped him. Made his blood turn to ice, made him search the low roofs.

A dark little gargoyle stared up at him. Crouched on the edge of the tiles, Kit watched him wide eyed, but then stared suddenly past him at the window above, at the sill he had just abandoned. Her voice was a terrified hiss. *"Jump, Joe! He's coming! Jump! He's opening the shutters! Jump now! Drop that thing and jump!"*

Earlier that morning, the kit had seen Joe Grey heading for the police department as she prowled the roofs alone thinking about Lucinda and Pedric, mourning them, deeply missing them. Wandering the peaks and shingles feeling flat and sad, she had seen Joe Grey below, galloping up the sidewalk, headed somewhere in a hurry. Coming down, she had followed him and when he galloped through the courthouse gardens, of course she had followed. But then he turned and saw her, and instead of his usual friendly ear twitch, inviting her to join him, he'd given her a hiss, a leave-me-alone snarl, and had cruelly sent her away again. Or he thought he had.

Slinking away through the bushes hurt and angry, she had turned when he wasn't looking, and followed him to the front door of the PD. Had watched him slip inside on the heels of the judge's secretary. The tall

blonde, delivering a sheaf of papers, took no notice of
the gray tomcat padding in behind her. The kit wanted
to follow, but he'd been so cross she daren't. And then
only a minute later a delivery boy hurried up the street
carrying a big white bag of takeout that smelled of pastrami and made her lick her whiskers, and she had
watched the dispatcher buzz the boy through.

Joe Grey had gone in there to share the captain's
lunch and had sent her away alone. Feeling incredibly
hurt and sad, and mad too—all claws and hisses—she
didn't even want to beg lunch by charming some likely
tourist in one of the sidewalk cafés as she so often did.
She felt totally alone and abandoned. She had no one.
Lucinda and Pedric were gone forever. And this morning, Dulcie had rudely slipped off without her. And
now Joe Grey didn't want her. How cruelly he had
driven her away.

All alone, with no one to care about her, she climbed
to the roof of the PD and hunched down in the oak tree.
There she waited for nearly an hour angry and lonely,
until Joe Grey came out again. But then, leaving the
station, he was not licking his whiskers, he did not look
happily fed. He looked so gaunt and hungry himself
that *that* made her feel better. Much better.

She watched him crouch in the geraniums drinking
hungrily from an automatic bubbler that watered the
courthouse gardens, then he took off fast, heading
across the village. The kit followed. Joe was so interested in wherever he was going that he paid no attention now to who might be behind him. He was all
hustle, dodging people's feet and up trees and across
roofs, his ears pricked, his stub tail straight out behind.
She trailed him five blocks to Ocean and across Ocean

among the feet of tourists and on again to the fine big house that looked like a museum from the front and was all glass at the back.

Sneaking low and carefully the kit had followed him around the side of the house and saw him go in through an open glass door. Hiding in the shadowy bushes that grew among the boulders, she watched him enter that big house through an open slider. Was that door open for *him*? He sniffed the door, then went right on in, as bold as if he lived there. When he had gone inside she pressed her nose against the door, looking.

Joe had disappeared. She peered into the room, then she followed her nose. Joe's scent led across the huge big room that had brightly colored caves all around, all elegantly furnished, so many places to play and to hide. She investigated one fascinating niche then another, rubbing and rolling, racing across the backs of the couches and trying her claws in the brocade. Sniffing leather and velvet, exploring every single object in every single room, she never did find Joe Grey. At last she approached the stairs.

But looking up that broad, angled flight, the kit stopped and backed away. What was up there? Joe had been up there a long time. What was he doing? She had heard no sound, no thump of paws, and she was frightened. She was standing undecided, looking up, when she heard a car park out in front, heard the car door open and close, then a man's footsteps on the stone terrace. Quickly she hid behind the closest chair, crouching against the thick, soft velvet.

The kit knew Marlin Dorriss. Didn't everyone in the village know him? He was a philanthropist, whatever that meant, and a womanizer. She knew what that word meant. Wilma said he was usually circumspect in his personal life and that meant quiet and careful like a hunting cat. Except he wasn't circumspect about Helen Thurwell. Marlin Dorriss was tall and slim, with a lovely tan, beautiful deep brown eyes, and short-clipped white hair. Handsome, and kind looking.

But as he crossed the big room and headed up the stairs where Joe Grey had gone, she felt afraid.

She couldn't race up the stairs past him to warn Joe. But she could slip out, and around to the front, and maybe, if she could gain the angled roofs and ledges, she could get inside.

Scooting through the bushes to the front of the house she clawed and scrabbled her way up bits of wall and across slabs of roof, looking above her for an open window—and then suddenly above her, a window *slid* open.

And there was Joe Grey. She saw his white paw slide the glass back, saw him press between the glass and the shutter with a huge packet in his mouth. He remained so for some time, staring back into the room. Then he crouched as if someone was coming and leaped into space twisting to land on a roof below. Above him, Marlin Dorriss appeared; she could see him at the next window. She choked back a cry. Joe stared down at her.

*"Jump,"* she hissed. *"He's coming! Jump! He's opening the shutters! Jump now! Drop that thing and jump!"*

Then everything happened at once. Dorriss closed the shutters and turned away, and Joe leaped to the next angle with the brown paper bundle, then leaped again to the concrete. The bundle split open just at the edge

of the bushes. In the wind, papers began to flap and
dance. Kit had never seen Joe move so fast. Grabbing a
mouthful of papers he pulled the package under the
bushes and was back again snatching up more. The kit
leaped.

And she was beside him snatching pieces of torn paper from the wind. Had Dorriss turned back? Was he
looking? Had he seen the package fall before Joe
snatched it away? The kit could not see Dorriss now,
his silhouette was gone from the window—but then
there he was standing at another window looking out.

Surely he couldn't see them beneath the bushes.
Had they caught all the papers? Like catching swooping birds from the rooftop. The kit stared at the papers
under her paws. "What is all this?"

"Evidence," Joe said, pushing little bits of paper
back into the torn envelope, trying to fold it around the
ragged mess. Kit helped him stuff papers in. Pressing
the envelope into folds with their paws they gripped it
between them, their teeth piercing the heavy paper as
they tried to hold it together. And when Dorriss turned
away, when the windows were clear once more, they
dragged it out from the bushes and away.

Keeping to the shadows along the sidewalk, they
tried to shelter their burden from the wind. It was a
long way to Joe's house, and already the package was
heavy. Trying to find a rhythm together, falling into an
unwieldy pace, eight paws attempting to move in har-
mony, they hauled their burden through an empty alley
and along the less-frequented backstreets. Kit's head
was filled with questions which, with her mouth full,
she couldn't ask.

The envelope grew heavier with every step. The

wind died as they left the shore, and that helped. But the day grew muggy hot. Kit wanted to stop and rest but Joe didn't pause, pushing on from shadow to shadow and from bush to bush. When a human appeared far down the street they dragged their burden under a porch or behind a fence.

It seemed to take hours to cover those long blocks. When at last they neared Joe's house, the kit's entire being cried out for water, food, and a nap. A pair of tourists wandered past, and they slipped deeper among the bushes where they rested a moment, panting. Peering out at the house, the kit *so* longed to be inside, *so* longed for a drink of cool water.

The Damen house looked not at all as it once had. When Kit first came there as a young cat, the house was a white cottage with only one story, what Wilma called a Cape Cod. Now with its new facade of heavy Mexican timbers and plastered walls, it was truly elegant. And the best part was Joe's tower high atop the new upstairs. Kit loved Joe's cat-size house with a view of the village rooftops—it was a cozy bit of cat heaven.

Lucinda and Pedric had planned to build a tower just like it. Atop their own new house. "You will have a tower," Lucinda had said. "A fine tall cat tower looking out at all the world just like Joe Grey's tower."

Now Lucinda and Pedric would never build their dream home.

The kit would give all the towers in all the world to have them back. A tear slid down, spotting the brown envelope and its papers as they hauled their unwieldy burden through Joe Grey's cat door.

Pulling the package through, the papers catching on

the door, they dropped it on the African throw rug and lay beside it.

"Heavy as a dead raccoon," Joe said. "Thank you, Kit. I guess you saved the day."

"What did we save? What are those papers?"

Joe Grey smiled. "With luck, this could be the claw that snags the big one. A killing bite to the slickest burglar this village has ever seen." He glanced toward the front door, listening. But the car he'd heard went on by. You never knew when Clyde might bring company, Max Harper or Dallas Garza or Ryan Flannery. "Come on, let's get it upstairs before someone walks in."

Dragging the envelope between them, they hauled it up the new stairway that had been built in half of the old guest room. The other half of that room was now a walk-in closet where Clyde kept all manner of oddments, from unused parts for his weight-lifting equipment to stacks of outdated automotive catalogs. At the top of the steps, in the new master bedroom, they dragged their burden across the new carpet to Clyde's study.

Hauling it up onto Clyde's desk, Joe pawed the papers out and carefully separated the various bills from the torn pages of the notebook. Fetching a rubber band from a box on the desk, he managed to secure the small bits of torn evidence. Watching him, Kit retrieved another rubber band, but he made her put it back. "Don't chew that, Kit. It could kill you."

"That little thing? How could it?"

"Just like string, Kit. You know about string. The barbs of your tongue hold it back, you can't spit it out, it gets wrapped around the base of your tongue, you swallow the rest and you're in trouble."

She spit out the rubber band. She'd been told more than once about string, that if she should ever swallow a string not to pull it out with her paw, that she could cut her insides doing that. Joe studied the stack of bills. Who knew which were of value? No one would know until they were compared with the dates of the burglaries. Even then, there would be a lot of play in the machinery. The Tyler family in Ventura, for instance, had opened their safe in January and not again until October when they found the antique diamond necklace missing; the burglary could have happened anytime in those nine months. The Von Cleavers, in Montecito, were in Europe for five weeks. Got back to find a glass cabinet broken into and a silver pitcher missing, a museum piece signed by a famous craftsman from the 1600s, but nothing else was gone. Each burglary was the same, the rarest and most expensive item lifted, nothing else touched. Marlin Dorriss himself had been at his Florida condo when his favorite Diebenkorn painting vanished from his Molena Point house—if it vanished, if that was not a red herring.

But what kind of thief took only one piece and left a houseful of treasures?

Joe Grey smiled. Someone out for the thrills, for the rarity or historical value of the items stolen, someone who didn't need the money. Who got all the money he wanted in other ways?

Impatient with the lack of solid answers to what he suspected, impatient for darkness so he could deliver the evidence to the law, Joe restlessly prowled the study.

But the kit had curled up in a corner of the love seat with her nose tucked under her paw, so sad and withdrawn that Joe paused, watching her. He stood worrying over her when a click from above made him stiffen.

The rooftop cat door made a slap, and Dulcie popped out of the hole in the ceiling, dropping daintily to the rafter beneath. Perched on the high, dark beam, she peered down at him—and her green eyes widened.

"You got the bills!" She dropped to the desk beside him with a delicate thud. "Tell me! Tell me how you did it. Dorriss didn't see you? Why are you frowning?"

He glanced across to the love seat. She turned to look at the kit.

"So sad, Dulcie. She keeps falling back into sadness."

Leaping to the love seat Dulcie nosed at the kit and washed her tortoiseshell face, washed her ears, nudged and loved her until at last the kit looked up and tried to smile. When the tattercoat had snuggled against Dulcie, Joe said, "Kit saved me from a bad trip, she warned me just in time." He gave her a brief replay that made Dulcie shiver and laugh, then he asked, "What did you find at Consuela's?"

"The cottage was locked. I tried everything. Finally balanced on the branch of an oak tree and clawed through a roof vent, in through a filthy attic and down through the crawl space. Had to claw away the plywood cover like we did when those raccoons chased us." She sneezed. "All dust and cobwebs. I got the plywood aside and slipped down on the closet shelf.

"Closet was empty, just some empty hangers. But the door was open. I looked out into the room, ready to hit the attic again and vanish. That cottage is just one big room, like a studio apartment. No one was there, nada. I searched the whole place. Found exactly noth-

ing. Checked the dinky bath and kitchen, fought open
every cupboard and drawer. Not one stolen garment.
Not much of anything else except mouse droppings.
It's just a crummy rental, no better than where a homeless would crash.

"I was so mad that I'd wasted my time. I could have
been hunting, or could have been tossing Dorriss's
place with you—*could* have been prowling the village
with Kit," she said gently, glancing down at the tattercoat. "I was about to storm out when someone opened
the garage door. Shook the whole house, rumbling up.
I crouched, ready to leap back to the attic. The garage
door closed again, and something metal clanged in
there. When the door between the garage and the house
opened, I whipped around and dove under the couch.

"I could hear them giggling before I got a look, Dillon and her two schoolmates. Consuela wasn't with
them. They got some soft drinks from the fridge, some
chips from the cupboard that the mice hadn't been at,
and they began to drag in clothes—from their car, I
thought then. New clothes, Joe. Beautiful clothes.
Leather. Cashmere. Silk. Piling them on the couch and
daybed and chairs.

"They pushed the closet door wide open—it has a
mirror on the inside—and they began trying on clothes
and giggling, vamping, hamming it up. All the clothes
had tags, tags hanging down from the couch in my
face, every one from Alice's Mirror.

"The blond girl, Candy, said they shouldn't take
anything, the cops would recognize whatever they
wore. Leah, the tall one, said that was stupid, how
would the cops be able to tell. It ended up, Leah and
Candy each took a couple of leather jackets and some

sweaters. Dillon didn't take anything. She tried on clothes but put them down again. They talked about another job tonight, only to do it really early, just after the stores close. A different MO, Candy said, to throw the cops off. What a dim brain. She thinks the law won't expect another job so soon, won't be watching."

"Did they say what store?"

Dulcie sighed. "The Sport Shop. But . . . I really don't want to . . ."

"Dulcie, it doesn't do Dillon any good to get away with this stuff. She's going to be in trouble sooner or later. Better she gets it over with, before it's something worse."

"I suppose. But there's more. I saw more." She rose and began to pace. From the love seat, the kit watched her quietly.

"I followed them into the garage and slipped under a workbench, watched them hang the clothes in metal lockers. That's the clanging I heard. They snapped padlocks on, and left. Five were already locked, Joe. They filled and locked four more. I didn't see if they had a car out front. Leah used the garage opener to get out. I saw her drop it in her pocket as the door came down behind them.

"When they'd left, I bumped against the lockers. Leaped and thumped at them. None sounded hollow, they all sounded dull, crammed full."

Joe was quiet. Then, "Do you want to call the station? Or shall I?"

She sneezed. "The whole scene makes me sick." Resignedly she moved to the phone, hit the speaker button, and pawed in the number of the station. And reluctantly she did the deed. When she had finished telling the dispatcher what she knew, she stretched out on the desk blotter next to the torn papers and ragged brown envelope, looking very sad.

"It's best," Joe said, his ears down, the white strip on his nose creased into a frown.

Dulcie studied the pile of bills and the torn pages. "It's all right for you to talk. You didn't betray a friend."

19

The shadows of night seemed reluctant indeed to tuck themselves down around the village. In Joe Grey's private tower the cats waited impatiently for darkness. Beneath Joe's paws lay a new brown envelope containing a gallon plastic freezer bag. They had stuffed Marlin Dorriss's bills and the torn notebook pages inside the clear container so that, when they delivered the evidence to the station, it would not cause a departmental panic. Would not trigger hasty emergency procedures to deal with a package that, at first touch, might blow the place sky high. Sealed with careful paws, and the excess air pressed out, the bag awaited only darkness to be hauled across the rooftops. Fidgeting, the messengers washed and groomed, willing night to hurry.

On the street below the Damen roof, a few tourists wandered in twos and threes and fours, and local residents hurried past heading home to hearth and supper. As the cats watched familiar cars turn up the side streets and disappear into carports or garages, Joe's thoughts were on Marlin Dorriss, on what might hap-

pen when Dorriss opened his file drawer and found the
bills missing, found the outdated substitutes in their
place.

"So what's he going to do?" Dulcie said. "If he finds
the bills missing and reports the theft, then we're stak-
ing out the wrong mouse hole. But if he's guilty," she
said, smiling, "you won't hear a word." She gave Joe a
long and appraising stare, her green eyes darkening in
the slowly falling evening. "He reports it, you can
write him off as a suspect. So what's the big deal?" She
touched his nose with a soft paw. "Relax, Joe. Relax
and roll with it."

But she gave him a narrow look. "You're all fidgets
and claws. *You* know this whole business is a gamble."
She leaned to nuzzle his whiskers. "I'll bet my best
wool blanket that you've nailed him, that you've got
your thief."

Joe looked at her and tried to shake off the edginess.
As he licked the last grain of sand from the Dorriss
front yard off his paw, dusk began to thicken slowly
around them, a gentler light to soften the rooftops. He
looked at Dulcie and Kit reclining on the new pillows
in his tower and he had to smile at how much they enjoyed a bit of luxury. And soon beyond the arches of
the tower the dark foliage of the pines and oaks began
to blur. In the east the gibbous moon began to rise, a
lopsided globe far brighter than they would have chosen for this particular trek. When at last darkness deepened across the rooftop shadows, the three cats rose
and stretched.

Leaving Joe's tower, Joe and Dulcie dragged the
package between them. Hurrying across the roofs from
concealing chimney to darkening overhang to shelter-

ing branches, they skirted around second-floor windows where some apartment dweller or late office worker might be idly looking out. They remembered too well how Charlie had first glimpsed them on the rooftops and had heard Dulcie laugh, and how she began, then, to wonder.

Walking home from a later supper, Charlie had looked up to see the cats running along the peaks and had recognized against the bright night sky Joe Grey's docked tail and white markings. Hearing a young, delighted laugh, she had been puzzled. That incident combined with several others had led Charlie to guess the truth about them—but Charlie was an exception. Most humans would not make that leap, would not be willing to entertain such an amazing concept.

Now, above the rooftops, above the hurrying cats the moon lifted higher, increasing its glow and diminishing the size of the shadows. The night wind blew colder. Their hard-won package grew heavier, pulling at neck and shoulder muscles, making their jaws ache. Joe and Dulcie pushed ahead, dodging patches of light, ducking beneath branches, their teeth deep in the heavy packet. The kit trailed behind, unusually quiet, not pressing to help them. Then just across the last street lay the long expanse of the courthouse roof and the roof of Molena Point PD, the rounded clay tiles gleaming in the moonlight.

The chasm of the street was wide. One ancient oak spanned above the concrete, its branches meeting the smaller branches of its counterpart that grew close to the opposite sidewalk. Dragging their burden across the thick, leafy limb, trying not to hang it up among the twigs or to drop it, Joe and Dulcie felt as graceful as a pair of clipped-wing pigeons flopping among the branches. The kit crossed on a branch above them, precarious and uncertain herself as she watched their unsteady progress.

Reaching the courthouse roof, the three cats together hauled their prize the long length of the courthouse, bumping on the round tiles and into the oak tree that stood beside the police department. Now they had three choices.

They could haul the envelope down to the front entry and prop it against the glass door. They could hike it around back, to the locked back door that opened on the police parking lot where Harper and the two detectives usually left their cars, where Harper himself would likely find it. But there was more traffic at the front door. The time was seven P.M. Watch would change at eight. Most of the officers and the dispatcher would leave by the front door, heading for their personal cars that were parked in the front lot. The first officer out would see the package and retrieve it, and go back to log it in and alert the watch commander. *Voilà*, mission accomplished.

Or, third choice, they could shove the plastic package through the high bars of the holding cell window. It would land behind the barred door, not ten feet from where the dispatcher ruled over the front of the station. Surely she would see it and take it into safe custody— if she didn't hit the panic button.

Looking through the depths of the oak leaves to the cell window, Dulcie was in favor of that route. "We drop it down there, no one outside on the street is going to see it and pick it up."

"Right," Joe said, padding along the branch to the

barred window and peering down inside. "Except that the cell's occupied. Can't you smell him?" He twitched his nose, flehming at the scent—but then, that cell never smelled like a flower garden.

Below them, stretched out on the bunk, lay a rumpled, sleeping body, his arms flailed out, one hand resting on the floor. A tall, thin guy maybe in his late twenties, with long dirty hair, dirty ragged clothes, and a handlebar mustache. He did not look or smell like someone they wanted to trust with the evidence. Even if he was indeed asleep, the thud of the dropping package would very likely wake him.

"Maybe he's just been arrested," Dulcie said. "Maybe he's waiting to be booked, then they'll take him on back to the jail."

"And maybe not," Joe said. "Do you see anyone down there getting ready to book him?" Beyond the bars of the holding cell door, the area around the dispatcher's counter and the booking counter was empty. They saw only the dispatcher herself in her open cubicle, talking on the radio, apparently to an officer who, somewhere in the village, was just leaving the scene of a settled domestic dispute—always a touchy call.

Dulcie watched the drunk sleeping below them. "I'll *take* the package in. I can drop down there with it, a lot quieter than we can toss it. I can haul it through the barred door without waking him, without anyone seeing me."

"And what if he isn't asleep? What a story he'd have to tell the cops, to trade for a quick release. 'I know how that package got in here, officer. I saw a cat drop down in here carrying that thing in its mouth.'"

"He's drunk, Joe. They're going to believe him? I can be in there and down the hall to Harper's office before his boozy head clears, before he figures out what he saw."

"And even if no one sees you, Dulcie, when Harper finds the evidence deposited neatly on his desk, what then? He won't ask how it got past the dispatcher? And past his new, state-of-the-art security system? He won't start suspecting one of his own officers?" He stared at Dulcie. "He starts suspecting Garza or Davis, who both know he wants those bills. *Then* it would hit the fan."

"He's going to ask questions anyway."

"He isn't going to ask questions if it isn't found inside."

"But . . ."

"Wait," Joe said. "Someone's coming."

And, like Diana smiling on sainted lovers, good luck smiled on the cats. They watched Officer Brennan coming down the hall, his uniform tight over his protruding stomach.

Below them, metal clanged against metal as Brennan opened the barred door, hustled the drunk awake, and marched him out of the cell. The guy half fell against the dispatcher's counter, staggered against the booking counter, then stumbled away in front of Brennan, down the hall toward the back door and the jail.

The minute he was gone the cats hauled the package through the oak tree's snatching foliage and over the sill and shoved it through the bars. It fell with a hushing, sliding thump just inside the cell door—that brought the dispatcher to her feet, startled.

This particular dispatcher was a full-fledged officer.

She was armed, and she approached the cell with her hand on her holstered weapon. Above her, the gun-shy cats backed away up the tree. They could see her studying the packet then staring above her, searching the high, open window. Then she whirled away, back to her station. They heard her quick footsteps, then the building's shrill alarm.

Officers came running from the back offices, and out the front door. Before the cats could leap across the moonlit roofs to freedom, cops were swarming out wielding handheld searchlights, shining them toward the roof and into the tree, and they hunched down deep among the deepest leaves, their reflective eyes tight shut.

Beside Dulcie, the kit was not secretly smiling at the commotion, as she usually would be. Her tail was not twitching and dancing with excitement. She was deeply quiet. The kit's grieving worried Dulcie.

When the torches swung away at last, to sweep on across the parking lot and gardens, within the prickly leaves the three cats peered out. Below them, patrol cars had swung around from the back of the building to angle across the driveways and along the street, blocking the escape of all other vehicles. And officers on foot surrounded the gardens, their searchlights leaping from bush to bush and into the parked cars. The lights shone across the moon-bright roofs behind the cats. They were trapped like treed possums.

But while the cats crouched within the heavy oak leaves wishing the moonlight and searchlights would vanish, wishing mightily for absolute darkness, Kate Osborne was doing her best to avoid the dark.

She had left work a bit late, finishing up some ordering and some computer sketches. It was just six thirty, but she was so tired and so ravenously hungry that she hardly cared if tonight a whole battalion of strangers followed her. Going down the elevator from her office to the parking garage, slipping quickly into her car and pulling out into the lighted street, half of her wanted to go straight home, wolf down a sandwich, and fall into bed. The other half wanted a nice, warming dinner that she didn't have to lift a hand over, wanted to sit at a cozy table and be waited on—wanted not to be alone for a while longer, but to remain safely among people.

For days after the Greenlaws' deaths she didn't think she was followed. She kept watch around her but didn't see anyone; but then on Thursday when she looked out her apartment window she had seen the same man standing in a doorway across the street. She did not simply imagine it was the same man. His sloped shoulders and stance were the same. And this time she had gotten a good look at his pale muddy hair, his sloping forehead and large nose.

If he meant to harm her, why did he just stand there? She almost wished, with a perverse cold fear, that instead of following, he *would* approach her, that he would come upstairs and knock on her door because she had grown more angry than afraid. Angry at this harassment, at this invasion of her privacy, at this hampering of her free, easy movement around the city.

Besides the pepper spray, she had begun to carry a

pair of scissors in her purse, a decision that was probably incredibly stupid. She wished she weren't such a wuss, that she'd learned karate or knew how to handle a gun, that she had some skill that would make her feel less vulnerable.

Both Hanni and Hanni's sister, Ryan, were comfortable and competent with firearms. Having grown up in a police family they had been trained early and well. And Charlie, too, since she married Max, had learned the same careful, responsible skills. Such expertise and confidence would be comforting now.

She decided to stop for dinner, and to hell with being followed. Driving through the crowded, narrow streets, she turned north up Columbus toward a favorite small seafood café. Dolphin's would be well lighted, and the sidewalk would be busy with pedestrians this time of evening. Just two blocks from the restaurant she was lucky to spot a car pulling out, and she swerved in.

Locking her car and hurrying up the street, she was half a block from Dolphin's when she glanced back and saw the same man following her. She was so angry she almost approached him, pepper spray in hand.

But then fear filled her, and she hurried on toward Dolphin's, trying to stay among people. She did not like living this way. She thought, not for the first time, of how it would be when she chucked city life and moved home to Molena Point. Where she could indeed feel safe again. Crossing the street away from him as he followed, she hurried on—but when she glanced in the shop windows where she could see behind her, he had crossed, too. He was pacing her, his thin reflection moving jaggedly from one square of dark glass to the

next. When she slowed, he slowed. When she quickened her step, so did he. When she reached Dolphin's
she slipped quickly inside and pulled the door closed
hard behind her. She'd have liked to lock it.

Her favorite waitress, Annette, looked up from
clearing a table and smiled, and nodded toward her
usual table. Annette was rotund, in her thirties, with
a slender, fine-boned face that seemed to belong to a
much thinner woman. She had lovely dark eyes and a
beautiful complexion. As Kate crossed the restaurant
between the crowded tables she kept her back to the
window. But when she glanced around, the man stood
outside looking in through the glass.

When she stared hard at him, he moved on. When
he'd passed beyond her view she sat down at the table
with her back to the wall, where she could see the
street. Annette brought her usual pot of tea and paused,
a question in her eyes. Kate said nothing. She ordered
a bourbon and soda as well, and a shrimp melt on
French and a salad. Annette stood a few minutes making small talk, as Kate continued to watch the window.

Annette and her husband, an army sergeant, had
moved to San Francisco when he was transferred to the
Presidio. She liked to tell Kate of the new places she
had discovered in the city, and Kate loved to make sug-
gestions. The absence of the man outside the glass did
not ease Kate's anxiety, he could be just down the
street waiting for her, maybe standing against the next
building just beyond the window. The early evening
street did not, tonight, hold its usual charm. The cozy
shops along this block presented, tonight, a more
threatening aspect of North Beach. She felt safe only
within the restaurant, she did not like to think about go-

ing out again. She thought, when she was ready to leave, she might call the police.

But what kind of complaint would she make? The man hadn't confronted her, he hadn't touched or spoken to her. She could only say she'd been followed. Very likely they would think she was a nut case, imagining things. She supposed she could go out through the kitchen, to the alley, slip around the block to her car. She closed her eyes, trying to slow her pounding heart.

When she opened her eyes she saw him directly across the street walking among a crowd of tourists. Same man, looking directly across to Dolphin's windows, his slumped shoulders and rocking walk making him easy to recognize. When he'd passed beyond her view she rose and moved to the front window, standing to the side where she wouldn't be seen.

He had crossed to her side of the street but was heading away; soon he disappeared. Had he followed her from her office? Followed her clear across town and somehow found a parking spot near where she parked? Or had he already known her favorite small restaurants? Had he simply swung by each, looking for her? Why hadn't she gone somewhere different, someplace she seldom frequented? She was still at the window when a young woman burst in through the front door, turning to look back at the street.

She looked familiar, and Kate watched her with curiosity. She was looking around for someone. When she spotted Kate she nearly lunged at her.

"Kate? Yes, you are Kate Osborne?"

Kate had started to back away—but she *did* know this woman. Nancy something, the design client who had approached her at the office, whom she had turned over to another designer. She was a delicate, elegant person, maybe in her early thirties. Beautifully groomed with a flawless creamy complexion, her face scrubbed clean, her blue-black hair smoothed into a simple chignon. She had wanted to do her apartment with South American furnishings; Kate had been sorry to turn down the project. The woman was simply dressed in a cream skirt and creamy sweater and carried a pale silk raincoat. Her dark eyes were huge. "You *are* Kate Osborne?" she repeated. "We met . . ."

"Yes," Kate said. "I remember. You— What's wrong? You look distressed."

"Could we step away from the window? There's . . . I think . . . I know it sounds wild, but I think a man has been following you."

Kate led her to the small corner table. The young woman sat down so that she, too, could see the street. "I'm Nancy Westervelt."

"Yes. I hope you found a designer you will enjoy working with."

"I have an appointment next week. Thank you." The woman chafed her hands together lightly, as if she were cold. "Tonight when I saw you on the street I thought I recognized you. When I turned to look, my attention was caught by a man who seemed to be following you. I watched him. When you came in the restaurant he drew back out of sight but then in a minute he slipped forward and looked in the window. Then he went on past, crossed the street, came back along the other side, and kept watching. He so bothered me that I knew I must tell you."

"I appreciate that. When did you first notice him?"

"I saw you get out of your car. He was in a cab right behind you, he got out as you were parking. He started right off following you, though I didn't realize at first what he was doing.

"Maybe it's nothing, but it frightened me." Nancy's voice was soft and well modulated. They sat a few minutes discussing her design project, waiting to see if he would return, both watching the window. Then, in the shadowed door of a T-shirt shop across the street the man appeared, as if perhaps he had been there for a while but had just stepped forward. Nervously Kate glanced toward the kitchen, where the back door opened to the alley.

The young woman's eyes widened. "Can you go out the back? If you could slip out that way, and around to your car . . . you could take my raincoat, there's a hat in the pocket, you could pull that down over your hair."

Kate almost laughed, the idea of a disguise was so bizarre. And what if he caught her in the back alley? She would like to call the police, she was really tired of this. She wished she knew the names of the two detectives that Dallas Garza had worked with here in the city. If they knew that she was a friend of Garza's, would they be more likely to help her? More likely to believe that she'd been followed, and to listen to her?

But she didn't know their names, and anyway she would be embarrassed to call the busy San Francisco PD and ask them to send out a patrol car for something so . . . something that, when she repeated it back to herself, seemed so without substance. *He has been following me for weeks, I see him standing in doorways . . .*

If her car or her apartment had been broken into, the police would take her seriously. But this . . . Well, she had to do something. Glancing toward the kitchen, she rose.

Nancy rose with her, handing her the raincoat. "I'll go out with you. He won't expect to see two women."

Sliding some money onto the table, Kate followed her toward the back. Watching Nancy, she tried not to warm to the woman's gentle manner—but why did she have to be so suspicious? Nancy Westervelt was only trying to help her, was only concerned for her. As they paused by the door to the kitchen, Kate pulled on the raincoat, then the hat, tucking her blond hair up inside. She felt better doing something positive, even if this was melodramatic. Nancy looked hard at her. "I was followed once." She was quiet a moment. "It wasn't nice. It wasn't something I'll forget."

A faint nausea touched Kate, a shaky sickness.

As they moved through the kitchen among the busy chefs, among hot, delicious dinners being prepared along the big stainless-steel tables, the workers frowned at them, puzzled. A round, dark-eyed chef appraised Kate so critically that she thought he would tell them to leave. But then Annette caught up with them, handing Kate a foil-wrapped package. Kate could smell the warm shrimp melt. And quickly Annette led them through the kitchen, shepherding them with authority. Between a stack of cans and boxes, and storage lockers, they approached the back screen door covered by a dark security grid.

"Wait here." Annette's thin, oval face was quietly serious. "Let me look out the back window." She disappeared into a storeroom, but was gone only a moment. Returning, she didn't ask questions. "There's no one there that I can see, the alley looks empty."

They slipped out through the screen door fast, Nancy going first, Kate staying close behind her shrouded in the cream raincoat, the slouch hat pulled down nearly to her eyebrows. She felt like Groucho Marx in drag; she wondered if the lame disguise would fool anyone. Hurrying beside Nancy along the faintly lit alley she headed for the side street that would take them to Columbus again and her car.

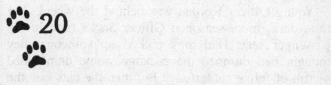

## 20

The roof of the courthouse reflected bright moonlight, offering no dark niche where a cat could hide. Along the edges of the tile roof, harsh searchlights scanned the night's shadows bleeding up into the sky. Only within the gloom of the oak tree's thick foliage, where the leaves caressed the roof of the Molena Point PD, was there safety. The three cats huddled down, blending as well as they could among the shadows, their paler parts carefully concealed from the dazzling beams. Joe Grey's white chest, nose, and paws were tucked under him as neatly as if he were a rolled-up ball of gray yarn.

It might seem overkill to send the entire department out looking for whoever had dumped that clear plastic package in through the holding cell window. But these days, any object tossed into a police building had to be regarded with suspicion. Anything, any time, could be a bomb. For too many, law enforcement had become the enemy.

Just when searchlights ceased to scour the parking

lot and progressed deeper into the village, a squad car pulled in from the street to park in the red zone facing the station. The cats watched warily.

Young Officer Rordan was behind the wheel. The thin, dark, more-seasoned Officer Sacks rode in the passenger seat. Had they picked up someone they thought had dumped the package, some unintended victim of feline subterfuge? But then the cats saw the three figures in the backseat.

All were female, slim, and young; one with pale hair piled on top of her head, one a tall girl with long dark hair tied back in a ponytail. And, a too-familiar figure with a sassy bob that, even in the glow of the vapor lights, gleamed as red as new rust.

Stepping from the vehicle, Officers Rordan and Sacks ordered the girls out. The three crawled out of the back, angry and disheveled, and were marched into the station, Candy and Leah scowling with rage. Dillon looked frightened and ashamed. Officer Sacks carried two large paper grocery bags crammed full of clothes; the cats could see bits of leather and velour, an expensive-looking running shoe. The officers and their prisoners disappeared inside, and the cats heard a metal door slam. Pushing through the oak's thick leaves to the high barred window, they peered down into the holding cell.

The girls sat sprawled on the stained bunk, all three now sullen and defiant. In the style of fashion-conscious young teens, none was dressed warm enough for the chill evening. Candy wore tight faded jeans, a white tank top that hiked well above her middle, and goose bumps. She slouched at the far end of the bunk watching as Officer Sacks booked Leah and then Dillon: name and address, parents' names, school, and any statement they cared to make. Leah's answers were so rude the cats wondered if she *wanted* to be locked up for the night or perhaps longer. Her thin, sagging T-shirt looked no warmer than Candy's tank top. Her lipstick was the color of raspberry jam. Only Dillon answered Sacks's questions with any civility, as she glanced past him into the station. Was she looking for Captain Harper, perhaps hoping he wasn't there? She was wearing red jeans and an old, creased leather jacket with nothing but a bra underneath. Her boots were thick and heavy, of the kind that, well aimed, could break a person's leg. When Sacks finished with the girls, they lounged on the hard bunk, scowling and silent.

Max Harper arrived some twenty minutes later. He hardly glanced at the dispatcher's counter but went directly to the cell, his expression tightly controlled, a look that the cats knew very well. A line in his cheek twitched with anger, with disappointment. Dillon Thurwell was, in many respects, as close to a daughter as Max Harper might ever have.

Opening the cell door, he summoned the two arresting officers and sent Leah and Candy back to the jail to be locked up there. Then he turned his attention to Dillon. Stepping into the cell and locking the door behind him, he stood looking down at her, studying the top of her head as she sat staring at the floor. Watching them, the cats crowded against the bars, their ears back, not liking the hurt they could see in Max Harper's stern face. When Dillon wouldn't look up at him, he sat down beside her.

"I called your parents." He took her chin in his hand, turned her face so she had to look up at him. Her scowl was fierce, and frightened.

"I want to hear your version. I want to hear exactly what you three did tonight."

"If you called my dad, why isn't he here? How come he's taking so long?"

"I called him on my way down to the station. It's been only a few minutes. Tell me what happened, Dillon. Tell me now."

"*I* know the drill!" she snapped. "It will go easier for me if I tell the truth. Everything will be cool if I tell you all about it. The truth and only the truth and that will make life just peachy."

"Which one of you broke the lock?" Harper asked quietly.

No answer.

His expression didn't change. "Who went in through the window?"

Nothing.

"You girls planned your other burglaries more smoothly than this one. I have to say, you accomplished some fancy footwork at Alice's Mirror. Even if it was all going to go against you, in the end."

She looked at him, surprised, then scowled harder. "*I* broke the lock. *I* went through the window. *I* handed the stuff out. Okay? So what? That's some kind of federal offense?"

"If it were a federal offense I wouldn't have to mess with you. I'd turn you over to the feds. Where's the fourth member of your little club? Where's Consuela? She slip out before my officers arrived? Leave you to take the heat?"

"She wasn't there," Dillon said. "She's off somewhere."

"Off where?"

"How would I know."

"Did she set this burglary up before she left?"

Dillon didn't answer.

"Or did you plan it yourselves, without her? You've been busy, haven't you, teaching yourself how to steal." He looked steadily at her. "Where do you plan to go with that?"

No response. She tapped her boot on the concrete in a steady and irritating rhythm.

"I don't have to spell it out for you, Dillon. You know how to make your own choices. You're building a life here. You don't get to go back and try again, you don't get to start over."

Harper looked up when Officer Sacks came through the front door carrying two big paper drink containers with straws stuck in the lids. As Sacks handed them through the bars to Harper, the cats sniffed the sweet smell of chocolate. When Harper handed a container to Dillon, she looked like she wanted to throw it in his face. He watched her, amused, while he sipped on his own malt. From above them, the cats watched Dillon, equally amused. She refused to touch the malt, though she was probably thirsty and hungry, and much in need of a sugar fix, after her anger and fear. A chocolate malt, to a young girl, had to be like a nice juicy mouse to a cat who was hungry and in need.

Max Harper sat with Dillon for some time not talking, finishing his malt. Dillon tasted hers at last, glanced ashamedly at him, and ended up slurping the contents as if she was indeed starving. Sitting on the bunk beside her, Harper put his arm around her. Dillon, letting her guard down, looked now on the verge of

tears. But she glanced up scowling again when the
front door of the station opened.

Helen Thurwell entered. The cats were pleased to
see that she had come, until they saw Marlin Dorriss
behind her. Talk about bad taste, talk about thoughtless
and rude.

The couple was dressed to the nines, Dorriss in a
dinner jacket, Helen in a long slim black dress with a
V-neck, a gem glittering against her throat, suspended
on a platinum chain.

Moving to the barred cell door, Helen stood looking
in at her daughter. Her frown of distaste included not
only the jail cell, but Captain Harper himself. Behind
her, Marlin Dorriss stood not five feet from the dispatcher's desk, his back to the sealed freezer bag that
lay in plain sight, displaying his paid Visa bills and the
torn pages of the little notebook. The cats, watching
the potentially explosive scene, were rigid, all three
hearts pounding in double time. As Dorriss turned toward the counter, Joe Grey sucked in a breath ready to
yowl, desperate to create a diversion—but at the same
moment the dispatcher slid the packet underneath the
counter out of sight. Both Joe and Dulcie went limp,
and their pounding hearts slowed.

Officer Jennifer Keen was a rookie who filled the dispatcher position when the regular dispatchers took time
off. She was a pretty brunette with a voice as hoarse as
sandpaper. Having glanced at the contents of the plastic
package, she had been adequately quick on the draw.

At the cell door, Helen looked from Harper to her
daughter. "Which one of you wants to talk?" Her look
at Harper seemed almost to imply that the break and
enter had been his fault. The cats wondered where Dil-

lon's father was. John Thurwell was the nurturing one, the wronged parent who stayed home with Dillon while her mother played fast and loose. It was her father who should be with Dillon now.

Within the cell, Max Harper sat quietly beside Dillon waiting for her to explain to her mother what she had been unwilling to tell him. Dillon was silent, staring at the floor.

Harper opened the cell door and Helen, with an expression of extreme distaste, stepped inside. Closing the cell door behind her, he stood to the side, just below the cell window. Across the foyer, Marlin Dorriss's expression where he stood beside the dispatcher's desk was cool with disdain, as if his relationship with Helen Thurwell really ought not to include involvements with the police, or with her errant daughter.

Watching him, Joe Grey wondered. What was it about Dorriss's expression? Filled with distaste, but something deep down, as well, seemed tense with apprehension. And as Helen tried to get Dillon to tell her what had happened, and Dillon remained silent and uncooperative, Dorriss began to fidget. At last Helen turned to him.

"I know you have to get to the airport, Marlin. I'll walk the few blocks home; it's a nice evening." Summarily dismissing him, she reached through the bars of the closed door. He took her hand, pressed her hand in both of his, but did not offer to kiss her.

Not in front of her daughter? Or not in front of the captain? Or did he not want to get that close to the bars of a jail cell?

When Dorriss left the station the cats slipped to the edge of the roof and watched him swing into his black

Mercedes. Heading for an evening flight, where? A trip that would remove him from the village for how long?

When Dorriss had gone and the cats looked again down into the cell, Harper was holding a police report, reading it to Helen in a gesture the cats thought was as much to shame her as to shame Dillon.

The burglary had occurred at the Sports Shop on Lincoln Street. The officers had found the lock on the back door broken, and the girls in possession of some five thousand dollars' worth of imported sweaters, leather coats, and top-of-the-line running shoes.

"How do *you* know how much it was worth?" Helen challenged.

"My officers can add," Harper told her. "They can read price tags. Mrs. Barker is on her way in." He looked at Dillon, repeating his earlier questions. "Who took the stuff, Dillon? Who handled the break-in, and who stood watch?"

"I took it! I broke in, I told you! They stood watch. I took the stuff. Okay? How come we didn't hear the alarm?"

"Silent alarm," Harper said. "It alerts the security firm. I guess, this time, you didn't do your homework." According to the report, the two officers arrived on the scene as Dillon handed out the first bag. Apparently neither Candy nor Leah had seen the two officers approach them among the shadows of the alley.

Max Harper's lecture to Dillon was short, to the point, and not appreciated by Helen Thurwell. "You are fourteen years old, Dillon. In four years you'll be responsible for your own physical, financial, and emotional well-being. It takes some effort and thought to equip yourself for that, for the time when you'll have no one but yourself to lean on."

He put his hands on Dillon's shoulders. He looked a long time at her, the kind of look as when she'd done something stupid that had endangered a good horse. He tilted her chin, again forcing her to look at him. "You've learned to handle a horse competently, under difficult conditions. Now it's time to remember your lessons, to treat yourself with equal respect.

"You cannot," he told her, "let someone else's emotional baggage cripple you. Even if that someone is your mother." He looked hard at her. "You cannot cripple yourself to teach your mother a lesson."

Helen Thurwell looked mad enough to hit Harper, looked like she would grab him, jerk him around, and punch him. Dillon glared at him, but angry tears were running down. He put his arms around her and pulled her close. Above them, the cats hardly breathed. They were so caught by the drama, they hung halfway in between the window bars. The vicissitudes of humanity were sometimes so overwhelming, the scene they witnessed was so emotionally draining, that when Dillon's father arrived to take his daughter home, the cats felt like three limp dishrags hung to dry in the branches.

21

Crossing the sidewalk quickly to the passenger side of her car, Kate unlocked the door meaning to slide across to the driver's side, hoping she wouldn't be noticed from across the street. Turning to thank Nancy, who had been more than kind to help her, Kate caught her breath.

Nancy came at her fast, pushed her hard across the console to the driver's seat, bruising her leg, and swung in behind her. "Move it! He's coming!"

Kate stared at the girl.

"He's coming. Let me out in a block or two. Give me the coat, maybe I can mislead him."

Kate started the car. For a second, the look in Nancy's dark eyes iced her blood, but then she saw him; he came running from between two buildings. She revved the engine and burned rubber, skidding away from the curb. As he ran beneath a streetlight she saw his face, but at an angle that startled her.

He looked like the waiter who had died in the gallery.

Oh, but she must be wrong. Driving as fast as she dared, she was too busy dodging cars to look again. As she maneuvered past other traffic, the two faces shone in her mind like two portraits flashed on a screen. The same high sloping forehead, the same large nose and thin face.

When she had seen the waiter that night, his looks had startled her. She hadn't known why. She even then must have seen his resemblance to the man who had followed her. Swerving around a corner heading home, she glanced at Nancy.

The woman was shrugging into the coat Kate had shed, pulling the hat down over her face. When Kate was some ten blocks from the restaurant, when she was sure that no car was following, she stopped at a well-lit corner beside an open grocery where Nancy might take shelter and call a cab. Kate had started to thank her when the girl shoved a gun in her ribs.

Her voice was less cultured now, quick and forceful. "He won't follow you now. Move it. Get rolling." The gun was a black automatic. Kate didn't know much about guns. She had no idea whether the safety was on or off, no idea how to tell if it was loaded, though she thought that the clip was in place.

"Where's the jewelry?"

"In . . . in my apartment."

"Try again. We already tossed your apartment. If we go there now and you can't produce the jewelry, I'll kill you."

"There's a ruby choker in my apartment. I can give you that."

"I have the choker. Where's the rest, the other nine pieces?"

Kate studied the traffic, wanting to jam her foot hard on the gas and swerve into an oncoming car, to cause such a wreck the police would be called and a crowd would gather. Stopping at a signal, staring at the gun, she was afraid to jump out of the car and try to run, afraid the woman would shoot. Warily Kate watched her. What was it about her face, something strangely familiar and unsettling?

The day Nancy Westervelt came to her office, wanting a designer for her new apartment, she had been waiting for Kate not in the reception area but in Kate's private office. Kate had come in to find her standing at the window looking out at the street, not four feet from Kate's desk and file cabinet. Had she been searching the desk?

She looked over defiantly into the woman's dark eyes, trying to imagine Nancy Westervelt's smoothly coiffed hair frizzled in a black cloud, imagine her eyes heavily lined with black, and thick, nearly black lipstick. When the light changed, Kate nearly ran into the car ahead: she was looking at the young woman from the village, at the woman who had come here to rob her.

Turning onto Stockton, where she had to stop for a cable car, she looked over at her passenger, trying to ignore the gun pointed at her. Surely, above the gun barrel, Consuela Benton looked back at her.

She should have known. Kate remembered cloying perfume, heavy, cheap jewelry, a low-cut tank top tight across her breasts—she should have known at once, there in her office or certainly the minute the woman walked into the restaurant. But this woman was a master of change. From a frowzy teenager to this sophisticate. Who would guess? Moving belatedly ahead with the traffic, she felt as if she was in some sadistic fun house, felt so off balance she nearly did wreck the car, skidding sideways into the next lane.

"Watch your driving! Answer me! Are they in your office?" Her voice was shriller, harsh with impatience.

"I rented another safe deposit box. After you stole my key and check carbon. Do you think the bank doesn't have your fingerprints? Do you think the police won't—"

"I wore gloves. You did not rent a new deposit box, not in that bank or any bank in this city."

Kate laughed. "That bank knows the story. You won't learn where from them; you won't get into that box."

Consuela poked her hard with the gun. "I'll ask you one last time. Where is the jewelry? You answer me or our friend will take over. He's directly behind us, in the gray car. Are the jewels in your office?"

"You're welcome to look if you like." Ignoring honking horns and skidding brakes Kate swung a U-turn in the middle of the block and headed across town for her office. Her head was pounding. She felt ice cold, then the next moment hot and flushed. She wondered if she could swerve the car hard and wrest the gun away. She wished she knew more about firearms. Driving in silence, trying to think of a plan, then at last pulling up beside the darkened office building, she felt totally defeated. She knew nothing about how to defend herself. As the woman instructed, Kate turned down into the underground parking garage.

In the greasy yellow glow of the vapor bulbs, the

garage was empty of all but a few cars. Consuela made her slide back across and get out the passenger side. The woman walked so close to her they could have been joined at the hip, the gun under her coat pressed against Kate like a scene from some gangster movie. Kate tried to imagine kneeing her in the groin, jabbing the heel of her hand to the girl's chin or nose, hurting her bad enough to crumple her. Imagined herself grabbing the gun—imagined herself, untrained and uncertain, making a mess of it and ending up shot, maybe dead. Inadequate did not half describe her sense of frustration; she hated her ineptitude and cowardliness. Ringing for the elevator and moving inside it with Consuela, she punched the fifth floor.

Unlocking the outer office door and switching on the lights, Kate crossed the reception area, with its pale, deeply carved carpet and its mix of antique and contemporary furnishings, its handsome potted plants and rich oil paintings. When she didn't move fast enough, the gun barrel poked her in the back. Unlocking the door to her office, she stepped directly to the file cabinet and unlocked that. There was no point in pretending the jewels weren't there. Opening the bottom drawer, she reached to the back, drawing out the plain little cardboard box.

"Open it. Pull the tape off."

Reaching for her desk scissors, Kate imagined stabbing Consuela more quickly than Consuela could pull the trigger, but instead, of course, she obeyed, cutting the tape and opening the lid, removing the little suede evening bag. Opening its clasp, she tipped out the nine pieces of jewelry onto the blotter. The silver and topaz choker she had worn to Charlie's party. A ruby pen-

dant, two diamond bracelets, a gold and onyx necklace, two rings, one set with diamonds, one with a sapphire, and an emerald bracelet and choker, the jewels
and heavy gold settings flashing in the overhead lights,
the strange medieval design fascinating Kate even now.

"Put them back in the box. Tape it up."

Kate put the pieces back into the blue suede bag, lay
that in the box, and fetched tape from her desk drawer.
When it was sealed she watched the girl work the box
into her raincoat pocket, never turning the gun or her
gaze from Kate. Did Consuela mean to kill her now,
and leave her body to be found by the janitor?

Consuela forced her back through the reception
room and into the elevator, shoving her out again into
the parking garage. "Unlock the car."

Kate unlocked it.

"Give me the keys."

Did she mean to shoot her here?

"The keys! And get in the driver's seat."

"You have the jewelry. What do you want now?"

"Give me the keys and get in the car."

Kate did as she was told.

Consuela got in, slammed the door, then handed her
the keys. "Drive directly to your apartment."

Kate swallowed.

If she were shot at home, as if she had walked in on
a burglar, she might lie there for a very long time before
anyone thought to look for her. She often didn't call in
in the morning but went directly out on house calls.

Turning on Van Ness, she watched a gray hatchback
staying close behind her. Turning onto Stockton, she
glanced at Consuela. "Are you connected to Emerson
Bristol?"

The girl just looked at her. "Who's that?"

"The . . . an appraiser."

Consuela gave her a blank look. Neither spoke again until they reached Kate's parking garage, where Consuela gestured for her to pull in.

Parking, Kate had her hand on the door when Consuela stopped her. "Give me your keys."

Kate's heart sank.

Consuela opened the passenger side window and threw the keys as hard as she could among the darkest, farthest rows of parked cars.

"Stay here inside the car. You will sit here for ten minutes after I leave, facing straight ahead. If you look around or get out you will be shot."

Kate glanced past her, to see the gray car waiting at the curb.

Getting out, Consuela moved quickly through the garage to the street and slid in beside the driver. Kate caught a quick glimpse of high forehead and prominent nose. And then they were gone, driving quietly up the dark street. The minute they were past her building Kate slid out, snatching her flashlight from the glove compartment, and moved into the blackness among the parked cars searching for her keys.

Why had Consuela left her alive? Because she didn't want to face a murder charge in case they were caught? But why had she bothered to bring her home? Did the woman think she would be less likely to call the cops if she were returned to her own apartment? That maybe she would run upstairs, collapse in tears, and that would be the end of it? Or at least if she did call the cops, they had a little time while she retrieved her keys—maybe a lot of time, if the keys had gone down through one of the storm grates in the garage floor.

She found them at last; it took her nearly half an hour. They were lodged on the hood of a big Buick, where the black grid of air ducts met the windshield, the keys half hidden beneath the edge of the hood. Retrieving them and hurrying up the closed stairway to her apartment, she flinched at every imagined shifting of the shadows above her, at every hint of sound from the upper landing. At her own door she fumbled with her key, pushing nervously inside. Slamming and locking the door, she leaned against it, her heart pounding.

When she looked up at her apartment, she felt her heart skip, and she went sick.

It appeared as if a tornado had touched down, flinging and smashing furniture, spewing the contents of every drawer in its violent tantrum of destruction. The couch and chairs lay upside down, the upholstery ripped, cotton and foam stuffing pulled out in hunks, even the dust covers shredded off the bottoms, revealing springs and webbing.

Numbly she moved through the mess feeling physically bruised. Along nearly every wall the carpet and pad had been ripped away to reveal the old wooden floors beneath. The kitchen looked like a garbage dump. She stood looking in, and did not want to enter. Every cupboard had been flung open, the contents thrown to the floor, spilled food mixed with broken china. A cold draft hit her, though she had left no window open.

Certainly not the kitchen window, which now stood open, letting in the damp breeze.

She wanted to race for the front door, fling it wide,

and run. Backing away from the kitchen, she crossed to
the fireplace and picked up the poker that lay incising
its black soot across a satin pillow. Clutching the
poker, she moved again to the kitchen, shaking with
shock and rage. She crossed to the sink and window,
glancing behind her to watch the kitchen door, wading
through debris that crunched under her shoes.

The window had been jimmied open four inches.
That was as far as the second, newer lock would allow.
Not wide enough for human entry. Examining the
older lock, she could see where it was broken, the
metal cracked through. Looking out at the adjoining
rooftops, she shut the window and jammed a long carving knife between the end of the sliding glass and the
wall.

She stood looking at the broken dishes and scattered
rice and cereal. Every container had been emptied,
flour and sugar bags lay atop the mess, along with a
coffee can. Had the thieves thought she'd keep the jewels in such places? With every new example of their
thoroughness, the monetary value of the jewels became
more certain in her mind. They were not paste. Why
her parents or grandfather would leave such a fortune,
taped into a cardboard box at the back of a safe, for a
child who might never see that fortune, was a mystery
she might never solve.

Moving back through the grisly mess, clutching the
poker, she ventured toward the rest of the apartment,
turning first to her study.

The two file cabinets were open, the drawers gutted,
files and papers flung everywhere. Books were toppled
from their shelves and were lying open, the spines
awry, pages ripped out as if in their search Consuela

and her friend had had, as well, a high good time. This was not searching; this was destruction. Maybe with people like this, it took only opportunity. Time and place invited, they seized the moment as hungrily as an addict would seize drugs. She was so angry that if she had her hands on Consuela now, gun or not, she would lay her out cold or die trying.

Picking up her office phone, she heard no dial tone. She hit the button, listened. Nothing; again the line was dead. Why did the phone company have to string its wires up the side of the building, prey to every prowler?

She had dropped her purse on the table by the front door. During the time Consuela had the gun on her she had toyed with the thought of trying to slip the phone from her purse and dial 911, but there was never a second when Consuela glanced away.

Still carrying the poker, she fished the phone from her purse and dialed 911 now. She gave the dispatcher her address and described the break-in, trying to make clear the extent of the destruction. The dispatcher told her to get out of the apartment until officers could clear it.

"No. I feel safer here. I was . . . I was kidnapped tonight, as well. They could still be out there." This sounded really weird, so strange that she felt embarrassed. The woman would think she was a nut.

"Can you go to a neighbor's?"

"I don't know my neighbors. I'll stay here."

"Where in the apartment are you?"

"By the front door, in the entry. I've searched part of the apartment, all but the bedroom."

"Officers are on the way. Please stay on the line.

When exactly were you kidnapped?" Was the woman patronizing her? Trying to assess her degree of sanity or insanity?

Well, she couldn't blame her.

Or did she simply want to keep her talking until help arrived? She repeated as briefly and clearly as she could the events since she entered the restaurant until she arrived home. She told the dispatcher about giving Consuela the jewels. She explained Consuela's change in appearance and gave her a description of her male partner, and of the car. That seemed to impress the dispatcher. She explained that Consuela had been in Molena Point and that the police there might possibly have some information on her.

Talking with the dispatcher, Kate pulled the foil-wrapped sandwich from her purse and moved into the kitchen. She was amazed that she could think of food, but she felt weak and faint, and knew she needed to eat something. Finding a saucepan among the rubble and an unbroken cup half buried in flour, she washed both thoroughly in hot soapy water, tucking the phone between her ear and shoulder. Filling the pan with water, she set it on a burner, brought up a gas flame, and searched among the debris for a tea bag.

Unwrapping the little bag of English Breakfast, she dropped it in the cup, poured boiling water over it, and carried teacup and sandwich into the little dining room, stepping over her nice place mats that were wadded on the floor. She needed to eat. She was weak; her diminished blood sugar dragged her courage even lower. She told the dispatcher where she now was in the apartment. She was pulling out her chair when a movement in the living room brought her up short. She turned, swallowing a cry of alarm.

A black cat sat on the overturned couch disdainfully watching her.

He was huge; his amber eyes blazed so fiercely they seemed filled with licking flames.

There could not be another like him, this cat who called himself the death angel, this cat who had stolen her safe deposit key and had stolen her signature; the same thieving cat that had arrived in the village last year with Greeley Urzey to steal from the village shop-keepers. The beast that, at supper after Charlie's gallery opening, had looked down through the skylight watching them. She stood beside the table facing him, as ice cold as if all her blood had drained away. She looked down at the phone in her hand, and quietly broke the connection.

The cat smiled. "Little Kate Osborne. Pretty little Kate Osborne."

"Why did you help Consuela? What do you get out of it? Why would a cat like you be interested in a hand-ful of costume jewelry with paste stones? Your thieving partner could steal anything you want."

"What partner would that be?"

"Old Greeley," she said, sitting weakly down at the table, cupping her cold hands around the warm teacup.

"I don't run with *him* anymore. She is my partner now, sometimes. I see that you gave her the jewels."

"How would you know what I gave her?"

"I saw her leave the parking garage. She would not have left unless she had the jewelry."

"And is he your partner, too? The man with the big

nose?" She sipped at her tea. Where were the police? What was taking so long? What would they do, now that she had hung up?

The cat's eyes narrowed to slits and his ears laid close to his head. "If the jewels are only paste, why do *you* treasure those pieces so highly?" His crouch was so tense she thought he would leap on her, biting and clawing.

"The jewelry is part of my past. A past that has no meaning for you, or for Consuela and her friend."

Again the cat smiled. "I could tell you about your past." He looked at her sandwich, which lay untouched in the open foil wrap, the melted cheese turned to the consistency of rubber. "You were told at the orphanage that McCabe might be the name of your grandfather."

"How would you know that?"

He rose and stretched, eyeing her dinner. "Is that shrimp I smell? Grilled shrimp?"

Defensively she picked up her sandwich. The cat leaped six feet to an overturned chair and leaped again onto the table. He stood on her dining table staring intently at her supper.

Removing half the sandwich from the open wrapper she shoved it across to him, leaving a greasy path on the nice oak. She'd have to have a cleaning crew in; she wasn't going to deal with this alone.

Gobbling greedily, the black tom was as messy as a stray dog. The sandwich was gone in six gulps. Licking grease from his whiskers, he eyed her half. She ate quickly though it was cold and rubbery. If in her uneasy hunger she gulped as ravenously as the tom, she didn't care.

"*I* can tell you about McCabe," the cat said. "*I* can

tell you about your grandfather *and* your parents, if you indeed want to know."

"How would *you* know about my heritage?" The cat's words deeply frightened her. Her search, which had started out nearly three years ago as a fledgling interest in her strange heritage, had turned into a nightmare of fear.

The black tom pricked his ears, watching her. "You'd be a pretty little cat, Kate Osborne. Oh, yes, all cream and silk. Maybe more willing than little Dulcie or that tortoiseshell. I do like a partner with my own talents."

His audacity enraged her. And the feline part of her nature deeply upset her. The joy she had once taken in those talents had vanished—to be a cat, rolling in the garden, racing over rooftops. Those changes had occurred only those few days when her life was threatened; they had not remained a part of her life. She looked at the tomcat. "Tell me why Consuela wanted the jewels. Why she would want paste jewels?"

"Shall we say she collects oddities?"

"She'll go to jail for robbing me, her fingerprints are on my safe deposit box, her forgery is on the bank records. That's a big risk, for oddities."

The cat's eyes grew as large as moons; he stared at her, keening a wild hunting cry, creeping toward her—she imagined his teeth in her flesh. Palms sweating, her heart racing, she rose and backed away.

He sat down suddenly on the table and began casually washing his paws, his expression one of deep amusement.

Watching him, she didn't know why she had launched herself into this search for her past, why she had opened this Pandora's box of perplexing connections, seeking matters that any sensible person would leave alone.

The black cat looked deeply at her. His purr was ragged. "You have amazing talents, Kate Osborne."

"Not anymore. That is past. I am no more than what you see."

The cat smiled. "You were under great stress at that time. Your life was threatened, your marriage shattered, your fear that your husband would kill you shocked and sickened you. Perhaps that was why the changes occurred—but what a lovely white and marmalade cat you must have been. And now . . . Perhaps the stress of present events will—"

"No!" Kate flung her cup at him; he leaped out of its path and it shattered against the wall. He sat down again facing her, his yellow eyes filled with a mad light. The cat *was* mad. There was no reason that such a beast, with the sentient skills of a human, could not be as stark raving crazy as some poor, demented human.

But she did want to know how he had learned about her, and what else he might know.

Watching her, he smiled. "The Cat Museum, Kate Osborne. There is more information there than you have found."

"I have been thoroughly through the archives."

"The oral tradition, among our kind, is reliable and useful." The cat's eyes narrowed. "Nothing written. Much that can be told."

She thought of the other cats prowling the museum gardens, and she shivered. She had wondered about those cats. But now . . . she would not, could not ever go there again, to that place she had loved so well.

"They do not like me there," he said. "Those cats who are like us, they do not like me." He looked deeply at her. "There is indeed a hidden world, Kate Osborne. That is the world I seek. That is your true home, the world where the jewels come from."

"What, some commune hidden back in the mountains? Some colony of crazies with guards at the gate?" *Where were the police?* She wanted this cat out of there, she wanted this unpleasantness over with.

"A world lying deep beneath this city, Kate, a world cavernous and vast. That is the world that should have been McCabe's. The world where I, too, belong."

She was certain that when the law arrived the cat would vanish the way he had come, that she would be rid of him—he wouldn't dare stay, he daren't sit watching while she answered the officer's questions, while she tried to skirt around the answers that she couldn't offer. Hurrying to the kitchen she removed the carving knife and opened the window again, providing for him the same four-inch escape route by which he must have entered. Sickly, desperately, she wanted this cat gone. What did he want with her? Moving quickly back into the dining room Kate found the cat still on the table, nosing at her cell phone. Snatching it up, she dropped it in her pocket. She wanted to snatch up Azrael and shove him out the window, but she was too afraid of him.

Surely when the patrol car came, if it ever did, then he would leave. The uniforms would do their work and go away again, and she would be alone. If she could ignore her ruined apartment, she'd take a long hot shower, pull some bedding together, lock her bedroom door against all possible intruders, and go to sleep. Tomorrow she'd muster the strength to pack what was fit to keep, send everything else to the trash, and . . . What? Move out? Abandon the city now, at once? Give notice at the studio and move back to Molena Point immediately, where she'd be safe?

Or she could transfer to Seattle, far away from the Bay Area, to work in the firm's new office there. She had not before seriously considered that option.

Watching her, the black cat yawned. "There *is* such a world, Kate Osborne, a world where all cats speak, a world of subterranean valleys and caverns where jewels are dug from the walls. Diamonds, rubies . . . Where jewelsmiths are as common as dust. Where do you think that strange work comes from that no one can identify? You know the old Celtic tales, the Irish and Welsh sagas. Do you think that ancient history is all lies because it comes to us in the form of story? Do you really *not* believe in those worlds, told of again and again throughout history?"

"They are *only* stories! Folktales! Flights of fancy, anyone knows that. There *is* no other world; such a thing is not possible." She stared hard at the inky beast. His amber eyes blazed back at her, as hot as the flames of hell.

"The jewels can lead us there," the cat said complacently. "If we can learn where they came from in this world, we can find the way down. A door, a passage down into that lost world." He looked at her intently.

"You are mad," she whispered. "There is no world but this. *This world! Here! Now.*" Snatching at the edge of the table, she tilted it so violently the black tomcat could only leap off. He landed on the buffet. She wanted to throw the table at him. "Leave me alone! *She* has the jewels! Go to Consuela. Take the jewels. Go find your mythical door. Get out of here. Go to that other world or wherever. But get the hell out of *here*, I have nothing for you!"

He stood atop the buffet glaring at her, panther-black and as powerful and sinewy as any jungle beast. "What bargain would it take, Kate Osborne, for you to help me find that world and enter it? You have talents that I do not. And the jewels themselves from that world are surely a badge of power . . ."

*"Get out!"* She swung around, grabbing the poker.

He stared at her unflinching. "There is a house, Kate Osborne. An old gray Victorian in Pacific Heights, an earthquake-damaged house, closed now and awaiting repairs. Cats live there, cats that do not fit into the dull gardens of the Cat Museum, beautiful, dark-souled cats who were driven out by their tame cousins. Those cats could lead us . . . or perhaps we will find the door there, in that wrecked dwelling, perhaps—"

"Then go there! Go to your rebel cats! Such beasts should welcome *you*. Go down to that world and leave *me* alone." The cat was mad, he was indeed Poe's black beast, as Joe Grey had once observed. "Go to *them*," she repeated. "I can't help you."

"They do not want me there. Those cats fear me; they fear my power. They rise like a tide against me."

"So what do you want from me? *I can't help you.*"

"Those beasts come and go freely from that world. Perhaps indeed a portal is there, in that ruined place . . . I have seen them appear out of the darkness of that house, I have seen their eyes. I have smelled the scent of deep, dank earth on them." His eyes burned with desire. "They drive me out, Kate Osborne. They do not want me in that world."

She watched him, chilled by his words but not understanding.

"Even the dark souls, Kate Osborne, make war among themselves, battles of jealousy and power. If that world has turned dark as I think it has, if the hell beasts now rule there . . . then only a badge of power can have authority." His yellow eyes gleamed. "I believe the jewels with their symbols of cats wield the power I want. A talisman of authority from that world . . ."

She shivered, drawing back. The cat was insane, driven by an ego bigger than any lost world—and yet despite her fear of him, his words and his cloying voice strangely quickened her heart. And a little voice deep inside her kept asking, *Why are there no public records for McCabe, or for my grandmother or my parents? What* are *McCabe's oblique references in his journals to some other world?*

She shook her head, turning away. She did not want to think about this; she did not want any of this.

But then she turned back, watching the tomcat. "Is *she* a part of this? Is Consuela part of this insanity? Does she believe in such a world?"

His laugh was cold, teeth bared with derision. "She knows nothing about my true purpose. She has taken the jewels for her lover."

"The man who followed me?"

The cat laughed again, a snarling hiss that gave her goose bumps. "That man is not her lover. Her lover is her partner, as am I. We are three in our ventures. The man who followed you is a pawn, a simple lackey." He watched her appraisingly. "If you want to know about her partner, you must help me."

The cat jerked around as footsteps sounded outside the door in the stairwell.

"Go!" she hissed.

The cat sat unmoving, his smile evil.

Kate was so enraged, so at the end of her temper, that she snatched up the beast by the nape of his bullish neck and his thick black tail and, holding him away from her, she hiked him through to the kitchen. She was sure he'd twist around and slash her—he could shred her arm in an instant.

But he did nothing. He hung limp, watching her and laughing. *Laughing.* Enraged, she shoved him through the narrow opening, forcing him through with her hand on his rump, then closing the window, wedging it again with the butcher knife. Then she went to open the front door. In her last view of Azrael, the tomcat sauntered boldly away into the black night of the rooftops.

# 22

In the presence of the two officers, Kate was foolishly embarrassed by the shambles of her apartment. Shaken by her encounter with the black tomcat, she felt dull and slow, as if her normal senses were muffled.

Of the two officers, the tall, thin one was young, maybe in his late twenties, with startling blue eyes. He stood in the open door, his smile reserved, appraising her and watchful.

"Mrs. Osborne? I'm Officer Harden. This is Officer Pardue." Harden's instant scan passed beyond her to the destroyed living room, seeming to record every small detail, every break and spill and tear, every gouge and stain.

Officer Pardue was shorter and older, perhaps in his fifties, the lines in his face sculpted into the look of someone with a perpetually sour stomach. His survey of the room seemed more wary, more attuned to watching for a hidden presence, for someone waiting out of sight. When she stepped back for them to enter, Officer

Pardue began at once to move through the apartment to clear it, his hand on his gun. Officer Harden remained standing with her, asking questions but sharply alert until Officer Pardue returned. Only then did Harden begin to fill in his report, walking through the rooms with her, then sitting with her at the dining table, avoiding the grease.

As Pardue waited by the door, Kate told Officer Harden that before she got home she had been followed, and that she had been kidnapped for perhaps an hour and then released in her own parking garage. It all sounded so hokey, so made up. She gave him the detailed circumstances and described the jewelry the woman had taken. He interrupted her once to call the station, to speak with a detective. He did not want her to clean up the apartment or to move anything at all until the detective arrived. That he was concerned enough to bring in an investigator, made her feel better. Harden wanted to know what she had touched after she got home. When she told him she had made tea and eaten a sandwich he seemed amused.

"I felt faint; I had to have something. I sat here, at the table." She did not, of course, mention her uninvited dinner guest. If, later, the detective found paw prints on the table, so be it. When Harden went to look at her phone line, he found that it had been cut just outside her kitchen window. He reported this for her through the dispatcher.

As he filled out his report, he made her repeat many answers. She did not like that he was testing her. He asked her three times whether she knew the man, and made her repeat that she wasn't sure. Asked her twice to describe how she knew Consuela. She would have to answer all this again, for the detective. She hoped he would not be as heavy-handed. Explaining that in Molena Point Consuela had posed as a teenager, she was most uncomfortable at how addled that sounded. She was relieved when Detective Jared Reedie arrived some ten minutes later.

His quick arrival surprised her, implying to her that this particular burglary might be important. Reedie was a shockingly good-looking young man with dark brown hair and brown eyes, dressed in cords and a suede sport coat, a young man so handsome that Kate immediately found herself mistrusting him. When the two officers had left, Reedie walked through the house with her, taking photographs, then at last he came to sit with her at the table as Harden had done. She told her story over again knowing he would compare it with what she'd told Officer Harden—as if she were the one on trial. She understood why this was necessary, but that didn't make her any more comfortable with the fact-finding process to which the law was committed.

Reedie said, "There was a report tonight of a woman being followed into a restaurant on Columbus."

She nodded. "I think the waitress, Annette, might have called. She helped me leave—helped that woman and me go out the back."

"You saw the car that followed you."

"A gray hatchback. I don't know what make. Fairly new, though."

"And you got a look at the man?"

When, for the fourth time, she described the man, she caught a gleam of interest from Reedie. He spent quite some time going over her description of him, and of the waiter in Molena Point. He seemed equally interested in her two very different descriptions of Consuela.

"You think they were the same person, this sophisticated Nancy Westervelt, and the teenager you described from Molena Point?"

"Yes, I'm sure it's the same woman." This was such a tangle. She had to tell him about the theft of her safe deposit key. She was nervous not to, because she had reported it to the bank. The detective seemed to sense that she was leaving things out, though he did not accuse her of that. When he kept questioning her about Consuela she said, "Maybe it would help if you talked with Captain Harper in Molena Point, or spoke with one of his detectives, with Dallas Garza or Juana Davis. All three know Consuela, and maybe they could shed some light. They should know if she's left the village."

"What is your connection to Molena Point PD?"

"I worked for Dallas Garza's niece, here in the city. While Dallas was still with your department. If I return to Molena Point to live, his niece wants me to join her again. She now has her own design studio there." She studied his handsome face, his expressionless brown eyes. "Captain Harper is a personal friend, as well. He was very helpful and supportive when my husband . . ."

She faltered, then, "Do you remember a money-laundering and car-theft scheme in Molena Point three years ago? They killed the owner of the car dealership when he found out what they were doing."

Reedie nodded. "I remember."

"My husband, James Osborne, was part of it. When I found out, he arranged with his partner to kill me. It was Captain Harper who broke the case. The two are now in San Quentin."

Her explanation seemed to put Detective Reedie somewhat at ease, and the remainder of his interview was less rigid. She described for him in as much detail as she could each piece of jewelry that Consuela had taken. She told him where she had had them appraised. By the time the detective rose to leave, he had a detailed account of her evening, had taken three rolls of photographs, and had a description of the man who had followed her. The detective seemed, in fact, so intent on the man that she wanted to mention the newspaper article she had read about the jewel robbery in the city and the escape of one of the thieves.

But he would know that; maybe that was why he was interested. When Reedie asked if she wanted to press charges against Consuela, she hesitated.

"If I press charges, and she's caught and the jewelry is recovered—if she actually goes to trial, I won't get the jewelry back until the trial's finished. Is that right?"

"Yes. And then only if you can identify it."

"I don't have photographs. Would my fingerprints on the jewelry count for anything?"

Detective Reedie smiled. "I can see that it counts for something—if she doesn't wipe them clean. Your description of the pieces will be taken into consideration. You might want to get a written description from the appraiser and a letter from the attorney who gave them to you."

"Yes," she said doubtfully. "If the attorney ever looked at them, if he ever opened that sealed box. But . . ." She looked up at Reedie. "I think I could draw them with some accuracy."

"That might be helpful. It couldn't hurt."

"If I don't press charges of theft, but report the jewelry taken, could I expect to get the jewelry back?" She didn't want to wait months or maybe years for the overcrowded San Francisco court system to release the evidence. "If I did that, what could you hold her on? Would you have enough to hold her?"

Reedie smiled. "You can press charges for kidnapping, for breaking and entering, and for malicious damage. But the case would be stronger if you charge her with taking the jewelry as well.

"It's not as if the jewelry went missing during the break-in," he said. "You were forced to give her the box. It would make a far stronger case if you laid it all out as it happened." He studied her. "But we have to keep that kind of evidence for the trial. It's not like, say, stolen merchandise where you can check the price tag, know the exact value, and return it to a store that has been robbed. The court would insist on holding it for actual consideration during the trial."

"Do I need to come into the station to file charges?"

He removed a sheaf of forms from the back of his clipboard and handed her two, offering her a pen. Kate gave him a grateful look and began to fill in the required information. She did not take time to run her phone messages until half an hour after Detective Reedie left.

When the police had gone, she took a long hot shower, made herself a bourbon and water, and tucked up in bed, locking her bedroom door. With her cell phone she called the message service for her home phone. Detective Reedie had reported her phone line cut, but she could access the service from anywhere. She supposed the land line would be repaired in the morning.

Alone and safe in her bedroom, jotting down messages, punching erase or save, she was torn by the thoughts that the black tomcat had stirred.

Yet, when she faced her decision to abandon the search into her family, to forget the past and settle down to real life, an emptiness yawned, making her feel very alone. To cut those nebulous ties to her heritage, no matter how strange that past was, made her feel totally cut off from the world.

Huddled up in bed, frightened again and lonely, she felt a deep need for her friends, for Wilma and Charlie, for Clyde, for Hanni and Ryan. Unexpected tears started flowing, and before she finished listening to her messages she hung up and dialed Molena Point.

Clyde answered. His voice was muzzy with sleep. She glanced at her bedside clock. It was nearly ten.

"I was reading," he lied.

"You were asleep."

"In my study, reading. Foggy out, really socked. Guess I drifted off."

"In your study with a fire burning," she said longingly.

"A fire burning, a glass of bourbon. All I need is you, it couldn't get any better."

She laughed. "You're such a philanderer. What about Ryan?"

"She's at home working on blueprints."

"And Joe is sprawled on your feet?" Kate wanted to keep him talking, keep hearing his voice so familiar and comforting. She wished she were there; she needed Clyde, needed a strong shoulder to lean on.

"Joe's out hunting, waylaying innocent rabbits. Damn cat. I hate when he hunts in the fog; it's the most dangerous time. But you can't tell him one damn thing; might as well talk to the wall. How are you, Kate? You sound . . . what's wrong?"

"I'm too tired to repeat it all again. The police have been here, and a detective. I had a break-in. I just . . . needed to hear your voice. I'll explain it all later. Trashed my apartment. I'm fine now, apartment's secure."

"Tell me the rest."

"Could I tell you tomorrow? I just . . . wanted to hear your voice. I felt so lonely."

"Don't leave me hanging. Talk to me."

"I'm just so tired."

"Try," he said unsympathetically.

"That girl from the village, that cheap girl running with Dillon? Consuela something?"

"Yes?"

She told him, starting with the theft of her safe deposit key. Joe Grey, in his typical tomcat secrecy, had told Clyde none of that. She left the phone once to refill her drink, and they talked for nearly an hour. Clyde's questions were endless. He said, "I'm coming up, Kate. First thing in the morning."

"That isn't necessary, I don't want you to do that. I just wanted to hear your voice. I'm fine, Clyde. The police have it in hand."

When she hung up, having convinced him at last not to come, she went to the kitchen and managed to find another tea bag. Taking a cup back to bed, she continued running her messages. That was when she got Lucinda.

She had erased the ninth message, from a client, having made the necessary notes. She had begun to play the next one when she sat straight up in bed. Holding the phone away from her, staring at it, she missed vital words.

She replayed it, unbelieving. At first, for an instant, she thought it was an old message that had somehow gotten saved.

"Kate, it's Lucinda. We weren't in that wreck, we're all right. We wanted, for a while, to not tell anyone at all, not even the sheriff. We'll explain it all when we see you, we're heading for San Francisco . . ."

*Alive? They were alive?* She felt cold with shock, then delirious with relief. She wanted to jump up and down on the bed, to turn cartwheels. Punching save, she ran the message four more times.

"If you're out late," Lucinda said, "if you try to call me back and we're asleep, leave a message. We're at the Redwood, in Fort Bragg. We don't want to come barging in tomorrow, if it's not convenient. We just . . . It will take a while to tell you all that's happened. But we're fine. We got out of the RV long before the wreck; we weren't anywhere near when it burned." Lucinda's voice sounded strong and happy.

"We'll be in the city in the morning, I made reservations at that little hotel just down from you. Maybe, if you're free, we can have breakfast?"

She listened. Played it again. Again. *Alive! They were alive!* Three days since the wreck and no word, *and now they were alive!*

This could not be a joke, she knew Lucinda's voice.

What had happened? Where had they been? Why *hadn't* they been in touch? *Why hadn't they called her, or called Wilma? Why hadn't they contacted the police?* She sat holding the phone, staring at it, her hands trembling; she was grinning like an idiot.

When at last she called their hotel, she got the message service. Well, it was after eleven, likely they were asleep. She didn't try their cell phone. She left a message, then tried to call Wilma but got a busy signal. Did Wilma know? Had Lucinda already called her? Were they talking right now? When she had talked with Clyde, he didn't know.

And most important, did the kit know? Did Kit know that the family she loved so fiercely was safe, the family for whom she had been grieving?

Lucinda's message had been left at 8:30 P.M., just about the time she had walked into her trashed apartment. She couldn't stop thinking of the kit, of how excited the little tattercoat would be. She tried Wilma again but her line was still busy, and so was Clyde's.


Before Wilma called to give Clyde the amazing news about Lucinda and Pedric, Clyde stood in his study wondering whether to throw some clothes in a duffel and take off at once, drive on up to the city, and give Kate some moral support, or whether to go sensibly to bed and take off at first light. Kate sounded in really bad shape, he had never heard her so weepy. Not even during that bad time when Jimmie wanted her dead and when under stress Kate had experienced the feline side of her nature in a manner that he still found hard to deal with.

Moving into the bedroom, he had snatched his leather duffel from the shelf in the walk-in closet and was stuffing in a couple of pairs of shorts and socks when the phone rang. Picking up the bedside extension, he could hear a cat yowling in the background.

Within moments he knew they were alive; Lucinda and Pedric were alive. Wilma was laughing and crying. He could hear the kit in the background yowling and laughing; she sounded demented. He sat down on the bed.

He had to tell Joe. Why wasn't he here? Where the hell was Joe Grey?

## 23

By ten that night, the fog had packed itself as tight as cotton wool into Molena Point, drowning the village trees and rooftops and gathering like an advancing sea along the sidewalks and against the faintly lit storefronts. The oaks that guarded Wilma Getz's house stood shrouded as pale as ghosts above the mist-flooded flower beds. Not the faintest smear of light shone in Wilma's front windows, but at the back of the house her bedroom bled golden light out onto the grassy hill.

Within the cozy room a lamp burned, and three small oak logs blazed in the red enamel stove. On Wilma's bed, curled up on the thick, flowered quilt, Dulcie and Kit lay limp and relaxed as Wilma read to them.

Wilma would not have chosen for the night's reading a volume of Celtic folklore, but the kit had begged for it. Those stories, so reminiscent of Lucinda and Pedric, made the kit incredibly sad, yet she demanded to hear them. The tale was deep into stone circles and underground kingdoms when the phone rang, its shrill sound jerking the three of them abruptly from those distant realms. The two half-dreaming cats started up wide eyed, visions from the story crumbling as Wilma reached for the phone.

Her hand paused in midair. Did she really want to answer? Could it be a sales pitch this late? If a salesman got the answering machine, he'd hang up—that's what the machine was for. The last time the phone rang late at night, it had been terrible news: the deaths of two dear friends.

But then, ever curious, ever hopeful that something wonderful was happening in the world, Wilma picked up.

When she heard the voice at the other end she caught her breath, her heart started to thud—then she began to smile, then to laugh. "Hold on," she said. "Hold one minute."

Hitting record, she reached out to the kit. "Come here quick. You were right," she whispered, gathering the kit in close to her. "Kit, you were right, they're alive." Cuddling the kit in her arms, she held the receiver so they both could listen. "They're alive, Kit! Lucinda and Pedric are alive." Then, remembering the speaker, she pressed the button. "Go on," she said. "We're all three listening."

Lucinda's voice sent the kit rigid. She stared at the phone that, she had thought a few months ago, was some kind of magic. She stared up at Wilma.

Lucinda was saying, "After I left a message on Kate's phone, Pedric and I went out to dinner. We just got back. I expect Kate has already called you. Well, we're fine, Wilma. We're just fine. Is the kit there?"

The kit stared at the speaker and touched it with a hesitant paw. Pressing against Wilma, looking up into Wilma's face, she tried to read the truth of what she was hearing. All her kittenhood suspicion of telephones and things electronic tumbled through her head, rendering her deeply uncertain. She couldn't stop shivering.

But that *was* Lucinda's voice, she knew Lucinda's voice.

"Kit? Are you there? It's really me, it's Lucinda. We're fine, Pedric is right here with me. We got out of the RV before the wreck. We're coming home, Kit. Coming to stay, to build our house for the three of us."

Kit shoved her nose at the speaker. *"Lucinda, Lucinda . . ."* And for once the kit abandoned all powers of speech and fell into mewling cries.

"We're in Fort Bragg," Lucinda said. "We'll be in the city tomorrow morning. We've left a message for Kate. There's so much more to tell her—so much to tell you. So much that I think we need to tell Captain Harper. Now. Tonight. Would he mind if we called him at home?"

"Of course he wouldn't mind. He'll be thrilled to hear your voices and so will Charlie. But what . . . ?"

"The man who stole our RV, who probably intended to kill us—we think we know him. We think this could be connected somehow to events in the village."

Wilma sat quietly listening to Lucinda's story, seeing the old couple locked in their bedroom in the RV as the man pocketed their ignition keys, as he unhooked the gas and electric lines, the water and waste systems from the RV parking slot.

"What time was this?" Wilma asked. "Didn't anyone in the campground see him and wonder?"

"It was early, just after dark. But no one could see our rig. We always choose a private space with just the woods around us.

"Well, when he started the engine and took off, we were locked in the bedroom. We crawled under the bed into the storage compartment and waited until he slowed to turn onto the highway, then went out the other side into the bushes, dragging a duffel with a few clothes and some money. And a blanket. No need to be cold; we slept all night in the woods."

"But what did he want?" Wilma said. Not that anyone these days needed an excuse for cold-blooded behavior.

"The jewelry," Lucinda told her. "That costume jewelry. Can you believe that? It's lovely, but it's only paste."

"Are you sure that's what he wanted?"

"It's what he told us."

"And you gave it to him?"

"We told him we'd put it in a safe deposit box in Eureka with some personal papers. He demanded our key and a sample of Pedric's signature. We gave him both."

Lucinda laughed. "The safe deposit key is not for a bank in Eureka. That's where he was headed when we bailed out of the RV. The jewels were in the storage compartment of the RV, we got them out in the duffel. Pedric—"

"You had them . . . have them with you?"

"Of course. We took them when we crawled out."

Wilma smiled at their resourcefulness, then shivered. "Do be careful, Lucinda. Why would he . . . Are you so sure they're paste?"

"Kate had hers appraised. Ours are just like hers; same style, same kind of setting. We couldn't have bought those pieces up in Russian River for the little we paid if the jewels were real."

Wilma looked at Dulcie. They were both thinking the same thing. Wilma said, "Lucinda, it's time for another appraisal. Meantime, please be careful. Even when you get to the Bay Area, miles from Russian River, you could still be in danger."

When Lucinda hung up to call Max Harper, Wilma sat holding the two cats close, the kit purring so loudly that she drowned out the crackle of the fire and the distant pounding of the surf. Wilma said, "Can you imagine Max and Charlie's delight when they find out the Greenlaws are alive?"

"I can imagine," Dulcie said tersely, "Captain Harper asking more questions than you did. What man? How do they know him? *How* is this connected to the village?"

"I didn't want to grill her. She'll tell all that to Max. Be patient, Dulcie. We'll hear it all from him, or from Charlie." Wilma straightened the flowered quilt, smoothed the sheet, and turned out the light. She and the cats were just settling down when again the phone rang. It was Kate.

They spent the next hour talking with her. The fire died down, the room grew chilly, and they wrapped themselves in the quilt. What an amazing night! Kate's break-in, her ruined apartment, Azrael entering through her kitchen window to open the door for that woman, then staying to harass her. Wilma didn't say it, but Kate sounded like a basket case.

"Consuela Benton," Wilma said, amazed.

But of course the kit and Dulcie had known. They didn't tell Wilma everything—not when that black tom had prowled her house so brazenly, not when Kate's key had been stolen right here in Wilma's own guest room, practically under Wilma's nose. Though they might opt to tell her soon, if Consuela and that beast returned to the village.

"So smooth and sophisticated," Kate said, "not a thing like Consuela. Hardly any makeup, her hair simple and clean, no ghoulish black eye makeup, no skintight jeans and bare belly button—"

"Kate, I'm going to call Charlie in the morning. See if I can pick up her barrette and take the two pieces to be appraised, here in the village. Maybe Lucinda would take her pieces to someone, maybe someone Dallas Garza could remember, in the city."

"I'll suggest it," Kate said. "I'll try."

They hung up. Wilma and the cats snuggled down again, and the kit fell asleep at once. So much excitement, so much wonderment and joy. Now she totally crashed, worn out, curled in a tangle of the quilt, dropping deep, deep under, exhausted clear down to her tortoiseshell paws.

**24**

The ringing phone woke Charlie. She was alone in bed, alone in the house. The time was 11:40. Muzzily she picked up the receiver thinking it was Max. The woman who spoke, her voice, her words, sent chills wriggling down Charlie's spine. *"Who?"* She sat up in bed, switching on the lamp. *"Who is this?"*

"It's Lucinda, my dear. Lucinda Greenlaw."

Outside the bedroom window, the thick fog was smeared yellow by the two security lights that illuminated the yard and stable. Clutching the phone, Charlie didn't speak.

"Oh dear, I don't mean to shock everyone. I thought Kate might have called you. We weren't in the RV when it crashed, Charlie. We're alive. We . . ."

What kind of scam was this? Charlie listened warily. If the Greenlaws were alive, Max would have known right away, from the sheriff. And Lucinda would have called Wilma at once. Charlie sat holding the phone, trying to figure out what was going down.

"Charlie, this *is* Lucinda. I didn't mean to frighten

283

you. I just talked with Wilma. I need to talk with Max . . . You're not on a cell phone?"

"No," Charlie said. "It's the be . . ." She caught her breath. She'd started to say the bedroom phone. She stared toward the hall, wondering if someone had gotten in the house, if someone was on one of the extensions, playing some insane trick. "Who *is* this?" She wished Max were there. There was no way this could be Lucinda. Max should be talking to this woman.

"It's Lucinda, my dear. Is the captain there? I just talked with Wilma—and with Kit, Charlie. I talked with Kit."

She pulled the covers up. "Lucinda?" She stuffed both pillows behind her.

"We weren't in the RV when it crashed and burned, Charlie, we'd already gotten out, before it reached the highway."

"But where have you been? Why didn't you call? The whole village is grieving."

As she listened to Lucinda's explanation and imagined the elderly couple crawling into the storage compartment and out the other side, slipping and sliding down into the muddy drainage ditch, Charlie began to grin.

She knew that Pedric had completed some work on the new RV to customize it before they ever began to travel, but she hadn't known how much.

"I didn't know," she said, laughing, "how sly Pedric could be. I didn't know with what foresight he did those improvements."

"Sometimes it pays," Lucinda said, "to have grown up in a family of thieves. Pedric knows every way there is to get into—or get out of—a house or trailer or RV."

"This is just . . . You two are incredible. Max will want to hear this. Call him now, Lucinda. At the station."

"It's all right to call there so late?"

"More than all right." Charlie gave her the number. "We love you, Lucinda."

Hanging up, turning out the light, and pulling up the covers, Charlie snuggled down. This was indeed a gift of grace—for the Greenlaws, for the kit, for all their friends. A deep sense of protection filled her, as powerful as when, on her and Max's wedding day, they had escaped that terrible explosion that had been set to kill them and most of the wedding party. Escaping that disaster, she had felt that all of them were blessed and watched over. She felt the same now, with this amazing reprieve.

Within the fog-shrouded police station, Max Harper and Detective Garza sat on either side of Harper's desk with Marlin Dorriss's phone and credit card bills spread out between them. Garza was busy recording pertinent motel stays or gas or restaurant purchases onto a chart, next to the corresponding burglaries. So far they had put Dorriss near the scene of seven thefts. Interestingly, during five of those, his motel bill showed double occupancy.

Harper said, "I hope to hell that wasn't Helen Thurwell. That would tear it. You want to check Helen's time off from the real estate firm?"

Garza nodded. The fact that Dorriss's bills had come to them through the holding cell window did not dampen the intensity with which the officers sorted through them—though how their informant had gotten away so fast off the roof, with uniforms blasting the sky with searchlights, neither Harper nor Garza cared to speculate.

As they studied the information, preparing to petition the judge for a search warrant, the informant himself looked down on their heads from atop Max Harper's bookcase. The tomcat appeared to be sleeping, his yellow eyes closed, his breathing slow and deep. Occasionally, one or the other of the officers would glance up at him, amused. No one knew why the cat was so attracted to cops.

The cat was good company, though, on a quiet late night. Probably he was addicted to the fried chicken and doughnuts that the dispatchers saved for him. Whatever reasons the cat might have, the nervy little freeloader had become a fixture around the station. As were his two lady pals, though the females didn't sprawl all over a guy's desk quite so boldly, nosing at papers and reports.

By the time Harper and Garza set the bills aside, they had eleven possible hits. Leaning back in his chair, Harper propped his feet on the desk, grinning at Dallas. "I think we've made Marlin Dorriss. We sure have enough for a warrant."

"But why the hell," Garza said, "if Dorriss also has a dozen false identities, with credit cards and drivers' licenses as our informant claims he does, why didn't he set up to use those for the thefts?" Their informant had, an hour after the Visa bill drop, called the station to relay the information about the false IDs to the captain.

Garza shrugged. "Guess he couldn't though. In every one of those thefts, there was some affair or charity dinner, so he had a reason to be there. How would he receive phone calls? And in a small town, if he checked into a hotel under a false name, there would be too many possible leaks."

Harper rose to refill their coffee cups. "This is some kind of game for the thief—some high-powered game. Steals one trophy piece from each residence, leaves a fortune untouched."

Garza shrugged. "Takes all kinds."

"I'll see the judge first thing in the morning."

Joe found it hard not to yowl with triumph, not to leap down and give the officers a high five. He listened, very still.

"You really think," Dallas said, "there's any point in searching his local residence? Why would he stash his take anywhere near the village?"

"Not likely, but we'll have to cover it. In fact, it wouldn't surprise me to find it right here. I went through his Molena Point house when it was being built. Contractor is a friend of mine. Dorriss doesn't know I was ever in there."

Harper's dry smile rearranged his lean, tanned wrinkles. "You know how the rich like to build with hiding places, foil the bad guys. That house has it in spades. All those different alcoves, it must have a dozen double walls, hidden dead spaces that no one would ever notice. Sealed up, no access you'd easily see."

"What about the contractor? Dorriss trusted him?"

"I think Dorriss had a little something on the guy." Harper set down his cup. "If the local search gives us nothing, maybe there's rented storage space, though I doubt it. More likely his San Francisco condo, or even Tahoe. I'll call Judge Brameir in the city, get him early in the morning, see if he'll issue a warrant for the condo."

Above the officers' heads, Joe Grey smiled. That was his thinking exactly. And, if Azrael *had* been in Dorriss's house, as he suspected, if the cat was welcome there, and if Azrael ran with Consuela, then was she Dorriss's partner? Had Consuela been Dorriss's companion in those double occupancy rooms while Dorriss pulled off his burglaries?

If Dorriss's stash was there at the condo, Joe thought, what about Clyde's antique Packard? Was it there, as well, hidden in a garage? Wouldn't that be a hoot. San Francisco PD goes out with a warrant, searches the place, and there's Clyde's valuable restored Packard sitting right there waiting for them. Joe's head was so full of possibilities he thought he'd explode. He had risen, faking a yawn, burning to leap down and go tell Clyde his theory, when the phone buzzed.

Harper hit the speaker.

The dispatcher said, "Thought you'd want this one, Captain."

When she'd put through the call and when Joe heard Lucinda's voice, he nearly fell off the bookshelf. *The Greenlaws were alive?* Not in the hospital, not harmed in any way, but alive and heading for the city?

Joe listened with the two officers to Lucinda's amazing story, watched the two men's pleased smiles, and listened to Harper's questions and Lucinda's responses: no, they hadn't yet talked with the sheriff, yes they were watching that they weren't followed. When Harper had the whole story and had hung up, he and Dallas were both grinning. This time, even without the law, it looked like the bad guy had got what he deserved. The sense of satisfaction that filled the officers and filled Joe Grey was thick enough to cut with a knife.

As the tomcat dropped from the bookcase to the desk, hit the floor yawning, and padded lazily out of the room, he was so wired that he could barely keep from racing up the hall to the glass door shouting for the dispatcher to let him out—by this time Dulcie knew, the kit knew, and he could hardly wait to hear the little tattercoat's excited yowls.

## 25

The Garden House Hotel had once been a pair of private residences, handsome Victorian homes each adorned with cupolas and round shingled towers, with diamond-paned bay windows and gingerbread trim along the intricate roof lines. To join the two houses, the architect had constructed a domed solarium, a large and handsome Victorian-style structure to accommodate the gardenlike lobby, the registration desk, and the patio portion of a casual restaurant. There were two elevators, one for each wing. Lucinda and Pedric Greenlaw parked in the small lot next door that was reserved for hotel guests. The time was 9 A.M. They had risen early, as was their custom, and had checked out of their Fort Bragg motel after only a quick snack for breakfast. Driving carefully in the dark pre-dawn for a while, they hoped to hit the lull before the late morning traffic that would be moving into the city across the Golden Gate Bridge.

Arriving at the Garden House, parking in the lot next door, and locking their rented Olds Cutlass, they hurried into the hotel carrying their only luggage: two small duffels, one old and scarred that had rolled with them out of the RV on that fateful night, and a new red canvas bag that they had purchased in a drugstore in Fort Bragg along with extra sweatshirts, socks, underwear, canned fruit, snack food, and half a dozen bottles of water. The two bags contained most of their worldly possessions, except for their CDs and investments. Approaching the door to the hotel, they were both thinking hungrily of pancakes and bacon and coffee when Lucinda, glancing up at the third and top floor of the hotel, stopped, laughing.

"How nice! They allow pets. Or maybe they have a hotel cat." A black cat sat in the window, staring down at them. They glimpsed the animal for only a moment before a woman picked it up, and both disappeared. Pedric looked at her, smiling. If Lucinda had a soft spot for anything in the world it was cats— though particularly their own tortoiseshell Kit, whom they had both missed very much during their travels.

Last night on the phone, the kit had nearly deafened them both, yowling and shouting with joy, so thrilled that they had survived the crash, demanding to know when they would be home and for how long. When Lucinda repeated to her, "For good, Kit. Forever and good," the kit had, as Wilma said, bounced off the walls with excitement. Now Pedric stood holding Lucinda's hand, both watching the high window thinking the cat might reappear, and admiring the hotel's domes and gingerbread and the soaring solarium; and the tall, thin, handsome eighty-year-olds grinned at each other like children. How pleasant to be in the city for a few

days before they headed home. For a few moments
they stood watching passersby on the street, too, and
seeing what shops were nearby and admiring the San
Francisco skyline against the blue sky.

But then, turning to approach the solarium lobby,
looking through the long, bright windows into the tiled
garden room with its lush plants, Pedric drew Lucinda
back suddenly.

"Come away quickly." Turning and pulling her
away, he hurried her down the street, into the first doorway they came to, into the entry to a used bookshop, a
low-ceilinged, shadowed niche where the morning sun
had not yet found access. "Give me your cell phone,"
Pedric said.

"It's in the car," Lucinda said, peering out, pressing
forward trying to see. But Pedric pulled her back and
inside, through the open door of the bookshop.

The store was small and dim, its shelves arranged
with unusual neatness for a used bookstore, and it
smelled dust-free and clean. Most of the volumes had
leather bindings and looked expensive and in fine condition. The gold lettering on the front window, when
they read it slowly backward, informed them that the
shop featured California History, for collectors.
Frowning, Lucinda peered out through the glass,
watching the street and the hotel entry.

"Didn't you see him?" Pedric said. "Look there!
Just shutting the trunk of that car! The man who stole
the RV."

"It can't be." Lucinda dropped her duffel bag by a
stack of books, craning to see out through the crowded
display window between the neatly arranged volumes.

On the curb before the hotel, a thin, sandy-haired

man was just swinging in through the passenger door of a pale blue Corvette. They could see a woman driving, could see her profile and a tangle of curly black hair. As she pulled away, a dark shape blurred across the back window as if a small dog had jumped up on the ledge behind the seat. Then the car was gone, losing itself in the traffic.

Turning back, Pedric snatched a business card from the counter and noted down the license. Slipping this in his pocket and taking Lucinda's hand, he moved with her deeper into the store, where the proprietor watched them—a short, thirtyish man with a round, smooth face, an unusually short haircut that let his scalp shine through, dark shirt and slacks, and a wrinkled corduroy jacket. When Pedric asked to use the phone, he passed the instrument over the counter at once with a gentle, almost Old World courtesy.

Within minutes, Pedric had called the police, had described the theft of their RV up in Humboldt County so the dispatcher could check police records, and had given them a description of the thief and the car, and its license number. The bookstore owner had turned back to shelving books, but was quietly listening.

A patrol car must have been in the neighborhood because by the time the elderly couple had walked back to the hotel and checked in, a squad car was pulling to the curb. They went out to join the two officers.

A young black woman officer emerged from the driver's side. "I'm Officer Hart." She looked like she was fresh out of college. The older officer, Sean Maconachy, was a ruddy-faced man with graying hair and a sour, closed expression.

"Let's step inside," Maconachy said. "Can you be certain that was the man who kidnapped you?"

"We are certain," Pedric said. "Yesterday evening we filed a complaint with the Humboldt County sheriff. Will that allow you to pick up the car and arrest the man?"

"According to our information," Maconachy said, "the accident happened last Sunday. Nearly a week ago. And you did not file the report until yesterday?"

"It's a long story," Pedric said. "We were afraid to file before. We had escaped the RV before the wreck, but afterward, when the thief wasn't found, we assumed he had escaped too. We didn't know where he might be. We holed up in a motel, afraid he might find us. Afraid, for a while, even to contact the sheriff.

"When the man didn't show, when we felt sure no one was watching the motel, then we called the sheriff's office."

Maconachy nodded. Turning aside, he made a call to the station, putting the blue Corvette on wanted status and asking for a copy of the report. He glanced down the street as if he would like to go after the car himself. But the patrol units in the area would by now have been alerted. Maconachy nodded toward the hotel entry, and Lucinda and Pedric went on inside with the officers.

The interior garden areas were planted with ferns and with the bright blooms of cyclamens, the floor laid with pale travertine, the seating areas furnished with cushioned wicker chairs arranged on Turkish rugs. The clerk behind the desk was Asian and very tall. Lucinda and Pedric, standing with the two officers, gave him a description of the sandy-haired man with the high forehead and prominent nose.

"They checked out just before you came in," the clerk said. "He wasn't registered but he has been staying with the woman. She registered for two. Clarice Hudson."

The officers looked at Lucinda and Pedric.

"The name means nothing to us," Pedric told them.

Officer Hart took Clarice Hudson's credit card information and home address from the clerk, information that very possibly would turn out to be of no value.

"The woman had a cat," the clerk said. "Big black cat. We welcome pets, it's our specialty, but . . . well, the cat stayed in the room all right when the maid did it up, but she couldn't work near it; it snarled at her several times. Really a brute. We need to take another look at the rules. Gave me the chills, that cat."

Moving across the lobby with the two officers, Lucinda and Pedric sat with them around a low table in the comfortable wicker chairs, answering questions as the officers recorded what happened on the night their RV was stolen.

"He may have been staying at the same campground," Pedric said. "We would see him walking through, but neither of us noticed him entering or leaving any vehicle. He'd say a distant good morning, or nod. Seemed pleasant enough but preoccupied."

"The night he stole the RV," Lucinda said, "we had gone out to dinner—we always pulled a '94 Saturn behind the rig, for transportation. We went into Russian River, to a place called Jimmie's. We got back to the campground around seven, later than we'd planned. We don't like to drive very far at night."

"We locked the car," Pedric said, "unlocked the RV. When we flipped on the lights there he was sitting at the dinette, a big black gun on the table pointed straight at us. An automatic, but I couldn't see what make.

"He didn't ask for money. He wanted, specifically, some pieces of jewelry that Lucinda had bought in Russian River on our last trip. That was more than strange, because it's only costume jewelry. At least, a friend has some like it that she had appraised, and hers is of no special value, a few hundred dollars for the gold work. But that was what he wanted. When we said we didn't have the jewelry with us, that Lucinda had left it in Molena Point, he didn't believe us. He grew really angry, started shouting."

"He began to search the RV," Lucinda said. "Tore everything up, banging cupboards, making such a racket that we hoped someone would come to see what was happening.

"But we always park off to ourselves, choose the most private spot," she said. "We like to look at the woods and wildlife, not at other campers. Well, no one came to help us and that was just as well, I guess, since the man was armed."

Pedric said, "He shoved Lucinda in the bedroom. When I hit him from behind he turned and threw me in too." The old man grimaced. "I'm not as strong as I once was. In my prime, I'd have taken that guy out. He demanded the jewels again, then demanded the ignition keys. When I didn't hand them over, he roughed me up pretty bad, jerked the keys out of my pocket, and locked us in the bedroom."

"Pedric still has bruises," Lucinda said. "All along his side and back. A wonder he didn't break something. Well, he didn't get the jewelry."

Officer Hart looked hard at them. "You had it all the

time, and you didn't hand it over, even though it was only paste?"

"We don't like being told what to do," Lucinda said, "and by that time we were both wondering if it *was* paste." She smiled at the officers. "What he didn't know was that Pedric had modified the RV."

"I lived most of my life on the road," Pedric said. "Traveling in trailers and all kinds of rigs." He grinned at the officers. "The reason isn't important, it doesn't apply right now, but one thing I learned early, you need more than one or two ways out of a rig—in case of fire, in case of a wreck, in case the law comes down on you suddenly."

Officer Maconachy grinned.

Pedric said, "That was a long time ago, but some habits don't change easily. I built two storage compartments into the RV that opened from both the outside and from within. One was the mattress platform. I had to do quite a lot of adapting, and give over some of the space for functional equipment, but I made it work."

"When he locked us in," Lucinda said, "we packed a canvas duffel with a few clothes, some money we kept stashed, and the jewelry—it was with the money in one of Pedric's special hiding places."

"Took him a while to unhook the rig," Pedric said. "Waste lines, water and gas and power. We just sat there on the bed, locked in. We didn't want to hide in the compartment until he took off; we were afraid he'd come back there again, wanting to know how to find some latch, how to unhook something.

"Well, he had no trouble. Must have known how an RV works. The minute he started the engine and got moving, we slid into the compartment."

Lucinda laughed. "We lay cramped in there bumping along as he drove out through the campground. We unlocked the outside door, and when he slowed to turn onto the highway, we dropped out of the rig and into the bushes dragging the duffel and our blanket—we didn't see any point in sleeping cold."

Both officers were smiling, with a gentle appreciation.

"We considered going to the camp manager," Pedric said. "Spend the night there. But we decided that wasn't smart. If this guy discovered us gone, if he'd stopped for something and opened the bedroom, that would be the first place he'd look."

"So we took off hiking," Lucinda said. "We went a good way from the grounds in the dark. When we were off alone by the river, we made ourselves a little camp in the bushes where we could see there wasn't any poison oak."

"We lay listening for a while," Pedric said. "Then we curled up under the blanket like two spoons, and went to sleep."

Officer Hart was laughing. Officer Maconachy sat grinning. "You did right well," he said. "Very well, indeed."

"According to the news accounts," Pedric said, "he wrecked the rig about four hours later. We had no idea whether he searched the rig before that, whether he knew we were gone."

Pedric looked at the officers. "I can't say I'm pleased that he got out alive. Seems to me that would have been a nice turn of justice, if he had died instead of the tanker driver. We feel real bad about that."

Lucinda said, "We left the Saturn there in the camp-ground. We were afraid if we took it, that night or later, and he came back looking for us, we'd be easy to follow."

"The next morning," Pedric said, "we walked into Russian River. We were going to go to the sheriff, but then we decided that wasn't smart, either. Decided to stay hidden for a while. We rented a car, drove over to Fort Bragg, and checked into the oldest and most inconspicuous tourist place we could find. Stayed there for several nights, and when no one came snooping around we headed down this way."

"We have a friend here," Lucinda said. "We'll be here with her a day or two, then home to Molena Point."

"Will you give me those addresses?" Maconachy asked.

She gave them Wilma's address and phone number in the village; but when she told them Kate's address just a block away on Stockton, both officers were suddenly keen with an unspoken watchfulness.

Officer Hart said, "When did you last speak with Ms. Osborne?"

"What is it?" Lucinda said. She leaned forward studying the two officers. "What's happened? We called last night. I didn't talk with her; I left a message on her machine. Oh my God. What's happened?"

"She's all right, she's fine," said Officer Hart quickly. "She had a break-in last night. Someone trashed her place."

Both officers watched them intently.

"What time was this?" Pedric said.

"Late afternoon or early evening. She got home and

found it around eight-thirty," said Hart. "Totally destroyed the place, overturned and broke the furniture. They were after some jewelry."

Lucinda looked quietly back at them, then hurried out to the car. She returned carrying her cell phone, shaking her head. There were no messages.

"She surely would have told us," Lucinda said. "Maybe she called our motel in Fort Bragg and left a message there. When we went to bed, we turned the ringer down. Maybe she left a message with the motel and somehow, checking out, we didn't get it."

The officers sat filling in their reports while Lucinda called Kate. Kate answered on the first ring.

"Kate? Are you all right?"

"I'm fine, Lucinda. My line was out last night. I didn't get your message until late. Where are you? I'm so eager to see you. The place is a terrible mess but I've straightened up the guest room—I think you'll be comfortable. Have you had breakfast? You did get my message? Where are you?"

"We're just down the street. No, we didn't get your message, but we know what happened. I'll explain when we see you. Do you know who broke in? Did you see anyone?"

"I know who she is," Kate said.

"It wasn't a man? You didn't see a man?"

"A man *has* been following me, Lucinda. Why? He stopped following for a while, and I'd hoped it was over. But now he's back. How do you— Why do you ask?"

"What does he look like?"

"He . . . he looks like that waiter. In the village. At Charlie's gallery opening. I told you about that. The waiter who—"

"The waiter who died," Lucinda said. "Yes, Captain Harper called us. Sammy Clarkman. I told Harper his name, and where we met him, but I didn't know anything more about him." She glanced at the attentive officers. "Clarkman died in Molena Point, of a days-old trauma," she told them. And, to Kate, "We'll be there within the hour, see you then."

"The man we saw this morning," she told the officers, "the man who broke into our RV, he surely looked like that waiter. Clarkman died two weeks ago, while serving at a gallery opening. Kate says that would describe, as well, the man who followed her.

"We met Sammy in Russian River a few months ago, when he was waiting tables at the hotel. Then in Molena Point we saw him at Jolly's Deli. Well, he helped cater the exhibit of a friend of ours there. He died while serving drinks, just fell over dead. The coroner said from a days-old blow to the head. He looked enough like the man who stole our RV to be his brother."

Officer Maconachy said, "Can you tell me the date of the opening?"

Lucinda thought a minute. "October twenty-fourth. A Sunday night."

He watched her thoughtfully. "Do you know anything about Clarkman, how long he lived in Russian River, or in Molena Point?"

"No, I'm sorry. Nor do I know what took him away from Russian River."

"Do you know if he ever lived here in the city?"

"He didn't mention living here. I don't remember that he mentioned San Francisco at all."

Maconachy rose. "After you've met your friend,

would you come down to the station and talk with the detective who's been in touch with Mendocino County? He'll want to hear what you have to say."

As the officers headed away, and the Greenlaws stepped to the desk to cancel their reservation, just a few miles south Clyde Damen approached the city driving a borrowed Cadillac sedan that was heavier and thus safer on the road than his antique roadster. On the seat beside him, Joe Grey stood with his paws on the dash, looking out at the approaching city with deep interest.

## 26

The time was 9:30, the morning sun burning off the last of the valley fog as Clyde and Joe Grey approached San Francisco. They had left the house at 7:30. The Cadillac still smelled new though it was a year old, a trade-in that Clyde had borrowed from the dealership with which his automotive shop shared space. A car more reliable on the freeway at high speed than Clyde's dozen vintage antiques, most of which were tucked away in the back garage awaiting Clyde's further attention in therapeutic engine mechanics, body smoothing, and, ultimately, cosmetic detailing and bright new paint. The sun, rising ahead of them, drenched the San Francisco skyline, offering, to Joe Grey, a far more inviting view of the city than the dim, garbage-strewn alleys of his kittenhood.

Peering out, Joe thought about the Greenlaws turning up alive, about Kate's trashed apartment, and about Marlin Dorriss's various enterprises. If these matters were connected, the thread that bound them was tangled enough to give anyone a headache. Quietly he glanced at Clyde—his housemate was in a better mood since he'd downed some caffeine; in San Jose they'd made a pit stop, picking up a cup of coffee, a cinnamon bun, and, for Joe, a quarter-pounder, hold the pickles and lettuce. Joe had taken care of his own pit stop under a tree behind the fast food emporium while Clyde kept an eye out for dogs, and they were on the road again. Their argument this early morning over whether Joe should accompany him had been stressful for them both.

Clyde said the San Francisco streets were dangerous for a cat. Had pointed out that Joe hadn't survived those streets very well as a young cat, that Clyde had rescued him from the gutter, half dead. Joe said he'd gotten along just fine until his tail got broken, and that on this present junket he did not expect to be running the city's back streets and alleys.

"You damn near died in that gutter."

"I'm not going back to the gutter."

Clyde had maintained there was nothing Joe could do in San Francisco to help Kate. Joe reminded him that Azrael was there harassing Kate and that Clyde, despite his many talents, was not skilled at getting up the sides of buildings or slipping through cat-size openings to chase a surly tomcat. But the fact remained that Clyde was deeply concerned about Kate. Joe watched his housemate with interest. His sense was that, no matter how much Clyde was put off by Kate's unusual feline talents, no matter how she had distanced herself from him romantically, they needed each other very much as friends.

The two went back a long way. They had been good

friends while Kate and Jimmie were married. The three were often together, though even then Clyde and Kate seemed close, laughing and having fun together and enjoying Clyde's various pets, while Jimmie hated cats and had always seemed the odd man out. Jimmie had often been sarcastic and patronizing to Kate, and that hadn't gone down well with Clyde.

It seemed to Joe that, when the beginning romance between Clyde and Kate went so quickly awry, the feelings that remained had slowly mellowed into a deep and needful friendship. And that was nice. Friendship between two of opposite sexes, without the need to crawl into bed, was one of the values of human civility and intelligence that Joe Grey had come to admire.

Joe did not reveal to Clyde his real reason for demanding to accompany him to the city, and that had deepened their early morning conflict. And of course Clyde had said, "What about Dulcie and the kit? Don't you think they'll be mad as hell when they find out we ran off to San Francisco without them? With all Dulcie's dreams of spending a weekend at the St. Francis? Of shopping at Saks and I. Magnin? As Dulcie would put it, like a grand human lady?"

"So I'll buy them a present from Magnin," Joe had said irritably, and that had been the end of the matter. Clyde had only glared at him, so annoyed himself that he'd refused to call Kate to tell her he was on the way. He said she'd only fuss at him.

But now, as they pulled into the city and Clyde

headed for Kate's apartment—with no other destination intended—Joe's thoughts were racing. He watched Clyde narrowly.

"I guess San Francisco PD should have a search warrant by now," Joe said. "I guess they'll be searching Dorriss's condo—Harper said he'd call the judge early." He watched Clyde appraisingly. "Maybe they've already found the Packard."

Clyde turned to look at Joe. "We didn't come up here to look for the Packard. That is so unrealistic, to think it's in the city. We came to help Kate, to give Kate moral support. What makes you think my car would be hidden in San Francisco?"

Joe shrugged. A subtle twist of his gray shoulders, a flick of his ears. "Call it cat sense."

*"What?"*

"That sixth sense the authorities talk about."

"What authorities?"

"Cat authorities. People who study cats, who write about our ability to sense an earthquake before it happens, or a storm or hurricane. Same thing."

Clyde glared at him, almost missing a red light, slamming on the brakes. "What's so great about that? A weatherman can predict storms and hurricanes."

"He can't predict an earthquake. He can't feel a storm in his paws like I can."

"A weatherman doesn't *have* paws," Clyde shouted.

"Same with the Packard," Joe said. "I have this really strong sense that it's here in the city. And I'm not the only one. Max Harper thinks it could be at the Dorriss condo. And Captain Harper is not given to what you call foolish notions." Joe looked hard at Clyde. "It wouldn't hurt to look. We could just—"

"We can't *just* anything. We're here for Kate, not on some pointless chase. Not to get involved in some police investigation that is absolutely none of our business and where we'd be in the way. If there's anything the cops hate, it's civilians messing around a search, not to mention some nosy tomcat."

"Dorriss's condo has to have a garage. If Harper's right, your precious Packard could be sitting there just waiting for you." He looked intently at Clyde. "The cops get to it first and haul it away to their lockup, no telling what kind of damage they'll inflict. What do they know about classic cars? Dent a fender, break one of those windows that you had such a hard time finding . . ."

"The police are trained to take care of valuable evidence."

Joe Grey smiled.

Heading up Stockton, Clyde tried to call Kate. She didn't answer her home phone or her cell phone. He hung up without leaving a message. "Maybe she's meeting Lucinda and Pedric, or they're out to breakfast." He glanced at Joe. "You think, if the Packard was there in Dorriss's garage, that some uninformed rookie might manhandle it? I'm not saying it is there, I'm . . ."

"The Dorriss condo isn't far, just up Marina."

Clyde tried Kate again. This time he left a message. "We're headed for your place, Kate. Going to stop up on Marina. Be along shortly." And again Joe Grey smiled.

As Clyde turned up toward Marina, his mind on his 1927 Packard roadster, just a few blocks ahead Kate and Lucinda and Pedric, in the Greenlaws' rental car, were heading for breakfast at one of the intriguing restaurants in Ghirardelli Square. The Greenlaws were far too hungry to stop by the San Francisco PD before breakfast.

Canceling their hotel reservation but paying a one-night penalty, the Greenlaws had arrived at Kate's apartment knowing that she'd had a break-in, but still shocked at the extent of the damage. Wading among the remains of what had been a handsome living room, stepping over lovely brocade cushions torn apart among broken pieces of cherry end tables, among upholstery stuffing scattered like snow, Lucinda shook her head. "Did they have to tear it up like this? What was the point?"

"Scum doesn't need a reason," Pedric said angrily. The old man seldom raised his voice. Now his words were filled with rage. Threading their way between Kate's hand-thrown lamps that stood on the floor where she had righted them, stepping carefully around heaps of designer's catalogs and fabric books tangled beneath the overturned couch and chairs, the couple made their way to the dining table, where Kate had coffee waiting.

She had cleared a space for them, had wiped off the chairs and table. Lucinda and Pedric sat down gratefully, breathing in the welcome scent of a good Colombian brew. Kate filled their mugs and passed a plate of shortbread and the cream and sugar. Lucinda considered the empty cardboard cartons heaped against the wall, and against the dining-room window, a collection of vodka, gin, tomato sauce, paper towel, and soup boxes.

"I just got back," Kate said, "snatched them from the corner market before they broke them down. Made two trips and I'm still out of breath, hauling them up the stairs. I'm going to have to start working out."

"That woman did all this?" Lucinda said. "Consuela, and that man? What kind of people are these?" She looked intently at Kate. "What do they want? Not a handful of fake jewels?"

"I don't any longer believe that those jewels are paste," Kate said. "But why would that appraiser . . . Emerson Bristol . . . He has such a good reputation. At least . . . I thought he did." She studied their thin, lined faces. "Even if I've been overly casual in some ways, I did use some caution. I gave him a false address. On a hunch, I guess. I don't really know why. Some little niggling feeling—not that it did any good apparently, as he had me followed anyway. Or someone did."

Kate sipped her coffee. "After being married to Jimmie, thinking it was a good marriage, I guess I lost faith in my own judgment. I sure lost faith in the apparent trustworthiness of other people."

She shook her head. "With that attitude, you'd think I'd have checked out the appraiser. But I believed fully in the knowledge of those who recommended him. Then, too, it was hard to imagine that anything of great value would be tucked away in that old safe all those years, nearly thirty years."

Lucinda nodded. Pedric looked as if he found nothing really surprising, only another interesting twist in the intricate fabric of the world. Pedric Greenlaw had seen a lot in his eighty-some years. He expected, before he died, to see a good deal more.

"I suppose," Kate said, "every few years someone in

the firm asked about the box in the safe, hauled it out and read the note again, checked whatever records they kept, then shoved the box back out of the way. Without the note tucked in the box, who knows what would have happened."

Kate refilled their coffee cups. "I have the name of another appraiser. I called Detective Garza this morning. He said San Francisco PD uses this man, and so do the San Francisco courts. Garza has complete trust in him. Steve Tiernan. Too bad I don't have the pieces now to take to him. Who knows if I'll ever get them back. But I wondered if you might like to have your own jewelry appraised, since the work is so very similar."

"We would like to do that," Lucinda said.

Kate fetched her sweater, and as they headed out to breakfast in the Greenlaws' rental car, Lucinda told her about the black cat that the young woman at the hotel had had with her.

"That has to be Consuela," Kate said. "So that's where she was staying. How convenient—the cat could come right across the roofs. I wonder where they've gone now. The cat was in here last night, it's that beast from Molena Point. Azrael, the tomcat that ran with old Greeley Urzey."

Lucinda shook her head. "Not just some ordinary cat."

"The cat broke in, then let Consuela in. Long after she left to come and find me, Azrael stayed behind. When I got home, after Consuela left me, that animal was sitting right there on the overturned couch staring at me."

"And what did he want?" Pedric said.

"He wanted me to help him. It was so . . . I'd think it funny, except that he terrifies me. He talked about some kind of hidden world that—"

The minute she said it, she was sorry. Both Lucinda and Pedric turned to stare at her. Lucinda drove in silence for some time. She was about to turn into Ghirardelli Square's parking garage when she spotted a space on the street. Parking, she said, "Did the beast imply that the *jewelry* came from some . . . hidden world? Did he say that, Kate?"

Before Kate could answer, Pedric said, "A world beneath the green hills." His thin, lined face was so intent. His eyes never left hers. Kate had to remind herself that this old man had grown up on the ancient Celtic tales, that those myths were an important part of his heritage.

"A world entered through a cave," Pedric said, "or through a door, or through a portal into a hill. A door that, in the old country, might be found hidden at the back of a root cellar."

Kate wanted to say, *Those are only stories, Pedric. Ancient, made-up stories.* But she couldn't say that to him. She glanced at Lucinda. The old woman touched her hand.

"Joe and Dulcie and Kit are real," Lucinda said. "In their amazing talents of speech and understanding, they are very real. Yet most everyone in the world would say that such a thing is impossible, that such a cat can be no more than myth."

The old lady cracked the windows so they could sit in comfort for a few minutes. Above them, the old brick buildings rose among their newer skylights and glass roofs, a charming complex of shops and restaurants where, it seemed, nothing bad could happen. Above the tall steps that rose from the sidewalk they could glimpse the courtyard restaurants and little shops that filled the three stories of the old chocolate factory; delights meant to be enjoyed in a safe and ordered world. But within the car hung the hoary shadows of a chaotic environment, and it seemed to Kate that around her writhed dark myths, chill and threatening.

Looking at Kate, Pedric said gruffly, "The kit believes in another world than this. All her short life she has longed for that world."

But then the old man smiled and shook his head. "Joe Grey wants nothing to do with such an idea. Joe says this world is quite enough for him. Let's go have some breakfast."

But, over breakfast, Kate could not leave such thoughts behind her. The Greenlaws had stirred anew her unease, mixed with the persistent small thread of interest. She thought about the black cat, about the old house he believed opened to that other world, thought how deftly the snarling tom had guided her unwilling thoughts. Last night after his visit to her apartment she had found herself, just at the edge of sleep, imagining such a world and falling into dreams where she wandered that exotic land—and she had awakened that morning lost and frightened.

Now, sitting comfortably at the little breakfast table between Lucinda and Pedric in the pretty café, she took Lucinda's hand, holding fast to the old woman's steadiness, holding fast to the real and solid world.

# 27

Marlin Dorriss's condo was in the Marina District with a fine view of the Golden Gate Bridge, Alcatraz Island, and the cold blue waters of San Francisco Bay. The complex was prime residential property and beautifully maintained. The sky to be seen from the condo's wide, clean windows this morning was streaked with wisps of white cloud that lay so low they threaded through the tall orange towers of the great bridge. The occupants of the condo, at the moment, were not enjoying the view but were cursing the brightness of the day.

The prominent location of the sprawling third-floor apartment was not an element that pleased them. Cops cruised that street routinely; and twenty minutes ago a silver gray Cadillac had parked across the street but no one had gotten out. Under the shadows of the tree that half hid the vehicle, they couldn't tell much about the man sitting in the driver's seat, but he had to be watching their building.

"Marlin could have bought a place away from the

main drag," Hollis growled. "There's another cop car."

Consuela shrugged. "Maybe they're watching the tourists, getting an eyeful of those short little skirts blowing up around their crotches, and no bras under their sweaters."

"Cops seen all that stuff. And you had to park right in plain view. Might as well put up a sign."

"They won't spot the car; they have no make on the car."

"She's got a make on it. How many blue Corvettes do you see? You should'a done her."

"That's so childish. I don't do things like that; that's stupid. I'd rather spend a few years locked up with free meals, free phone, and laundry service, than to burn."

"You don't burn in California. Get a lawyer, you're out before your clothes start to stink."

"If you'd find the key to the garage, we could get the car out of sight."

"*You* should know where he keeps the key, you spend enough time here. I'm surprised you stayed in that fancy hotel across town."

"That place was perfect, a block from her apartment." She glanced up to the top of the armoire. "Damn cat liked it fine. In and out of her window, and I didn't even have to open the door for him."

From atop the armoire, the damn cat fixed Consuela with a look that came close to doing *her*. If looks could kill, she would be squirming like a decapitated cockroach.

Hollis, picking up a cloisonné lamp that stood on a carved end table, put it roughly on the floor, and sat down on the table, straddle-legged, looking out the window to the street below. Munching on a quarter-pounder, he dripped an occasional slop of mustard and greasy meat juice onto the oriental rug. Consuela, sprawled in a leather chair beside the phone, munched French fries and chicken nuggets that she had dumped onto a porcelain tray and sipped a Coke, leaving rings on the burled maple. She had been dialing Marlin Dorriss's cell phone for half an hour. They had dropped their jackets and canvas duffel and the takeout bags on the brocade couch.

The condo, which had smelled subtly of furniture polish and fine leather when they first entered, now smelled of fries and mustard, rancid grease and raw onions. Atop the tall, hand-decorated Belgian armoire, the black tomcat had already slurped up his burger. Digging his claws into the hundred-year-old cabinet, he studied Consuela and her disgusting friend, wondering how long he wanted to tolerate the pair. He didn't mind working with Consuela, this randy master of shifting identities, as long as she was associated with Dorriss. Only under Dorriss's influence—or because she wanted to influence Dorriss—did the little slut put on any class. She'd far rather dress like a streetwalker than make herself up for Kate Osborne, even if her turnout had been nearly flawless.

Hollis, on the other hand, was always scum. No one could clean up Hollis Dorriss or make him into anything more acceptable. No wonder Marlin had all but disowned his useless pair of sons. No wonder he preferred that they go by the name Clarkman.

Dorriss had used them whenever they came around, then paid them off and sent them packing. Now of course he had only one to deal with, and good rid-

dance. That last fiasco, here in the city—Sammy team-
ing up with that cheap gang of third-rate jewel thieves
and getting hit on the head—that had been the ultimate
stupidity. Sure as hell it was Sammy's ultimate stupidity; that little caper got him dead.

But then Hollis flubbed it even worse stealing that
RV and hitting that tanker. Too bad the jerk got out
alive. Well, it didn't matter; Hollis was just marking
time until some cop slapped the cuffs on him—jail
meat waiting to happen.

You'd think, with the number of ventures the two
had tried, they'd have put away some kind of stash. Instead, Hollis and Sammy had spent whatever they
stole. Having done everything from residential break-
and-enter to mugging old ladies, the two hadn't
learned much. He'd heard it all from Dorriss; the man
did not seem the kind to go on about his personal life,
particularly to a cat. But a few drinks, late at night, and
Dorriss's soft underbelly showed. The sophistication
peeled away and he let it all out, his disappointments—
and his grandiose and elaborate plans.

Well, you had to admit, those carefully thought-out
burglary scenarios were not hot air. Marlin Dorriss
could pull off the most bizarre operation without a
flaw—thanks, in part, to yours truly. Azrael was quite
aware that he had spectacularly increased the range
and possibilities of Marlin Dorriss's ventures.

Fixing his gaze on the display wall that so tastefully
filled the north end of the living room, on Dorriss's ex-
hibition of rarities as he called it, Azrael studied Dorriss's acquisitions from a year's worth of inspired and
masterful burglaries: a fortune in stolen treasures.

Each piece of jewelry was elegantly framed, behind unbreakable glass. Each larger item, the historic silver pitcher, the antique porcelain pieces, the contemporary sculpture, was appropriately set into a thick glass cubicle. A display so elegant, and of such value, that it might have graced the wall of Tiffany's. The man was insane to keep the stuff here, even if the wall was normally hidden behind locked panels. He had been insane to give Consuela the combination of the panel locks—if he had given it to her. Maybe she'd filched it.

The four panels, each four feet wide, had been slid back into their pockets allowing Consuela to view the master's work—not because she idolized Dorriss's expertise, but because she'd had a hand in the thefts. Traveling with Dorriss and Azrael, performing various supportive chores, she had played backup as Azrael himself and then Dorriss entered the chosen residence. Between the tomcat and Dorriss, no security system was invulnerable.

Once inside the house, a diamond choker in a lady's boudoir, for instance, required no more than the silent feline paw, the quick feline wit, while Dorriss kept watch. A locked safe? There Dorriss himself was the master. Consuela did the outside work, waiting with the car or SUV, keeping lookout with the cell phone, which would send a silent vibration to Dorriss's phone.

Of course, if their target was a painting or a larger piece of sculpture, Dorriss did the removal. But he could not have functioned so flawlessly without Azrael's unique talents.

The black cat yawned, licking his paw and purring with satisfaction. He liked this life of luxury. Since he had parted from drunken Greeley Urzey, and then from the insipid blonde he'd met in Panama, he had come into his true calling. Marlin Dorriss treated him royally, and Dorriss fully respected his erudite and resourceful talents. The man was quite cognizant that Azrael's feline skills were far superior to the cleverest human thief. Trusting Azrael, Dorriss had no idea that his feline partner might harbor an agenda of his own.

Both Azrael and Dorriss had been intrigued with the photographs of Kate's antique jewelry that had been forwarded by Emerson Bristol; Dorriss was certainly considering the jewels for a future project. He had no notion, at this moment, that the matter had already been taken care of.

While Consuela's hunger to curry Dorriss's increased favor was totally juvenile, her desire had made her useful. Her stealing these jewels for Dorriss rather than for herself had worked very well into his, Azrael's, plans.

And after all, it was Consuela's jealousy of Helen Thurwell—after Consuela played matchmaker between the two—that had driven her to this theft, that had made her so wild to impress him.

Suggesting that Dorriss use information he could gather by getting friendly with Helen Thurwell, Consuela herself had helped to launch Dorriss into this new operation. But then his resulting cozy affair with Helen had enraged Consuela. Humans could be so amusing.

Well, that series of capers, which had nothing to do with the recent jewel theft, was now ripe for harvest. In fact, this very morning Dorriss should be making his first moves.

Too bad the plan for the new project did not include

feline assistance. However, the timing had worked out
very well. While Dorriss was busy fleecing a flock of
brand-new sheep, he, Azrael, was carrying out his own
agenda. He might, a few days hence, be exercising his
considerable talents in an environ far more fascinating
than this poor world. Yawning again, he was considering a nap when Consuela and Hollis started bickering.
So boring, so loud and childish.

Beyond them out the window he could see another
cop car cruising. Didn't the law have anything else to
do? Bastards made him nervous. He was just curling
up, despite the annoying argument, when the doorbell
rang.

Alarmed, he dropped off the armoire and leaped to
the windowsill where Consuela stood looking down,
trying to conceal herself behind the shutter. A second
cop car stood just below, in the red zone. The bell rang
again. Consuela glanced at her purse where she'd
stashed the jewels.

"The panels!" Azrael hissed at her. "Shut the panels."

Hastily she and Hollis slid the wall panels in place
and locked them, then she stood with her hand on the
intercom, undecided.

"You better let them in and play dumb," Azrael said.
"Stash the jewels first."

"What are they doing here?"

"Maybe they have a warrant," Hollis said stupidly.
"Maybe that woman made you, figured out who you
are, linked you up with Dorriss—and that led them
right here."

"Linked *you* up with Dorriss," Consuela snapped.
"*You're* his son."

The bell rang again. Consuela snatched up her purse, pulled out the small blue evening bag that held the jewels, and looked at Azrael. The tomcat looked back at her, jolted by a rush of adrenaline. This gig was working out just fine.


In the silver Cadillac, on the front seat beside Clyde, Joe Grey stood up on his hind paws peering through the windshield. The condo building was of Mediterranean design and was fairly new, with well-maintained gardens and fresh cream-toned paint. It was lent an air of hominess by the many roses blooming in raised planters against the building's walls and in the entry foyer. He watched the two officers from San Francisco PD enter. The taller one, who was in uniform, reached to ring the bell. The other guy was in plainclothes, but he had cop written all over him. Detective, Joe thought, smiling. A moment after they rang, at a third-floor window, a black cat appeared beside the dark-haired woman who stood half concealed behind the shutters. The cat was huge, as black as cinders; the woman's hair was curled in a cloud around her pale face. The way the morning light struck the window and shone down through a skylight, Joe could see clearly a portion of the high-ceilinged room behind them.

As the woman turned away, Joe watched her sliding some sort of wide panels across an elaborately decorated wall. He saw light hit the decorations glancing from them in a flash of brilliance, then they were hidden as the panels closed.

In the window, the cat moved as if trying to see better down into the street. When he pressed his face against the glass as if watching their car, Joe slid out of sight beneath the dash.

Beside him, Clyde had the phone to his ear, leaving another message for Kate. Hanging up, he studied the black cat in the window, then looked down at Joe. "You're afraid of that clown?"

"Not at all," Joe said testily. "I don't want him to know I'm here. Whatever they're up to, I'd rather not be made before I go snooping. Did Consuela let the cops in? What's the cat doing, can you still see him?"

"You're not going out there. You're staying in the car." But Clyde dug the binoculars from the glove compartment. "I came over here to look for my Packard, not to chauffeur some self-designated feline busybody bent on making trouble."

Joe slid up on the seat again. The two cops had disappeared, presumably buzzed through to the stairs or elevator. The black cat had vanished, too. Stepping onto Clyde's legs, Joe was prepared to leap out the open window, when Clyde grabbed the nape of his neck.

"Let go! I'm just listening!" With his head out the window, he tried to catch a word or two when Consuela opened the upstairs door to the officers, but he could hear nothing over the sound of a passing car. Glancing back at Clyde, he lifted a paw, claws out, until Clyde sensibly loosened his grip.

Having closed and locked the panels, Consuela shoved the blue suede evening bag at Azrael. "Get in the bedroom. If they start to search, take it up the trellis. Hide it on the roof."

"You better unlock the French doors." Azrael lifted the bagful of jewelry, bowing his neck. Damn thing weighed a ton. She fled past him for the bedroom; he heard the French doors open. As he dragged the bag up the hall, she hurried out again.

"Get a move on," she snapped over her shoulder. "If I don't let them in, and if the bastards have a warrant, they'll call the manager to unlock the damn door."

Taking the bag in his teeth, he dragged it across the bedroom and onto the balcony. The weight of all that gold nearly dislocated his spine. How did she think he was going to get that thing up the trellis? Damn humans. As much as he wanted a few select pieces, he didn't need to take it all, not for his purposes.

But there was no time to try to dig the bag open. Chomping down securely on the blue suede, he leaped onto the trellis and tried to climb.

The trellis was a frail thing, and the vine was just as thin, hardly strong enough to hold a good-size sparrow.

A sturdy enough pine tree stood beyond the window, its branches rising above the building, but the trunk was too far away for a leap, even without his burden. If the cops arrested Consuela and Hollis, he had two choices. He could secure the jewelry for Dorriss, and could pretty much write his own ticket: hide the bag on the roof and, when the law finished searching the condo and took away those two losers, call Dorriss. What could be easier?

Or he could choose the most impressive piece or

two, a bracelet or choker that would fit around his neck perhaps. Dump the rest on the roof for the pigeons, then go on to follow his own plans.

Dragging his burden off the trellis onto the clay roof tiles, he could hear, below, businesslike voices from the living room as the cops questioned Consuela.

## 28

The binoculars had been Joe's idea. Clyde had to admit, the 7×35 lenses gave him a sharp, almost intimate view through the third-floor window of the condo where Consuela and the uniformed officer stood talking. "I don't see the plainclothes guy."

"See the cat?"

"Not a sign of him."

That made Joe nervous. "What are they doing in there? Wish you could lip read. Why don't you call Harper, see if he got the warrant, see if that's what this *is* about."

Clyde lowered the binoculars, looking at Joe. "Harper doesn't need to know I'm here. And how would *I* know about a warrant?"

"Just play dumb. Tell him you came up to the city because you were worried about Kate—tell him the truth, Clyde. He doesn't need to know what else you're interested in, or where you are at this particular moment."

"So when I tell him I came up to see Kate, he's going to offer gratis information about a search being conducted by San Francisco PD?"

"Feel him out, draw him out. You can do that. Maybe those guys are just fishing—that's more than *we* had time to do."

Their plan had been to walk through the complex trying to see into the garages that occupied the first floor beneath the apartments. They'd thought maybe there'd be windows in the back. But they hadn't had time to look for the Packard before they saw Consuela and the black tomcat, and then the cops showed. Now, as the uniformed officer moved out of sight, Clyde's cell phone rang.

"Damen," he said softly. Then, "Where are you?"

Joe leaped to the back of the seat to press his ear to the phone. Kate was saying, "We're at Ghirardelli Square for breakfast, waiting for our order. I've made an appointment with an appraiser, for Lucinda's jewelry, just before noon. I just stepped outside to do that, and to check my messages; the shops and little gardens are so beautiful. You didn't have to come, Clyde. Where are you?"

"Just up from you, opposite the yacht harbor. Do you—Hold on."

Above them in the condo, Consuela had left the window. But the black cat had appeared at the other end of the condo on a balcony. Clyde felt Joe's claws digging into his shoulder as together they watched Azrael climb up a bougainvillea vine, clawing his way toward the roof. The black cat moved slowly, dragging something heavy that was dangling from his clenched teeth. "What is that thing?" Clyde said. "Something blue. Looks like a woman's purse."

On the phone, Kate gasped, "That's . . ."

But Joe was out the window, slashing Clyde's hand when Clyde tried to grab him, dropping to the street behind a passing car. He could hear Kate shouting into the phone as Clyde bailed out behind him, swerving into the path of a cab. Joe was safely across when tires squealed, and then Clyde was across, yelling as Joe headed for the end of the building where a pine tree rose, as bare as a telephone pole, its high, faraway branches brushing the roof where Azrael had disappeared.

Storming up the tree, Joe leaped for the roof, his claws scrabbling and slipping on the slick, rounded tiles. Ahead of him among a maze of heating vents and chimneys a black tail flashed and was gone. Watching for the tomcat to show again, Joe studied the shadows among the rooftop machinery.

Joe waited for some time, then slipped in among the pipes and wire mesh boxes, sniffing the air. All he could detect was the smell of machine oil, ocean, and fish from the wharves.

But then, where the shadows of two chimneys converged, he saw a faint movement. He remained still, his heart pounding.

Azrael appeared suddenly, leaping to the top of a wire cage. Dropping the blue bag between his paws, he hunched low over it, watching Joe. Crouched in attack mode, his amber eyes were slitted, his teeth bared. At this moment, against the sky, he looked as huge and fierce as if the beast did, indeed, bear the blood of jaguars as he boasted.

Warily, Joe approached him. As he rounded on Azrael, he heard from the apartment below a crash that sounded like furniture breaking, heard Consuela swear, then a softer thud, and one of the cops shouted. At the same instant, Joe made a flying leap onto the mesh box and straight into Azrael's claws. Burying his teeth in the tomcat's shoulder, he bit and raked, ripping his hind claws down Azrael's side. Azrael, twisting with the power of a thrashing boa, bit into Joe's belly. Below them glass shattered, a cop barked an order, and then silence, sudden and complete.

Coming at Joe with all the screaming power of an enraged jaguar, Azrael slashed at Joe's face; Joe tasted blood. Clawing at each other, the two toms slid across the tiles rolling and scrabbling. And as Joe leaped for the black cat's throat, the pounding of hard shoes came running, sliding, and Clyde loomed over them, diving for Azrael. Azrael gave a violent surge that hurled Joe sideways, slashed Clyde's arm, and twisted out of Clyde's hands, snatching the bag where it had fallen among the shadows.

Weighted by his burden, Azrael sailed off the roof into the overhanging branches of the pine and was gone, scorching down in a shower of pine bark. Joe streaked down after him, hitting the ground with a thud that knocked his wind out. Already Azrael was half a block away flashing through the condo gardens and up the hill at the back, his neck bowed sideways as he dragged the blue suede bag. As Joe leaped after him, he heard Clyde running across the roof above, and down wooden stairs somewhere at the back.

And as Joe fled after the black tom, intent on Kate's vanishing jewels, down the coast in Molena Point, Dulcie and Kit lay quietly in Detective Juana Davis's office observing a material witness to the death of James Quinn. Listening to the woman who, though in part responsible for the real estate agent's demise, seemed without knowledge of that fact.

Dulcie lay curled in Juana's in box as unmoving as a sleek toy cat. Across the desk from her, the kit lay sprawled across a stack of reports, belly up, fluffy tail dangling over the edge of the desk, her long fur tumbled in all directions like a ragged fur piece. Detective Davis sat at her desk between the two cats, apparently amused by the pair, making no effort to evict them. Across from her, settled at one end of the couch, Helen Thurwell looked up at Davis, calm, composed, and puzzled.

"I thought I'd told Detective Garza everything that might help," Helen was saying. "It wasn't much, but . . . you're still thinking that it might not have been an accident? That someone *killed* James?"

Neither cat opened her eyes. Neither cat allowed her ears to rotate following the conversation. Both seemed deeply under, twitching occasionally as if wandering somewhere among mysterious feline dreams.

"I understand that this is painful," Juana was saying. "But I believe you can help. Quinn was your partner for how many years?"

"Nearly ten years," Helen said. "He was a good partner, always careful in his record keeping, always cordial and considerate of our clients, never impatient with them—never stepping on my toes in a transaction. You don't work with someone that long, and that closely, and not grow to care for them."

"No one is suggesting that there was any problem between you."

Dulcie slitted her eyes open just enough to watch Davis. Juana Davis was a no-nonsense sort of woman in her fifties, squarely built, with dark hair and dark eyes. She was a steady, commonsense person, but along the way she hadn't lost her sympathy for another human being. She was just very selective as to who deserved it. Dulcie thought that Juana was still making up her mind about Helen Thurwell.

On a hunch, Dulcie unwound herself from the in box, sat up yawning, and leaped to the couch to settle down beside Helen, curling up close to her, to see what she would do.

Davis's couch was old, tweed-covered, and smelled of cocker spaniel from some past life before she bought it at the Pumpkin Coach Charity Shop. The city did not pay for items the city fathers considered luxury purchases. Dulcie didn't see why a couch would be considered a luxury; but then, she wasn't the city manager. On the coffee table before Helen lay a thick briefcase. Before she reached for her files, Helen turned to stroke Dulcie.

She seemed to know how to pet a cat, so gentle and reassuring that Dulcie began to purr. Interesting that Helen wasn't this reassuring with her daughter—but then, maybe petting an animal helped to ease Helen's tension. And dealing with her daughter did not?

When at last Helen opened the briefcase, she removed a large black ledger. "This was what you wanted? The record of my work days?" Rising, she passed the ledger across the desk.

Juana opened it, studied several pages, and nodded. "Do all real estate agents keep this kind of record?"

Helen shook her head. "The agent who trained me,

the man I worked with when I first started out, he taught me to do that. He'd had a court case once where he had to testify about the specific circumstances of a sale. I guess it got pretty ugly. He couldn't be sure of some of the times involved and, as it was a murder case, he felt he hadn't been very helpful.

"Some of our documents are marked with the time of signing as well as dated; others are not. In a case like his, he'd had to go through them all, do the best he could to remember specifics. After that, he began to keep a log. He trained me to do that, and I've done it ever since." Helen looked at Juana inquiringly.

Rising, Juana moved to the credenza. Turning over two clean cups, she poured fresh coffee from a Krups coffeemaker. "Cream and sugar?"

"Neither please. Just black."

Setting one mug on the coffee table and the other on her desk, Juana picked up a sheaf of photocopies that lay on the blotter and stood looking down at Helen. "These are copies of the pages of a notebook." Juana handed the papers to Helen. "The original pages had been ripped in quarters. We taped them together and made copies, then locked them in the evidence room. Do you recognize the handwriting?"

Helen examined the first few pages. "It's James's handwriting. But these entries . . . these are the names of my clients." She looked up at Juana. "We both had our own clients. We simply worked backup for each other." She examined several more pages.

"I think these are the dates that offers were made, or maybe that a client went into escrow. I'd have to check the ledger." She looked up at Juana. "I don't understand. Why would James keep this? This information is all recorded in my ledger. And in the various papers that are on file."

"You notice the little symbols before each entry? What are those?"

Helen shook her head. "I don't know. Asterisk. Pound sign. Circle. Repeated over and over. I haven't any idea. I don't understand why James would keep any kind of list of my clients."

"Can you find any pattern? Remember any special circumstances about these particular meetings? Would the symbols indicate whether you met with the client in the office, or somewhere else? Whether anyone besides your office associates was present? Anything at all out of the ordinary?"

Helen studied the entries for some time, sipping her coffee. When she reached absently to pet Dulcie again, her hand had grown tense and cold. She sat a minute with her eyes closed, as if thinking. As if trying to remember, perhaps to make sure of something. When she looked up at Juana, her hand had grown very still on Dulcie's fur. And her cheeks were flushed.

"I think . . . I'm pretty sure there was someone in the office during each of these transactions."

Juana sat watching Helen, her square, tanned face impassive. Helen's hand on Dulcie's shoulder was so tense that under other circumstances Dulcie would have risen and moved away. Helen said, "Marlin Dorriss was . . . was in the office during each of these meetings. I'm sure of it. Waiting for me somewhere in the office."

Juana continued to watch her, in silence.

"Sometimes, he'd be sitting reading in a client's chair, beside some empty desk. Sometimes in one of the chairs against the wall just beyond my desk. You know how our office is, each desk with space enough to draw up chairs and sign papers, but no separate conference room for the signings."

"Anyone besides Marlin Dorriss?"

"No." Helen's face colored. "Waiting for me to go to lunch or maybe dinner."

Dulcie was pleased that Helen had the grace to feel ashamed.

"After your clients finished their business and left, did Marlin usually come on over to your desk?"

Helen looked surprised. "Yes, he did," she said thoughtfully. She gripped Dulcie's shoulder so hard that it was all Dulcie could do not to hiss. Dulcie watched Helen, fascinated.

Had Helen never once questioned Dorriss's presence in her office? Had she never wondered if Dorriss would snoop on a client's personal information that was all laid out on her desk? Dulcie imagined him retrieving bank names, memorizing street addresses, information from loan applications, social security numbers. Had he been able, as Helen turned away perhaps putting her papers in order, to jot down bank account numbers, business references, mother's maiden name—a regular buffet of vital information?

"When the clients left," Juana said, "and Dorriss came to your desk, their papers might be still lying there?"

"Yes," Helen said shakily. "Sometimes." She pressed a fist to her mouth. "But he wouldn't . . . He wouldn't have . . ." She realized she was clutching Dulcie, and took her hand away.

Juana said, "Do you have a restroom in the office?"

"Yes."

"Did he usually use it before you left for . . . lunch or whatever?"

"Always. But he . . . he is very careful about germs, almost a fetish."

*Right*, Dulcie thought. She could imagine Dorriss in the locked restroom busily recording all the vital information from Helen's clients. This smooth snooping had to be the setup for identity theft. She licked her paw, thinking.

Identity theft could go on for many months before the victim had any clue. Who knew how soon the recipients of such attention would wake to find their houses mortgaged or sold, their CDs cashed, their bank accounts stripped, and their credit destroyed? How many people had he already swindled?

And Dorriss had left town last night, had caught a flight somewhere. Setting out to transfer other people's funds, to collect cashier's checks secured by other people's real estate?

Dropping down from the couch she leaped to Juana's desk where she prowled innocently among the detective's stacked papers. Juana, watching her, moved her cup so as not to have cat hair or maybe a cat nose in her coffee. As Dulcie turned away she spotted it, lying on a stack of papers: The photocopy of a flight schedule, with the name of a local travel agency at the top, and Marlin Dorriss's name beneath.

Pretending to play, gently pawing at the papers, she studied the schedule. Dorriss or the agency had thoughtfully typed a cover sheet, a condensation, on one page, giving seven destinations and dates. The pages stapled behind it would surely give departure and arrival times, airline, airport, flight number. Well, the cover sheet was all she needed. She couldn't help it; she looked up at Davis, smiling and purring. Oh, the detective was on top of it; Detective Davis had run with her suspicions before ever interviewing Helen Thurwell. Dulcie could imagine Davis calling all the travel agents in town until she hit pay dirt.

Dorriss had flown out last night to LA. Two days in LA, then to San Diego where he'd pick up a car. He must be driving back up the coast, because the next flight was out of San Francisco, heading north. The itinerary gave not only flights and car rentals, but hotel reservations in Laguna, La Jolla, then Santa Barbara, and Sacramento, before he caught the San Francisco flight. The entire trip would take just under two weeks.

It must be nice to enjoy such a long working vacation. Was this another string of strange burglaries? Or a chorus of well-planned securities sales or purchases and bank withdrawals, all in names other than Marlin Dorriss?

Lying down on the desk, Dulcie watched as Juana rose to see Helen out. Helen looked pleadingly at Juana; she was very quiet now, very subdued, understanding at last that she had been the unwitting collaborator in a high-powered criminal undertaking. The detective put her arm around Helen. "We'll get to the bottom of this. You did nothing deliberately. Try not to worry."

"I was *deliberately* stupid," Helen said. "So criminally stupid that I got my partner killed." She looked miserably at Juana. "I have no doubt, now, that his death was not an accident."

She shook her head. "James was not careless, he would not have left the gas on like that. He was not forgetful, not even in the smallest matters." She found a tissue in her pocket and wiped her eyes. "I have been stupid for a very long time." She was crying in earnest, her shoulders shaking.

The expression on Juana Davis's face was a mixture of discomfort, sympathy, and a cop's restrained look of triumph. Taking her arm from around Helen, Juana touched Helen's shoulder, heading her into the hall.

And Dulcie, watching the two women, found it hard to muster much sympathy for Helen Thurwell. All the empathy in the tabby's heart was for Juana Davis as the detective set out on what could be a difficult task, heartbreaking for many more people than Helen Thurwell.

Dulcie knew, from listening to Dallas Garza and Captain Harper, that the crime of identity theft might be uncovered and the culprit apprehended; the perp might even be prosecuted, but the damage done might never be undone, the victims' money might never be recovered.

29

Streaking between the complex of condo buildings and up the hill behind, through the gardens of expensive estates, Joe drew nearer the black tom but then lost him again among a cluster of smaller homes. Racing past two houses that were still boarded up from the last earthquake, Joe paused in their neglected gardens seeking Azrael's scent.

There: the black beast appeared suddenly crossing the street while dragging his burden, leaping clear of a car. The cat was slowing and tiring. Swiftly Joe closed on him. He was about to leap and grab Azrael, when behind him a car slid across both lanes and screeched to the curb; Joe caught a glimpse of Lucinda bent over the wheel, and Pedric beside her. The back door opened and Kate slid out.

She caught Joe up, snatching him in mid-stride and kept running, chasing the black tom, clutching Joe to her so hard he could hardly breathe. Ahead of them Azrael was a smear of black swerving away from the street through the bushes and heavily over a fence.

Kate, running along the fence, found a gate and fought it open. Crossing the yard clutching Joe, she lost minutes finding the way out.

"Let me go, Kate! You've lost him!"

"No! I can catch him!" She glanced down at him, her blond hair plastered with sweat, her eyes frightened.

"He has the jewels," Joe coughed, half strangled. "Ease up, I can't breathe."

Tightening her grip on the back of his neck, she eased her hand on his chest. He gulped for air. "I didn't know you could run like that. How did you find us? Where's Clyde? Why are you . . . ?"

She didn't answer. Glimpsing Azrael swerving into an alley, she flew after him across someone's patio and through another garden. Lucinda's car was lost beyond the yards and fences. They passed a boarded-up house, then soon another, not derelicts but nice houses; Joe thought they were somewhere in Cow Hollow where there had been a lot of damage in the earthquake. Ahead on the sidewalk, the black tomcat appeared suddenly; he stood panting as if at the end of his strength, the blue bag at his feet. Joe tensed to leap down.

It was here that Lucinda found them and pulled to the curb. Azrael snatched up the bag and disappeared into the bushes, heading for a boarded-up house as Clyde's car swerved in behind Lucinda. Kate dropped Joe and lunged through the bushes after the black tom. The beast bolted up the steps and through a broken window between crookedly nailed boards, dragging the blue evening bag.

The faded Victorian house listed to the left, supported by a scaffolding of rough lumber all along one side. All the windows were secured with boards over the dirty and broken glass. Two boards were nailed across the front door, and there was a chain barrier across the front steps. The trim on the three stories was splintered along one side, and shingles had fallen into the bushes.

Slipping under the chain barrier, Kate was working at the doorknob and pushing at the door. The house must once have been a comfortable home for a big family. Joe wondered why these houses had been let sit for so long. Through the broken window where the black tomcat had gone, Joe could see pale shadows moving. Kate put her shoulder to the door, sent it flying open, ducked under the boards, and disappeared inside.

Warily Joe followed her. He didn't like the place; he didn't like its deep hollow silence. It smelled of something dank and foreign. As he moved up the steps, Clyde thudded up behind him. They entered together, Clyde ducking beneath the boards.

Only a dull light seeped through the dirty, boarded-up windows. They stood for a moment in the gloom, then moved on in, the floor creaking beneath Clyde's feet, the dry dust puffing up beneath Joe's paws—dust that was marked all over with paw prints. Beyond the dim living room, in what appeared to be the dining room, Kate stood facing a tall china cabinet that towered in the darkest corner, a folded mattress leaning up against it amid a tangle of ragged lumber.


Kate stood looking up through the shadows at the black tom. Crouching atop the tall cabinet he stared down at her, his amber eyes narrowing as if waiting for her to speak. The blue suede bag lay between his paws; he loomed over it, fiercely possessive. A split second and he could leap down squarely into her face, clawing and biting; his eyes blazed and threatened, making her tremble.

Around her the house was silent. It stunk of cat. Heaps of trash were piled in the dark corners, papers, wine bottles, beer cans. She thought there would be hordes of mice to feed the pale cats she'd seen slipping away. To her left a broken stairway led partway up to the floor above, where a ragged hole gaped. A pale cat peered down, then was gone, a cat that looked as hard of body as a dog, and with a lean killer's face. Beneath the stairs blackness loomed so dense, so complete that she felt as if the house floated in a void, as if the floor on which she stood had nothing but emptiness beneath. The room was cold, a coldness that went to the bone. Watching the cat, his hints of another world that had so stirred her dreams now filled her with fear. How could she have wanted any such world, how could she want any world to which this beast was drawn?

But she wanted her property back; she was not willing to turn away from what was hers. Moving closer in among the leaning boards, she thought that if she stood on the humped and folded mattress, she could reach the bag and snatch it away.

He watched as she began to climb, his smile slow and amused. And suddenly grabbing the bag in his mouth, he leaped directly past her face. She lunged, snatching the bag from his mouth—and felt claws like knives down her arm. The suede ripped open, too, under her spurting blood. The jewels spilled, falling away to vanish among the boards. Dropping down, she snatched at a bracelet, quickly kneeling among the boards reaching to catch the slithering chain of a locket. Snarling, the black tom came at her—and Joe Grey came flying, toppling boards and knocking Azrael among them. Jewelry scattered and fell between the fighting tomcats, lost in the rubble, hidden beneath falling boards.

Snatching up the emerald bracelet, Azrael spun and ran, leaping for the blackness beneath the stairs.

Kate rose to follow but Clyde grabbed her, drawing her back.

They stood at the edge of the hole staring down beneath the stairs into total blackness. They could see nothing, no hint of foundation, no broken timbers or tumbled earth. Only emptiness falling away, deep black space that seemed to go down and down as if it spread out beneath the house, black and endless, as if perhaps the quake had shifted the earth, leaving a cavern beneath that part of the house. Kate backed away, dizzy. Leaning against Clyde, she leaned against Joe Grey as well where Clyde had snatched him up, holding him safe from that abyss. In Clyde's arms Joe met her stare with the same deep fear that filled Kate herself; and from somewhere within the blackness, Azrael spoke to her.

"You would do well to follow me, Kate Osborne. You would do well to come with me." Was he crouched on some ledge or fallen timber that was invisible to her? She stared and stared but could see nothing, no glint of his yellow eyes. Then beside Kate something moved among the rubble, and from the shadows a pale cat leaped past her into the blackness, then another, an-

other—and they too vanished. And from deep within
that dank space, Azrael's purr rumbled. "You will forever regret your cowardice, Kate Osborne, if you stay
behind. You can see that they accept me now. Because I
took the jewels. Because I bear the emerald choker.
They will lead me now, down into that world." The cat
purred louder, his rumble echoing. "Come with me,
Kate Osborne. Come now . . ."

Kate backed farther away.

"If you will follow me, I will lead you home, Kate,
where hidden rivers run beneath the earth among green
meadows, where you can dig jewels from the cavern
walls, all the wealth you want, for the taking." A cold
breath touched Kate, a stink of damp sour earth as if
stirred by movement somewhere deep within that void.
And Azrael did not speak again.

She stared down into the empty dark that waited just
beneath her feet, and she turned away sickened, leaning into Clyde's steady grip. He pulled her away, putting his arm around her; she could feel Joe's heart
pounding fast between them. The relief on the tomcat's
face was comical.

Behind Clyde, Lucinda and Pedric stepped from the
shadows. Whatever they felt, whatever they had seen,
they did not speak. The four of them knelt, searching
for Kate's inheritance among the rubble and broken
lumber, while Joe Grey sat washing blood from his
paws.

Moving one splintered board at a time, they uncovered and retrieved nine pieces of the jewelry. When
Pedric got a flashlight out of his car and shone it under
the stairs, they could see only blackness, as if indeed,
beneath the house, a vast area of landfill had shifted

away, leaving the building on some earthquake-riven ledge. There was no sign of the choker, no answering flash of gold and green from those murky depths.

"Out," Kate whispered, backing away, the true sense of danger coming home to her. They moved swiftly out beneath the door's barrier, into the fresh air.

A police car was pulling to the curb. As Detective Reedie stepped out, Joe Grey slid from Clyde's arms into Lucinda's, and under her jacket, out of sight. And the old woman wandered away with him.

Kate, smoothing her disheveled hair, smiled at the detective and held out her folded sweater, in which she had wrapped the jewels and the shredded blue bag. "We have them!" she said breathlessly, trying to invent a plausible story that did not include a thieving black tomcat. "How did you find us?"

Reedie looked at the jewels and at her bleeding arm, at her dirty hands and streaked face. "I saw you running," the detective said warily, "from the window of the condo. What was that you were chasing? *A cat?* It was carrying that blue bag?" The handsome young detective looked hard at her. "You want to tell me what happened?"

Kate didn't know what to say. He watched her, waiting. His thatch of brown hair made that handsome face look even more boyish; his brown eyes looked half angry at being scammed, half filled with curiosity.

"I saw Consuela's car," she said, "we were coming back from breakfast. The blue Corvette? I pulled over, hoping it was hers, and saw something running—a big black cat—from under a pine tree at the end of the condo. I couldn't believe . . . It was dragging something blue. My bag, I knew it was my bag. I just . . . jumped out of the car and ran."

The detective turned, glancing toward Clyde. "And your friend in the silver Cadillac?"

He had obviously seen Clyde parked in front of the condo. Kate explained that Clyde had seen the Corvette, too, that he had been sitting in his car watching the building where it was parked, wondering if it belonged to Consuela. She was faltering when Clyde took over.

Clyde seemed truly amazed that the cat had grabbed the blue bag; he thought Consuela must have thrown it out the window when she knew the police were at the door. "I was turned away," he said. "I thought I heard something hit the ground among the dead leaves. When I looked, I saw a snatch of blue. But why that cat would grab it up . . ." Clyde shook his head, at a loss to explain the black beast. "Cats do weird things. Well," he said, grinning, "Kate got her jewels back." He studied Reedie. "Was that Marlin Dorriss's condo? I'd heard it's in the Marina. Was Consuela connected with Dorriss?"

"It is Dorriss's condo," Reedie said stiffly. "What made you ask?"

"A hunch," Clyde lied. "I saw them together once, in Molena Point, and wondered. Are you going back there now?"

"I am. You have some business there?"

"I would like to follow you back, talk with you."

Reedie glanced at Kate, then nodded.

Kate just hoped Reedie wouldn't go digging for more answers than he needed.

Well, her story sounded plausible to her. The best

lie, sometimes, was the truth, with the incriminating
parts left out.

After Reedie left, Lucinda dropped Clyde and Joe back
at the condo. There, Joe quietly slipped into the Cadillac while Clyde talked with Reedie, then went with
him to look for the Packard—but only after Reedie
called Molena Point PD and talked with Harper.

Clyde told Reedie that he had no proof of any mis-
conduct on Dorriss's part. Just a feeling, Clyde said. A
hunch that Dorriss might be involved in the thefts. He
lied to Reedie, and through Reedie he lied to Harper,
and all to protect Joe Grey. He said to Reedie innocently that, if the officers had found any stolen items in
the condo, then maybe Dorriss had the Packard as
well. In short, Clyde wove a tangle in a way that he ab-
horred, all for the gray tomcat.

Kate said later that she wished Clyde didn't have to
stir up so many questions for Reedie, when the detective would be talking more than once with Harper and
Garza about the case. But it couldn't be helped, if
Clyde wanted to look for his Packard—and Clyde
loved that Packard.

She did wonder privately sometimes if any woman
ever in Clyde's life would stir the possessive emotions
generated by those abused and neglected old cars that
he made whole and new again.

Dropping Clyde off at the condo, Kate and Lucinda
and Pedric, feeling suddenly nervous at carrying all the
jewels with them, headed for the Greenlaws' appointment with the appraiser, hoping he would see them
though they were nearly an hour late. They agreed to

meet for lunch either at Kate's favorite sidewalk café, or across the street at I. Magnin where Clyde—after he found the Packard, he said, as if he was certain he'd find it—had a bit of shopping to do. Off Kate and Pedric and Lucinda went, carrying with them what might be a fortune wrapped in Kate's sweater; and Clyde and Joe Grey went to shop, all as if this were a perfectly ordinary morning.

## 30

The women's accessory department of I. Magnin smelled subtly of expensive perfumes and, if one had a feline's ability to detect fainter scents, of fine leather and silks and velvets and imported wools. Joe Grey was not visible, but the customer looking at cashmere scarves and evening stoles carried a large, apparently heavy backpack, one of those models with netting set into the sides.

Though the subject was clean-shaven and his short dark hair well cut, though he was neatly dressed in sport coat and slacks, a store detective watched him. The unobtrusive observer stood several counters away appearing to be selecting a woman's sweater. His skilled surveillance was hardly noticeable as he waited for the guy to lift a hundred-dollar scarf and slip it in the backpack. If the prospective shoplifter seemed to be talking to himself, he could be a bit strange, or that could be a ploy, a weird but deliberate distraction. The detective watched him lift one scarf from the rack, hold it suspiciously up to the backpack, wait a minute, then lay it back over the rack. The customer had been perusing the merchandise thus for about ten minutes, one scarf or stole after another. The clerk waiting on him was patient, but she was not smiling; the man made her nervous.

But then a woman joined the customer, a striking blonde, and the subject's solitary remarks became part of normal conversation. Now the blonde held up the scarves, one at a time, and she seemed almost to be talking to the backpack. The store dick moved closer.

Just as he decided to approach the pair, two elderly folk joined them. Their behavior, however, was equally bizarre. Sometimes he wished he'd stayed working warehouse security, where life had been simpler. Now the tall wrinkled woman held up scarves, going through the same routine as the other two; and the strange thing was, all four of them seemed to be losing patience. The detective glanced at his watch. This charade was cutting into his lunch hour. Moving away into women's shoes but keeping an eye on the party, he saw to his great relief that the guy with the backpack had finally selected two cashmere stoles. One was ice blue, one amber. Making his purchases, he paid cash. If he was passing counterfeit money he wouldn't have made such a spectacle, would have been in and out fast. Wanting his lunch, the detective turned away—if the backpack contained stolen merchandise, the electronic gate would pick it up and signal an alarm. It was an extremely touchy procedure to confront a customer for shoplifting while that person was still in the store. Abandoning the group, he headed out a side door and up the street for a quick hamburger.

The four people followed him out and headed down

the block for their own lunch. Only the passenger in the backpack had paid any attention to the store dick. Watching him through the mesh, Joe was highly amused by the man's frustration.

When the detective had disappeared, Joe nuzzled into the package that Clyde had dropped into the pack, sniffing deeply at the expensive wool. Dulcie would be thrilled; so would the kit. Ice blue for Dulcie, amber for Kit, both stoles softer than bird down. Joe had never before purchased a gift of any kind, certainly not a two-hundred-dollar stole for his lady.

He had, of course, not paid directly for the gifts. But as Clyde had offered a reward for information leading to recovery of the Packard, Joe figured he'd earned that amount, and more.

Swinging back by the condo after chasing Azrael, they had found Consuela and Hollis already removed to the city jail, and the uniforms still searching the apartment. The officers had found the hidden locks on Dorriss's sliding wall panels, and were photographing the stolen items. They had called for, and had posted, a guard of five additional officers, and the street was crawling with police cars. The condo manager, who lived on the premises, had gone around with Clyde and Detective Reedie to open the doors of Dorriss's three single garages.

They had found two empty. The third contained a vehicle lovingly protected by a thick waterproof cover made especially for a 1927 Packard roadster. Clyde might never know whether Dorriss had bought the cover some time before he stole the Packard, fully intending to possess that particular car, or whether he rashly ordered it from an automotive specialty shop after the deed was accomplished.

Leaving the garage and parting from Detective Reedie, Clyde had returned to the Cadillac grinning with success.

Joe Grey had said nothing. But with every line of his body, the angle of his ears and the slant of his whiskers, the look in his eyes, he had given back to Clyde a cool and judgmental I-told-you-so.

Now as Clyde and Kate and the Greenlaws took their seats at the sidewalk table, Clyde carefully set Joe's pack on an empty chair beside him and opened the flap.

Yawning, Joe looked out as Clyde read several items from the menu. With a twitch of his ears at the right moment, he gave Clyde his lunch order, then curled down again on the soft I. Magnin package. He had almost shut out his friends' small talk when Lucinda said, "It makes me feel very much easier with those people in jail, particularly now."

Joe slitted open his eyes. *Particularly now, what?* What had he missed? *The appraisal*, he thought, coming up out of the backpack.

Lucinda leaned over to speak softly to Clyde, waiting until the waiter set down their onion rings and beer. Joe had thought the appraiser would keep the pieces for a day or so before returning them with his evaluation, but apparently not.

"They're real," Lucinda said softly to Clyde. "Our seven pieces, and Kate's nine. All of fine quality, the appraiser said. Thank goodness we were able to rent safe deposit boxes, this time with more security we hope than Kate's box had, and with some extra precautions."

The idea of another safe deposit box alarmed Joe. But where else was there that would be more secure? Watching Kate, he expected her to be radiant with the news but she didn't seem to be, she was very quiet as Clyde laid his hand on hers.

"What?" Clyde said.

"Just . . . reaction, I guess," she said softly. "Yes, it's wonderful, the appraisal, having that treasure to fall back on, to tuck away for some emergency. I just . . . need to get over all the rest of it." She squeezed Clyde's hand. She looked, Joe thought, deeply introspective. Maybe she'd celebrate her new fortune later, maybe wildly. But right now she needed some downtime, maybe to get used to the idea of what such wealth might mean.

Well, he understood that. He had no idea what he would do with a large wad of cash—but then, Joe thought, there wasn't much chance he'd ever need to worry about such matters.

He was surprised Clyde hadn't asked how much the jewels were worth. Clyde hadn't; not then, not there on the street. Joe was burning to know—not that it was any of his business, or Clyde's either.

Watching Kate, he knew she needed to settle back into the real world, after the dark sorcery of the black tom, after the touch of a beast who would take great pleasure in destroying Kate's natural joy of life, a beast who worshiped only destruction.

The waiter brought their sandwiches, and Kate's salad and Joe's shrimp cocktail sans sauce. Joe ate with greedy concentration, standing up in the backpack with his front paws on the table, lifting each shrimp out where he could chomp it more handily. If he garnered glances and smiles from nearby diners, he ignored them. Finishing the shrimp he had a little wash, then, yawning, he curled down inside the backpack again, against the soft package. It had been a busy morning. Drifting off, he wondered where Kate would go from here? Back to Molena Point, to work for Hanni? Or Seattle, as she'd told Clyde she might, to work there for her present firm?

But she'd be alone in Seattle, no friends around her. She'd told Clyde it was only a short flight down to the village, maybe two hours to San Francisco, then thirty minutes to Molena Point. But how often would she come, once she was caught up in that new life? How often would she return to the village to be among friends who were like family?

*She'll be all right*, Joe told himself. *No need to get protective and soft-minded over a self-sufficient, beautiful, and soon to be wealthy human. Kate will do just fine.* And Joe Grey slept, the deep dreamless sleep of contentment, the untroubled sleep of one who had changed a life or two. He didn't wake to say good-bye to Kate and the Greenlaws, but somewhere in sleep he heard Clyde and Kate as she lingered for a moment by the car.

"Back there in that old house," Clyde said, "I was afraid you wanted to follow him."

"Maybe, for a moment," she said softly. "There are two drives in all of us, Clyde. One toward heaven, one toward hell. It's our choice that matters. What I truly wanted, deep down, was to be done with the beast. With everything he believes in. If there ever was such a world, and if that beast is drawn there, then it must be dark and twisted and terrible. Maybe," Kate said, "maybe it was different once, long ago, when McCabe wrote of such a place. When perhaps my parents wandered there. I don't know, Clyde. But that is not my world; *this* is my world. This world is full of more wonders than I can handle." She was silent a moment, then, "Thank you, Clyde, for coming, for being here. Thank you, Joe Grey." Joe felt her fingers caress his head and ears, then heard her turn and walk away.

Joe didn't stir when Clyde tucked the backpack onto the passenger seat and fastened the seat belt around it. He didn't wake in San Jose when Clyde stopped for a cup of coffee, didn't wake until they passed Gilroy, when Clyde swerved hard and hit his horn. Yawning, Joe crawled out of the backpack looking blearily around. "What was that about?"

"Some drunk went over the line," Clyde said angrily. "Damn near sideswiped me." Then he smiled. "There's a black and white behind us, they just pulled the guy over." He glanced down at Joe. "You were out like a light."

Joe yawned and didn't answer. Settling down atop the backpack for another snooze, he didn't wake again until they were pulling into their own drive. It was just dusk, the falling light among the trees and cottages soft and inviting, the smells of cooking along the street bringing Joe wide awake. He was starving. And what was this? Why was their house lighted up?

Every light must be on downstairs, bright behind the drawn curtains. Joe stared up at Clyde. "What did you do, rent out the house?"

Clyde looked back at him, then at the street where Charlie's blue Chevy van was parked. "Something's wrong." He swung out of the car fast, but held the door open for Joe. Joe paused. Crouching on the seat ready to leap out, he saw Dulcie in the window, standing tall on the sill, looking.

She did not look distressed. In fact, her whiskers were straight out, her ears sharply alert—just glad to see them home. She disappeared as Joe leaped from the car; and when he hit his cat door Dulcie and the kit were there, pushing out to greet him.

It was a very small, very private party. At first, just Wilma and Charlie and Clyde, Joe and Dulcie and the kit. Dulcie and Kit licked his ears and whiskers as if he'd been gone for weeks, but then the kit was all over him demanding to know about Lucinda and Pedric. Where were they, why hadn't they come back with Clyde, when were they coming home and did they really mean to stay this time? She wanted them here in the village safe and she didn't want them to roam anymore.

The aroma of spaghetti sauce filled the house from where it was simmering on the stove. When they all moved into the kitchen, Charlie put the pasta on to boil, and got out the grated cheese and salad dressing. The table was set for six. A big basket of Jolly's best French bread waited on the counter beside a huge salad. And in the middle of the round table stood a cake decorated with one candle and with red lettering on white icing. The sentiment portrayed in Wilma's inimitable cake-decorating style said,

WELL DONE, JOE GREY! YOU ARE A PRINCE AMONG CATS.

Joe was just rearing up to blow out the candle, not an easy move for a cat, when the phone rang. Charlie hit the speaker.

It was Kate. "They get home okay?"

"Just got here," Charlie said. "He's blowing out his candle. We only have enough time for Joe to cut his cake and have a toast or two before Max and Dallas and Ryan get here."

"Drink cheers for us," Kate said. "Lucinda and Pedric are here, helping to clean up the apartment. Tell Clyde and Joe thank you. Lucinda and Pedric say thank you. We love you all."

When they'd hung up, Charlie opened a bottle of champagne and they toasted Joe Grey for helping recover Kate's jewels, for finding Clyde's Packard, and for operations of a clandestine nature in the investigation that should soon break Marlin Dorriss's identity theft scam. Then Clyde cut Joe's cake, which was a delectable combination of goose liver and cream cheese. This was served on crackers with the champagne—and for the cats, warm milk. Dulcie and Kit's cashmere stoles were presented by Joe himself, the tomcat hauling them out of the I. Magnin bag and laying them at the ladies' feet: blue for Dulcie, amber for the kit. Dulcie's green eyes caressed Joe lovingly. Clyde's four hundred dollars could not have been better spent. The kit's round yellow eyes were wide with excitement as she patted at the soft, folded cashmere then curled down to roll on it, loudly purring.

Before Max and Dallas and Ryan arrived, all evidence of the celebration had disappeared. The officers and Ryan came in laughing, Harper and Garza very high indeed with the way the Dorriss cases were shaping up. And Ryan too, hugging Clyde, was filled with excitement. An upbeat atmosphere at the station always put her in a happy mood—her uncle Dallas had helped raise her, she was practically a cop's kid; the ongoing drama of his work was an important part of her life.

"You saw Kate," Ryan said, taking Clyde's hand. "Will she be all right? She got her jewels back!"

"She'll be fine," Clyde said. "I guess the jewels will make her a wealthy woman." He searched Ryan's eyes for a glint of jealousy, but he saw only concern. Ryan was Kate's friend. Kate had worked a long time for Ryan's sister, she was like part of the family. He put his arm around her, liking the smell of fresh sawdust that clung to her hair.

Ryan's arm came around him bolder than Kate's caress would be, and somehow steadier. When she looked at him, her green eyes beneath her dark lashes were filled with humor, and with challenge. Clyde liked that, he liked challenge, in the right woman.

As they took their places at the table, Max was still smiling. Clyde liked seeing his old friend happy; and it was not only the resolution of the three cases that made him grin. Since Max and Charlie married, Max had come back to life in a way Clyde had not seen since before he was widowed.

"Consuela and Hollis are in custody," Max said, "and that bizarre display in Dorriss's condo has been dismantled—San Francisco PD e-mailed us a copy of the video they took of Dorriss's trophy wall.

"They've locked the stolen items in their evidence

vault. Every piece that was reported missing—including a green Packard," he said, grinning. "Reedie says they lifted that baby onto a flatbed, *treated* it like a baby, and stored it in a safe corner of the police garage." He looked at Clyde. "Not a chance of damage, Reedie staked his life on that."

"On the stolen IDs," Dallas said, "with Dorriss moving around the state right now making purchases, we've contacted every city on or near his itinerary. They've put out flyers to the escrow companies, contacted the banks. Soon as a complaint comes in, local detectives will be on the case, and we go to work with that jurisdiction."

"A long, slow process," Clyde said.

"But effective," Dallas said. "We're lucky to have this information; the snitch really put us onto this one. It's a damn sight more than you ever expect to get on these cases."

Garza looked at Max. "It would be nice to have an ID on this snitch. And to know how he operates, how he gets this stuff . . . how he *knows* to get it." The detective sipped his beer. "I'd give a lot to know what made him suspect Dorriss in the first place. Or maybe," Garza said, leaning his elbows on the table, "Maybe none of us *wants* to know. This guy is a gold mine. Sure as hell, no one wants to discourage him."

"Whoever he is," Harper said, "he was shrewd enough to substitute old credit card and gas bills in Dorriss's file for the current ones. Not leave the empty file for Dorriss to spot the minute he opened the drawer."

Lying on the kitchen counter, Joe Grey kept right on washing his paws, though he did allow himself a hidden smile and a glance at Dulcie.

Harper said, "When we went through the house this afternoon, we found five bits of torn paper as well, that match the torn pages of Quinn's notebook. Found them near the hearth in the master bedroom. That," Harper said, smiling, "makes Dorriss a prime candidate not only for the burglaries but for Quinn's death."

"The notebook," Dallas said, "plus a partial finger-print on Quinn's back doorknob that has been identi-fied as Dorriss's. As if Dorriss may have slipped his glove off for a minute, working on the lock."

"Found a set of lock picks in his dressing room," Harper said, "taped inside a hollow tie rack." The cap-tain smiled. "We've got the evidence, and we're hop-ing, when we get Consuela back down here, we can get her to talk as well."

Dallas said, "I have a feeling she'll talk, and Hollis, too, to save his neck. Hollis will be facing charges for kidnapping the Greenlaws, as well as vehicular theft. If he thinks it will go easier for him, I'm guessing he'll tell us all he can about his father."

Joe Grey watched his human friends finish supper, then he raced with Dulcie and Kit upstairs, up to the rafters, and out to his private tower. The kit came last, dragging her cashmere stole up into the tower where she patted it into a little mound and lay down on it looking smug.

Clyde had replaced the cushions in Joe's tower with new ones. There was no smell left of the black tomcat, and, through Joe's cat door, the breeze off the sea was fresh and cool. Lying on the pillows looking out over the rooftops, Joe thought that the next weeks would be highly interesting, as the Molena Point PD worked on the multitude of charges against Dorriss, Consuela, and Hollis that the district attorney would ultimately prepare for the court.

"And what about Dillon?" the kit said sadly. The little tattercoat was painfully aware of her own part in Dillon's arrest.

"She wasn't booked," Dulcie said. "Didn't you know that, Kit? Leah and Candy were booked. Not Dillon. She was remanded over to the custody of her mother, under Captain Harper's supervision."

"Big deal," Joe said, "if Helen keeps on as she has been."

"I don't think she will," Dulcie said. "Dillon's parents are going away for two weeks, on a cruise. They arranged for Dillon to stay with Max and Charlie. Before you got home, Charlie told us Dillon was up there today, and she and Charlie went riding. Dillon wanted to know if she could still go to work for Ryan. I think that maybe it will come out all right."

Smiling, the kit curled down on her cashmere stole and was soon asleep; and Joe and Dulcie looked at each other contentedly. The next weeks would indeed be interesting, with all the action at the department, with indictments and hearings. But the best thing of all was to be together and to be among family. Dulcie said, "That black beast won't be back?"

"We've seen the last of him," Joe said. "I'd bet on it." He imagined Azrael wandering among dank stone vaults beneath granite skies or maybe only among the cellars and ruined underpinnings of San Francisco, of that many-faceted city. And he looked intently at Dulcie.

"If he did come back here, he wouldn't stay long, Dulcie. Not in our village. We've had enough of his kind."

Please turn the page
for a sneak peek into the
next delightful Joe Grey mystery.

CAT CROSS THEIR GRAVES

On sale in hardcover from
HarperCollins Publishers
January 2005

Ten minutes before the sirens blasted, the tortoise-shell kit awoke just as startled and off-center as Charlie, just as eerily scared. The sirens jerked her up from her tangle of cushions, in her third floor window seat. Pressing her nose against the cold dark glass she stared down past the lower balconies to the inn's blowing gardens. Gardens and patio were softly lit but deserted.

The time was near to midnight. Beyond the inn's enclosing walls, a haze of light from the village shops shifted in the wind as indistinct as blowing gauze; against that hazy smear, the black pools of trees rattled and shook; and above the solid village roofs' chimneys, above the black pools of wind-tossed trees, the distant stars burned icy and remote. Impossible worlds, it seemed to Kit, spinning in a vastness that no one could comprehend.

What had waked her?

Below her in the patio, nothing moved but the puppets of the wind, nothing moved against the wind; and she heard no faintest sound.

361

She and Lucinda and Pedric had been at Otter Pine Inn since before Christmas, enjoying the most luxurious holiday the kit had ever imagined. Over the hush of the wind, from deeper within the darkened suite through the open bedroom door, she could hear Lucinda and Pedric's soft breathing; the old couple slept so deeply. Lucinda said that was the result of a good conscience. The kit, staring down again through the bay window to the courtyard and sprawling gardens, studied the windows of the bar and the dining room and the tearoom.

The tearoom was closed at this hour, and the dining room looked deserted; she thought it was about to close. No one came out of the bar, and the bar's black smoked windows were too dark to see through. But no sleepy couple had come out, and no one was returning through the wrought iron gate from the street, ready to settle in for the night. Pressing her nose harder to the glass, her whiskers and ears sharply pricked, her every sense was alert.

Otter Pine Inn occupied nearly a full block near the center of the village, just a short stroll from Ocean Avenue. Its wrought iron gates, its three wings that formed a U, and its creamy stucco walls surrounded winding brick walks and bright winter blooms. The roofs of the inn were red tile, mossy in the shady places, thus slick to run on; slick all over when they were wet.

There were four third floor penthouses. Patty Rose's suite was at the back. Kit and Lucinda and Pedric's suite looked across the patio to the front gate. In the other two penthouses this weekend were a young couple with three cocker spaniels, and a family with two children and a great Dane, a dog the kit avoided but only because she didn't know him. The cockers were more her size, she could easily bloody them if the need arose. Or she could terrorize them for amusement, if she liked. If Lucinda didn't catch her at it. She did not like to offend Lucinda or Pedric.

Since before Christmas Kit had enjoyed such a lovely time with her adopted family. The three of them had indulged in all manner of holiday and post-holiday pleasures, concerts, plays, long walks, and amazing gourmet delights. But most wonderful of all was their reunion, after Kit had so painfully mourned the old couple's death. To have her beloved Greenlaws back from the grave, as it were, was a never-ending wonder to the small tortoiseshell. When Lucinda and Pedric showed up alive after everyone thought they had been killed in that terrible highway accident, the kit had nearly flown out of her skin with joy.

Settling into Otter Pine Inn for the holiday, visiting with their friend Patty Rose, the kit had every possible luxury, her own cushioned window seat, her own hand-painted Dalton china dinner service, and anything at all that she cared to order from the inn's gourmet kitchen or from attentive waiters in the dining patio.

Twitching an ear, she listened harder. Had she heard, on the instant of waking, angry human voices?

Below her, the bar's lights went dimmer still, and three yawning couples emerged, maybe the last customers, heading for the upper rooms. Molena Point was not a late-hour town; even the tourists turned in early, many to rise at dawn for a walk with their dogs or a run along the white beach. The shore in the morning was busy with wet, sandy dogs.

The lights went brighter in the bar, and she could see the waiters starting to clean up, wiping the tables; the cleaning staff would arrive soon to sweep and scrub. Above the village, storm clouds were starting to move in again and she could smell rain through the cracks around the side window. She could hear voices now.

Hushed and angry. An argument from somewhere beyond the dining room. Maybe from the stairs that led down to the parking garage? She hated the garage; that vast concrete basement made her shiver with unease, she didn't like to go there. Once when she was little she had thought that caves and caverns were wonderful places peopled with amazing and mythical beings. Now such places frightened her. Angrier and louder the voices came, though maybe too faint for a human to hear. Burning with curiosity and a strange dread, she pressed the glass of the side window with an impatient paw until it opened.

A man and a woman arguing. She didn't recognize him, but the woman was Patty. Patty Rose. She had never heard Patty so angry. Nosing the window wider she pressed against the screen. Yes, the way the echoes bounced and fell, she thought they were on the stair that led down to the garage. Their words were deflected by the inn's plastered walls, but Patty's retort was accusing. ". . . all that time . . . never once . . . just. . . . Then on to do . . ." Kit could make out nothing more, and what she heard didn't make sense. She was pawing at the screen's latch when three sharp reports barked between the walls, echoing, reverberating back and forth across the patio. She slashed hard down the screen, ripping a jagged hole.

Behind her, she heard Lucinda thump out of bed.

Before the agile old lady could stop her, Kit forced through the screen tearing out hanks of fur and dropped to a second floor balcony. Below her, doors banged open, people were running and shouting. She heard a tiny click as Lucinda snatched up the bedside phone; she heard Lucinda alert the dispatcher as, likely, a dozen people were trying to do.

"Three shots, that's all I know," Lucinda said as Kit slipped beneath the rail. "Yes, shots, my dear," the old woman said testily. "That was not a backfire. I know gunshots when I hear them. And there was no smallest sound of a car engine."

Kit dropped onto the back of a bench and into a bed of cyclamens. Racing across the brick walk and through the taller flowers, she listened for the shooter running. All she heard was her own fur brushing through the foliage. Skirting a bed of geraniums, her nose tingled to their smell where they lay crushed.

Strange, the stairwell that led down to the parking garage was dark. The little lights along the steps that led down to the garage had been turned off. As she reached the top of the stairwell she heard running below. The faintest footsteps fast descending the concrete stairs: soft shoes heading for the parking basement. She caught a whiff of geranium mixed with the sharp-iron smell of blood, heard the squeak of rubber soles on concrete.

In the blackness of the stairs below her, a body lay sprawled head down on the dark stairs. Shivering, staring at the mutilated woman, Kit glimpsed far below a running shadow disappear through blackness into the garage. But Kit's attention, her whole being, was centered on the dead woman.

Patty Rose lay tumbled head-down, unnaturally twisted down the concrete steps, her white silk dressing gown slick with blood. Her face was turned away but was reflected in the steel hood of the recessed light: bloody, distorted. The smell of blood filled Kit's nose, she could taste the iron-heavy smell. Sirens screamed across the village, muffled by the wind and by the walls of the buildings. Heart pounding, she crept down the steps to Patty.

Her friend couldn't be alive. Kit did not want to know that. The sirens were louder, louder, coming fast and loud. Trying not to look at Patty's poor torn face as she reached out her nose searching for breath, knowing there would be none. Sirens screamed around the building so loud she thought her ears would burst.

They ceased as suddenly as they had begun. Car doors slammed. The night was filled with the static of police radios, footsteps pounded across the patio above her, running cops started down the stairs. She ran, pelting down into darkness.

Crouched far down the steps in blackness, she smelled Patty's blood as strong as if it was on her own whiskers. Her tail was between her legs, her whole being felt shrunken.

Patty Rose had held Kit on her lap and loved and petted her, Patty had shared tea with her and fed her bits of shortbread all buttery warm, Patty had talked so softly to her. This kind woman had talked and talked to her and had never known that Kit could have answered.

That seemed terrible now, that Patty had never known. Patty Rose would have been thrilled.

Below her she heard another scuffle of footsteps near the door to the parking garage, a faint squeak as of rubber soles on concrete. And now below her in the garage she heard the cops surging down its two ramps and inside.

Kit longed for Joe Grey and Dulcie, for the strength of the big gray tomcat and for tabby Dulcie's mothering. She was nearly a full-grown cat, but right now she needed badly to push close between them like a lost kitten. The two cats and their human friends had cared for her ever since she abandoned the wild bunch she ran with. Always picked on, she hadn't had the courage to leave until she met Joe Grey and Dulcie, and Lucinda and Pedric. Oh, then her life had so changed. To find two speaking cats like herself, and to find humans who understood—that had been an amazing time.

But right now this minute, she ached just to feel Dulcie's nose against her ear, to hear Dulcie and Joe Grey tell her that everything would be all right—she longed, most of all, for this terrible thing to have never happened, for Patty Rose to be alive and unharmed.

Above her, two medics knelt over Patty's poor bloody body. Kit's nose was sour with the smell of death. Far below her she could hear the faint scuffs and faint voices as the officers searched. She'd heard no car screeching out to escape. Was the killer hidden among the parked cars or under them, or in a car, waiting for the cops to search and somehow miss him, meaning then to slip away? She imagined him creeping out later through the confusion of police cars and rescue vehicles and somehow eluding them. Was that possible? Oh, the officers would find him.

But still . . . she knew something they didn't.

Racing down she hit the bottom step and fled into the garage dodging a confusion of swinging spotlights, the officers' torches burning leaping paths through the blackness.

Crouching in shadow under a small black car, she listened. Her paws were slick with sweat. At last she began to creep along between the cars, scenting the concrete, seeking the smell of crushed geranium, listening maybe for the sound of softer shoes slipping away accompanied by that little squeak of rubber against concrete.